Dear Read

The no
years by
Rosemary
McBain are accountable to one thing above all
others: Avon has never tried to force authors
into any particular mold. Rather, Avon is a
publisher that encourages individual talent and is
always on the lookout for writers who will
deliver *real* books, not packaged formulas.

In 1982, we started a program to help readers
pick out authors of exceptional promise. Called
"The Avon Romance," the books were
distinguished by a ribbon motif in the upper
left-hand corner of the cover. Although every
title was by a new author, and the settings could
be either historical or contemporary, they were
quickly discovered and became known as "the
ribbon books."

In 1984, "The Avon Romance" will be a
feature on the Avon list. Each month, you will
find novels with many different settings, each
one by an author who is special. You will not
find predictable characters, predictable plots and
predictable endings. The only predictable thing
about "The Avon Romance" will be the superior
quality that Avon has always delivered in the
field of romance!

Sincerely,

Walter Mead

WALTER MEADE
President & Publisher

NOW & AGAIN

JOAN CASSITY

AVON
PUBLISHERS OF BARD, CAMELOT, DISCUS AND FLARE BOOKS

AVON BOOKS
A division of
The Hearst Corporation
1790 Broadway
New York, New York 10019

Copyright © 1984 by Joan Cassity
Published by arrangement with the author
Library of Congress Catalog Card Number: 84-90896
ISBN: 0-380-87353-2

First Avon Printing, June, 1984

AVON TRADEMARK REG. U. S. PAT. OFF. AND IN
OTHER COUNTRIES, MARCA REGISTRADA, HECHO EN
U. S. A.

Printed in the U. S. A.

WFH 10 9 8 7 6 5 4 3 2 1

To my daughters
Cheri, Janelle, and Colleen;
my mother Alice Shooter,
and all my good friends who stood behind me.

NOW & AGAIN

Chapter One

"He peddled the goddamn bid!" Shawn McCullough recognized her father's booming voice even before she raised her eyes from the set of landscape design specifications that had held her undivided attention for the past several hours. One look at his face set her blood boiling. She didn't even have to ask who had upset him. It had to be Bellows. Andrew Bellows, the largest and wealthiest building contractor in the Bay Area. He'd done it again, and she hated him with a passion.

Jack McCullough stomped over to the drawing board opposite his daughter, grabbed the Arcadia Lane specifications, and jammed them into a wastebasket, his big hands crumpling the massive roll, his florid face mirroring his anger. When he was angry, he seemed to be six inches taller than his normal six feet two inches, and his eyes were a piercing, steely blue. Shawn could see the veins pulsating in his temples, and furious as she was, she knew that he needed her as he had always needed her.

"McCullough, your blood pressure!" she warned.

"To hell with my blood pressure," he roared. "Right now I'm so goddamn mad at Bellows . . ." Suddenly his face paled, and his white-knuckled hands clutched the edge of the table.

Shawn was beside him, a wave of concern ebbing her

anger. "McCullough! Forget the lousy no-good character. He isn't worth it."

"Isn't that the goddamn truth," he muttered as he slumped down in a chair, unconsciously rubbing his arm.

Shawn's deep blue eyes searched his face. He looked exhausted, and she knew he had counted on winning this contract. McCullough wasn't the biggest landscaper in the San Francisco Bay Area, but he was an honest one who didn't cut corners and bury the evidence. There were lots of ways it could be done, and it happened all the time. She knew the Arcadia Lane mall would be a prime example with Andrew Bellows covering the shortages right alongside his protégé, L and C Landscaping. L and C, Lenard and Cramer, my foot! Liars and Cheaters was more accurate, she thought. She moved behind her father, rubbing his broad shoulders with hands that seemed Lilliputian next to his muscular frame. Yet they were delicately attractive and well groomed with a splash of rose on the nails, the ultimate accent to her ivory skin.

"You're tense," she said. "Come on, boss man, relax. Where's the old spark? Remember what they say about a good man? Well, it goes double for the Irish, you know. We'll show him, though I don't know how," she stated, and the anger returned. For a moment she forgot her concern for her father's health, and she could feel his muscles begin to soften as her fingers bore down on his tight back.

"Um," he said. "I wish I could bottle this feeling and drink it. It's almost better than good Irish whisky."

A hint of a smile crossed her pretty face, and she playfully swatted his shoulder, moving her five-feet-two-inch frame to face him. "Enough for now," she said. "I must have that bid ready by two P.M. tomorrow."

"The park?"

She nodded as the door opened and Antonio Rizzo walked in. Shawn could tell he'd been hard at work again, his dark curly hair askew, beads of sweat covering his deeply tanned forehead and staining his plaid shirt. At thirty, Tony was the field supervisor. He oversaw all of the field operations, making a daily check of each job McCullough Landscaping was working on, helping the foremen to iron out problems. The men respected him and enjoyed his lighthearted bantering. Shawn was well aware of his value to the corporation, yet she never felt totally comfortable around him unless her father was present. She sometimes felt that he resented her for being a woman in a man's world; not only that, but a woman with a great deal of influence over his boss.

"Well, what's the good word?" Tony said, but the smile slipped from his lips as he saw the frown that creased McCullough's brow. "He did it again, huh?"

Jack McCullough nodded, and the muscles in his cheeks tightened, the creases in his forehead deepened. Shawn could see him tense again. She shook her head at Tony, and the warning was clear.

"Hey, come on, Jack." He shrugged his broad shoulders and went into his familiar Italian semantics. "You wanna me to putta da contract out on him?"

"I'm damn tempted," her father said flatly.

"Eh, justa letta me know," Tony said. "I taka care a him quick." Then looking at his serious face as Jack rose from the chair, he added, "Sorry, I know how you were counting on the Arcadia contract to see us through the winter."

"You know what this means?" the older man asked.

"Yeah, a layoff." He reached over and patted the slumped shoulder of his boss. "We'll get the next one, by damn. I got a good feeling about the park specs that Shawn is working on."

"If only that would solve it," Jack said, running his fingers through his salt-and-pepper hair with a weary sigh.

Shawn had never seen her father look so tired. Even the cleft in his chin seemed taut. She glanced at her watch; it was twelve-thirty P.M. "McCullough," she said, giving him a gentle push toward the door and looking for all the world like an ant trying to move a watermelon, "have some lunch and go home to rest. You're tired. Tony and I can handle things here."

"Yeah, you've been at it too hard lately," Tony agreed.

"We'll see, after I make a few phone calls," her father said, but she knew he wouldn't. He was a workhorse, stubborn as a mule, and he had a determined set to his jaw that no amount of coaxing could change. She watched him go into his office and turned to Tony. "See if you can't ride herd on him and get him outta here, huh?"

Tony smiled. "You know as well as I do that that damn Irishman's not gonna do anything he doesn't want to."

She nodded in defeat. "I suppose you're right."

Tony picked up a set of plans. "See you later, got to run by the baseball field."

"Norton School?"

"You got it. Oh, did you get a call on that soil sample yet? It's critical, you know."

"No, better check with Audrey. I told her to hold all the calls till I finish working up this bid. I don't need to tell you how important this one is now."

"Um," he said, and left her office. Shawn watched him saunter out, brushing against the potted philodendron, whose huge, shiny leaves occasionally interfered with passing traffic.

Shawn's concentration had been broken, and the anger she tried to suppress kept pounding away at her brain like a miniature jackhammer. She pulled out the sandwich she had tucked into her huge canvas bag that morning and unwrapped it. More often than not, she ate with the rest of the office crew, but today she needed solitude. She absent-mindedly dropped the sandwich to her desk and strode to the hall where she poured a cup of coffee. She moved with the grace and confidence of a primed athlete, her dress curving to the lithe lines of her figure.

The white background of her dress, supporting bold stripes of violet, orange, and aqua, enhanced the brilliance of her blue eyes. A woven white belt gathered the garment in at her waist while slits on both sides of the skirt tantalizingly exposed her attractive legs.

Half an hour had passed, and the sandwich was barely touched. Shawn pushed it aside. She wanted to finish the bid before she left that evening. She went back to her calculator, and with iron determination, she pared the figures to the bone. They needed this job, and she would get it. At least the odds were that L and C wouldn't bid on this one now. They would be crazy to, particularly now that they had won Arcadia Lane. Talk about big, it was well over a million-dollar job which would eat up at least six months and keep a sizable number of men working. She wondered just what their competitor's bid was. Perhaps $500 or $1,000 low. They could easily make up that and more just by skimping on the sandfill around the irrigation pipes. For the first time in the four years she had worked for her father, Shawn was tempted to cut the figures on the park more than her estimates called for. She knew that if they got this job, there would be only the usual winter layoff instead of having to let go key people, which was all too probable in light of today's loss.

She picked up her pencil and stared at it. No, the owner of McCullough Landscaping, Inc. would not allow any shenanigans, no matter what. *I wish I were back in college*, Shawn thought glumly. *That damned Irishman should have had a son. Maybe I'm not tough enough after all.* She picked up the plan and reached for the specs, breathing to herself, "I know, McCullough, I guess we're both damn fools!"

It was several hours later before she thought of her father again. She had checked and rechecked the figures, but something about the concrete gnawed at her. She read the specifications again and it all seemed to tally, but still it bothered her. Shawn slid her chair back, grabbed the plans and specs, and darted into her father's office. "McCullough, something isn't right here," she said, pushing the black curls off her forehead.

His desk was the usual disarray of papers and half a cup of coffee perched near the edge. Shawn's eyes lingered on the picture of her mother, an older reflection of herself with the same deep indigo eyes fringed with long, dark lashes; the luxuriant, gray hair that had once been as dark and radiant as her own; and the mischievous smile that she remembered as a young child but which, in later years, had diminished with pain. She could almost hear the Gaelic brogue, and she stood rooted to the spot, her eyes fastened on her mother's lips as if expecting them to utter words of wisdom. How long it had been since she had heard that gentle voice. A moment of sadness gripped her, and she had to remind herself that her mother had lived a full and loving life despite her premature death. Shawn shivered and pulled her gaze from the picture.

Her father wasn't at his desk. She peered out the window and realized that the September sun's glow was fading and that his car was gone. "I'll be damned! He really did leave early. Maybe he does have some sense after all," she said fondly to the empty office. She was relieved he had gone, yet she couldn't shake a feeling of eerie apprehension. If only her mother were still here.

Shawn's dark blue Spitfire slipped through the evening traffic as she covered the twenty miles home. The September wind whipped at her long, ebony curls as the convertible slowed to freeway-exit speed. Shawn consciously tried to relax. It wasn't like her father to leave early, even with her urging. Perhaps he was more tired, more upset than she had realized. What he needed was a vacation, she thought and decided that she would convince him to take a few days off to rest. She turned up the long, winding driveway to their Los Altos Hills home and glanced at the recently cut lawn. It smelled fresh and was a rich jade green that spoke of knowledge of the soil. The surrounding plants and shrubs were trimmed to perfection and the hedge exactly in keeping. Rhododendrons lined the opposite side of the drive in a shower of fiery pink and red. Farther up by the garage, pampas grass predicted the end of summer with its towering feathers, dried and swaying in the early evening breeze. She braked to a stop alongside her father's white Cadillac. Then she strode across the paved walk and through the polished double doors.

"I'm home," she announced, swinging the door shut behind her.

The house was silent. "That slave driver's probably up there catnapping while I worked my fingers to the bone," she said to herself with an impish grin. She crossed the terrazzo entryway and ascended the stairs, her heels barely marking the plush mahogany-colored pile. She reached her father's room, fully expecting his thunderous snores to be rattling every fixture, yet the silence of the house was deafening. Shock washed over her in a single frigid wave at seeing him crumpled on the floor. "McCullough!" she cried with urgent disbelief as she rushed across the room to kneel beside him and grasped him by the collar. "Damn you, Irishman!" she yelled. Then, searching frantically for a pulse, she squeezed his wrist as if she could will him to life. Panic-stricken, she shook him violently, but his limp form gave no response. An ear to his heart, a silent plea to God and—nothing. Nothing except the cold feel of his flesh and the realization, his soul, his mind, so vital, so caring, had escaped her.

Shawn threw back her head, tears stinging her eyes as heart-wrenching sobs wracked her body. Through the tears, her eyes darted back to his face searching desperately, illogically, for the slightest trace of expression. "Daddy?"

Chapter Two

It was one of those crystal-clear September days when the faintest sound or scent is carried on the warm breeze, but as she stood watching the others depart, Shawn felt only numbness. Her eyes moved over the multitude of bright flowers that were draped about the casket. Their pungent odor filled the air and stuck in Shawn's throat like nausea.

"Shawn, honey." The voice jarred her, and she felt a soft touch on her hand. It was Elsa Sommers, the dearest friend she and her father had. "Come on, I'll take you home," Elsa urged.

Shawn shook her head. She wasn't ready to return to the empty house. "No," she answered. "I have my own good-byes to say."

Tears clouded Elsa's soft brown eyes, and her voice was tremulous. "Yes, I understand," she said, and looked away. Then, regaining her composure, she said compassionately, "Stay as long as you like, dear. I'll take care of the guests back at the house." For a moment the two women clutched hands before Elsa hugged Shawn to her breast, then walked slowly over to the casket and extracted a single red rose. "I love you, Jack," she murmured, holding the blossom close to her heart. As Elsa walked to the car, she barely heard the reassuring, masculine voice of Matthew Monroe.

"Don't worry, I'll see her home," he promised.

9

Shawn forced her hesitant feet into motion. The crisp, gray linen of her suit and the silken black of her curls emphasized the pale, frozen set of her features. Her eyes seemed to stare through the casket and beyond it. Shawn squared her shoulders and she gently touched her fingers to her lips and placed them on the coffin. The coldness of the lacquered mahogony struck her with a hard finality. The flowers, the sadness, engulfed her. Shawn turned away abruptly, her eyes fastening on a small stone bench partially hidden under a giant willow tree. She felt like crawling into a hole and hibernating, and her feet instinctively followed her thoughts. It was only beneath the willow that tears broke through her barrier of composure. Shawn dropped to the bench sobbing.

When her tears were spent, she murmured, prayerlike, "Oh, God, Daddy, what will I do without you? I feel so alone."

"You're not alone," a strong voice answered.

Shawn looked up into the sympathetic green eyes of Matthew Monroe as he extended his hand to raise her to her feet.

"You must be cold, you're shivering," he said, and peeled off his suit jacket to drape about her shoulders. "If you're ready, I'll take you home."

In the car Shawn became aware of the man next to her. Matt Monroe, the teenage boy with the enchanting green eyes whom she had so adored as a child of ten. It was kind of him to wait for her, and yet she could not rouse herself to thank him. Instead, she sat quietly studying his features. There was strength in the jawline, a hint of the breeze in his rich brown hair lightly flecked with gold, and a gentleness in his eyes as he looked over and grinned at her. "Do you still like Oreos?" he asked.

Despite her grief, a faint smile crossed her tight lips as she remembered a scorching summer day when she and her best friend Valerie had sat twittering about him, gorging themselves on the cookies, unaware that he had been listening. Suddenly, she could again feel the heat that had flushed her face and neck when he suddenly appeared from nowhere to catch them. His question made her feel like a child again, protected and loved.

She reached over and touched his arm. "It's nice seeing you again, Matt. You always were around when I skinned my knees," she said softly.

His heavy brows arched in thought. "How long has it been? Ten or twelve years?" The wrinkles in his forehead smoothed as he looked over at her and his smile exposed even white teeth.

He always did have straight, beautiful teeth, and she remembered how conscious she'd been of her own metallic smile in those days. "All of that," she said. "As I recall, the last time I saw you was right before you left for UCLA."

"Your memory is better than mine. About all I remember are the holiday dinners when our folks dragged us back and forth to each others' homes, and of course, certain little incidents," he said meaningfully.

She smiled briefly, then wrinkled her brows. "Let's see," she pondered, "there's about seven years difference in our ages. You must be about thirty-three."

"Um, pushing thirty-four," he admitted. He looked over at her and started to say something else, then hesitated, his eyes appraising her delicate features before he glanced back at the road. It wasn't the time to tell her she was beautiful.

Trying to keep her thoughts occupied, she asked, "How is it being a corporate lawyer? Bet you're a smashing success."

He laughed. "I wouldn't exactly say that, unless success is synonymous with busy."

She nodded her agreement. "It seems to follow. And what then brings you to town? Is it a permanent move?"

"No, 'fraid not. I spend most of my time in L.A. Just needed a little R and R."

"You have been away awhile. Are you staying with the folks?"

"Mom wouldn't have it any other way."

In the distance, Shawn could see cars lining the street near her house, and the moment of shared reminiscences gave way to the present. She felt herself stiffen and whispered, "I can't go in."

Matt slowed the 450SL to a halt, then held her hand gently, giving her a minute to steady herself. "I'll be right beside you," he assured her. His steady gaze held hers, and she relaxed for the first time that day.

The next morning Shawn awoke from a restless sleep, thinking she was late for work, then realizing it was Saturday, the day after the funeral. She had invited Elsa to stay the night, the women drawing comfort from each other's company. Exhausted, they had gone to bed early, and now Shawn wanted to lose herself again in the warmth of the comforter and hide from the cold light of day, but the ticking of the clock made her edgy. Throwing back the quilt, she stumbled into the bathroom, splashed cold water on her face, and silently challenged the mirror to describe her feelings. She felt seared by her loss, a terrible loss that not even the mirror could completely expose. And yet no damn Irishman was worth his salt if he couldn't get a handle on his feelings, she told herself firmly. Her father was gone, and his daughter would have to accept it. Then, ignoring the tears trickling down the side of her nose, she threw the hairbrush down and said, "To hell with you, McCullough. I don't care what you demanded in the past, I'll cry if I feel like it, and I'll never get over missing you." She brushed haphazardly at the tears that spilled out of blue eyes the color of sapphires. Sell the business, he had said. "Don't be a slave to it." Was that what she wanted to do? Her mind was a jumble; perhaps in a few days she could evaluate her position. Everyone would give her time, surely even her father's lawyer.

The telephone intruded into her thoughts, and she picked it up reluctantly. "Hello?"

"Hi," Matt's soothing voice came back. "How are you?"

"You want the truth or shall I make up a tall one?"

"Hm"—he seemed to contemplate for a second—"the truth."

"I feel lousy, just plain lousy," she despaired.

"In that case, come out with me for the day," he offered.

Shawn was hesitant. "I don't know, Matt, I'm really a wreck, no sense spoiling your day."

"Just say yes. You need to keep busy, and you'd be doing me a favor as well. Don't know if I can stand all this R and R," he confessed.

Suddenly, Shawn felt the grief begin to lift at his lighthearted teasing, and she had to admit that she needed something different to occupy her mind. Even Elsa had warned against making decisions right away. Take a little time, she had said, but like most things, it was easier said than done. Shawn was impulsive by nature and not inclined to procrastinate. Still, she knew it was good advice and she needed a diversion. "Well, I suppose—"

"That's good enough. Don't say anything more," he interrupted. "Dress casual. I'll pick you up in half an hour."

Shawn couldn't help laughing at his rush of words.

"Did you know you have a beautiful laugh?" he said gently before hanging up.

She replaced the phone with a small smile. Strange that he should come back into her life right now. Still, his bantering was uplifting, and she pushed the fingers of guilt aside, hurrying to brush her dark strands of hair to a glossy radiance, then applied a touch of color to her pale lips and cheeks. McCullough had had no patience with mourning. She pulled off her nightgown and rummaged through the closet, choosing a pair of neatly tailored white pants and a bright blue sweater. Electric blue made her eyes glitter, everyone said. She glanced in the mirror and had to admit that the color made a difference. Her eyes were black-fringed blue velvet; her cheeks and lips had lost their pallor. Shawn smiled faintly at her reflection and left the room.

When she entered the kitchen, Elsa was already dressed and sitting at the white wrought-iron table having coffee. Her beautiful silver-gray hair formed a halo around her aristocratic features, and when she smiled up at

Shawn, her golden brown eyes were gentle, her smile caring.

"Good morning," she said as if it were any other normal day.

"Did you sleep well?" Shawn asked.

"No, but I think I'll make it, how about you?"

For a moment the two women's eyes met in mutual understanding. Then Elsa broke the silence. "You look mighty pretty," she said. "Going somewhere?"

A guilty twinge gripped Shawn and she was tempted to call Matt and cancel, but she knew Elsa would protest. "Yes, Matt called," she answered. "I don't know where we're going, but he'll be here soon. Do you mind?"

"Mind? Of course not. He seems to be just what you need. Now, I don't want any explanation, just enjoy the day. I have some errands to do, but I'll be here when you get back." She poured a steaming cup of coffee and handed it to Shawn.

"Did anyone ever tell you that you're a great lady?"

Elsa smiled in reply and gazed out the window. "Your gentleman caller is here," she said. "I'll let him in."

Shawn's stomach tightened in a knot, and her hand rattled the coffee cup as she set it on the glass tabletop. What was she feeling? Had she never gotten over the ridiculous school-girl crush she had had so long ago? Why, she hadn't even thought about him through the years except when she'd heard of his broken engagement and later a rumor about a beautiful blond he was supposedly romancing. Her thoughts were interrupted by the pleasantries exchanged between Matt and Elsa. She smoothed her hair and pulled at her sweater nervously, then smiled as he walked into the kitchen.

His green eyes sparkled at the sight of her, and she was glad she'd worn the bright blue. "Are you ready?" he asked.

"Ready as I'll ever be," she said.

"Then come along, my dear," he said, taking her arm. "'Bye, Elsa."

"Have a good time, you two," Elsa returned.

"See you tonight," Shawn said. "And thanks again for everything."

Elsa waved her hand in protest. "I love you, remember?"

The statement brought tears to Shawn's eyes, and she hurried out the door without another word. Once inside the car, she was silent. Matt looked over and touched her arm reassuringly. "I'm all right," she said in a small voice. "Just an emotional jerk. I promise, I won't let it spoil your day." She forced herself to smile and added, "Now, Prince Charming, just where are we going?"

"To the castle and pull up the drawbridge. Then I'll have you all to myself." He gave her a feigned lecherous grin and twirled an imaginary handlebar mustache.

This time she smiled genuinely. "Still the charmer," she said, and for some odd reason she wanted to ask about his broken engagement and the blond, but she wasn't sure she wanted to hear about it, so she concentrated on the freeway traffic. Matt was quietly listening to the stereo, but she was keenly aware of his presence next to her. A navy pair of pants set off his kelly green polo shirt, which pulled taut across his muscular chest. His tanned, powerful arms gave her a steadying feeling yet unnerved her all at the same time. His profile was a portrait of strength: the firm jawline, the arch of his heavy brows, the straightness of his nose, and the clarity of his eyes made her curious about his love life. Was he gentle or demanding? A small laugh escaped her.

"That's what I want to hear," he said, glancing at her. "Private joke, or can anyone join in?"

"I was just thinking how odd that we haven't seen each other in so long. Living so close by, we must have just missed each other."

"Strange, isn't it? But then, who would expect to find such beauty in their own backyard?" he said pensively as though thinking aloud. Then he added in a less sober tone, "But it's just as well, I had a lot to learn about women."

"Oh, really?" she said, refusing to be serious. "And what did you learn?"

"Not a hell of a lot, I guess." He laughed. "But I keep trying."

"I'll bet you do."

He raised his brows but didn't comment as he hummed along with the stereo. Shawn could see Marriott's Great America in the distance, and she knew without asking that that was where they were going. A tingle of excitement stirred within her as Matt turned into the parking lot and concentrated on the parking attendant's hand movements for direction. When they were eased into a space, he smiled over at her. "Are you ready for this?"

"Why not? I love amusement parks," she said.

For an instant, his eyes held hers, and he reached over to gently caress the soft line of her jaw. "Still a little girl at heart," he said fondly. "You make me feel so damn good."

His touch made her flesh tingle under her sweater, and she was glad he didn't notice. Somehow she knew he didn't expect a reply, but if he had, she might have said the same thing about him.

"Come on, little girl, we're gonna ride everything."

"Everything? Not the Demon!"

"Uh huh, I said everything."

"Matt Monroe, that thing scares me to death!"

"Don't worry, I'll hang on to you," he promised.

"You won't have to. I'll cling so close to you you'll think I'm your Siamese twin!" she promised indignantly.

His expression was innocent as he asked, "Oh? Just where would we be joined?"

She reached over and swatted him playfully. "Forget it. You might be Robin Hood, but I'm really not Maid Marian," she stated with the emphasis on *maid*.

He laughed uproariously. "You know, I think I believe you. That's a hell of a shame," he said, shaking his head all the while he sized her up with obvious approval.

Shawn could feel her face flush as his hand engulfed hers and they joined the milling crowd at the ticket office. Shawn's excitement built as she watched the laughing

teenagers and a little boy who stood next to her tugging at
his mother's sleeve. "I wanna ride the merry-go-round,
Mamma, the biggest, blackest horse, okay?"

Shawn stooped to his level. "A black horse?" she said. "I
thought all princes rode white chargers."

"No, lady, my mom says black is beautiful, but it's okay,
you can ride a white one."

She looked down at his smiling black face and grinned.
"You're absolutely right! Why didn't I think of that, faith
and begorrah, and me being black Irish at that!"

He gave her a quizzical look but laughed along with her.
As she straightened up, she saw Matt watching her with
an amused smile.

People were everywhere—kids carrying balloons, eating hot dogs, and sundaes piled high with whipped cream
and chocolate syrup. For the moment, Shawn forgot about
yesterday. This was an amusement park, a fantasy world,
and she was caught up by the mood of the crowd. Her eyes
scanned the little shops and lingered on the double level
merry-go-round.

"Well, what are we waiting for?" Matt asked noticing
her glance.

When the calliope music stopped and the riders dismounted, Shawn immediately headed for a pinto, and her
newfound small friend claimed the horse next to her.

Matt could hear Shawn giggling and was pleased to see
that her attention was devoted to the little black boy
beside her. She seemed to be enjoying herself as much as if
it were a real animal beneath her, slapping the reins and
nudging the flanks as she pointed to various rides and
chatted with her young acquaintance. Gliding around the
carousel ahead of Matt, she appeared vibrant, her beautiful oval face the picture of enjoyment, and her eyes
sparkling with gaiety, her shiny dark hair flowing in the
breeze. He noted the graceful curves of her body, the
tininess of her waist, and the entrancing ease with which
she moved. He caught himself wondering if that flawless
ivory complexion extended from head to toe. He was sorry
when the ride ended and she dismounted. For a moment,

he sat watching her as she bid farewell to Jason, her new little friend.

"Hey, remember me?" Matt was beside her now. "You sure get involved, don't you?"

She realized he was smiling, and nodded. "Yes, I've been known to." For the first time in several days, she felt some of the tension slip away. For the moment, she could lose herself with this handsome man next to her. "Isn't it gorgeous?" she said, stretching her arms to encompass the whole park.

"Yes, you sure are," he blurted out, then hastened to add, "What's your next pleasure?"

"I don't know, surprise me!"

For the next few hours, they wandered through the shops, viewed the park's enormity from the Ferris wheel, and delighted in the cool spray of water that sifted back into their faces on Loggers' Run. When they returned to earth from the lofty cages of Sky World, Matt suggested a late lunch, and her gnawing stomach agreed.

They ate at Harbor Inn. Shawn enjoyed watching the people while she savored her shrimp along with the New England atmosphere. She scarcely noticed that Matt was quiet too. The food was delicious, and she was glad that he'd talked her into coming, even though a faint rush of guilt kept cropping up whenever they relaxed. He seemed to sense her change of mood and hastened her back to the happy throng of people, suggesting that they ride the train to the park's opposite end. The cool breeze felt refreshing, and she was almost sorry to disembark until she spied the huge, stuffed dinosaurs hanging from the ceiling of one of the concessions.

"Matt, win me one of those?" she said impulsively, pointing to the wildly colored animals.

His eyebrows shot up. "Sounds easy, doesn't it? Well, let's give it a shot." For the next twenty minutes, Matt pitched dimes with Shawn fortifying him with stacks of change until he began talking to the silver coins. "Get in there, you little son of a gun! Oh, damn, don't bounce." Try as he might, the dimes continually ricocheted off the dishes. And he felt as though every dinosaur in the place was staring at him, taunting him. He was relieved when Shawn gave up reluctantly and tugged at his arm.

"Never mind," she said disappointedly.

Matt pitched the last dime without looking as he turned to go. "You did it!" Shawn jumped up and down, clapping her hands gleefully, and impulsively hugging his big frame. "I'll take the orange one," she announced to the attendant with outstretched hands.

"Oh, dear," she said, slightly bowing under the stuffed animal's cumbersome weight.

Matt laughed and easily lifted the monster into his muscled arms. "This thing's damn near as big as you."

"You're right," she admitted. "Thank you, kind sir."

"It's quite all right. Now it's time you did something for me," he said fiendishly.

"Oh? What's that?"

"Ride the Demon."

Her face paled. "Do we have to?"

"Uh huh." He clasped her small hand in his large, firm one and pulled her toward the line.

Shawn followed his lead reluctantly. "We can't," she said. "Whatever will we do with Timothy?"

"Timothy? Oh," he said, looking at the mass of orange plush cradled in his arm. A frown crossed his brow. "Just a minute," he said, and walked back to the booth with Shawn trailing behind him. He handed the smiling ticket-seller a dollar bill to watch the stuffed animal while Shawn searched her mind frantically for another excuse.

Almost instantly, he was back at her side, his arm guiding her to doom. There was no mistaking his determination. Shawn resigned herself to fate and allowed herself to be led through the gate. After they were belted in, she held her breath all the way to the top of the first upside-down loop on the roller coaster, then let it out in one big scream that lasted the entire way down and around again. Matt threw back his head and laughed, his arm tight around her, and as they came out of the loop and went into

a corkscrew, their bodies molded together. As they topped
the second loop, Shawn drew in her breath, and her eyes
grew wide and she gasped,"Oh God, hel-l-p!" She hardly
noticed when Matt pulled her closer, his mouth pressed
against her hair. When they finally slowed to a halt, he
turned to stare silently at her, his brow furrowed.

Her eyes went a blue blaze. "What the hell are you
thinking?"

An amused smile returned to his lips. "I was just
wondering if the way you express yourself would be more
effective if you weren't so little."

"Who cares?" she retorted. "Right now my heart's
pounding hard enough to crack my ribs!"

"Can I feel?" He raised his hand.

"No!" She slapped teasingly at his fingers. "I think I
need a tranquilizer," she groaned.

"Got just the thing." He helped her out of the car and
ushered her to a bench. "You wait here."

Shawn was glad for the reprieve as she suddenly felt
fatigued. She tried to relax her tightened muscles by
watching the passing people and enjoying the scenery.
Her eyes rested on the pansies behind a foot-high,
wrought-iron fence when thoughts of yesterday crept into
her mind. She tore her gaze away from the brightly
colored flowers and turned her back on them.

"This will give you a new burst of energy," Matt
promised as he sat beside her and placed a huge cone of
cotton candy in her hand.

Cotton candy, oh, God, McCullough had been like a big
kid about cotton candy. She remembered shortly after her
mother died, he had taken her to the boardwalk at Santa
Cruz and bought it for both of them, knowing that she
loved it too. He had tried to ease her sorrow by carrying on
when his own heart was breaking. Shawn could feel the
tears welling in her eyes, but she managed a polite,
"Thank you."

Matt took a bite of the fluff and licked his sticky lips
before he noticed that she hadn't touched hers and that
tears were trickling down her pretty face as she stared at

the pink foam in front of her. Somehow he knew it had triggered memories of her father. He took the cone from her limp hand and walked over to the trash can, depositing both pink reminders. When he returned, Shawn was still sitting rigidly, silent tears coursing down her cheeks.

Matt reached out and pulled her to his chest. "Cry, Shawn, go ahead and cry, honey," he whispered, and she couldn't help obeying.

When the tears began to ease, she pulled away from the protection of his shoulder and looked at him through red-rimmed eyes. "I'm so sorry, I ruined your day after all."

"No," he said huskily, "it's been a wonderful day. Come on, I'll take you home now."

Shawn hardly noticed that he scooped up Timothy in one arm as he led her out of the park with his other arm wrapped around her. She sat quietly during the drive home and at intervals, she could feel his eyes upon her in the dim light of the dashboard. But she had nothing to say, and he gave her the right to her memories. And for a brief instant, his thoughts shifted to another beautiful woman.

Back at her home, she took his hand getting out of the car and rested her head against his shoulder going up the walk. The night was warm, and the moon played elusive tricks with the trees and shrubs, and Matt's heart ached with longing for the little shadow of a girl as it had never ached before. For the first time in his life, he was at a loss for words. He wanted to hold her close and never let her go, comfort her with kisses, with love.

She managed a smile and a polite thank-you at the door, but her mind was elsewhere. Matt reached down and kissed the tip of her nose gently. "Sleep well," he said. "I'll stop by in the afternoon tomorrow around two. Maybe we can do something quiet, okay?"

She raised his big hand that was holding her small one to her cheek in a strange, little gesture almost like a hug, and nodded. Then she was gone, and he stood staring at the door, wishing he could hold her next to him. "Good night, Shawn," he whispered. "Tomorrow's a new day."

Chapter Three

Sunday, Shawn was up before dawn, pacing the floor of the empty living room, completely absorbed by thoughts of the future. She reached for a cup of coffee from the silver tray, her hand shaking as she brought it to her lips. She was bone-weary, and try as she might to relax her mind, she couldn't silence her thoughts. What about the McCullough Landscaping business? The question kept pounding at her, and she knew that Tony Rizzo and all her dad's employees were worriedly asking themselves the same thing. Of course, they had all been considerate at the funeral, not even the slightest question as to her plans for the company, yet they would be anxious.

If she sold the business, what would she do? Stay on as an estimator under new ownership? Could she work for someone else, or would she be at odds with a new owner, always thinking that McCullough would have done things differently? If the boss were someone like Andrew Bellows, she knew they would be at swords' points in one hell of a hurry.

The very thought of Bellows angered her. If ever a man was well known in landscaping, Bellows was. Strangely enough, she had never met the man, though he was the talk of the industry. His building projects alone contributed a vast share of work to Bay Area landscapers. The newspapers occasionally featured write-ups on his various enterprises, and she had seen his picture once but couldn't remember now what he looked like.

Shawn put the coffee cup down on the table and sank to the sofa, her hands cradling her chin as she stared out the window at the brightening sky. It was finally morning, and she had all kinds of options. She could sell the business, making money enough to walk away and start something new, yet her concern for the employees nagged her, and with winter coming up and the loss of the Arcadia Lane shopping center contract, the prospect of a sale right now seemed dismal. It would take time. On the other hand, who said she had to sell? Could she really totally enter a man's world and run the operation herself? She had to admit that landscaping was a big part of her life, just as it had been of her father's. She had trailed after him enough since she was knee-high, gaining considerable experience with the best of teachers.

Then she'd grown up and was no longer her father's sidekick in the field. She was suddenly a young lady involved in social activities that monopolized her time, and later she was busy at Stanford working on her B.A. Only after graduation did she reenter the landscaping world and once again become her father's assistant, only this time on the inside.

Suddenly she wondered if she could still run a backhoe, and she was surprised that today she could think of McCullough with a little less pain. She would talk to Elsa about it. Elsa could advise her if anyone could. She glanced at the stately grandfather clock, whose melodious chimes she had been ignoring for the past several hours. Ten o'clock. She would fix a fancy brunch for Elsa. She rose from the sofa, tightened the sash of her pink satin robe, slid her feet into the fluffy white scuffs she'd kicked off earlier, and went to the kitchen to start brunch.

"Good morning, honey. Can I help?" Elsa offered from the doorway.

"No, it's my turn to pamper you, but you could give me some advice."

"You know you can talk to me anytime," Elsa returned with a smile.

"Well, Elsa, I'm worried about the business. I know McCullough wanted me to sell it, but, Elsa, I'm concerned about the employees and"—she hesitated—"I guess I have to be honest, it's too much a part of me, of Dad. Do you think I could run it?"

"Look, young lady, you can do anything if you want to badly enough," Elsa stated. Shawn nodded in agreement and waited for Elsa to continue. "However, consider that working directly with the men wouldn't be easy."

"Yes, but Tony Rizzo would still be dealing with the men on the outside," Shawn said as she pulled the quiche out of the microwave, cut it into slices, and scooped out a portion onto a plate, then set it in front of Elsa.

Elsa sniffed its mouth-watering aroma. "Umm, that smells scrumptious."

Pulling out two bowls of fresh fruit from the refrigerator, Shawn said, "I guess you're trying to tell me that even with Tony, there would be times when I would have to intervene in the tougher situations just because of the hat I'd be wearing."

"I think you said it. And don't forget, a business of that nature is still essentially a man's world. It wouldn't be easy. On the other hand, you could take the money if you sell and invest it in something with fewer headaches." Elsa ate with obvious relish while she talked.

"Yes, I suppose you're right," Shawn said with resignation and lowered eyes. She paused, then emphatically slapped the table. "I'll sell it! There comes a time when logic must overrule my Irish temperament." Relieved at having made her decision, she slid back her chair and gave her adviser a grateful hug.

An hour later, she was dressed and bidding Elsa goodbye when the phone rang. "You go ahead and answer, honey, I'll give you a call in a day or two," Elsa urged from the doorway. "If you get lonesome, come spend a few days with me. I'd love it!"

"I will," Shawn said, and hurried to pick up the receiver.

It was Tony Rizzo wanting to know how she was faring and if she would be at the office tomorrow. Elsa was scarcely gone, and loneliness had already set in. Work would be good therapy, and besides, Shawn wasn't one to procrastinate. "Yes, I'll see you at seven," she said. "There's a lot we'll need to talk over. Thanks for calling, Tony." She replaced the phone thoughtfully.

It was still several hours till Matt's arrival. She had made up her mind about the business, and she didn't want to think about it anymore—or the way that she was beginning to feel about Matt. She'd been in love only once before and it hadn't worked. Jim had been a nice fellow, unfortunately plagued by a domineering mother and no will to oppose her. Shawn had broken off the relationship, and for a while she was downhearted. Her closeness to her father and her work filled the void satisfactorily, she told herself, and for the past year, she had more or less avoided serious involvements. No more heartaches. She would keep it that way with Matt, too, she resolved. Shawn picked up the novel she'd begun reading more than a week ago and attempted to lose herself in someone else's life.

It was one P.M. when she put the book aside to get ready to meet Matt. She automatically glanced into her father's study as she walked by, a pang of loneliness gripping her as she hurried up the stairs. Perhaps a dress, a bright print to boost her spirits. She showered quickly and chose a soft silk with red and navy splashes against a white background. She was putting the final touches on her makeup when the door chimes announced Matt's arrival.

"Hi," she said, smiling as she opened the door to greet Matt who was lounging against the railing, dressed in a casual plaid sport shirt and chinos.

"Hi, yourself," he said, leaning forward to give her a paternal peck on the forehead, then stepped back for a long look at her. "You're more beautiful today than yesterday."

"Is that one of your standard lines?" she chided, determined to keep the mood light.

"Only with you," he said seriously, then an easy smile flashed across his face. "Oh, just a minute, I almost forgot again." With that, he was momentarily gone, reappearing in the doorway to hand her yesterday's winnings from the amusement park.

She giggled as she hugged the plush monster before depositing the dinosaur on the terrazzo and turning to Matt. "Thanks for your thoughtfulness."

"It's nothing." He shrugged. "He needs a home, and as I recall, you wanted the critter."

They both laughed. "It's good to hear you laugh," he said. "Grab your bathing suit and let's go!"

Shawn gave him a quizzical glance, but as she followed him to the car carrying her beach bag, she muttered, "It's insane, my goose bumps will have goose bumps. It must be all of sixty-five degrees."

In the car, she waited for his explanation with growing impatience. "Okay, we're on our way to where?"

"Uncle Neal's. He's not really my uncle, but I've called him that since I was a kid. Actually, he and Aunt Millie are close friends of the family. They live in Woodside, up among the redwoods. I want to show you their place. Very unique. Quiet and peaceful, just what you need."

"I see," Shawn said, suddenly uneasy about meeting his old friends. She felt comfortable with Matt—he had seen her at her worst—but was she ready to socialize with strangers? She sat silently, admiring the scenery as the Mercedes easily took the horseshoe curves up the mountain roads.

"Quarter for your thoughts," Matt said, smiling over at her.

"That's a penny."

"What about inflation?"

She laughed. He knew just how to loosen her up, and she liked it. "How long are you staying?" she asked.

"Hopefully another week; that is, unless duty calls. This time I hope old T. J. can manage on his own. I'm enjoying every minute of this trip," he said quietly.

His intimate look made her feel warm, and the curve in the road shifted her closer to his side. She moved away and snapped on her seatbelt.

"You afraid of me?" he asked with a teasing gleam in his eyes.

"No, just used to precaution," she said, but an inner voice told her differently. Here was a guy she could love so easily, it said, a man who was in command, yet one who could hurt her, not like the men, who up to now she had been able to control.

"Well, here we are," he said, turning into a scenic cul-de-sac. He got out and opened a wrought-iron gate while Shawn's eyes followed the curve of the driveway to an immense redwood home that was set deep among the trees.

As they drove up the tree-lined lane, Shawn couldn't help thinking how different this beauty was from the plans that she was used to bidding where spacing of trees, shrubs, and flowers was sometimes too precise. Here, nature had scattered ferns and wild flowers, yet the overall effect was astounding beauty that could never be achieved on a drawing board. She was so caught up in the wild splendor of the place that it was a moment before she realized that they had arrived and that Matt already was getting something from the trunk. Shawn got out and smiled with pleasure. How difficult it was to grow ferns just a mere ten miles away. Yet on King's Mountain they grew in lush abundance.

Her eyes traveled the length of the house. A set of stairs led to the first of several decks that were obviously designed to view the magnificent canyon to her left. She could easily see why the builder had incorporated so much glass in the redwood construction. Who would want to miss the morning sun on the tree-studded canyon walls?

"Well, what do you think?" Matt said from behind her.

"It's got to be the enchanted forest! This house—it's so magnificent." Only then did she notice the two bags he was carrying. "What's that?"

"Dinner." He went up the stairs across the deck to the front door with Shawn trailing behind him.

"Dinner?" she said, watching him juggle the bags while reaching for a key to unlock the unique hand-carved door.

"Matt, will you tell me what's going on here? Where are your aunt and uncle?" she demanded.

He returned her frown with a grin. "Virgin Islands, I think Mom said. They'll be gone for several weeks and she's house-sitting. Seemed like a good idea to relieve her of the chore and be able to enjoy it too, don't you agree?"

"You mean we'll have this mansion all to ourselves?" she said incredulously.

"Uh huh," he said with a gleam in his eyes that suggested ulterior motives.

For a moment Shawn let herself imagine how it would feel to be held in the arms of Matt Monroe, till the old hurt of her broken romance abruptly returned to mind. Loving Matt could be even more painful, yet she was finding it harder and harder to resist his charm. Still, she wouldn't give him the satisfaction of knowing her indecision.

Thoughtfully, she followed him into the living room, which was decorated in a blend of warm earth tones that lent a coziness, yet an elegance, to the room, despite the high-beamed ceiling. Two matching sofas done in a blue-and-rust print on an ivory background formed an L around an ornately carved coffee table in front of the fireplace. He hurried her through a regal dining room, stopped to leave the groceries in the kitchen, then ushered her down a hall. He threw open a set of hand-carved double doors. "The pool, my dear," he indicated with a theatrical sweep of his hands, allowing her to enter first.

Shawn took two steps and stopped, her eyes darting about the room in awe. The redwood ceiling arched high overhead, culminating in a huge, dome-shaped skylight that filtered sunlight to the potted miniature palms scattered about on the first level of the white marble floor. The yellow pots enhanced the foliage, and the kelly-green-and-white print pillows that were strewn about. At the far end of the first level along a glass wall sat several wicker-footed, glass-topped tables with matching high-backed chairs and yellow print cushions. Directly ahead of Shawn were three steps that led to a sunken pool surrounded by a white marble walkway large enough to contain white wicker lounges with the same colorful print cushions. In the center of the beautiful pool was a magnificent recirculating fountain. Richly stained redwood walls gave warmth to the white marble floors.

When Shawn's eyes had fully absorbed the splendor of the room, she turned to Matt, who was watching her reaction with delight, the same pleased expression that he had worn when he first opened the door for her. The smile she returned was radiant. "I love it, *love* it!" she declared enthusiastically. Not waiting for a response, she descended the steps to the pool and stood watching the misty bubbles cascading from the fountain. The entire pool seemed to be alive with frothy foam and dancing water, illuminated by what appeared to be a circular lighting system beneath a shower of glittering moisture.

Minutes later when she came out of the dressing room, Matt already was sprawled on one of the lounges on the pool level. His lean, muscular body diverted her attention from their surroundings. He was tanned, handsome, virile, and confident, and she ignored the sudden urge to brush her fingers through the dark hair on his chest.

When Matt looked up, the tacit approval in his eyes brought a blush to Shawn's cheeks almost as if he had read her mind. She tried to take his appreciative stare at her bikini-clad form in stride. "You sure look great in red," he said. "Even if there isn't very damn much of it."

Suddenly she became self-conscious in her tiny swim suit and terribly aware of his disconcerting gaze. She dropped her towel on the lounge beside him and quickly dove into the water. Instantly, he was on his feet and into the pool after her. They splashed and played in the refreshing bubbles, swimming at intervals until Shawn was weak with pleasure. "I don't know if I have the strength to get out," she breathed.

In one easy motion, Matt scooped her up in his arms, carried her to a lounge, and deposited her gently on it. Then, reaching for her towel, he dried her legs and arms, ever so slowly, as he sat on the edge of her couch. Shawn was oddly unnerved by his touch and avoided his eyes when he bent to brush a light kiss on her shoulder. He suddenly rose to his feet, insisting she sit and enjoy the sun setting behind the tree-studded hillside, its radiance delicately frosting the upper edge of the canyon with a golden hue as the gray dusk overtook the valley floor below. Shawn wasn't aware of how much time had passed until he reappeared in the doorway with their plates. She couldn't help wondering how many women he had plied with his gourmet skills plus his charming attention. The steak was rare and juicy, the asparagus hollandaise light, the salad crisp.

For the next hour they chatted like old friends while savoring the perfect dinner, until night finally cast its shadow of darkness, and the only illumination was the flickering glow from the fireplace across the open room. Shawn felt totally relaxed as she sipped her wine and sat back lazily in her chair. "That was excellent, Matt! I couldn't eat another bite!"

"Oh, but you must! I've prepared a special dessert for you," he announced. "Just sit tight, you wouldn't want to miss this," he insisted, pushing back his chair. When he returned, he was carrying a crystal pedestal cake plate with a silver cover and an elegant cake server.

Shawn's stomach gurgled in protest as she watched him place the elaborate setup before her and raise the cover with a flourish. *"Voilà!"* he cried, and with a sweep of his hand unveiled his masterpiece.

Shawn's eyes grew enormous for a moment before she began giggling so hard it was a long pause before she could speak. "Oreos!" she gasped between fits of laughter. "You're too much," she said. "Won't I ever live down that Oreo Caper?"

"I hope not," he said with a chuckle. "I rather liked what you and Valerie said about me that day. Tell me, do you still think I'm—what was it you said—gorgeous?"

"Oh, all of that," she teased, unaware of his subtle mood change as he looked at her.

Matt rose from his chair, and in one easy movement was behind her, his arms encircling her waist, his lips brushing her ear as he gently raised her to her feet. "The hell with the Oreos," he whispered, his mouth seeking hers. Shawn's lips yielded beneath his searching, demanding kiss before she gently pulled away.

"No, please Matt, it's all too soon. I've always dreamed of this, but I'm in such a state right now that I don't know if it's real or only a dream. I don't want this one to fade."

Chapter Four

The next morning Shawn swung into the parking lot and leaned her elbows on the steering wheel for a moment, but the familiar security was gone, replaced by a sense of anxiety. Her eyes immediately traveled to the office door. McCullough Landscaping, Inc. Sadness welled up in her throat, and she realized that if she let her emotions rule, she would change her decision to sell. Quickly, she got out of the car, entered the building, and suddenly she thought about the park bid that she had labored over on the day her father died. For an instant, she told herself the outcome didn't really matter, but she couldn't divorce herself from the welfare of the employees or her own highly competitive spirit.

She averted her head from her father's closed office door and headed for the familiar sanctity of her office with its potted, shiny philodendron near the door, the drawing board in one corner, and several gold upholstered chairs centered around a coffee table in front of a neatly kept desk. A pang of regret stirred. It would not be for much longer that she would use the books shelved in the mahogany case behind the desk, nor would she enjoy the sun filtering in the window.

"Good morning," Tony Rizzo said from the doorway, his black eyes questioning her mood.

"Hi, Tony," Shawn returned, managing a light smile. "How goes it this morning?"

"Not too bad," he said in a more relaxed tone as he entered the office. Then a smile broadened his mouth. "Oh, I damn near forgot, we got the park!"

A surge of enthusiasm coursed through Shawn. "That's great!" she said, and motioned for him to sit down. "Now tell me, how much money did I leave lying on the table?"

Tony grinned. It was always the first question every contractor asked because of fear that they had over-looked something and "bought a job" in the jargon of the industry. "You were right in the ballpark," he said. "Bradford and Collins missed it by seventy-five dollars, and the other bids ranged to around five hundred dollars over. Right on, I'd say. We're still in business," he kidded.

Shawn felt mixed emotions. "Still in business" he'd said. This would make the impending sale easier, and yet she hated to break the news. "Tony," she started, then glancing out the office window, she saw Steve Nelson, one of the foremen, get out of his truck and saunter into the office. The daily routine had begun; the news of her decision to sell would have to wait.

"Get back to me when you have some spare time," she said. "Oh, and thank you, Tony, for looking after things while—"

"Hey, no thanks necessary, boss lady," he interrupted.

She looked up at his tone and the familiar endearment, knowing that he had transferred from her father to herself his full support. Tears made her eyes a deeper blue, and she couldn't speak.

"You know something?" he said, reaching across the desk to touch her shoulder gently. "You got what it takes, or you wouldn't be here this morning. I'll swear, you Irish are all guts."

His compliment boosted her spirits. "You bet we are," she said in a suddenly confident voice, and brushed away the tears impatiently.

Tony smiled. "Hey, why don't we have that discussion at lunch? Charley Brown's around noon?"

Shawn nodded. "I'll be there," she said in a firm voice.

Andrew Bellows's sharply defined features clearly registered his annoyance as he leaned on the restaurant's railing overlooking the fireplace and observed the brisk flow of lunch traffic. It was eleven forty-five A.M., and not a sign of Sam Goldberg. He drummed impatiently on the railing with his fingers, then pushed up a well-tailored sleeve to glance at an expensive gold watch.

Time was, as usual, in short supply. With his vast fortune, it was the one thing he could not buy, and he hated to waste a microsecond of it. There wasn't one gray strand in his wavy blond hair, and at thirty-six, he had the physique of a twenty-five-year-old, a fact which he attributed to his daily workouts. There were only two things, apart from work, for which Andrew Bellows allowed time: his health regime and attractive women. He rarely missed morning laps around the pool even at times when he had been out till sunup. Bellows had a playboy reputation, and almost every single woman on the peninsula found him desirable, although extremely elusive, generous, and a very unwilling candidate for marriage. Why get married? He had his choice of women, and in all fairness, neither the time nor the inclination for a lasting relationship.

He was a self-made man, having acquired his money through building contracts and a very sharp business acumen in real estate. Early in his dealings, he had purchased vast land holdings in numerous states. Bellows's fortune began to grow with his construction of multistoried groups of town houses, and it didn't stop there. He seemed to have a sixth sense about timing and proved it over and over again by holding onto property until appreciation coupled with volume had made him a powerfully rich man. One thing separated him from his competitors, however. While his peers mainly specialized in one or two areas of construction, Andrew Bellows built everything from high-rises to shopping centers to huge freeway projects, and his challenges extended to the international level.

Again, he tapped his fingers on the railing, pondering about going to the bar for a drink. No, he would wait for Goldberg; Bellows rarely had more than one cocktail for lunch. A smart businessman kept his wits about him, undulled by alcohol, and he knew that cold, hard fact better than most.

His attention was diverted by a lovely young woman entering the restaurant. As he stood admiring her walk toward the hostess, he was impressed by her grace; she seemed to move effortlessly. His intense blue eyes took in all of her and listened as she informed the hostess that she would wait, someone was joining her shortly. Another socialite with nothing better to do than gossip over lunch with a friend, he decided, but he had to admit that this one was in a class by herself. In her navy blue linen suit and bright print blouse, she was chic and beautiful. He watched intently as Shawn approached the waiting area where she glanced at her watch.

"We seem to have the same problem," he said by way of introduction. "Would you care to join me for a drink?" Bellows sized her up with interest, all the way from her shiny black hair to her ringless fourth finger and slowly on down to her size six shoes, deciding that she was something different all right.

"I seldom drink at lunch," she countered his frank evaluation flatly. "And never on a working day."

"Oh," he said with growing curiosity. "Perhaps you'd be so kind as to enlighten me as to what you do."

"I'm not always noted for my kindness," she returned in a mockingly sweet voice. Then spying Tony coming through the door, she left Bellows to ponder her retreating figure, and as she and Tony were ushered to the dining area, the look on Bellows's face stated very clearly what he was thinking.

Andrew Bellows was seldom turned down, by anyone,

but of course, she didn't know his identity. Why hadn't he thought to introduce himself? The thought that the beautiful woman had eluded him was depressing, and he was relieved to see Goldberg finally make an appearance.

"Will this table be satisfactory, Mr. Bellows?" the hostess inquired sweetly.

At the next table, unseen, but back-to-back with Andrew Bellows, Shawn drew in a deep breath at the mention of his name and recognized the voice of the man who had tried to buy her a drink earlier. It couldn't be *the* Andrew Bellows!

Shawn toyed with her spinach salad, only half-listening to Tony as he filled her in on current job status. She commented at the proper times, although her attention kept straying to the next table. Was the man behind her actually the infamous Bellows? The back of his blond head didn't tell her a thing, yet she shamelessly eavesdropped.

"Now, tell me, Sam, what do you think about that suit Bernard Johnson slapped on me?"

"He'll collect, one way or another. It's an open-and-shut case. The man did, in fact, get hurt on your job even though it was L and C Landscaping's fault." The gray-haired lawyer shrugged. "But that's why you have liability insurance. Only thing is, it's been a series of stupid incidents with Lenard and Cramer that makes you look bad."

Sam's client frowned, and his icy, blue eyes clearly registered his irritation. "I don't need that kind of undeserved reputation," he said in disgust. "There's no way of controlling those goddamn subcontractors."

Sam Goldberg smiled. "It's a fact of life," he said. "Maybe you ought to consider buying your own landscaping company. You sure could keep them busy."

"I don't have time to fool around with starting another new company right now," Bellows snorted.

"There are easier ways." The attorney made a subtle yet well-placed suggestion and flashed Bellows a sly smile.

"You mean buy an established corporation?"

"Why not? You'd have control and experience."

"And just where am I going to find a landscape outfit worth a damn that's up for sale?"

"What about McCullough Landscaping? Old man Mc-Cullough just died, and no doubt left it to his only daughter. I expect it'll be on the market soon."

Shawn almost choked.

"McCullough Landscaping, huh?" Andrew Bellows's brow wrinkled in thought as he sipped his scotch on the rocks. "Oh yes, they're the ones who did our town houses in Palo Alto. Not a bad suggestion, Sam!" He took a bite of his filet, narrowing his eyes as he chewed. "You know, the idea is tempting. L and C are sloppy, and they've gotten out of control. I've just about had it with them." He rubbed his chin and looked at the attorney. "A daughter, huh? How old?"

Goldberg shrugged. "How do I know? You're the guy who keeps track of the ladies. Probably twenty-five or thirty, I'd guess."

"Hm. I'm feeling charitable today. We might be able to get it for a song. It's damn probable she can't run the business, probably doesn't know the first thing about it," he pondered aloud. "A woman running a landscape outfit would be asinine."

At the next table, Tony and Shawn's conversation stopped abruptly at the mention of McCullough Landscaping. As they listened, Tony could see cold anger blazing in Shawn's eyes, and as she took a deep breath and put her fork down with deliberate calm, he wondered how she would handle this. By the look on her face, Bellows was about to get a reaction. What kind was anybody's guess.

Shawn reached in her purse with a shaky hand muttering, "For a song, huh? Asinine, huh? I'll show that, that . . . owoo, I can't even think of a rotten enough word!" She drew out one of her business cards and a pen. Tony dared not smile as he watched her slash a line through *Estimator* and write *Owner,* but he grinned to himself as she rose from her chair. The McCullough Irish was up.

With seething calm, Shawn tapped Andrew Bellows on the shoulder.

As he looked up in surprise, an eager grin lit up his handsome face when he recognized the beauty who had turned him down earlier.

"So you're Andrew Bellows. Since I'm feeling exceptionally charitable myself today, I shall present you with my card," she said in a rigidly controlled voice as she placed the card in front of him.

His grin widened. *His* name, that was all it took to get a response from the lady. His eyes focused on the card, and his charming smile was quickly replaced by shocked realization as he slowly looked up at her.

Shawn nodded her head and smiled sweetly. "For a song, huh?" she purred. "I think not. You see, I don't happen to dance to anyone's tune at any price." Then turning to Tony who was beside her, she said, "Let's get back to work. Somehow the atmosphere in here today is . . . rather repugnant." As he followed Shawn out of the restaurant, Tony couldn't help chuckling over the look on Bellows's face. The building magnate stared after them, his mouth agape. Even Goldberg couldn't repress a snicker as he reached over and raised Andrew's chin with his fingers to close the open mouth.

Chapter Five

Andrew Bellows stomped into his office without a word to Jill, his secretary, who raised an eyebrow at his mood. In his office, Bellows sat staring out one of the richly draped windows of the forty-storied, San Jose office building that he had constructed several years earlier. Originally, the entire top floor had been occupied by Bellows Enterprises, and in recent months, his staff had extended to the next level below. Generally, in the posh setting of his domain, Andrew felt as though he were king of all he surveyed; however, at the moment, he was still finding it difficult to swallow his pride and admit to himself that perhaps he had deserved Shawn McCullough's wrath.

He couldn't remember when he had felt so frustrated. Didn't that outrageous—but gorgeous, he had to admit—female realize that he could destroy McCullough Landscaping in the blink of an eye if it suited his whim? A few calls to suppliers and a talk with L and C Landscaping to set them up for low bid on any job that she bid, and McCullough Landscaping would be wiped from the face of the earth. Yet his annoyance with L and C still rankled. The sloppy outfit was making him look bad, and no matter what, Andrew Bellows took pride in his reputation as a master in the building trade. That meant that everything, including the window dressing, must be top-notch.

Bellows discarded his navy silk tie on the chair and paced back and forth on the gold, lush-pile carpet. What was it she had said? She couldn't be bought at any price? He'd heard that before, but when the money was on the table, how quickly they changed their tune. Hell, everybody has a price. If he offered her a fair amount, would she accept it? He peered out the window, eyes narrowed, remembering the determination in her voice and her absolute control. For the first time in his life, he wasn't so sure. Reluctantly, he rather admired the little scrap of a fighter.

The annoying buzz of the intercom shattered his thoughts. "Yes, Jill, what is it?" he muttered impatiently.

"Bill Cramer of L and C Landscaping is on the phone, Mr. Bellows," her pleasant voice came back. "He says it's urgent."

"He couldn't have picked a better time. I need a word with that boy." Andrew flipped on the speaker. "Bellows here," he boomed.

"Hello, Andy. Say, we've run into a bit of a problem on our end."

"Oh? What kind of a problem, Bill?"

"Arcadia Lane. You know all those palm trees that have to be moved in by crane?"

"Yes, yes, what about them?" he demanded.

"Well, Mitchell Crane has upped their price by six thousand dollars. Thought you ought to know about the additional cost before I come by this afternoon to sign the contract."

"I see. You got another verbal on the phone, huh, Bill? Sounds to me like Mitchell's getting wise to you, too. When are you going to learn that you don't do business without written bids?" he asked heatedly.

"Hey, Andy, it's only six thousand on a million-dollar job. You can handle that, can't you?"

"Yes, Bill, I can handle it, but I shouldn't have to, nor will I," he snapped. "I'm tired of supporting you, and Goldberg has a full-time job keeping my butt out of trouble entirely on your account. As far as I'm concerned, your bid stands as is! There'll be no money under the table and no shortages on this one, my friend. I'll be personally checking it."

"Listen, Bellows, don't pull this on me. You know damn well that we're the only firm that can pull the landscaping off in time for your opening!"

"And you, my friend, should know better than to threaten me!" Bellows said angrily. "Now, you have the terms and I want an answer. No ifs, ands, or buts! What's the verdict? Do you want this job or don't you?"

There was a long pause on the other end before Bill Cramer said, "I don't!"

"Fine!" Andrew clicked off the speaker and heaved a disgusted sigh. Arcadia Lane would open on time, even if he had to go out and make certain himself. Normally, he would have turned a problem of this nature over to one of his staff, but this was suddenly personal. Nobody threatened him. He buzzed his secretary. "Get me a rundown on the Arcadia Lane bids," he snapped.

Back in her office, Shawn was still seething. Two hours had passed since leaving the restaurant, and all she could think about was the colossal nerve of Andrew Bellows. Can't run a landscaping business, indeed! She would show him, for her father's sake, if for no other reason. Yet she suddenly knew that even without Andrew Bellows's goading remarks, staying with the business was right for her.

Bellows had merely been the catalyst prompting her decision reversal, and she felt complete satisfaction remembering his stunned look. "Well, if you're going to show him," she told herself, "you'd better get down to business." Shawn shrugged out of her suit jacket and dug out the contract on a job that her father had arranged with a small contractor a month ago and was reading the specs when the intercom claimed her attention. "Yes, Audrey?"

"You have a visitor," the secretary said.

Before Shawn could answer, a resonant male voice from

the doorway announced, "A rather unwelcome one, I
suspect."

Shawn's deep blue eyes darkened perceptibly as they
narrowed at the sight of Andrew Bellows. She had gotten
to him all right, or he wouldn't be here, and the feeling of
triumph was most satisfying. For a flickering moment, the
temptation to calmly invite him to leave entered her
mind, but this was a business office, and he probably
expected her to lose her temper and act like the stereotypi-
cal hysterical female. No amount of inner turmoil and
rage would force her to give him that satisfaction. Instead,
she let a sardonic grin blossom and countered with, "For
once, you're absolutely right."

Bellows shrugged slightly and walked into the office
quickly. "May I?" he asked as he shut the door.

"Yes, perhaps you'd better," she said in a way that
clearly showed her hostility toward him. "Now, just what
is it that brings the great Andrew Bellows to this humble
establishment?"

An amused grin curved his mouth, and he cleared his
throat. "I deserved that," he admitted as he seated himself
in one of the gold chairs opposite her desk and shuffled
through the papers he was holding.

Shawn raised one eyebrow. "You'll find no argument
here, so please continue. You have the floor," she said
coolly as she picked up her coffee and willed her hand not
to tremble as she brought the cup to her lips. No way
would she let him glimpse how he had unnerved her, or
the seething anger that his presence aroused.

"You have me dead to rights. I'm here to apologize. I had
no right to assume anything. Truce?" He extended his
hand across her desk.

Shawn looked at the proferred hand, then looked him in
the eye a long, deliberate moment before she rose from her
chair to walk over to the window, purposely letting him
hang as she silently turned her back on him. Then, having
gotten her temper under control, she turned to face him.
"There is no need for an apology, Mr. Bellows. You have a
right to your opinion just as I have. Though, if I were you,

I would be a bit more discreet about airing those opinions loudly in a public restaurant. Now, if you will excuse me, I have a great deal of business to organize."

"That's the second reason I'm here. Business, I mean."

"Business? I thought I made it quite clear that Mc-Cullough Landscaping is not for sale at any price," she snapped.

"Yes, as a matter of fact, you did. You impressed me enough that if you think you can handle it, Arcadia Lane is yours."

Shawn gaped at him speechlessly as he handed her the contract while grinning a bit sheepishly.

It was a long moment before she regained enough self-control to say, "Oh?" with an inadvertent lilt to her voice as she calmly lowered herself to the chair facing him. What ulterior motives were behind this? And what about L and C who supposedly had gotten the Arcadia Lane contract? Would Andrew Bellows stop at nothing to get what he wanted and what exactly did he want? She had made it definitely clear that her business was not for sale.

Anticipating her next question he said, "It's very simple. L and C reneged on their bid, and you happened to be next in line."

She carefully searched his face in an effort to read any underlying meaning. Did he intend to buy her with this job? But Andrew Bellows was the original poker face.

"I haven't time to put it out for rebid," Bellows went on. "Do you think you can handle it?" he asked with a challenge that said perhaps she was all empty talk, now that the chips were down.

"If we couldn't handle it, Mr. Bellows, we would never have bid it in the first place," she purred condescendingly as she picked up the contract and scanned it while striving to regain her composure, which had evaporated with his sudden, startling announcement. How she secretly wished her father could have been here to confront Bellows! Could they really handle Arcadia and the park job, too? The shopping center would be the biggest job McCullough Landscaping had ever contracted. Yet, they had already decided they could do both jobs before they had considered going after the park. A little shiver of exciting uncertainty rippled through her, and she hoped that Andrew Bellows's penetrating eyes hadn't caught it. "Well now that's settled," he said with a smile that seemed genuine. "It's my custom to buy the subcontractor a drink over a big one like this. Anyway, I would like to get to know you better. After all, we will be working together on a sizable project. What do you say?"

"No, thank you. I don't drink during working hours. It would seem that you have a short memory."

He glanced at his watch. "It's four-thirty. When do you call it a day?"

"When I'm through. And Mr. Bellows, I may be doing business with you, but it's just that, business."

"Andy, call me Andy. Listen, I realize I was wrong before, but you have to understand, I've just never met a woman like you—and I did apologize. What in hell else can I do?" He ran his fingers through his hair and looked her in the eye. "Do you hold grudges?"

The way he asked that brought a smile to her lips despite herself, and she did have to admit that he'd gone out of his way to apologize. Most certainly, Andrew Bellows didn't deliver contracts personally every day.

The intercom interrupted before she could speak. "I have Mr. Monroe on the phone for you," Audrey announced.

Shawn picked it up. "Hi, Matt," she said with a smile that indicated her less businesslike feelings.

Andrew Bellows noted her tone and sat quietly listening with a pensive expression on his handsome face as he tried to picture the man on the other end.

"Oh, that's too bad," she said. "When are you leaving?"

With that, a hint of a smile brightened Bellows's face. "That soon?" Shawn said, frowning, then her face lighted.

"Tell you what, I'll leave here in half an hour and drive you to the airport. We can talk on the way. I have a lot to tell you," she said softly into the phone.

Bellows cleared his throat when he heard her say in a more personal tone, "Yes, I'll miss you, too." Before replacing the phone, Shawn turned to face her new business associate. "I'm afraid the drink is out. But then, you heard the conversation," she added with a pleasant smile. "Perhaps another time, Mr. Bellows."

His mouth widened in a confident smile. "I can be an exceedingly patient man when I've a mind to be," he said, rising to leave. "Someday we'll have that drink."

"Someday, Mr. Bellows, can be a long way away," Shawn blithely answered with a demure smile.

She was still feeling smug about the way she had handled the situation when she picked up Matt. They were scarcely a block en route when Matt said in a mock-demanding voice, "Pull over to the curb, woman!"

"Why?" Shawn asked, wondering what was wrong as she glanced at him questioningly.

Again he commanded, "I said, stop the car!"

It was an order, and it rubbed Shawn the wrong way, particularly after her encounter with Andrew Bellows. She queried sharply, "What for?"

His expression took the sting out of the demand. "Because I want your full attention for what I'm about to say."

When the car stopped, he gazed at her tenderly and said, "You know, I hate leaving now that I've found you."

Startled at the intensity of his expression, she nodded in tentative agreement as their eyes penetrated each other's for a time-stopping moment. It was Matt who broke the silence. "Come with me. Let's spend some time together. You have nothing to keep you here. Let's get married if you want," he begged impulsively.

She could feel the blood surge in her cheeks as she brushed a lock of her hair from her eyes and blinked in astonishment. "Matt—" she began, her thoughts going to the enormous contract she'd just approved.

"Yes?"

"It's just so sudden, I'm overwhelmed."

He touched her hair caressingly.

An uncertain smile warmed her lips, and her eyes held a faraway look as she stared out the car window. She said softly, "It can be wonderful, Matt, but it's too soon for the decision you want."

"Darling, I know I'm rushing you. I have no right to expect you to make that kind of choice right now, but I had hoped—"

She turned to face him and in a wistful low voice she whispered, "Please, Matt, I don't want to be hurt; don't mistake sudden desire for love."

"You surely don't think I'm a love-'em-and-leave-'em type?" he snapped.

She didn't reply; instead, she turned the key in the ignition. "You'll miss your plane. Now, tell me, why do you suddenly have to go?"

A sigh slipped from him as he scowled. "They moved up an important court date, and I need to really be on top of this one, you know, last-minute developments and such."

"When will you be back?"

"I don't know. It could drag on, but with any luck, a couple of weeks." Then in a compassionate voice he asked, "How'd it go at the office today?"

It was the first mention of her work that he had made since they'd met, and she eagerly told him of her first decision to sell and the reasons for changing her mind. Matt listened intently but didn't comment until she related the incident with Bellows in Charley Brown's restaurant. "Sounds like you really put him in his place. But that doesn't mean you still can't sell McCullough Landscaping."

She realized that he couldn't understand her feelings about the business that had become her way of life. "I can't explain, Matt, but it wasn't really Bellows that changed my mind. I suppose I was secretly looking for a reason to throw away logic and go with my heart. Do you understand what I mean?"

"I understand only one thing right now, and that's my feelings for you. Would what I said make any difference to your decision?"

"No, I suppose not," she said softly.

His eyes searched hers. "Then if you won't come with me yet, please, promise me one thing."

"Is it a big promise or a little one?" she teased.

"I'd say a very important one. Take good care of yourself and don't work too hard while I'm gone, okay?"

The concern in his gentle green eyes gave her that same feeling of warm protection and love that he'd given her before. A sudden pang of loneliness filled her. She nodded and smiled tremulously. Then, noticing that they were almost there, her focus returned to the busy airport. "I sure hope it doesn't take as long as usual to park. Got your ticket?"

"Nope. This is a sudden trip, remember? Maybe you'd better just drop me off and go on. No sense going through the hassle of parking. I'll just barely get squared away and have to board."

Shawn pulled over to the curb. A note of sadness crept into her voice as she said, "I wish we had more time."

He reached over to cup her face in his hands and smiled into her glistening eyes that seemed to search his. "Shawn, I know how I feel about you. Is it possible that you could love me, too?"

"Matt, don't— I need time, time to be sure that we're not just caught up in the thrill of a new romance."

He nodded in understanding as his arms drew her close, and his lips held hers for an instant. Then he was out of the car. She pitched the key to him. "Your luggage, don't forget."

He removed a black suit bag from the trunk, deposited it on the curb, and returned to her open window to drop the key in her palm. "Remember what you promised," he reminded, and pecked her forehead. "I'll call you." Then he was gone, lost in the milling throng of people.

Chapter Six

Noticing the seat belt sign fade out, Matt quickly released the buckle and adjusted his seat to accommodate his long legs. Though he had hated to leave, he was on his way back to the stimulating pressures of a court battle with one of Los Angeles's best attorneys, Norman Pollard, a man with a reputation for inventing legal loopholes. Although he regretted having to cut short his vacation, he was intrigued with the upcoming challenge, and confident that the strategy he had planned would be ultimately victorious in the courtroom. Yet he felt cheated by having to leave Shawn so abruptly.

His eyes closed. How he wished he could have spent a few more days with her. He yearned to hold her in his arms once again. So much had happened the past few days, feelings that he never knew he possessed had surfaced. And yet, there was that incident on the way to the airport—almost a small battle of wills—and then her reference to business. Was he really as important, as all-encompassing to her as she was to him?

"May I get you something to drink?" the flight attendant unwittingly interrupted.

As he opened his eyes, Matt's daydream gave way to the pretty blond who leaned over him. "Yes, thanks, a gin and tonic, Beefeater's if you have it," he said.

"We do," she assured with a smile, and as he watched her get the drink, he was reminded of another blond, one he had barely thought of since the day he had helped Shawn McCullough to her feet under the willow tree. Patrice! She was picking him up at the airport!

Patrice Guzman, T. J. Lewis's right-hand girl and PR agent, was a willowy, flaxen-haired beauty of twenty-nine. She and Matt had gotten to know one another several years earlier when Matt, having recently passed the bar, was hired as an associate attorney with Gilmore and Taft. Being the junior member of the firm, he had prepared briefs, filed motions, and compiled information regarding disputes or settlements for the firm's senior members who, in turn, handled the actual courtroom action. At that time, T. J. Lewis Enterprises was a growing corporation that sought legal counsel from Gilmore and Taft. In the course of legal entanglements, Matt found himself frequently involved with the highly efficient Patrice and was soon to discover her many talented facets.

She was a powerhouse of energy with total recall and the ability to immediately put her finger on any information he might require, completely in her element, managing the intricate affairs of the conglomerate. He could easily understand what made her so valuable to T. J. Lewis. Where most men in T. J.'s position would have dealt directly with their attorneys, he rarely did, save by phone, and as the corporation continued to expand, the most that anyone at Gilmore and Taft saw of Thomas James Lewis was his signature on legal documents, picked up and delivered by Ms. Guzman.

Matt had encountered T. J. several times and was surprised that on one occasion the old man had taken time to sit down for a detailed discussion relating to a particular case. Matt had been instantly drawn to the older man. Had it not been for the elaborate office and executive desk before him, one would never have guessed that T. J. Lewis was a man of great means. Short and with a moon face, full beard, and an infectious laugh, he gave the appearance of Santa Claus, lacking only the red outfit. His suit was probably Savile Row, though he wore it with an open-necked sport shirt and no tie. Matt had been instantly drawn to the older man.

He smiled to himself as his thoughts shifted back to Patrice and the morning when he had been introduced to an unsuspected side of "Miss Professional." That day, walking into the conference room at Lewis Enterprises, he was shocked to find her sobbing, her soft brown eyes blurred by weeping, the blond curls becomingly disheveled at her brow. At the far end of the massive table with papers in disarray all around her, Patrice Guzman was the exact antithesis of all she had previously presented.

"Sir, would you like another gin and tonic?" The flight attendant's voice intruded upon his reverie.

Matt gestured at the empty glass and said, "Sure, why not?"

They'd had two gin and tonics that day at lunch while Patrice poured out her heart. Her nerves had been stretched to the breaking point over countless details involved in a multimillion dollar suit against T. J. Lewis that she and Matt were putting together for Taft's court defense. There had not been enough hours in the day for Patrice to stay on top of it and still successfully carry out her other responsibilities, yet she had refused to give in to human frailties, until she had reached the proverbial final straw.

Matt had gone to T. J., stressing the importance of the case and requesting that Patrice's other duties be minimized until the litigation was resolved. The corners of Matt's closed eyes crinkled in a smile as he recalled the old man's reaction.

For a moment after Matt had finished talking, the rotund man across the desk had seemed lost in thought. Then the leonine head jerked up, and his eyes narrowed. "I had no idea she was in such a state. I'll lighten her load. And now the case. Just who in the hell is going to try it in court?"

"Jim Taft will represent you."

"Well, aren't you going through all the preliminaries?"

"Yes, that's standard procedure for any junior member of the firm."

Lewis looked at him speculatively. "That's always been a puzzle to me. It seems that if you're capable of putting something of this size together, you ought to know more about it than anyone else." He studied the young attorney's face for a long, hard moment. Then with a scrutinizing eye, he asked, "What do you think about corporate lawyers?"

There was little hesitation on the young man's part. "In all honesty, with as much legal work as you have, it's time you hired one."

Matt could almost read the old man's analysis as he watched his brow furrow in calculation.

With a quick judgment, born from years of experience, Lewis preferred his hand. "That's what I think. Congratulations, my boy! I like your style, you're hired!"

And so he had begun his corporate career with T. J. Lewis Enterprises, and in working together, he and Patrice had gradually developed a comfortable and intimate relationship.

He took a big gulp of his drink and closed his eyes again. How could he tell her about Shawn? How could he tell Patrice that their relationship was not all that he had thought it was? Could he make her understand that although he did love her, there was some element missing and that now he thought he had found it elsewhere?

"Sir, would you please raise your seat to the upright position? We're about to land," the flight attendant requested.

Matt looked up to see the seat-belt light on. He reached for the safety mechanism, buckled it in place, and steeled himself mentally for Patrice. He would tell her right away, but as he walked up the ramp and saw her radiant smile, his determination evaporated.

"Matt, darling! How I've missed you!"

Automatically, his arms opened to receive her embrace, and holding her close, he knew it would be tougher than he had imagined, for he did care for her. Too, their careers were so entwined, and their relationship had been a wonderful one with neither party making demands.

Now Matt felt a strong ambivalence—part of him longing for the raven-haired pixie with whom he'd spent so little time and a part of him enjoying the warmth of a familiar embrace.

"Matt?" she said as she pulled away from him. "You seem so— Are your folks all right?"

"They're fine," he said, forcing a smile.

"What a shame you couldn't stay at least another week. It's been so long since you saw them. I really did hate to call you." She reached up and gave him a peck on the cheek. "If they're anything like you, they must be great! Next time, take me with you, okay?" she said with an impulsiveness that totally surprised him. Then, not waiting for an answer, she grasped his hand. "Come on, let's get your luggage. I fixed a special dinner for you, darling. It's ready to pop in the oven. New recipe, you'll love it."

Her eyes were a brown sparkle of affection, and her enthusiasm overwhelmed him. It wasn't her style to be so demonstrative, nor had she ever before displayed her feelings publicly. Matt was glad he had had two drinks and right now wished for a third.

"I have to talk to you," he blurted.

"Yes, I know, love, I have a million things to tell you, too," she rattled on in a merry banter, "but all that legal stuff can wait. We're more important, don't you think?"

"Uh huh," he said, unable to mask the concern in his voice. "Let's get the hell out of here, I feel claustrophobic."

"You know, that's a great idea," she said with a suggestive smile.

"Um," he said, and wished he'd already told her that their relationship was over. What had come over her, anyway? This was going to be a lot harder than he'd thought. Matt took the keys from her hand. Perhaps driving would temporarily take his mind off the problem.

In the car, Patrice was as bubbly as she had been at the airport, and try as he might, he could not respond to her excitement about his return. Even with the buffer that the gin afforded, he found making light conversation difficult. She was different somehow, warmer, or was the alcohol making him misread her feelings? He definitely would tell her after dinner.

"Matt?" she interrupted his thoughts and reached over to squeeze his arm as he drove.

Matt jerked his arm away. Would his news hurt her badly or would she understand as she always had?

"I have a surprise for you," she blurted with pleasure.

He grinned. He'd never seen her so vibrant. She resembled a little child spilling over with anticipation, and it tickled him. Beyond her, his eyes glimpsed a car careening around the corner to her right. Suddenly it was as if life were reduced to slow motion. The out-of-control car was inexorably heading for them, and in the dreamlike state in which he was trapped, he wanted to hold the runaway automobile away with his hand, yet he was powerless to do anything to avert the oncoming crash. All he could do was to stare helplessly and watch it happen. Frozen for a moment before flooring the accelerator, he cried out, "Look out, Patrice!" In that same split second, the sickening grind of metal rang in his ears, and the car spun wildly from the force of the collision, smashing his head against the door frame.

As his eyes slowly began to focus, Matt shook his head groggily. Excited voices were beginning to penetrate his mental fog. What had happened? Then, remembering the sound of crunching metal, his first thought was Patrice. "Oh, my God, Patrice!" he uttered in horror.

The sight of her wedged under the dashboard by twisted metal was sickening. Panic engulfed him as he realized he couldn't free the limp form that only a moment before had been so animated.

Matt staggered from the car, dizzy and nauseous. "Call an ambulance!" he screamed to the gathering onlookers, then someone clutched at his arm.

A frightened, quavering voice was pleading shrilly, "My

brakes went out! The children were in the middle of the street and I *had* to turn or they'd all be dead now! Are you all right?"

Matt turned to see a small, shaken, gray-haired woman whose broken glasses hung askew on the tip of her nose, and the confusion that had blanketed his mind a moment ago was quickly overcome by her concern for him.

"Yes, I think I'm okay, just hit my head, but my friend is unconscious and I can't get her out!"

The woman suddenly blanched, and her hands rose to cover her mouth as she uttered a panicked, muffled cry.

Help arrived quickly, but it seemed like hours to Matt as he sweated through their removal of the metal that imprisoned Patrice. His heart beat a painful staccato as he stared at her chalk-white face and saw the bright red stain that saturated the pink dress she wore. Blood was oozing from the deep gashes that scarred her legs, and an involuntary gasp came from his throat. She was dying, and only moments ago she had been so happy. If only he had reacted sooner!

Matt helplessly watched paramedics place Patrice on a stretcher. Hurrying to her side, he held her limp hand and walked next to her.

"Oh, honey," he said, wishing she could speak.

Her eyes opened for a fraction of a second and hazily focused on his face.

"I'll stay with you," Matt murmured, and pressed her hand gently. "You have to be all right, I love you," he said, feeling anything but a need to clarify his statement.

A faint smile barely parted her pallid lips as tears welled, and he wondered if she had understood. Her grip on his hand tightened momentarily before she winced with pain and her fingers went limp. Her golden brown eyes fluttered shut. Never before had Matt felt so desolate.

The ride to the hospital was an agonizing eternity. A nameless terror engulfed him, a nightmare that all the pacing in the waiting room, all the fragmented prayers couldn't alleviate. A storm of fear had gripped his heart

and ravaged his mind, and he couldn't shut out that last
glimpse of her broken body. Could it have been his fault?
Could he have reacted faster if he hadn't had the two
drinks on the plane? The airlines do give doubles—had he
really consumed four drinks? He ran his fingers nervously
through his hair as if they could stop his brain from
pounding.

More than four hours later, Matt was still deep in
gloomy thought when he felt a hand on his shoulder. "Mr.
Monroe, I'm Dr. Davis. You're Ms. Guzman's friend?"

Matt nodded. "How is she?" he asked anxiously.

"I won't kid you. She may have a long recovery and
probably some difficulty walking, due to some nerve
damage. Usually therapy and determination can overcome this type of injury. Every patient varies, you understand. But right now, she needs every drop of her strength
to recover from some pretty extensive internal injuries, a
lot of moral support, too," he hastened to add. Rubbing his
bleary eyes, the weary surgeon went on, "The cuts were
mostly superficial. I don't think there's any need for
plastic surgery on her legs, they should heal nicely." He
gave Matt a tired smile. "She's young and strong. I have
high hopes for a complete recovery."

Patrice would live! Relief from his pent-up dread and
self-imposed guilt engulfed Matt. He trembled from weakness as he uttered, "Thank God! And thank *you*, Doctor."

The surgeon laid a sympathetic hand on his shoulder.
"It's three A.M. Why don't you go home and rest? She'll be
sedated for hours. You can see her in the morning for a few
minutes."

Matt turned the key in the lock and flipped on the light.
His exhaustion gave way to stunned disbelief as his eyes
focused on every detail. "Oh, my God!" She'd had his
apartment redecorated! A lump welled up in his throat
as the impact of what he was seeing hit him full-blast.
Every idea he had expressed only weeks before had
suddenly materialized. It was her surprise. It was too
much. Matt stumbled to the wet bar and grabbed the

nearest bottle. Pouring half a glass, he walked dazedly around the rooms.

In the kitchen, a bottle of imported champagne rested in an elegant ice bucket next to an exquisitely set table. Matt ran his fingers through the cold water that had started out as crushed ice, then shook the moisture from his hand. Absentmindedly, he lifted the cover from a casserole resting on the counter. She had planned dinner perfectly. He had no heart to investigate further. Seeking familiar refuge, he returned to the living room and the comfort of his favorite chair, which had suddenly metamorphosed to an orangish rust. His eyes wandered the length of the room, coming to rest on a picture of Patrice on the mantel. Her photographic smile was in stark contrast to the horror of the last few hours. Matt's last ounce of control deserted him, his face crumpled, and the empty glass slipped from his fingers and fell to the newly carpeted floor.

Chapter Seven

Tuesday morning, in her kitchen, Shawn toyed with her coffee cup. An inexplicable uneasiness robbed her of her usual morning energy, and she found it difficult to concentrate on anything other than the expected phone call from Matt. Logic told her that he had a great deal on his mind regarding the upcoming litigation, but secretly, she felt disappointed that he hadn't called immediately upon his arrival in Los Angeles.

The worst part was, she didn't even know how to reach him. Their relationship of the past several days had been almost a fantasy; strangely, they had not discussed such unromantic practicalities. Still, she knew he would call her the minute he was free. She smiled to herself, savoring the memory of his kiss and his protective arms encircling her, and the mere thought was a tonic.

Shawn put her cup in the sink and smoothed her hair as she passed the entryway mirror. "Good morning, Timothy," she said in a lilting voice, and chucked the dinosaur playfully under the chin with her fingers. The ring of a bell jarred her from her reverie. The phone! Matt! Her feet took wings and she reached eagerly for the receiver, but the moment she picked it up, the buzz in her ear shattered her daydream. The ring had been the door bell! Who on earth would be at her front door at this early hour? Annoyed, she glanced at her watch. Seven A.M. She walked slowly toward the door to confront the intruder.

A hand proffered the morning *Chronicle.* "Paperboy."

"A drop in status is one thing, but this is ridiculous," she jibed, though she couldn't help grinning at the sight of the expensively clad paper bearer before her.

Andrew Bellows chuckled as he deposited the newspaper into her outstretched hand. "I expect payment on receipt of merchandise. Got a cup of coffee?"

"What in blazes are you doing over here so early? Haven't you anything better to do with your time than pose as a newsboy? I was just on my way out."

"Good! Then I'll buy you breakfast."

Shawn stared at him amusedly, her blue eyes noting his eager expression. "What's it going to cost me?"

"Hell, I don't know, but I'll think of something."

"No thank you; I've already had coffee, and I really do have to get to the office."

"Well, we'll have dinner tonight then."

Shawn frowned. He certainly was presumptuous. What did she have to do to convince him, hit him over the head with one of his own two-by-fours? "Perhaps a business luncheon later on in the week if I can work it into my schedule," she said cheekily.

A flicker of indignation flushed his face as he turned and abruptly went back down the steps. "Do you think you'd have time to answer the phone if I called?" he asked sarcastically over his shoulder.

Shawn smiled inwardly. "Depends on when you call," she said sweetly, and laughed aloud at the sight of Andrew Bellows storming down the walk, his sport jacket billowing in the morning breeze and his Polo tie barely keeping pace.

"You are something, Bellows!" she said, still laughing as she closed the door.

Shawn breezed into the lobby. "Good morning, Audrey. Seen Tony?"

"I believe he's in your office."

"Great, I need to talk to him." She brushed by the philodendron, and upon entering her office, found Tony Rizzo staring at the Arcadia Lane blueprints that covered the drawing board.

Before she could speak, Tony turned to face her. "What are these doing here? I thought Jack threw them out!"

"Tony, why don't you sit down? There's been a rather interesting development."

"Oh?"

"Yes. I signed the contract yesterday afternoon on Arcadia Lane!"

"You're putting me on. Now tella me da truth and I'll see you notta get hurt," he teased, using his favorite phony dialect.

Shawn laughed at his parody. "No, it's the truth. I really did sign a contract with Bellows."

Tony's face sobered. "Bellows? What the hell's happening?"

"Pretty simple. L and C blew it, and we're next in line."

The young man's face darkened. "You gotta be kiddin' me!"

Shawn's eyes flashed in sudden irritation. "Hey, look, Tony, yesterday we were talking about laying off some of the crew. Now there's no need for that."

"But with Bellows, for Pete's sake!" he shouted. "What about what happened yesterday at the restaurant? What changed your mind?"

"My friend, don't think this was an easy decision, but we need that contract. Anyway, I think a lot of what we've heard about him has been overblown."

"I can't believe this is you talking, Shawn!"

"Well, you had better believe it because my name is on that contract, and we are going to fulfill our agreement starting next Monday!"

"Christ! I just lined up everything to start Sun Haven Park tomorrow. That's a damn big project, too, ya know. How in the hell are we gonna start both jobs at once?" And with that, Tony grabbed the plans and specs. "I'll need to study these if I ever get a spare minute," the young supervisor growled as he brusquely left the office on his way out.

"I certainly would appreciate it, Tony," she called after him with repressed sarcasm.

"Well, damn," Shawn said in disgust, "sometimes you just can't win!" Maybe he's right; maybe Dad was right, she thought. Had her concern for the employees affected her judgment? Yet she couldn't help remembering Bellows's blunt honesty in their conversation. Honesty was one thing she appreciated, and a far cry from the picture his reputation painted. As a matter of fact, ironically, her dad and Bellows actually had a lot in common.

An hour later, Shawn was studying a plan when Audrey came on the line. "Mr. Bellows on line two," she said with a twinkle.

Shawn rolled her eyes impatiently. "Oh, Lord, not him again! Shawn McCullough," she said, lacking her usual exuberance. "I thought I was supposed to call you later in the week regarding lunch."

Unruffled by her obvious irritation, Bellows's now familiar voice came back. "Oh, that—that's not why I'm calling."

"Well then, Andrew—"

"I was hoping you could spare an hour or two to acquaint yourself with the actual site of Arcadia Lane. If we're going to work together as a team, you should meet my superintendent and go over the progress to date on the construction. It's essential that your people and mine coordinate."

Shawn sighed. Was this meeting necessary at this time? Right now, her irritation caused by the disagreement with Tony and a subsequent telephone call from her lawyer requesting a meeting were uppermost in her mind. Besides, it would be Tony, not she, who would be working directly with Bellows's superintendent.

"Andrew," she stated, "I am not in the habit of overriding my field superintendent, Tony Rizzo. He's the man who will be working closely with your people. I realize the importance of your suggestion, and I will spend some time with Tony on the job later on. However, right now, I think it would be far more beneficial for you to meet with him."

There was a pause on the other end. "I'm used to dealing only at top level, Ms. McCullough, and I do have at least twenty other pressing matters for the day."

"Mr. Bellows, just how important is this project to you?"

"Important enough to merit my full attention, and I was hoping, yours. However, I can see the point in your argument."

"I'm glad to hear that you can apply a little rationale when necessary."

"Is there something about me that just plain irritates you? I thought we were friends or at least amicable business associates by now!"

Pausing for a moment and mentally conceding that she had been more than a little rude, Shawn then replied in a more congenial tone. "I'm sorry, I guess this is just one of those days when everything hits at once. Please forgive my abruptness. I'll get back to you after I corral Tony."

"You still drive a hard bargain, but I'll respect your chain of command. Let me know what you can set up with your man."

There was a click at the other end and Shawn replaced the receiver, her mind returning to the impending appointment with her attorney. She grabbed her purse and brushed by Audrey, who called after her, "Where will you be, Shawn?"

"At O'Halloran's office. Keep trying to get Tony. I have to talk with him when I return."

"Well, when will that be?"

"Hell, I don't know," she muttered as she left.

Audrey shrugged: "I swear this week has two Mondays."

Some of the morning's irritation evaporated when Shawn saw the smiling, ruddy-faced, bald-headed Patrick O'Halloran. She walked over quickly and gave him a friendly hug. "It's good to see you, Uncle Pat."

The older man, attempting to mask his concern, returned her hug and motioned her to a chair beside him. "I was surprised to find you back at work already."

Shawn shrugged her shoulders. "No sense procrastinating, there are too many loose ends."

Her old friend and confidant raised his eyebrows and decided to launch into the reason he'd called for this meeting. "You're right about that! I've been checking into things while working on the probate, and your dad's accountant informed me that Jack, unfortunately, was in arrears on several bank payments."

"Several! Pat! What do you mean by several? I know Dad had sometimes borrowed in the past to meet payroll . . ."

"Shawn, it isn't that simple," he interrupted.

Thoughts raced through her mind as she unconsciously fingered the gold-spike paperweight that decorated his desk. Then raising her eyes to meet his, she said, "Maybe you had better spell it out for me. Let's have the facts and figures."

O'Halloran pushed back his chair and made his way to the window.

Shawn approached him, gently touching his arm. "Is it that bad, Uncle Pat?"

The seasoned lawyer frowned in response to her question. "I'm really not sure, Shawn, but I think you need to be aware of this since it could adversely affect selling the business."

"Pat, I have no intention of selling the business."

O'Halloran's gray eyes widened in amazement. "Are you telling me that you are intending to run it? You must really believe in leprechauns."

Shawn smiled, despite the seriousness of the situation, and said, "There must be at least one with a pot of gold."

"By God, I hope so. It looks like we'll need about two hundred thousand in that pot."

"Two hundred thousand?" Shawn was shocked. "How could dad possibly be two hundred thousand in arrears?"

O'Halloran picked up a sheet of paper and handed it to her.

Shawn's brow increasingly furrowed as she scanned the ominous figures before her. "My God. No wonder Dad was so tense!" Tears started to well. "Oh, how I wish he had shared his burdens with me. I never dreamed he had such problems. No wonder he was counting so on Arcadia Lane."

O'Halloran laid a comforting hand on her shoulder and simply said, "Nobody expects to die when they do. He didn't want to worry you, honey."

She brushed angrily at the escaping trickle on her cheek, saying, "That was my dad."

Pausing only a moment with her thoughts, she said impulsively, "The house is free and clear. I'll sell it."

"But Shawn, that takes time. From what I understand, the bank is ready to foreclose."

"I take it that you've already talked to them about an extension?"

"Yes, I have talked to the loan officer and explained that this matter is in probate. I had no idea that you wanted to keep the business."

"I know, Uncle Pat, it looks like it's not going to be easy, but I think the bank will take my house as collateral."

"Your dad talked about paying it off several years back. Are you sure he did? I haven't gotten into that yet."

"We're all right there. He paid off the loan when he put the house in my name. Dad wanted the house free and clear for me, and he expected me to sell the business." The words were out of her mouth before the irony of the reversal of his wishes struck Shawn, but she dared not dwell on it.

"There aren't any more surprises?" she asked.

He shook his head. "No, if you can convince the bank some way, somehow, that you can repay them soon . . ." His voice trailed off doubtfully.

"I've *got* to," she said in such a positive note that it made him smile.

On the drive to the bank, Shawn's thoughts were on her father. He had been a very stubborn man, and as much as she knew he would have been against her keeping the corporation, she also knew that he, too, had been a man of his convictions and had always fought hard for what he believed. How could he have expected any less of her? She knew he could have easily borrowed the money on the house but hadn't to preserve her legacy. Well, now she had to follow her chosen path, and as much as she loved the house, she didn't need it. The sale would bring in approximately half a million dollars, enough to see her through the crisis and also enable her to buy a small condominium with the remaining proceeds.

As she walked into the bank, her confidence was slightly daunted by the sepulchrally cold atmosphere that surrounded her, and she wondered if anyone here would even consider her proposal.

Randomly, she approached one of the loan officers, who was seated behind his desk, engrossed in paperwork, and she lowered herself to a chair facing him.

It was a moment before the man acknowledged her presence and asked, "May I help you?"

"The name is Shawn McCullough of McCullough Landscaping, Inc., Mr. Trusdale," she said as she glanced at his nameplate. "I would like to speak with the president of your bank," she requested with some urgency.

"Is there some sort of problem, Ms. McCullough? Perhaps I could help you."

"No," she stated. "I must speak with your chief executive. Would you mind telling Mr. Kendall that I'm here and that no one else will do?"

Trusdale was taken aback by her insistence and her outwardly confident manner, but his training prompted his reply. "Mr. Kendall does not normally deal with the average customer."

Shawn's blue eyes deepened with determination. "This is not an average problem, I assure you, and I shall remain here until he's free."

The impeccably dressed bank officer grimaced as he rose from his chair. "I'll see what I can do. What would you suggest that I tell him?"

Shawn immediately thought of Andrew Bellows's words, and without hesitation, stated, "Tell him that I deal only at the top."

Shawn's confidence slowly ebbed as she heard a loud voice coming from the private office, and she wondered if she were about to ask the impossible. Impossible or not, she would see it through.

"We can't have her sitting out there the rest of the afternoon!" the disgruntled voice ordered. "Send her in. I'll give her ten minutes."

Ten minutes, indeed! He would give her as long as she needed! She rose and straightened the maroon silk of her skirt and blazer, the fabric whispering as she entered the president's private lair. "Mr. Kendall, I believe." She extended her hand. "I'm Shawn McCullough."

He rose from his chair and gave her a professional smile. "I'm pleased to meet you, Ms. McCullough. I'm told that you deal only at the top."

"That's right. Please sit down." She gestured imperiously as though she were in command as she seated herself across from him. "Now, then, since I have only ten minutes to state my case, I'll tell you what I have in mind, and perhaps we can dispense with the trivia."

The distinguished gentleman's smile evaporated, replaced by a surprised, if not quizzical, expression as he eased himself back into his chair.

Shawn's stomach did a flip-flop. Was she being a little too overbearing? Yet what did she have to lose? They'd already vetoed an extension. "My father, Jack McCullough, has done business with your bank for many years." Then quickly scanning the posh office for effect, she continued, "And has promptly repaid a number of loans to your rather profitable institution. Unfortunately, he's now dead, and I inherited and am taking over the business. This delinquent loan comes as a surprise to me, but I am not going to fold up the corporation because of it. Too many employees are dependent upon this outcome, and I have the solution."

"Just a moment, Ms. McCullough. I must acquaint myself with the particular loan. Do you have the account number?"

Shawn snapped her fingers. "Oh, damn, I left it at O'Halloran's. May I?" she asked, reaching for the phone.

"Please do," he said with a half-smile, and though it was incomplete, it bespoke genuine amusement.

She dialed O'Halloran, who gave her the information. "Thanks, Uncle Pat," she said as she wrote the account number down. Replacing the receiver, she handed the information to the speculative executive, who then buzzed one of the clerks to request a copy of the legal document while carefully studying the small and spirited young woman in front of him.

Shawn watched his expression as he frowningly scanned the legal paper.

"It seems there have already been several extensions on this loan with interest-only payments having been allowed by the board. Ms. McCullough, I'm afraid this is a great deal of money that you're talking about. What exactly do you think a bank operates on?"

"Cash flow and interest, of course!" Shawn returned.

"Hm, and at what point would you say that a loan becomes a bad risk?"

Shawn could not divine his thoughts, nor could she anticipate what he expected her to say, but unwilling to step into a snare, she replied, "I'm certain that you would know the answer to that much better than I. However, I do know that if you foreclose, it would create a good many obstacles for you to sell off the equipment and the building. However, I have a five-hundred-thousand-dollar home, free and clear to put up as loan collateral. My intention is to sell it and repay the bank loan as quickly as possible."

"Ms. McCullough, what makes you think that even if I can get the board to grant another extension that you will be able to sell that priced home within, say, thirty to sixty days?"

Suddenly, the impact of selling her home hit Shawn. "Blind faith, I guess." Then, angry with herself for allowing her vulnerability to show, she added, "You know, Mr. Kendall, some things are worth fighting for, and I firmly believe this is one of them." Then salvaging her dignity, she extended her hand to him. "I'll send you copies of two large contracts that McCullough Landscaping Inc. has acquired so that you'll have an idea of our future cash flow. I am a very determined woman on behalf of my firm and my employees, and I have solid experience in this line. We're a going-places business!"

As he took her outstretched hand, the president's face relented. Her enthusiasm impressed him. Quite a woman, he thought. "I can't make any promises," he said, "but I'll see what can be done and call you in a few days."

Shawn pulled out her card and crossed off *Estimator,* wrote in *Owner,* and handed it to him.

He smiled as he read her correction.

"Sorry about that, but I have more important problems to solve right now than ordering new business cards," she said with a blush.

He laughed genuinely. "Yes, I'd say that you have your priorities in order!"

It was four P.M. when Shawn returned to the office to find Tony waiting for her. "Oh, hi, Tony, I'm glad you're here. Hold on just a second, I need to make a call."

Tony seated himself in one of the gold chairs and nervously tapped his fingers on its arm as he scowled at her.

Shawn thumbed through the directory and rested her finger on Classic Realty, then dialed the number.

Across from her, the glowering Tony's head snapped up as he heard her say, "Yes, I want to list my home immediately. Could you arrange an appointment for this evening regarding an appraisal?" Then, giving the proper information with cold professionalism, there was a pause on Shawn's end before she closed the conversation with, "Seven P.M. will be fine."

"It's probably none of my business," Tony blurted, "but what the hell is this all about? I thought you loved that house!"

"No question about that, Tony, but something has come up that I wasn't aware of, and the corporation needs money badly."

"Shawn, what is it? What's happened?" Tony's usually lively animation was replaced by genuine concern as he listened to her explanation of the company's financial bind. "Christ, I had no idea things were that tight," he said in a stunned voice. "You could always declare bankruptcy."

The young woman's eyes mirrored a reserve of inner strength, and her voice was definite as she shook her head. "Dad would never have done something like that, and I'm not going to, either. I don't need the house; some things are more important!"

Admiration shone in the field superintendent's eyes as he said with a note of proprietary pride, "You know, I think you're one hell of a lady! Jack would be damn proud of you!"

Shawn smiled, and with renewed faith in their relationship, she felt free to approach the subject of the shopping center. "Tony, did you have a chance to look at the prints and specs on Arcadia Lane?"

"To be honest, I was too busy, and my hot head didn't help. I only glanced at them briefly. But hell, if you're willing to sell your house to save the business, I guess the least I can do is keep an open mind about Bellows."

Shawn smiled and knew that Tony was wholeheartedly behind her.

Chapter Eight

T. J. Lewis entered the hospital with a flourish. Laden with a huge floral arrangement, he wasted little time on inquiries. "ICU, second floor," he repeated after the volunteer had answered his question as to Patrice's whereabouts.

Upon entering the low-lit room he drew in a deep breath at the sight of the woman who had always been quick, lively, and almost perfectly efficient. Appearing to be in a light, restless sleep, she lay immobilized, several bottles dripping life into her veins. He set the flowers on the counter next to her bed, and the sorrow he felt brought a lump to his throat. She was his right hand, and she actually had more knowledge of business details than anyone else connected with the conglomerate, to say nothing of his personal feelings for her. It had been hard to believe when Matt had called him that this had really happened.

"Patrice," he uttered helplessly, and his hand sought to gently pat hers, momentarily blotting out the presence of the nurse as she entered.

"You can only stay five minutes, sir. She's still on the critical list."

T. J. Lewis stepped back and barked, "Where is her doctor?"

"He should be in to see her shortly."

"That's not good enough! I want to know her condition now!" With that, he stormed out of the room to the central desk and demanded, "Page Dr. Davis."

"Sir, is there a problem? Maybe I can be of assistance."

"No, dammit! I want to know her condition, and I'm certain that you're not authorized to tell me."

"S-sir," the flustered nurse stuttered. "Oh—here's her doctor now," she breathed with a sigh of relief and pointed to the distinguished-looking man coming out of the elevator.

The entrepreneur lost no time in confronting Dr. Davis. "I'm Thomas James Lewis, President of T. J. Lewis Enterprises, and I would like a prognosis on Patrice Guzman."

The surprised surgeon gave him a quizzical look. "Are you family, sir?"

"Since her parents are in Europe at the moment and she spends three-quarters of her time working for me, you might say I'm her guardian. Now, does that give me the right to privileged information?"

Dr. Davis smiled. "Yes, I suppose so."

"Well, then?"

As the surgeon spoke, Lewis's brow knit with worry. "That bad, huh? Thank you, Doctor. I appreciate your honesty. Now I'll tell you something. That little girl means a lot to me. I don't give a damn if she never works for me another day in her life; she's to have the best money can buy. A private nurse and a hell of a lot of your attention. I've looked into your credentials, and they tell me you're the best. If she recovers completely, you can expect a new therapy wing named after you. I'll be back later when she's awake." With that, he turned on his heel and pushed the elevator button. The door promptly opened as if on cue. The flabbergasted doctor stared after him.

"How are you feeling?" the soft, comforting female voice inquired.

Patrice's eyes fluttered open, and she fought against the sedation that had kept her on the dark side of conscious-

ness since the night before. An abrupt pain shot up her
spine, and a groan escaped from her pallid, dry lips.
"Water," she moaned.

It seemed ages before the nurse returned with a styro-
foam cup full of ice chips and attempted to spoon some
between the parched lips of her patient.

A few minutes later, Dr. Davis entered the room, and
Patrice's usually bright eyes were dull and remote as he
explained her injuries.

After the doctor disappeared down the hall, his words
echoed in her mind, yet she was too weak, too groggy to
comprehend the seriousness of what he had said. Slowly
her eyes fluttered shut, and the medication provided sweet
relief from the searing pain and the confusion of a nightmare come to life.

The next time she opened her eyes, it was in the soft
light of evening, and a shadow beside her bed gradually
came into focus.

Matt smiled ruefully. "Well, hello there, pretty lady. I
was beginning to think you might sleep the night away."

"Matt, oh, Matt! You're here!"

He held her hand, patting it gently. "You should have
known I'd be here."

She smiled wistfully. "Yes, I guess I knew you would
come," she agreed. The concern in his eyes was comforting, but as she began sorting out what the doctor had said,
doubt and bewilderment poured into the recesses of her
mind. Too, she wondered if Matt knew how very much she
loved him. If only she had had a chance to express it
earlier. Everything was different now. She shuddered, and
tears welled in her eyes. Matt needed someone whole and
healthy, and the ache in her heart became more overpowering than the pain that wracked her body. Hours of
minutes passed as she relived her bad marriage, and she
felt the despair of not being in control of her own destiny
once more.

And there was Matt's pity, too. She winced. A sob
escaped her dry lips, and she closed her eyes as if she could
blot out the cold, miserable truth. Matt would no doubt

feel obligated to marry her now, but she would never be sure of his love. Silent tears cascaded unchecked down her cheeks, and she was furious with herself, furious with the wretched twist of fate.

"I think you'd better leave now," a pleasant voice said from behind Matt. "She needs rest. Tomorrow she'll be a little stronger. Why don't you come back then?"

Matt nodded, and as he walked down the long hospital corridor, every step accented the ache of guilt that weighted his spirit.

Wednesday morning dawned with an overcast sky, and Shawn still had not heard from Matt. She tried to brush her doubts aside and went about organizing her work for the day. While her fingers tapped out the numbers on the touch-tone phone, she mentally sorted out the upcoming activities.

"Good morning, Bellows Enterprises," Jill answered. "May I help you?"

"Yes, this is Shawn McCullough. May I speak to Andrew Bellows, please?"

"One moment, Ms. McCullough, I'll see if he's in," the secretary returned.

Apparently, he had just arrived, and before Jill pushed the hold button, Shawn could hear his exuberant response. "I'm here. Put her through to my office."

"Good morning, Shawn," he said. "You're certainly starting the day off right. Does this call mean you'll join me for lunch?"

She laughed. "What an ego! No, it does not. It simply means that I talked with my field superintendent, Tony Rizzo, and if you can make it late Thursday afternoon, he'll be at the site."

"I'd still rather it was you."

"Sorry, but you yourself said it, chain of command."

"I know, I know," he muttered. "Tell him three o'clock. I hope he's cooperative."

"Why on earth would you say that? We're all cooperative at McCullough Landscaping," she returned sweetly.

"Not as cooperative as I'd like," he hinted.

"Oh, I'm sorry that you feel that way."

"Perhaps we could remedy the situation with dinner on Saturday night?"

"You don't give up easily, do you, Andy?"

"I never have, but that's not an answer."

"I think I've already answered your question a time or two," she laughed, admitting to herself that she was beginning to feel flattered by his persistence.

"Not to my liking. I'll call you Friday." There was a click, and the line went dead.

Shawn laughed to herself and wondered if he would remain half as interested if she were to consent. Men, she thought, a smile curving her full lips.

Tony grumbled to himself as he scanned the massive building site that was to eventually become Arcadia Lane. "How in the hell does Shawn expect me to find a black Lamborghini in all this mess?" To his left was a huge mountain of soil that had been excavated in preparation for footings to support the largest enclosed shopping center to date on the West Coast. Looking around the site, Tony noticed stacks of metal reinforcement, lumber, and pipes. It was hard to visualize the end result, even for a man of his expertise. God, we've done it this time! What a prize, he thought. Bellows. Where's Bellows? Where's that damn car?

Finally spotting the Lamborghini, Tony parked alongside, and as he got out, his eyes appraised the sleek black lines of the expensive machine. He fought a subconscious twinge of jealousy. "I'll bet this damn machine takes dictation, too," he said admiringly. Presently the sound of loud voices drew his attention to a group of men, one of whom he assumed was Bellows.

"What the hell kind of a job is this?" demanded the man, who was obviously not one of the workmen.

"What the hell's the matter with it?" demanded a man wearing coveralls splattered with concrete.

"Don't you realize that that concrete is too porous? Hell,

it wouldn't even stand up under the weight of my automobile, let alone bear the stress of the buildings it's supposed to support!"

"Well, it's according to specs!"

"Don't give me that bull, I know those specs by heart. There's no way that's the proper mix, and it sure as hell won't pass inspection. Now get on the other end of that jackhammer and let's do this job right!"

Man, that guy knows how to take charge, Tony thought with a chuckle of admiration. I wonder, could he be Bellows? Tony approached the men who were all making tracks in different directions. "I'm Tony Rizzo," he announced to the man in the sharp blue pinstripe suit. "I'm looking for Andrew Bellows. Could you point him out?"

"I'm Bellows, what's on your mind?"

The field superintendent wasn't surprised. "Mr. Bellows, I believe we have an appointment."

The dynamic man gave Tony a momentarily perplexed look. "Oh, yes, you're from McCullough Landscaping. Let's take a walk, and I'll show you what's going on here. My superintendent will be here shortly."

Tony grinned and glanced at the footings. "Does look pretty rotten."

"You overheard the conversation?"

Tony nodded.

"That's the kind of thing I won't tolerate on any of my jobs. You know what would happen to a structure on that lousy footing if we had even a slight earthquake?"

"It sure as hell wouldn't help the landscaping."

Bellows laughed appreciatively. "Yeah, you'd have to replant a helluva lot of posies in your planter boxes!"

By the time they had walked over a quarter of the site, Tony Rizzo's appraisal of the building magnate had taken a hundred-eighty-degree turn. He was surprised that a man with the number of business commitments that Bellows must have, would actually take time to talk to a landscape superintendent personally. He had expected merely to be introduced to Bellows's man in charge and to discuss pertinent matters only with him. Instead, the tycoon seemed to enjoy personally talking with Tony.

An hour later he was grinning with admiration as he watched Andrew Bellows walk over to his sleek Lamborghini with the confidence of a man who had well earned his position and knew it.

It was Thursday night when Matt turned the key in his apartment door. Upon entering, he was greeted by the haunting aura of Patrice. His feet automatically took him to the refrigerator where he abstractedly rummaged through its contents. "Aw, the hell with it," he muttered. As the door slammed on the refrigerator, Matt headed for the living room. "Everything's gone to hell!" His law case, Patrice, Shawn—oh, damn! He hadn't called her! He stared at the phone, wishing it could speak for him. What could he say to her now? His thoughts were all disconnected. At this morning's confrontation with his wily opponent, Norman Pollard, he had suddenly felt totally inadequate. Even his brilliant, preplanned strategy seemed futile now. For the first time in his law career, he was just going through the motions at the pretrial hearing. Thoughts of Patrice had engulfed him and destroyed his concentration. Now he really needed her competence and moral support. He hadn't realized how much he had depended upon her till all of a sudden the tables were turned and she was dependent upon him.

In the Los Altos hills, Shawn was immersed in comforting bubbles after a long hard day when the ringing of the phone broke into her languor. "Oh, damn, if that's Bellows again, I'm gonna drown him!" She ignored the disturbing instrument until its insistent ringing suddenly brought Matt to mind. Quickly, she reached for a plush towel to wrap about herself as she hastily padded down the hall.

"Hello?"

There was a moment's silence before Matt's voice came through. "Shawn?"

"Yes, oh, Matt, it's so good to hear your voice!"

"It's good to hear yours, too. I meant to call earlier, but things seem to have gotten out of hand. This case has turned into a can of worms."

"I understand Matt, but I'm glad you called. When will you be back?"

There was a hesitation before Matt spoke. "I really can't say, honey. I have a lot of things to straighten out first."

"Matt, is there something wrong? Your voice sounds so strange."

"No, no, I'm just tired."

"Poor baby, I should have called you, if I had had your number," she purred sympathetically.

"This lawsuit has me running around so much I'm hardly ever home. You probably couldn't have gotten me, anyway. It's better if I call you."

"Surely you aren't tied up every weekend? I know! I'll fly down in a week or two, and we'll do something relaxing together." Impulsively she rushed, "Never mind the week or two, I'll catch a plane tomorrow night. There's so much I want to tell you!"

"Honey, this weekend is bad, but if I can work something out, I'll call you before noon tomorrow."

Disappointment colored her voice. "You mean you couldn't even give me a few hours?"

"That's not it. I just can't explain it all to you now."

"Matt, you sound so remote. Are you sure everything's all right?"

"I'm fine and I really do miss you, but I can't count on what's happening from one day to the next."

There was a desperation in his voice that Shawn couldn't comprehend, and she suddenly felt a distance between them that was more than mere miles. "Matt, please give me a call one way or the other tomorrow."

"I said I would, sweetheart. Before noon."

Chapter Nine

Shawn was at work early Friday morning, and the next time she glanced at her watch, it was eleven-thirty A.M. "My gosh, time really flies when things are going smooth." She looked at the phone and pleaded, "Come on, Matt, time's a wasting."

By five minutes to twelve, Shawn began to get edgy. Trying to keep her mind occupied, she started going over correspondence. She looked up to see Audrey's head poking in the door.

"How about joining us for lunch?" the secretary invited.

Shawn hesitated only a second. "No, I'm expecting an important call. Go on without me and I'll cover the switchboard. Maybe next week I'll have more free time. Raincheck?"

"Hope so, we miss you."

Shawn's outward smile hid the inner turmoil that would have destroyed a perfectly good luncheon, anyway. Could her watch be wrong? she wondered as she checked the desk clock. Sadly, the timepieces coincided. With a sigh, she went back to her correspondence and scrawled a letter to be typed, but as she proofread her work, even the letter seemed to reflect her dismal mood. Quickly wadding the paper up, she threw it forcefully into the wastebasket, again glaring at the unrelenting clock. It was then that

Matt's peculiar evasiveness of the previous night returned to mind. "Five minutes," she fumed, "that's all it takes! Damn you, Matt, pick up the phone!" Her disappointment in Matt gradually changed to a smoldering anger that she found difficult to rationalize even as she told herself there had to be a good reason for his not calling.

Many miles farther to the south, at that same instant, Matt Monroe had just excused himself during a luncheon engagement with Norman Pollard. He walked to the pay phone, then, fishing in his pocket for some change, he lifted the receiver to fulfill his promise to Shawn. Yet as he stared at the instrument, his thoughts were no more coherent than they had been the night before. How could he ask her to come when the fact was, there was no way he could tell her anything? Slowly he returned the receiver to its hook and abruptly turned back to the sanctuary of the dining room to resume negotiations with Pollard.

Andrew Bellows picked up line one. "Bellows here."
"Well, how ya doing, Andy? I haven't seen you since the last Chamber of Commerce meeting." The hearty voice was that of his friend, Frank Kendall, president of State-wide Bank.
"I keep busy. What's up, Frank?"
"I have a copy of one of your contracts."
"What the hell are you doing with one of my contracts?"
Kendall chuckled. "Some cute little Irish gal loaned it to me."
Andrew Bellows's brow furrowed as his quick mind picked up Kendall's hint. "That wouldn't be Shawn McCullough, would it?"
"As usual, you're extremely perceptive, Andy, my friend."
"So? What's your opinion of the project?"
"Good-sized. Should keep you and McCullough Land-scaping going for a while," Kendall replied.
Andrew laughed. "You're right. Now then, Frank, just

what the hell's the story here? How do you fit into the picture?"

"That's why I called you. Fill me in on Shawn Mc-Cullough."

"What precisely would you have me tell you? Her dimensions?"

Kendall laughed. "My eyes aren't that bad yet. I'm referring to her financial integrity."

"Well, if you mean, have I checked her out with Dunn and Bradstreet, the answer is no, but her dad's firm has had an outstanding reputation for years. You're the money man, what the hell are you asking me for?"

"Simply because she's in a financial bind and needs another loan extension."

Andrew pondered but a moment. Then in a conciliatory tone he said, "Frank, I think you'd better tell me the whole story."

As he listened intently to Kendall's explanation, he drummed his fingers on the massive mahogany desk and frowned. When the banker had finished, Andrew Bellows got right to the point. "Hey, old buddy, from what you're telling me, it's a loan incurred by her father, and it sounds as though she's more than willing to pay the honest debt. She didn't declare bankruptcy. I don't think you need to worry about it. That woman's got a lot of grit. I'd put my money on her anytime, and if necessary, I'll be willing to co-sign that loan, though knowing the fiery little lady, I'm sure she wouldn't agree to that."

"I expect you're right. She seems to be a very determined young woman. The problem is, I need something concrete to present to the board to validate another extension."

Andrew paused for a moment then replied, "If needed, I'll advance her progress payments. I think your board will find that a satisfactory arrangement and show that Bellows Enterprises has enough faith to stand behind her."

"Thanks, Andy, you've got me convinced. I'll see if I can

get by without a document from you. Great talking to you."

"Anytime."

Bellows reached for the intercom, suddenly surprised by the way his feelings regarding women in business—especially landscaping—had changed. "Jill, would you hold all calls until I tell you otherwise?" Leaning back in his huge executive chair, Andrew Bellows stretched his arms, then laced his fingers behind his head. He didn't know the details of Shawn's situation, but he could understand how she must feel. Like a damned orphan. He could relate to that. "Just a minute, Andy," he admonished himself aloud. "You sure as hell better find out what kind of problems she has." He continued to ponder silently. If she went bankrupt, it could easily put a crimp in the opening of Arcadia Lane. Hell's bells, Arcadia Lane be damned! He surprised himself by the discovery that Shawn was more important, and he wondered just how far in the hole she was. Frank had hinted at a couple hundred grand. That was a bunch of money to catch up in the landscaping business.

Leaning forward, he grabbed the phone, quickly dialed McCullough Landscaping, and as he waited, mentally pictured the tantalizing raven-haired Irish temptress.

"Yes, Andy." Shawn's impatience, which had built to a crescendo, penetrated the phone.

"You sound like this has not been one of your days!"

"I'm sorry, but you're right. I've seen better ones. This has been at least a day and a half."

"Had a few of those myself. They can be pretty damn wearing. Actually, the reason I called was to ask you out to dinner, but I can tell by the tone of your voice that what you need is a stiff drink and a good night's sleep."

"Andy, for once you're right. I don't know why I'm telling you this, but I do need some rest. God, I'm tired."

Exhaustion and worry came through in her voice, and

he suddenly longed to hold her in his arms and soothe her.
Instead he said, "Go home, Shawn. Tomorrow's another
day, and dinner will keep."

"You know, I think that's the best advice I've gotten all
day."

"Then take it, and I'll call you in the morning."

Shawn plunked the coffeepot on the counter. Then,
reaching for the cup she'd just poured, she spilled it and
wailed, "Oh, damn! Don't tell me this is going to be an
instant replay of yesterday!" Quickly, she mopped up the
counter and took the cup out onto the back patio where, in
the past, on a Saturday, she had basked in the morning
sun while sharing coffee with her father. Somehow the
ritual wasn't the same. The concrete beneath her feet
seemed so cold, and the sun not as warm. It was as though
loneliness had become her twin. A mental vision of her
father seated opposite with a coffee cup in his massive
hand was as real as life itself. The need to ease the awful
loneliness overwhelmed her. She shivered with apprehension borne of uncertainty. There was nothing certain in
her life at this point, nor could she depend on Matt.
"Shawn McCullough," she said to herself, "stop wallowing
in self-pity and at least enjoy the sun's warmth." She set
her coffee on a nearby ledge and bent down for the
sprinkler key, turning it on fully. She might as well water
the thirsty lawns.

"Jesus Christ!" a thundering, masculine voice roared,
thoroughly startling her.

Shawn's eyes lit upon the unexpected intruder and
found a very damp and sputtering Andrew Bellows. An
inadvertent giggle escaped her.

"Do you furnish towels? Bathrobes? Spare shorts? Lock-
ers?"

"You'll get the first one," she said between spasms of
laughter. "I'm hardly set up for unexpected male guests."

"I'm not exactly unexpected," he said indignantly, shaking his wet head. "I told you that I'd call today."

"Call, yes. Appear, no. I thought you would phone like any normal human being, but I am glad to see you," she added to placate him.

"You mean you'll condescend to share a cup of coffee this morning?"

She laughed. "It's the least I can do after your impromptu shower."

He nodded righteously as he pulled a newspaper out of his back pocket and dumped its soggy remains in her palm. "Your paper, madam."

"Sorry about that," she said in amusement, then more seriously, "are you cold?"

His eyes penetrated her flimsy white lace gown and peignoir, and his eyebrows lifted in admiration. "You must be kidding! Not while I'm looking at you in that outfit, Shawn McCullough."

Instantly, Shawn felt acutely uncomfortable. She hastily clutched the front of the filmy robe, and a rose blush flooded her cheeks. "Andrew, the coffee's in the kitchen. Help yourself while I get dressed."

"Must you? You look great the way you are," he said, grinning.

Her answer was an exasperated grimace, but he noticed that her step had a lively bounce as she disappeared up the stairs. Andrew Bellows poured himself a cup of coffee and let his imagination run free. Some women he might have followed up the stairs, but somehow she was different. Right from the start, she represented a challenge. He was still mulling over his frustrations while absentmindedly sipping coffee when she returned clad in a snug-fitting red cashmere sweater and pearl-gray slacks that accentuated her trim and sensual body, causing him to inhale sharply.

"Did you find the cream and sugar?" she asked.

"What? Oh—no, I like it black."

"You look so serious, Andrew. Is there something wrong?"

Her smile was warm for once, and he wanted to crush her in his arms. She was unlike any woman he'd ever met, and his unaccustomed yearning was overwhelming. "Yes, something is wrong. I thought you were going to call me Andy, not Andrew."

She laughed. "All right, Andy. Now then, would you stop staring holes through me?"

"Oh, I'm sorry. I didn't realize that I was."

"As I said, Andy, I am glad to see you, but why are you here?"

Her rare, friendly tone put him at ease, and he answered impulsively. "It's such a beautiful, lazy day. Let's take a drive somewhere and let the sun dry me out. Besides, we need to talk business."

"Andy, I've had my fill of business this week, but I could go for a little diversion. The ride sounds good."

"Well, then," he said, guiding her toward the door, fingers gently touching her waist, "let's go."

Shawn nudged his hand away and smiled. "Friends, remember? Not bosom buddies."

He conceded good-naturedly. "Okay, I'll settle for friendship, for now. Come on." He led the way to his sleek black Countach, and as if by remote control, released the door.

"Andy, this—this car is positively stunning," she exclaimed in awe as she watched the door lift skyward, revealing the exotic interior furnished with tasteful white leather seats and upholstery, and black suede trim on the top of the dash and around the windshield and windows. The headliner was soft, white suede. "It's beautiful, but how on earth does one get in?"

"Practice, my dear. Just like easing into a custom-made Italian shoe—the first time requires a little body English."

Shawn frowned as she gingerly slid into the seat. "My heavens, does this car have a periscope?"

He grinned. "You aren't going to believe it, but yes, it does."

Bellows got in and started the car with ease.

Intrigued by the array of colorful flashing lights, Shawn remarked, "Are you sure we have clearance for takeoff?"

He laughed. "Would you really like to fly?"

"Don't tell me that you have a plane, too!"

"Oh, I might be able to get hold of one long enough to take you to lunch one of these days," he said.

"That sounds inviting," she said as she settled back into the body-hugging, contoured seat. Somehow their destination wasn't important. The elegance of Andrew's Lamborghini seemed to isolate her from her problems. She had entered the luxurious world of the very affluent, and she meant to enjoy it to the hilt. Letting the sleek car's expensive upholstery caress her, she couldn't remember having been so relaxed.

"I hate to bring up business when I'd much prefer spending my time enjoying your company, but I am concerned," Andrew interrupted her reverie.

The spell was broken. Shawn stiffened in her seat. "Concerned about what, Andy?"

"Well, Shawn, I have to be honest with you. I received a call from Frank Kendall yesterday afternoon."

"I expected that. Does that bother you?"

"Only to the extent that I want to help."

She studied his face. "You're sure it's not that you're afraid I'll file bankruptcy and cause Arcadia Lane to suffer?"

"Shawn, I'd be lying if I said I wasn't concerned about that possible factor with a deadline staring me in the face."

"I have the same deadline, remember? Andy, I'm not a quitter! Why in the hell do you think I went immediately to the bank?" she bristled.

Bellows frowned as he looked at her. "I think you're misunderstanding me again. Personalities aside, we are business associates, and if you have a problem, it also affects me and I'm hoping I can help."

"What are you going to do, Andrew? Give me two hundred thousand dollars?" she sweetly inquired.

"The thought had crossed my mind, but I knew you wouldn't accept it, so I just want you to know I'm here to help in any way that I can."

Shawn's eyes softened apologetically. "Andy, I'm sorry

to be so quick-tempered," she said. "That's one hell of an offer, and thanks. I appreciate the thought, but I need to work this out by myself. Don't worry, we will meet that opening date."

Her expression told him that she was genuinely touched that he understood her feelings regarding integrity. "You know," he said, "I believe you."

"Good. Then please let's forget problems for now and enjoy this beautiful, lazy day as you promised."

"I'm all for that. Why don't we run down the coast to Carmel?"

"And browse in all the little shops?" she said enthusiastically.

"Browse? I'm no shopper," he returned with a mock frown.

"Bet you could be," she challenged.

Andy answered her with a grin as he pressed a button, engaging the stereo.

The soft romantic music touched a chord in her heart, and against her will, thoughts of Matt flooded her mind. What kind of game was he playing that he couldn't even call late last night? To hell with Matt, she decided, I'm here to relax, and that's exactly what I'm going to do. She settled back in her luxurious seat, grinned, and turned her attention to the ocean at her right. Down on the shoreline below, the waves vented their fury against the protruding rocks, sending showers of spray in all directions. In her mind, it was as if her feelings were the waves breaking against the cold hardness of Matt's indifference. Again, she tuned Matt out, vowing not to give in to such negative thinking. Instead, she closed her eyes and rested her head against the supple leather. The wind kissing her hair and the sound of the tires on the pavement lulled her into a strange euphoria.

For the remainder of the trip, Andy concentrated on the curves in the road and enjoyed the stereo with only an occasional glance at the distractingly beautiful woman beside him, while Shawn, deep in her newfound tranquillity, was totally unaware of those hungry glances.

Several pleasant hours later, after thoroughly exploring picturesque downtown Carmel, Shawn found herself surprised by Andy's enthusiasm for shopping. After initially grumbling that shopping was a woman's domain, he fell into the spirit and seemed to be enjoying himself. Every once in a while she would catch him watching her with a smile on his face that she didn't quite understand.

"Let's see some of their paintings," she said late in the afternoon while tugging him in the direction of an art gallery. "You know, painting is something I've always wanted to try. Oh, look, Andy, look at that oil! It's the very same scenery we passed on the way down. I *love* it!"

Andrew Bellows critically scanned the seascape. "You know, it is well done. Would you like it?"

Shawn's eyes fastened on the price tag. It read seven hundred and fifty dollars. "Are you kidding? You're talking to somebody who needs two hundred thousand dollars," she said, laughing.

"Oh, forget the damn price. If you want the picture, I'll get it for you." He stretched to remove the seascape from the wall.

Shawn caught his arm. "No, Andy, that's ridiculous. I just thought the canvas was pretty. Somehow, it captures the mood of the day, but I don't want you to buy it for me."

"Are you sure, Shawn? I'd really like to."

She shook her head. "But I will let you buy dinner. These hills are about to do me in."

He laughed. "I know of a nice French restaurant."

"Sold!" she said. "How far?"

La Terrasse was exclusive and candlelit, a touch of Paris in the fall with its outdoor tables set upon a brick terrace. Gay, scalloped canopies above each table gave a feeling of seclusion, and the dimly lit wrought-iron lamp posts decorating the charming scene lent just enough light to make sure the diners got full enjoyment from the trees and flowerbeds adorning the terrace.

Shawn breathed a sigh of relief that could only mean

that she had kicked off her shoes beneath the table. "Oh, that feels good!"

Andy smiled. "You're quite a shopper."

"I don't know about that. I didn't buy a darn thing."

"True, but I've never seen anybody enjoy browsing so much."

Her smile was quick. "It *was* fun, wasn't it?"

His amused expression and the way he blinked his eyes in agreement told her that Andrew Bellows was not entirely the ruthless businessman he portrayed. His face reflected honest enjoyment, and a flicker of gentleness shone in his eyes.

"Would you care for a drink?" he asked.

"I would love one," she said. "Andy, this has been a wonderful day. I don't know when I've felt so relaxed!"

He leaned to touch her hand across the table, his fingers tracing its small outline, his eyes examining her face admiringly. "You're incredible," he said. "How do you do it?"

"Do what?"

"Make every little happening a special event. You really put your heart into everything you do, don't you?"

She looked at him in serious consideration, then wrinkled her nose and broke into a grin. "Sure, and why not?" she said with a touch of the brogue. "But mind you, it often gets me into trouble!"

"Somehow I think it's worth it." He laughed.

Shawn listened while Andrew ordered with practiced ease in fluent French. She was delighted with the resultant feast, and her appreciation and enthusiasm were clearly evident. Andy sat enthralled, watching her appreciatively savor each morsel while at the same time extolling the delectable wine sauces and delicate seasonings.

He leaned back in his chair as he eyed Shawn with obvious pleasure, weighing his thoughts at the same time. Reaching for the vintage wine, he replenished their glasses. Then his gaze returned to her. "I have a serious question for you. Do you mind?"

She raised her brows, and her expressive blue eyes gleamed in the dim light. "As long as it's not too personal."

"Shawn, I wonder . . . Oh, hell—is there any chance of getting beyond this purely platonic business relationship of ours?"

She suddenly looked away, disconcerted by what his words implied. "Why spoil a good thing?"

"Because you excite the hell out of me, and to be blunt but honest, I want to take you to bed, preferably tonight."

"Oh, do you? Now, just what kind of an answer do you expect to that statement?"

He wasn't sure what the tiny quirk in the corner of her mouth meant. "Yes would suit me fine," he said, picking up the cigar he had ordered after dinner.

"Is that why McCullough Landscaping wound up with Arcadia Lane, to bed McCullough's daughter?"

He lit his cigar. "Hell, no, this has nothing to do with business. It's strictly pleasure! You are a very alluring woman, Shawn McCullough!" His eyes riveted her unmercifully as he took a long drag on his cigar.

"I don't believe this," she said incredulously, ignoring the shiver sent coursing down her spine by his penetrating gaze. "Pleasure, you say? What ever happened to love or commitment?"

He shrugged, and little puffs of smoke rose from the expensive cigar as he looked at her with that infuriatingly amused expression of his. "Amazingly, with you, it's all synonymous."

"And just what is it that you're offering me?"

"The chance of a lifetime."

"Oh, I see. I'm certainly glad you clarified this great opportunity. I always like to know where I stand. Is this a one-nighter with options?"

He burst out laughing. "I doubt that even I could settle for that little with a woman of your charm and beauty and the obvious capacity to make me a happy man."

Her eyes appeared almost black in the dim light, and a strange sort of smoldering anger coursed hotly through her veins. "And how would you know?"

"That's one thing I do know—women."

"Perhaps not as well as you think. Tell me, with a blunt line like that you must have a bed partner to warm your penthouse every night. Just how many women anxiously await your favors?"

"Um—one, maybe two."

"Indeed? I'm disappointed. Don't you think they would be upset?"

"Of course."

"My sympathies to them."

"Shawn, you are very beautiful, and I admire your fire. I could become very attached to you. Why not move in with me?"

The abrupt suggestion caught Shawn off guard, but she quickly recovered. "So you could give me financial security, a warm bed with satin sheets, and a release for all my inhibitions?"

He looked at her evenly. "You scarcely seem to be the inhibited type."

She ignored his remark. "And just what happens when I turn you down?"

He grinned, obviously enjoying the verbal sparring. "Back to business."

"Oh, that's great! I'd hate to think our contract would suffer!"

"No problem."

There was a wicked sapphire gleam in her eyes as they bored into his cool blue ones. "Naturally, I'd have to have all the things a well-kept mistress deserves: diamonds, furs, clothes from the finest couturier in Paris. Perhaps we should put it in writing. I'm sure I can come up with a multitude of other stipulations."

He flicked the ashes from his cigar. "It would seem that you're not so inclined."

She smiled patronizingly sweet. "How did you ever guess?"

He nodded and rose from his chair, taking her hand to raise her to her feet. "The offer is open."

"Andrew Bellows! You are the most egotistical,

infuriating—" She quickly withdrew her hand, hotly sputtering.

"Chauvinist?"

"No, son of a bitch!"

He laughed. "And you, Shawn McCullough, are damn cute when you're mad. I didn't mean to rile you, honest."

"Then stop it, Andy, before I tell you to take your million-dollar job and shove it clear to your navel."

He threw his head back and roared with laughter. "You're one of a kind!"

A smile played upon her lips in spite of herself. "I can't make up my mind whether I've been insulted or complimented."

"You've never been a mistress, I take it?"

Her face turned the color of her sweater. "Well, damn! I hardly think that it's anyone's affair but my own!"

He grinned agreeably. "You're absolutely right, of course. But I do intend to have you. Come on, I'll take you home."

She shied away from him, demanding, "No stops along the way?"

"Honest. Truce, again?" He waved a white linen hankerchief in mock surrender.

Looking into his steel-blue eyes, she perceived an honesty and she knew that for all of his talk, he wouldn't press the proposition. "All right," she said, and was halfway out the door before she realized her feet were bare. "My shoes," she exclaimed, running back to retrieve them.

"It's just as well you turned me down," he said with a sigh. "Your feet are probably like ice about now!"

They both laughed as she slipped into her sandals and gaily took his arm.

Chapter Ten

It was a brisk October morning. On her way into the office building, Shawn pulled out her comb and ran it through the dark strands that had been tousled by the early morning breeze. The weekend had been a happy one. Andy had made her well aware of his desire, and it was an exhilarating feeling. She flushed, wondering what it would have been like had she taken him up on his offer.

"Good morning," Audrey said.

"Yes, isn't it?" Shawn said with exuberance.

"Tony's in your office."

"Good, there's a couple of things we need to go over." She hurried down the hall, poured some coffee, and entered her office.

"Hi, boss lady," Tony greeted her. "I thought I'd better touch bases with you before I get on with the job."

"How's it going with Sun Haven? Did you tear out the old landscaping?"

"Should wrap it up today. That's one thing the guys are good at." He laughed. "Sure comes out easier than it goes in."

"I'll bet it does! You know," Shawn said, suddenly wistful, "it's kind of a shame to tear out an existing park just to modernize it, but I guess it's been there since day one."

"Yeah, the play equipment was so rickety, it was dangerous. The new facilities will be a hell of a lot safer if we can keep the kids out of our hair long enough to install them."

"What's the problem?" Her jubilant mood was sobered by Tony's tone.

"Just the usual. I had Patterson rough-grading on the far end on Friday, and the kids pulled up all of his grid elevation stakes as fast as he put 'em in the ground."

"They're just having fun. Can't you explain the reason for the stakes? Surely they'll understand."

"Hell, I can't catch 'em long enough to tell 'em anything, but it's not the first time. We'll work it out."

"I have no doubt." She smiled. "Strange, you'd think the kids would be delighted with the prospect of a new park with all kinds of the latest play equipment."

"Who knows?" Tony said with a shrug. "This bunch seems to be pretty ornery. I just hope they stay the hell out of the irrigation trenches once we get going on them. Oh, by the way, the city has to install the water meters on Friday if possible."

"That soon?"

"We don't need any delays in getting the irrigation in. The sooner, the better. I'd at least like to close the trenches before the first big rain."

"Yes, that would be great. It's due any day now. Speaking of rain, how will that affect the shopping center?"

Tony shrugged. "There's no way we can get ahead of it on Arcadia. A job that size takes a while to get started. Nelson's our foreman for this job and he's still trying to figure out how to run a job that big, and I'm not too damn sure myself." He laughed. "But don't worry, boss lady, we'll get our ducks all in line. Well, I better get going. See ya later."

"Right. Have a good one."

After Tony left, Audrey poked her red head in the

doorway. "There's a delivery man here with a package for you. He needs your signature."

"For me? Must be something for one of the jobs," she wondered aloud as she hurried to the reception area.

"Ms. McCullough?" the man asked, thrusting a delivery slip under her nose. "Sign here, please."

Excitement began to build as Shawn quickly scrawled her name on the sheet. "Thank you," she said, returning the signed paper.

The crated mystery package intrigued her. What could possibly be in a six-foot-long by maybe four-foot-tall container, one that was probably no more than four or five inches deep? It certainly wasn't anything for the jobs, or it would have been so indicated on the delivery slip. She studied the carton, trying to decide the best procedure for uncrating her surprise.

"Well?" Audrey said expectantly, "I'm dying of curiosity. Aren't you going to do something?"

Shawn grinned. "You bet I am! Ralph," she called, spying the maintenance man, "can you find something that will pull huge staples?"

"Be there in a minute," Ralph replied, and disappeared into the garage.

"Now, what can I help you with, Ms. McCullough?" the tall, thin man asked when he reappeared.

"This box. Can you open it?" Shawn asked anxiously.

"Sure, no problem." Ralph bent to pry the staples loose. It seemed to take forever as Shawn impatiently watched his slow, methodical removal of the packaging.

When she could no longer bear to watch him make the trip over to the wastebasket with each staple, she brought the trash container over and parked it beside him.

Ralph tugged at the end lath. "Oh, damn! Cut my finger," he muttered, and fished in his pocket for a handkerchief while Shawn tapped with exasperation.

"Ralph. Ralph, will you just open the crate? I'll get you a Band-Aid in a minute," she said with all the petulance of a small child.

He gave her a frown and jerked the protective wood loose. Pulling out the contents to view, he said, "Now, isn't that pretty?"

"I should say," Audrey said. "It's absolutely beautiful!"

Shawn stared at her gift. It was gorgeous, even lovelier than she had remembered. A tingle of excitement, of genuine pleasure, coursed through her. How very thoughtful of Andrew. She smiled at Audrey. "It is beautiful, isn't it, but far too expensive." Suddenly her delight was overcome by her common sense, and a trace of annoyance surfaced because of Andrew's facing her with such temptation. She whirled around, strode briskly into her office, and reached for the phone all in one determined movement.

"It's a lovely seascape, Andrew, but I thought we understood one another. I simply can't accept that kind of gift." Her voice held a slight tone of irritation even though she was secretly pleased by his thoughtful generosity.

"Hold on now, don't throw it on the ground and do a Mexican hat dance on it just yet. Giving expensive gifts to my friends is one of my many frivolous foibles. Do you think that you should be excluded simply because I happen to be lusting for your body?" Andrew asked.

Shawn laughed uproariously but at the same time wondered how on earth she could possibly respond to that statement. Gathering her wits, she said, "Reaching for unattainable goals, Andy, only tends to increase one's reach rather than to better one's grasp."

"My arms are far longer than you know, Ms. McCullough."

"You are an impossible, egotistical, extremely frustrating man, Mr. Bellows."

"But of course. Did you expect otherwise?" He paused and then grew serious. "But really, Shawn, I want you to have the painting. Let's just say it's part of a day that I enjoyed very much. Honest, no strings, I swear! If it makes you feel any better, let's call it a good-will token between business partners."

"No, let's say that I'll hold it until you find the right spot for it."

"I already have, but whatever you wish."

"Thank you, Andy," she murmured, "you are very thoughtful, even if you are impossible." She heard him chuckle as she replaced the receiver and a grin lit up her lovely face.

"That's fantastic!" Shawn fairly shouted into the receiver late in the afternoon. "When can I expect a copy of the extension?"

"Couple of days," came Kendall's reply.

"That'll be fine," Shawn bubbled. "Thank you, Mr. Kendall. This is the perfect ending for a perfect day." She clicked the receiver in place, swung her chair around, and kicked her foot in the air in one easy motion. As the shoe flew off her foot, she exclaimed, "Saints be praised! I knew I could count on those 'little green fellows,' my guardian leprechauns!"

The shoe caromed off Tony's leg, eliciting from him a rather loud, "Ouch! What the hell's going on here?"

"We got it!" Shawn shouted exuberantly, then quickly rose from her chair and lurched toward him with a discernible tilt.

"Got what?" Tony muttered perplexedly.

"The loan extension, for heaven's sake!" She grabbed her superintendent and whirled him around in a joyous little dance.

"Hey, son of a gun, that's great! Looks like we're still in business!"

"You bet we are! Now, if only the house would sell quickly so I can pay off the loan." Even the thought of her precious house on the market couldn't dispel the excitement.

Watching Shawn, a grin broadened Tony's face. "I think we should celebrate. Come on, I'm buying."

Chapter Eleven

Tuesday morning, Dr. Davis smiled reassuringly at Patrice. "Well, my dear, are you ready to go home?"

The smile on his face did little to alleviate her fears. A frown wrinkled her brow, and her voice was clearly frightened. "But, Dr. Davis, I can barely walk with crutches."

"What did you expect from only two therapy sessions? To become a ballet dancer?" he teased.

"I am impatient, aren't I?" she admitted.

He nodded his head. "You've come a long way since the night of the accident. Why, soon you'll be as good as new. I have therapy set up for you on Mondays and Thursdays at two o'clock. Do you have someone to bring you?"

"I'll work it out, Doctor."

"Good. Then call me anytime if you have questions. I'll see you in my office in three weeks. I've prescribed some pain medication for you, which you can pick up at the pharmacy when you leave."

"Thank you, Doctor." She squeezed his hand. "You saved my life."

"No," he said, "somebody up there likes you, but you helped a lot on your own recovery."

His confident words gave her a boost in spirit, and it

wasn't until he was gone that the realization of her going home struck full-force. How would she manage on her own? Perhaps she should have taken T. J.'s offer. A private nurse would solve a lot of problems and also be company. Yet her resistance to that idea had been based upon her wanting independence. Maybe for a week or two, she would accept T. J.'s help but only until she was stronger.

As Matt entered the hospital room, he sensed something wrong even before he reached her, and his handsome face darkened with concern. He heard the depression in her tone as she explained about the nurse. Compassion infused his voice as he smiled comfortingly at her. "Why would you worry about that when you're coming home with me?"

She dropped her eyes, and in a disconsolate voice said, "I can't do that to you, Matt."

"What are loved ones for if not to help? Tell you what," he said in a lighter tone. "Just stay with me until you've regained your strength. Now how's that?"

She smiled wanly. "All right, Matt, but only until I'm stronger."

He nodded agreeably. "Well, what are we waiting for? I've already talked to the doc. He says we're going home."

That same evening, lying on his sofa, Matt reflected on the day's events. Patrice seemed to bloom from his attention while he found himself gaining strength from her presence. She was the old Patrice with her keen insight, and she offered a tremendous amount of encouragement. He found, as always, a certain quiet strength that she radiated. She seemed to anticipate his needs, and as he tucked her, childlike, into bed, he felt at peace with himself. Yet now, in the solitude of the darkened living room, the old doubts began to surface.

What a hell of a fix! There was no alternative other than to call Shawn, to tell her the entire story, the sooner the better. She might call and get Patrice. His fingers quickly traced the numbers and he cleared his throat in expectation, but the muffled ring reached no listener. Matt sighed. Perhaps he was overreacting to the whole situation, and hell, Patrice would only be with him a short while.

Late Friday afternoon in her office, Shawn studied the job costs on Norton School. They had saved money on laying the sod. It had been a good week, discounting Matt's failure to call. She wasn't about to keep wondering; she would call him tonight.

Her thoughts were interrupted by Tony's entrance. "You look totally engrossed. Anything I should know or not know?" he quipped.

Shawn looked up and smiled. "As a matter of fact, I was just thinking about Norton School and your starring role. You beat the time on laying the sod by half, and the job as a whole made twenty-eight percent. Nice work, Tony!"

Tony's shoulders straightened, and his face became radiant. "Hey, thanks, boss lady. Things are lookin' up."

"What's doing on Arcadia?"

"We'll move the trencher over there first thing Monday for the underground. I think Nelson has figured a plan of attack to get things rolling."

"That's what I like to hear," Shawn said. "Are you still going to be able to swing those palms in before they close the courtyard?"

"Yep, I talked to the source the other day, and he said he'll have them at the right time. All we have to do is notify him a few days in advance."

"That's good news."

"Uh, huh. Well, that about wraps it up. I don't know about you, but I'm ready for a nice relaxing weekend," Tony said as he rose to leave.

"Have a good one." Shawn glanced at her watch and picked up her purse. "See you Monday," she said to Audrey, who looked up from her typewriter.

"I'm glad to see you leaving at a reasonable time for a change," the secretary remarked.

Shawn grinned. "Necessity, I'm afraid. I need to get

things ready for the open house tomorrow, and you know what that means."

It was eight o'clock when Shawn put the vacuum away and breathed a sigh of relief. The house looked picture-perfect and smelled of pine. "Oh, I know," she said to herself. Quickly, she got the clippers and went out to the garden. Cutting perky white daisies, velvety red roses, puffy yellow marigolds, and some sprigs of greenery, she arranged them in an elaborate crystal bowl and placed the lovely arrangement on the dining table. Then stepping back to admire her handiwork, the whole thing suddenly hit home. The house might sell tomorrow, and she had no idea where she would live. The very thought of leaving the home she loved was depressing. She would lose so much that was dear to her. Even stuffed Timothy might have to become extinct again. She walked over and impulsively grabbed the dinosaur, hugging him to her. "There'll always be a spot for you," she said defiantly. Despositing him back on the terrazzo floor, she was reminded of Matt.

"Matt, oh, damn!" She had meant to call him earlier. Still wondering why he didn't call, she hesitated but a moment before going quickly to the phone. Anticipating his voice quickened her heartbeat as she listened to the annoying ring that went on and on. Where could he be? He surely wasn't working on the case at this hour. Depression mixed with irritation and loneliness gnawed away at her happy mood of only a moment ago, and a flick of her fingers silenced the frustrating sound. Immediately, she dialed Elsa, refusing to give in to her strong desire to call Andrew Bellows.

"How would you like company tonight?" she asked in response to Elsa's warm greeting. "It's getting me down, rattling around this big quiet house."

"Love it! Come on over, honey. Bring your overnight bag, and we'll have a long talk over some hot rum toddies."

"Sold! The realtor is holding open house tomorrow, and

I'd just as soon pass." Within minutes of the conversation, Shawn was out the door.

Tony braked to a stop in front of Shawn's garage and quickly stomped to the door. "Sorry, boss lady, you can't sleep this morning," he muttered as he rang the bell. "Wonder what the hell is really going on at Sun Haven? I'll bet it's those little kids who kept trailing the crew around. Come on, Shawn, time to rise and shine." Impatiently shifting his weight from one foot to the other, he leaned on the door bell. "Hm, there's nothin' stirring around here," he noted with a frown. He hurried back to his pickup, shuffled through his glove compartment for a scrap of paper, settling for an envelope, and grabbed a stubby piece of yellow marking crayon off the seat to scrawl a note. "Shawn, city called, Sun Haven flooded, on my way to check it out now, but from description, advise building an ark. Tony. P.S. If I'm not there Monday A.M., come bail me out."

A few minutes later, as he stood at the edge of the park, Tony shuddered. Water was gushing furiously, and the whole place was under water. Bubbling torrents of water had overflowed into rivers cascading down the street. Tony stared in disbelief at the cars plowing through the spreading pool that had formed in the intersection.

"Hey, you're washing out my new lawn clear across the street! Do something, dammit! I'm gonna hold you responsible for replacing it!"

Startled at the sound of the angry voice, Tony spun around, lost his footing, and fell awkwardly into a waist-deep trench. The complaining man's mouth fell open. Furious, Tony mounted the ledge, struggling to hoist himself out. Despite his efforts, the saturated ground gave way again and again under his weight, and he slipped helplessly back into the quagmire, mud splattering his nose.

Seeing his predicament, the man who had attacked him a minute before splashed toward Tony. "Can I give you a hand?" he asked with a touch of sympathy.

Tony reached gratefully for the outstretched hand.
"Watch it!" he warned. "The edges are really soft."

"I'll bet they are," the man said as he tugged at Tony's
mud-covered hands, and after a brief struggle, managed to
drag him out.

"Hey, thanks, buddy, don't worry about that lawn, we'll
take care of it later. Right now I gotta plug a couple of
holes." With that he hurriedly made his way to the valves,
yanking at the operating handles mistakenly left on by
the plumber, an open invitation to vandalism. To Tony, it
seemed the water would never stop, and when he finally
managed to reduce the torrent to a trickle, he heaved a
sigh of relief and muttered, "Wonder where the hell the
nearest phone is so I can rent a pump?" His eyes searched
the area, coming to rest on a black Lamborghini pulling in
behind his truck. There was only one person he knew who
drove a Countach. "Bellows. What the hell is he doing
here?" Tony muttered.

As if to forestall more bad news, Tony put his hands on
his mud-caked hips, then watched defiantly as a leg clad
in well-tailored gray trousers and a short black dress boot
extended itself from the car and came to rest squarely in a
large murky puddle.

As Andrew Bellows extracted himself from the car, he
felt the cold water seeping through his shoe leather and
shrugged in resignation. "And me without my tackle box."
Then, addressing Tony he called, "Good morning, Mr.
Rizzo, I see you have a little problem here."

"Looks like a hell of a problem to me," Tony retorted
shortly. "Don't tell me there's something wrong at Arcadia, too!"

Bellows laughed. "No, not that I know of. It just so
happens that I eavesdropped on your note to Ms. McCullough, and since she's not home, I thought maybe I could
give you a hand."

Tony grimaced. In his Yves Saint Laurent sport sweater
and trousers, Andrew Bellows appeared to be anything
but a helping hand. "I don't think you're dressed for the
occasion, Mr. Bellows."

Andrew laughed. "Circumstances dictate procedure, my friend. Now where do we begin?"

Four hours later, the drains were unclogged and pumps were emptying out the trenches when Andrew noticed Shawn's Spitfire pull up.

"Andrew," Shawn said as she closed the car door. "What on earth are you doing here?"

"Well, somebody had to play boss while the boss was playing. Got your wading shoes on? I trust you'll want to talk to Rizzo. He's monitoring the suction pump." His gaze fell to her sandal-clad feet. "Hm," he said. "Those aren't going to cut it." With that, he scooped her up and carried her across the muddy terrain, careful to avoid the collapsed trenches.

Shawn struggled to be free of his muscular arms. "Andrew, put me down! Can't you see everyone is staring?"

"So? Let 'em stare! And I suggest that you stop squirming, or I might accidentally drop you. Do I make myself clear?"

"Quite clear," she answered rather haughtily despite the devilish surge of enjoyment she experienced. The spicy masculine scent of him could not be obliterated by the dried splatters of mud that sought to camouflage his handsomely sharp features, and she found herself almost enjoying falling victim to his strength and vitality. She wondered wickedly if he were that overpowering in bed.

"Now that's better," he said when she had stopped struggling to be free. "Just relax. I'm not going to bite you, and if you're worried, this is sure as hell no place to get romantic. I'm simply being practical."

Shawn felt somehow deflated when he deposited her on the hood of Tony's truck.

"There," he said. "Now you can survey everything; that is, if you care to."

Shawn's eyes darted about the muddy shambles of a week's work. "Damn!" she exclaimed vehemently. "What happened, anyway?"

"I got my suspicions," Tony grumbled, pointing across the park at a group of kids on their bicycles.

"But how could they do all this?" She stretched out her arms helplessly.

"Hell of a mess, isn't it? It'll take a couple of weeks to dry out, and we'll have to close all the trenches and start over," he said wearily. "Those little sons of bitches had better steer clear of me," he threatened, "or I'll bury 'em in the damn trenches."

Determination flicked in Shawn's ice-blue eyes, and she hopped off the hood, striding deliberately toward a small black boy who was frantically trying to realign the chain on his bicycle while the other boys took off in all directions. As she approached, the boy, in one swift motion, raised the kickstand, grabbed the handlebars, and quickly started walking his bike in the opposite direction. With each slippery, wet step, the distance narrowed between them. Caught in the certainty of capture, fear showed in the youngster's huge brown eyes. "What do ya want me for? I didn't do it!" he yelped defensively.

"Maybe not all by yourself, but I'll bet you had a hand in it." Shawn gasped for breath as she grabbed his collar and spun him around to face her.

"Honest ma'am, it weren't me at all. Me and my friends don't do stuff like that!"

Shawn studied her squirming captive. "You sure look familiar to me. What's your name, anyway?"

Recognition beamed in the boy's dark eyes, and a hopeful smile broadened his mouth. "I'm Jason, Jason Brown. Don't you 'member we rode horses at Marriott's a little while back?"

"Indeed I do!" She patted the handlebars of his bicycle. "Is this your latest black charger?"

Jason grinned warmly. "Yep, only I got a problem with the chain sometimes. Keeps slippin' off somehow." He lowered the kickstand and attempted to maneuver the chain back to its proper alignment on the sprockets without success. His big eyes rose to meet hers. "See what I mean? Just doesn't work."

Shawn stared at the little boy, who appeared to be about eight years old.

"Ms. Shawn, that's your name, isn't it?" the boy said, squirming uneasily under her steady gaze.

"Yes, Shawn McCullough," she said smiling.

"Well, uh, I guess what I want to say is I'm sorry 'bout all of this. You're a nice lady."

"Thank you, but you didn't do it, did you, Jason?" she probed.

"Oh, no, ma'am, I didn't. But I can't tell. The Renegades—" He clapped his hands to his mouth.

"The Renegades? Who are the Renegades?"

"I don' know," he said defensively.

"Are you afraid of them, Jason?"

"You mean chicken?" He squared his small shoulders and puffed out his chest. "No, I just don't fink, that's all. Anyway, Ms. McCullough, I know people has to have places to live, but did you have to wreck our park to build one of those big condo—minums."

"You mean condominiums? Is that what they think we're doing?"

He nodded. "Aren't you?"

"Oh, no," she said, "whatever would make you think that?"

"That's what all the kids are saying. They say we won't have a park anymore."

"But you will—a better park than ever, with all the newest play equipment. It'll even have a baseball field, a barbecue area, and a recreation building. That is, if I can get those little monsters to stop destroying things long enough! Maybe you could tell all the kids what we're really doing here."

"I will, I'll tell 'em," Jason said, beaming over the newfound information.

"Great! I sure would appreciate that." Then, sensing Andrew Bellows's presence, she added, "I'll bet the man over there can help you with your bike so you can go tell the kids what's happening."

Andrew Bellows cocked an eyebrow and cleared his

throat as he stepped off the curb from where he had been listening amusedly to the exchange. "Ms. McCullough, I don't mind getting dirty, but must I grovel in it?" he said with feigned sarcasm.

She laughed. "It'll be good for your soul to help a kid for a change instead of a damsel in distress," she teased good-naturedly.

Andrew frowned. "But where's the incentive? *He* can't keep me warm on a cold night."

Jason, puzzled, looked from one to the other. "It's okay, mister, I'll just walk it home," he said resolutely.

"Oh, hell no, son, I can fix it in a minute," Bellows assured the boy as he pulled off his mud-spattered sweater and tossed it to Shawn before kneeling next to the bike.

As Shawn watched Andrew deftly maneuver the chain back to its mounting, she couldn't help but admire the rippling muscles of his back under the thin custom-made monogrammed shirt, and she fleetingly wondered if his reputedly active sex life contributed to his virility. He was ruggedly handsome with his sharply chiseled features and blond wavy hair, now encrusted with mud. The rolled-up sleeves gave evidence of time spent outdoors exposing tanned and well-developed biceps. Shawn's thoughts as she listened to his banter with the boy were a mass of confusion. Would he do all of this just to take her to bed, or was there a lot more to Andrew Bellows than his reputation would have everyone believe? Just why was he here?

"There you go, son. I think that will do it," Andrew said as he rose from his squatting position.

"Hey, thanks, mister," Jason said enthusiastically as he mounted his bike. "I'll be sure to tell 'em, ma'am, 'bout the park," he called back over his shoulder while swiftly pedaling off.

After Jason disappeared into the distance, Shawn turned to Andrew. "That was nice of you to help him. You know something? You're really a nice man."

"Who, me? What are you trying to do, ruin my image? I just know what it's like to be a kid like that, that's all."

For an instant Shawn caught a note of longing in his voice, and it occurred to her that she knew very little about this dynamic man beside her. "You do, Andy? Is your father dead?"

"Yes," he said, "but that's beside the point."

Sensing his reluctance to continue the conversation, Shawn said, "Someday I hope you'll tell me about it, but right now I'm wondering what brought you out here today."

"Oh, I just stopped by to deliver your paper," he said, "and saw Tony's note on your door. Thought I might be able to lend a hand."

Shawn smiled warmly and grasped his hand. "That you did! Thank you, my friend."

"If you really want to thank me, you can go out to dinner with me tonight."

Shawn laughed. "You never give up, do you, Andy? Well, this time I'm going to surprise you. The realtor is showing the house today, and I was considering McDonald's. Join me?"

He frowned. "I think we can do better than that!"

"Not unless you change your clothes."

"Your place or mine?"

"Andrew Bellows, you're incorrigible!"

"You rang the bell, sweetie! I'll pick you up around seven. If Rizzo's still here, we'll bring him a doggie bag."

Jason suddenly felt important, surrounded by all the members of the Renegades. For the very first time, he had their full attention.

"What'd that woman want? That one that was talkin' with you?"

"That's my friend," Jason explained. "I met her at Marriott's, Sam."

"Little brother, you wanna be careful! Now what did she want?"

"She wanted to know if I knew who flooded the park."

Sam Brown roughly grabbed his little brother by the shoulders and lifted him off the ground. "You didn't tell her, did ya?" he demanded.

Jason's eyes turned to white saucers. "Let me go, Sam! She says they're fixing it up to be a better park."

"You *did* tell her, didn't you? How could I have such a dumb brother? You're not only dumb, you're too little to be hanging around with us," the older teenage boy decided.

Jason shrank from the sea of hostile faces surrounding him and stifled the urge to cry. Suddenly he felt very small with the other boys towering over him.

Chapter Twelve

Shawn tossed the note back on the foyer table. A good offer, the realtor had written. Why wasn't she pleased? This sacrificial sale would enable her to repay the bank loan, yet a sinking feeling clutched her heart, and her feet felt leaden as she trudged up the stairs to change her muddy clothes. Passing her father's door, her gaze automatically settled on the bedroom's masculine contents, and she was drawn to the familiar surroundings.

Tears blurred her vision as she ran her fingers across the cool tile of the plaque that framed an old Irish blessing. "Why?" she uttered. "Why did you have to die?" Her thoughts pulled her to the window, and as she drank in the late October setting sun, she suddenly realized that she was repeating something that she had seen him do a thousand times. Having been a true lover of nature, he had always been attracted to the outdoor panorama and what it had to offer each changing day.

As if to close out her melancholia, Shawn abruptly left the room, yet the memory of her father stayed with her. "Damn you, Shawn, stop feeling sorry for yourself when you know that that crusty Irishman is in the palm of God's hand!" Shawn sighed dolefully realizing that she wanted to speak to someone who had known her father. Shawn knew that Elsa was coping with her sadness; it wouldn't be fair to add to her sense of loss. "Oh, Matt, how I need you now!" she whispered as she reached for the instrument that would bridge the gap between them.

His answering voice was the tonic she had been needing. "Matt, darling, how I wish you were here. I think the house is sold."

"Oh, that's good news," he returned noncommittally while carefully concealing his eyes from Patrice, who was within arm's length.

"Matt, you sound so distant. Why didn't you call me back? Did I catch you at a bad time? Do you have company?"

"Well—yes," came his strained response.

"A friend?"

"Yes, someone I work with."

"Is she blond and weighs about a hundred and ten?" Shawn joked, her voice sounding brittle in her ears.

"You have a vivid imagination," he replied uncomfortably.

His cool tone brought Shawn up short, causing her inexplicable uneasiness and budding anger. Why was he so defensive? The whole conversation became suddenly depressing, and her retort was sharply edged. "I'm sorry to have bothered you at a bad time. If you ever get a spare moment, call me." Her hand shook as she dropped the phone.

Matt stared at the dead instrument in his hand, and a deep sadness coursed through him.

"You seem upset, Matt. Was it someone from the office?" Patrice inquired.

"No, just a friend," he mumbled as he wandered to the wet bar. "Honey, can I fix you a drink?"

"No, I'm fine. Remember? I'm on medication. You go ahead."

When Matt returned to her, Patrice noticed the drink trembling in his hand. "Are you sure there's nothing wrong?"

"No, nothing. I'm just tired," he replied, unaware of the puzzled glance in his direction.

When Shawn opened the door to Andrew Bellows, he could not conceal his surprise. "I thought I gave you enough time to change!"

Shawn glanced down at her still muddy attire. "Oh, Andy, I'm sorry! I don't know where the time went."

"Never mind, you've had a bad day. It won't bother me to wait. I'll just fix a drink while you dress."

The elegantly tailored three-piece suit that he wore told Shawn that he had planned a night on the town. She forced a cheerful note. "Andy, you look very handsome. Any woman would be proud to be with you tonight, but I feel like hell, and I just want to be by myself. Do you mind terribly?" she finished gloomily.

A frown rippled his brow. "Of course I mind. I just got reservations with Greg at La Tour. Anyway, it'll do you good to get out tonight."

"Andy, I'm just not up to an elegant restaurant."

Her usual lilt was missing, and as he studied her more closely, he dropped his bantering tone. "Then we'll go wherever you want. Did you say the golden arches?"

Shawn laughed despite her depression and patted his tie. "They'd think the Prince of Wales walked in! Tell you what, I know of a nice little Italian place that everyone says has the best scallopini in these here parts."

Andrew grinned. "And red-and-white-checked table-cloths with chianti-bottle candleholders?"

"How did you guess?"

"I'm just brilliant, what can I tell you?" he teased.

Her smile faded. "Oh, but you'd look so out of place."

"That's no problem, versatility is my middle name," he said, removing his suit coat. "How's that?"

Shawn scrutinized his appearance. "Um, maybe the vest and the tie, too," she said as she helped relieve him of the garments.

The sweet smell of her hair assailed him, and he could

barely keep from pulling her into his arms. Instead, he
said, "You can undress me anytime."

Shawn gave him an elfin grin. "You're just not my type."

"Curses, foiled again! If that's all the cooperation I can
get, you might as well go get dressed."

The cozy atmosphere and the friendly faces at La Scala's
served as balm to Shawn's badly stretched nerves. While
Luigi busied himself in the kitchen, she and Andrew
sipped the robust red wine that he had ordered. As the
wine made itself felt, Shawn found herself unburdening
her thoughts about the house, the business, talking to
Andrew about everything except the heartache of Matt.
Andrew seemed delighted with the newfound shared inti-
macy and gave her a sympathetic ear. His attentiveness
showed a genuine concern for her welfare, and she began
to feel a bit selfish. Impulsively, she laid her hand over
his, noticing at once how fragile hers looked next to the
strength of his. "I'm sorry to have inflicted you with my
depressed mood earlier," she apologized slowly. "It's just
been a day and a half the way everything piled up. You've
become a good friend, Andy, and thanks again, too, for
your help at the park."

Desire filled his blue eyes, and the usually overly
confident grin was replaced by a languorous smile. "I
think you know the reason I was there," he said quietly.
Then in a lighter tone he added, "Besides, it was good for
me. I'd almost forgotten the exhilaration that comes from
physical accomplishment."

She smiled, relieved at the change in subject. "I'll bet it
has been a while since you manned a shovel."

"Quite a while," he admitted.

"But you stay in such good shape. How?"

"Exercise, swimming." He shrugged.

An interested gleam lit her eyes as she said, "You know,
I scarcely know anything about you. What exactly makes
up the great Andrew Bellows, his childhood, the early
years? Were you born with a silver spoon?"

He laughed. "Hardly. It was tin-plated all the way!"

She couldn't put her finger on it, but she was sure she

detected a hint of bitterness despite his hearty laugh.
"Tell me about your childhood; how you got to be the
biggest building contractor in the Bay Area," she gently
prodded.

"Not much to tell," he said.

Shawn's curiosity was piqued. "I can't believe that a
dynamic man like you hasn't got all sorts of yarns to
unravel. You must come from an interesting family; what
are your parents like?"

Andrew's eyebrows inched up, and his clear blue eyes
turned to ice, almost as though she'd struck him. "Haven't
seen them for years, my father's dead," he stated, obviously displeased with the subject. "If you don't mind, I'd
rather live in the present." His tone had the sound of a
firmly closing book, but in the next instant his somber
gaze came alive again in the candlelight, and he raised the
wine carafe to refill her glass. She wondered if she had
imagined the glacial change of the moment before.

"You needn't worry about finding a place to live," he
said out of the blue as he deftly maneuvered to change
the subject. "I have a condo in every city on the peninsula."

Had she imagined the curtness in his voice a moment
earlier, or was there something within herself that made
the men in her life evasive? "Good for you," she said.
"What is that supposed to mean?"

"Just what I said. Tell me where you want to live and
you shall have it," he said magnanimously.

"But Andy, I can't afford your kind of living! From what
I've heard, your sort of condo is pretty exclusive. By the
time I pay off that business loan, I'll have to settle for
something rather modest."

"You won't let me help you? I don't understand a woman
like you."

Her sapphire eyes challenged his equally blue ones over
the flame of the candle. "That's because you evidently
never before met a down-to-earth female!" She took mali-
cious pleasure in getting in a dig at his society butterflies.

"You're certainly right. Little 'Miss-Do-It-the-Hard-

Way!' Why can't you just relax and be like the rest of your sex?" He was being unfair, he knew, but she did goad him.

A quick surge of anger engulfed Shawn. "The sort you're used to?" she retorted. "Andrew, I didn't come to dinner with you to be insulted. I thought you were my friend."

"I *am,* Ms. McCullough, but this is all your fault. If you weren't so damned beautiful sitting there, it would be a hell of a lot easier to not try to pierce your armor. I'm sorry, I shall behave myself. Now," he said with an exaggerated sigh, "perhaps I can help you find something that you *can* afford."

Tickled by his expression and the left-handed compliment, she told him brightly, "That's a possibility. But first I'll have to figure out just what I can afford. There seem to be so many unexpected expenses with the business that I don't know at present how I'll handle things. All that water damage will probably drain the profit from the park job, and with winter coming on . . ." She took a deep breath and slowly released it as if letting off steam from a boiler. Then, thinking aloud, she said, "I really need some backup capital to cover the winter months. I'm afraid I'll be as bad as Dad was about laying off some of the men."

Andrew studied her tightly drawn features. "It's all part of the construction trade. The men expect it when it's raining. After all, if you go broke, they won't have a job."

"I'm not going broke," she snapped.

"It was merely a hypothesis," he returned. "No offense. Try this soup. It's mighty fine."

"Am I really that touchy tonight?" she asked.

Andrew shrugged. "You've had a hard day, and admittedly, I can be pretty pushy. Truce?" With a winning grin, he took her hand and lightly ran his thumb along her palm.

"You've got a deal," she enthused, certain he could see through her bravado to the weakness caused by his touch. She picked up her spoon and ladled the thick minestrone into her mouth. Then she impulsively reached for a hot pepper from the antipasto that they had ignored in favor

of the wine and took a bite. "Oh, my goodness," she gasped.
Fanning her open mouth wildly with her hand, she quickly swallowed the fiery morsel and followed it with a wine
chaser.

Andrew grinned. "Hot little devils, aren't they?"

"Whew!" Shawn said. "I'm ready for ice cream!"

"Not yet. You save the spumoni for later," Mama Luigi
interrupted as she flourished two heaping plates of pasta
and two equally large salads in front of them. "Hot
peppers, eh? Try this, to put a little flesh on you. Such a
pretty girl," she said in a motherly fashion as she touched
Shawn's hair, "but too skinny. We'll take care of that! Lots
of Luigi's pasta and scallopini." She gave Andrew a big
smile. "You bring her often. We'll put some color in her
cheeks and make her bloom like a rose." She playfully
nudged Andrew's shoulder as she directed, "Listen to
Mama Luigi, you'll have more to love."

Andrew laughed. "I don't know, Mama, she may be
pint-sized, but she's got more fire than those peppers!
Don't know if I could handle any more woman."

Color rose to Shawn's cheeks almost as though Mama
had willed it, and she dutifully twirled her fork in the
steaming, aromatic spaghetti. "I could get used to this in a
hurry," she remarked after savoring the tasty mouthful.

"See, what'd I tell you?" the old Italian matron said with
a friendly smile. "Luigi good cook!" She picked up Andrew's empty soup bowl and made a face at Shawn's full
one. "It's probably cold. I'll fill it with some hot minestrone."

"No, no, Mama, it's fine. I've had plenty," Shawn assured. "I want to enjoy my scallopini, too."

By the time Andrew paid the check, Shawn felt like a
stuffed duck waddling out the door. "Good night, Mama,"
she said. "You're right, Luigi is a great cook."

"That's a good reason to come back," the buxom woman
with the warm smile replied.

"You can bet on it," Andrew chimed in as he scooped up
the change, leaving a ten-dollar bill on the tray.

At Shawn's front door, Andrew took the key from her

hand, released the lock, and swung the door aside. Shawn
was lost in thought. It had been a most enjoyable evening,
and unlike Matt, Andy seemed to have been interested in
everything that concerned her. The same resentment that
she had harbored when she had spoken with Matt earlier
in the day returned, and she shivered involuntarily. What
was Matt doing? Was it conceivable that there was another woman? Could that possibly be the reason for
his apparently cool disinterest? Yet, in the deep recesses
of her mind, she tried desperately to shut out that possibility. But her common sense demanded, does he really
care?

She was lost in a confused maze when Andrew kissed
her tenderly on the cheek, bringing her out of her reverie
with a jolt. "Good night, Tiger, I'll call you," he said softly.

Suddenly she didn't want to be alone with her thoughts.
She needed to draw on the strength of his presence. The
words were out of her mouth before she realized what she
was saying. "No, Andy, don't go. Please stay for a brandy,"
she said half-pleadingly. "I'm much too full to go to bed,
and I'd like company. Do you mind?"

"Not in the least. Though, if I get comfortable, you may
have a houseguest for the night," he said, pleased at the
invitation.

Shawn sighed. "I don't know when I've ever been so full!
We should have brought Tony a doggie bag. He would have
thought he was in Italian heaven, and we'd both feel
pounds lighter right now."

"I don't think Mama Luigi would have allowed it. The
old gal took quite a shine to you. Cute, the way she wanted
to fatten you up."

"Immobilize me, you mean. Andy, you don't mind if I get
into something more comfortable, do you?"

He drew his head back to look at her, a teasing light
entering his eyes. "I'd love it," he said, the eager glint in
his blue eyes adding more meaning to his words.

"Andrew, dear, are you lusting for my body again? I'm
not talking about that sort of thing," she was quick to
explain. "I'm afraid you have a few misconceptions." She

patted her stomach. "My pasta seems to be expanding. Brandy's in the bar. Make mine light please," she requested as she turned on her heel and ascended the stairs with a smile. This man made her feel very desirable, and the feeling was stimulating—not that she was interested especially after the letdown that Matt had given her. The way things were going, it seemed to Shawn that Matt's only interest in her might have been purely physical. That could be a beautiful part of their relationship, but it wasn't enough. How could she have misjudged him so? "Is that all that men have in their heads? She pulled a soft green velvet one-piece lounger from her closet and slipped out of her clothes. The velvet caressed her skin, and she quickly peeked in the mirror to see if the absence of a bra was too obvious. "Who cares?" she murmured rather defiantly. "At least I can breathe now."

When he saw her, Andrew's face grew pale beneath his burnished tan, his tightened jaw revealing the tumult of emotions that he suddenly experienced. Her beauty was astounding, the long dark curls cascading over the emerald velvet-clad shoulders, the sapphire blue of her eyes accentuating the radiant features as she descended the last step. He downed his brandy in one quick gulp and expelled a long, ragged sigh. In three steps, he was across the room. Pulling her close, a shudder rippled through his body, and his arms tightened possessively around her. She hadn't had a chance to stop him before his searching mouth sought hers to deeply drink from those lips that had teased him too long. She felt his hard lips, tasting the brandy on them, then his tongue probed between her teeth. Even so, when he released her, there was anguish in the one word that she whispered.

"Andy."

She knew if she allowed him to continue, she would succumb to the exquisite thrill he kindled in her as no other man had. He had the power to evaporate her defenses, and she believed one unguarded moment could alter everything. Her voice clearly expressed both her desire and pain. His face twisted in torment, and his eyes reflected the torture within as he reluctantly loosened his grip on her. Even though every part of him was hungering for her love, for the marvelous feel of her, this was not the way to win her. For all his talk, she was nothing like the other game-playing women in his life, out for what they could get—namely, his money, if they couldn't capture his heart or his name.

For the first time in Andrew Bellows's life, here was a woman who was more important to him than the need to satisfy his sexual ego. Even if he kicked himself in the morning for the lost opportunity, sex between them could only happen with mutual love and desire—nothing else could stand between them.

His hands dropped listlessly to his sides. "I'd better go," he said quietly as he turned, picking up his coat, tie, and vest from the chair where he'd carelessly draped them earlier, and he departed without another word, leaving Shawn shaken and speechless.

Chapter Thirteen

Andrew Bellows walked out into the night with a paradoxical empty sensation in the pit of his full stomach. Suddenly he felt like the orphaned little boy who had so hungered for love but who had had to build a wall of toughness for survival. Automatically, he guided the Lamborghini to its reserved parking space beneath the concrete shroud of his penthouse. Impatiently stabbing the elevator button as if there were something pressing to do at this late hour, his mind was a jumble. Memories poured past him as he unlocked the door and dropped his tie and vest on the rich damask chair. He gazed about the apartment detachedly.

He had attained everything he had once thought he wanted—knowledge, wealth, a respectable name—and what good was it all? Who would have thought that he could get so bewitched by this beautiful woman. But now, in the emptiness of his luxurious surroundings, his disquieting thoughts forced him to reevaluate his life. What had happened to the little boy who, long ago, had so desperately wanted to attain what Andrew had now, and who had decided then, that love wasn't important if you had enough money? Yet, now as his eyes surveyed the thick carpets, the expensive furniture, and creature comforts that would have meant so much to a little boy without a dime in his pocket, Andrew felt strangely cold and dismal, and somehow, poor again.

He strode to the wet bar, poured three fingers of Chivas Regal, and downed it in one gulp, furiously throwing the expensive crystal into the fireplace with a resounding crash. His money didn't mean a damn thing to Shawn; it hadn't made a bit of difference, and he didn't know whether that angered or pleased him. She only wanted him to be her friend but no more than that, and the thought was debilitating.

Andrew paced the living room, pausing briefly at the floor-to-ceiling window to gaze at the city below. A symphony of lights moving in all directions sprinkled the night with glistening dew, striking a dissonant chord in his finely attuned mind. "Andrew, you damn fool," he berated himself as he abruptly returned to the bar and poured another drink, this time sipping it as he mulled over his thoughts.

The next morning Andrew Bellows pulled into San Jose Airport. As he strode to the general aviation parking area, he was again awestruck by the needle-nosed, tiger-shark elegance of the Lear jet, its sleekness almost making it appear to be in motion, if not for the airstair being extended and breaking the smooth lines. Triple-niner Lima's brilliant white Imcron paint with its bold blue striping gleamed in the morning sun. Like everything seemed to do these days, even the beauty of the plane somehow reminded him of Shawn's sparkling blue eyes and enticing body.

"Good morning, again," Steve Grodecki said as he poked his curly-haired head out the plane's door. "She's all preflighted and ready to fire up anytime you are, though I must say, it wasn't easy arranging it for you. Jim Kraff planned to fly this baby to the east coast Monday for a board meeting in New York and wouldn't have given it up for anyone else."

Andrew smiled. Jim Kraff was one of his right-hand men in international holdings and second only to Bellows himself in the hierarchy of Bellows Enterprises. The Lear was often used by members of the board as a convenient airborne boardroom. Bellows had made a great number of

decisions and put together million-dollar deals over a
Scotch on the rocks in the jet's luxurious cabin. To him,
this was a very private place where his mind was at its
sharpest, uninterrupted by the continual demands of the
office. He needed time to unravel his thoughts, and more
than that, he wanted solitude from the frustration Shawn
had inadvertently caused. And to top it all off, it was
pretty plain that it was a frustration he couldn't shed as
long as he was close to her. Who knows? In a couple of
weeks, he might gain a new perspective. He hadn't even
informèd his secretary, Jill, as to his whereabouts, only
that he would call in daily.

"So she's all ready to go? I knew you'd work it out, Steve.
Thanks," he said to the man who had taught him to fly a
number of years back, first in Vietnam flying helicopters
and later, general aviation aircraft. The short, wiry guy
could fly anything.

Grodecki grinned. "I have to admit, a couple of weeks in
San Juan sounded too damn good not to shuffle things a
bit!"

Andrew laughed as he boarded the jet, pulled up the
airstair, and went through the three-phase lock, then
entering the cockpit, he did a little sidestep around the
console before taking his seat as co-pilot.

Steve fired up the engines, doing the usual instrument
check while Bellows's keen eyes followed him through as a
double check, both men well aware of the routine's importance.

"Looking good," Bellows said, almost as though he were
now the instructor.

Steve nodded, pressed the mike, and called ground
control for taxi instructions.

Once up to the runway, the same feeling of elation that
always overcame Andrew on takeoff surfaced, and as the
tower cleared them, he smiled at his cohort.

Neither spoke as the jet rolled onto the runway, and the
experienced pilot fed in the power. Bellows reached over to
cup his palm over Grodecki's knuckles in a commonly
practiced reinforcement for takeoff. Even a strong man's

grip could inadvertently be jerked free during the maximum acceleration needed to become airborne.

"Let's get this thing moving," he said, and the steady whine of the engines rose in a crescendo. Both men felt nailed to the seat by the tremendous power as the Lear attained flying speed and climbed out at four thousand feet per minute. Andrew was happy. There was nothing in this life, not his money nor anything else, that gave him the feeling of power like that of takeoff and a breathtaking climb in the jet.

As Grodecki throttled back and leveled out, Andrew's mind returned to Shawn. God, he'd like to get her up here with him. There wasn't anything more beautiful on a clear day except, perhaps, Shawn herself. His frustration from his unrequited love refused him peace, even in the sky that he loved, and the more he thought about her, the more he silently brooded.

It wasn't something that he wanted to discuss with Steve, much less anyone else. The bachelor image that he had purposely created had not lent itself to sympathy, nor did he now want advice. The only one whose advice he accepted was Goldberg's, and damn, it was Goldberg who got him off on the wrong foot with Shawn to begin with. Damn fool lawyer!

Abruptly, Andrew rose from his seat in the cockpit. "She's all yours, Steve. I'm gonna stretch out in the lounge for a bit," he announced.

Steve looked over and grinned. "What's the matter, you get up too early or go to bed too late?"

"Both," Bellows grumbled. "If you need a break, call me."

He dodged the console on his way out of the cockpit and stopped at the wet bar to his left. For an instant he hesitated, then pouring a glass of Chivas, he stirred the ice with his finger as he headed for one of the rich leather seats next to a window. Sinking into the soft padding, he tried not to think of the reason for his quick departure. But it seemed that all his thoughts somehow reverted to

Shawn, who without trying, had turned his world upside down. He stared at the drink in his hand.

"Oh, hell!" he snorted, and was out of his reclining position and over to the bar, slamming the drink on the thick mahogany. Then he burst into the cockpit to take command.

Steve shot Andy a perplexed look. "Something bothering you?" he asked.

"Hell, no! I always cancel twelve business appointments and refuse to show up at board meetings because of a damn fool woman! I'd rather not discuss it," he growled.

Steve gave him a sidelong glance that asked if he was capable, in his present mood, of flying the airplane. "I thought you said this was a pleasure trip," he remarked. "It sure as hell isn't starting off to be!"

"Don't worry. I can handle the controls. Just ignore my foul disposition for the time being. I'll work it out."

"I'll count on it," his longtime friend returned.

That same Sunday morning, Shawn awoke with her head feeling as though it were held in a vice that was slowly being tightened. Sleep hadn't come easily after Andrew's abrupt exit. The intensity of his kiss had taken her completely by surprise, sending little shivers of enjoyment through her veins like a tonic that she so badly needed for her blue mood, yet leaving her feeling empty and confused. The nagging question of why he had turned and left without a word kept bouncing around in her brain. His kiss, almost rough, as if he were fighting an inner battle that she somehow unknowingly was a part of, had left her shaken and puzzled. Men, Shawn thought, are such complicated creatures. Who needs them? Even so, she could not control the longing that crushed her insides, and she had to get out of bed and stop thinking of Andy, stop wondering where her feelings for him were taking her.

Her eyes widened in surprise as the phone rang and she flung back the comforter. "Hello?"

"Honey, it's Matt."

"Yes, I recognize your voice," she coolly returned. "I guess you found that spare minute," she said, her tone even.

"Shawn, I had to call you! I'm sorry if I sounded edgy last night," he said plaintively. "I really have been under a lot of pressure. Please try to understand and forgive me, Shawn."

"Well, I'm getting damn tired of your evasive act, Matt," she said crossly. "Your complete lack of communication makes me feel insignificant and unimportant to you. Be honest with me, Matt. Is there another woman in the picture?"

"No . . ." He paused slightly. "I simply haven't been myself lately. Please trust me. There's something I need to straighten out."

"I'm sure I wouldn't know about that unless you tell me."

"I'll explain it all when I see you."

"What's stopping you from sharing it with me right now?"

"It's too involved, honey, but we'll make up for it. It won't be long before I can spend some real time with you."

"You promise?"

He laughed. "You bet! There's nothing I'd rather do!"

Shawn forced the doubts into her mind's inner recesses as she gently replaced the phone and sprang out of bed, a surge of exhilarating energy replacing the lethargy of only a few moments earlier. The paper, she thought; I must look for an apartment. She hurried to the front door, and without giving her attire a thought, padded down the steps in her sheer nightgown. As she reached for the folded paper, a smile crinkled the corners of her eyes at the remembrance of Andrew saying, "paperboy," and for a fleeting second, she half-expected him to appear and hand the daily to her. She dismissed a twinge of disappointment. This would be a good day, so quickly changed by Matt's call, not like the confusion of yesterday. Impulsive-

ly, she plucked a daisy from the colorful border along the
sidewalk and pulled a petal from the flower. "He loves
me," she said with gaiety. But she was afraid to admit to
herself yet that it was Andrew who loved her deeply,
passionately, and patiently.

It was seven-thirty on a Friday morning more than a
week later when Tony Rizzo checked the progress of the
work at Sun Haven Park. The park was peaceful, and the
morning sun felt warm on his back as he walked the
park's perimeter. Tony whistled in pace with his steps as
he skillfully hopped the caved-in trenches and made his
way across to the far end. The disaster was as bad as he
remembered, and this would be a job for a very savvy
operating engineer to handle. "Oh, hell," he quickly
decided. "I can straighten this out a lot faster myself. We
gotta get rolling! The rains can't hold off much longer." He
strode back to the truck and radioed Nelson, one of the
foremen.

"Move the Fergie right away," he commanded.

The next time he glanced at his watch, it was nearing
noon, and Tony was pleased by what he had accomplished.
It was time that he took a well-deserved lunch break.
Shutting down the piece of equipment, he jumped to the
ground. At the sight of the truck, the Italian's eyes
suddenly flashed fire, and he grabbed the door handle,
angrily jerked it open, then flipped the key and snatched
the mike. "Nelson!" he shouted. "I need a ride to the
office."

"Something wrong?"

"Hell, no, I just like the sound of your voice! Now
goddamn it, get somebody up here!" Tony slammed the
mike in place.

Neatly dressed in tailored navy slacks and a white silk
blouse, Shawn took the stack of opened mail from Audrey's desk corner. Heading down the hall to her office, she
noticed an envelope marked Bellows Enterprises. Its con-

tents, upon examination, included a sizable check. Shawn did a double take, dropped into her swivel chair, and pulled out a set of Arcadia Lane specifications from the shelf. She quickly scanned the payment section and realized that Andrew had mailed the check prematurely. She had not heard one word from him in almost two weeks, and it upset her to think that perhaps she had lost a friend who had really been a lifesaver. Yet there was little she could do about it. Andy knew how she felt about him, and if he wanted to continue the friendship, it would have to be on her terms. Only he could bridge the gap that he had created—but not with money, even though McCullough Landscaping could definitely use any amount due them.

Was this his way of saying he was sorry? She had surprised herself with the realization that she missed seeing him, talking and teasing with him on the phone. There was a void in her life, and her mind couldn't will her eyes not to scan the yard for her "newsboy" each time she picked up the morning paper, and she couldn't help but smile to herself when she enjoyed, so often during the day, the seascape decorating her office wall. Even the thought of his incorrigible ego danced through her head, yet that might be the reason that he was staying away. Andrew was not used to being denied anything, and though he had kissed her, and the thought of that penetrating kiss still caused her face to flush, they hadn't gone to bed. That had to annoy such an assertive man.

Was the check an apology or was she reading more into the payment than was warranted? He knew that she needed money. Was he reminding her of that fact? No, it was too petty. Shawn sighed. The past week had been a lonely one without any masculine company save Tony's, and she realized how much she missed the teasing and provocative conversations that she and her father had always enjoyed. Andrew would have liked her father, she decided; the two of them had a great deal in common, a heart of gold under the rugged exterior.

A smile lit up her face, and she was still daydreaming

when Tony burst into her office, his face aflame, eyes shooting sparks.

"Shawn!" he yelled. "Goddam it, we have to do something!"

"Hey, slow down, Tony! Do something about what?"

"Those little bastards at Sun Haven Park. You know—who the hell are they? The Renegades?" He was shaking with anger, his dark eyes blazing intensely.

Shawn shrugged. "You haven't told me a thing. I don't know what you're so excited about, for gosh sake! Calm down and make some sense, Tony. It can't be that bad!" she said soothingly.

He collapsed in the office chair. "They spray-painted my truck, replaced McCullough Landscaping with some choice words that I needn't repeat, and slashed all four tires."

"What?" She jumped from her chair, knocking it over. "That's an insult! I'll kill 'em! Nobody blackens this Irishman's name without a fight! Much less with a can of spray paint!"

Tony couldn't resist. "I thought it couldn't be that bad."

"You're right! I can't kill 'em, but I can sure as hell think of something to make 'em miserable!"

"Like what?"

Shawn frowned. "I don't know, but it has to be painful! Just how did they manage to do all that with you right there, Tony?"

"I was running the tractor. You can't hear a thing when that's running. I'll tell you one thing, it's gotta stop. I don't have time or patience to put up with any more of this shit!"

"What about money? Tires and paint aren't cheap!"

"Think I saved the paint job with some thinner I had in the truck that was left from Norton School's backstop." Tony gave her a hard stare. "We'd better forget about your young friend, Jason, and get the cops on this! I haven't time to stand guard," he fumed.

"Neither do I," she said, angry disappointment propelling her actions. She snatched up her purse. "I'm going to see the police," she said over her shoulder as her high heels beat in staccato down the hall and out to her car.

Shawn backed up the Spitfire, and in a puff of dust and exhaust, took off, splattering gravel in all directions. As she drove, her temper began to cool, and while she waited for a red light, she thought of Jason. He hadn't gotten through to the Renegades, but she was sure Jason had tried. As she slowed for the police station coming up on her right, the boy's words came back to her: "I don't fink." Suddenly Shawn felt like a rat. Her foot gradually eased off the gas as she racked her brain.

She jammed her foot on the accelerator, swiftly made a U-turn and headed for the printer's.

"Harvey," she said, taking a form from a box on the counter and quickly scrawling a message on it, "do you think you can make up two signs, say about four by four, in block letters?"

"Don't see why not. When do you need them?"

"ASAP. I'll be back for them around three-thirty this afternoon."

Harvey glanced at the scrawled words and raised his eyebrows. "You're almost as impulsive as your father was," he said.

Shawn smiled. "Would you believe more?"

At about four P.M. that afternoon, Shawn planted her challenge to the Renegades, a sign at each end of the park. Harvey had done a good job with the bold black print on a white background. There's no way they can miss these, she thought as she stepped back to reread her message and smiled smugly. Well, she would play their game. Going to the cops wouldn't actually have solved the situation and probably would have aggravated it. She'd been in and around the landscaping business long enough to know that vandalism was one of the most difficult things to prove. Generally, the contractor either had to absorb the cost or turn it over to the insurance company. But she was going to attempt to get through to the vandals, turn their thinking around. She certainly was stubborn enough to give it a try. Shawn picked up the small sledgehammer and marched briskly to her car.

As she flipped the key, she debated about returning to the office. She'd had about enough for the day, she decided, but if she went home, it would mean another lonely evening. While the motor idled, she took out the letter from Matt, which had arrived that morning and reread it. He'd postponed returning to Los Altos for at least another week, and suddenly her impulsiveness got the better of Shawn for the second time that day. She picked up the mike and called Audrey. "See if you can book me on the seven-thirty flight or any flight out tonight for L.A. Right now, I'm going home. Call you when I get there."

"Will do," Audrey replied. "I'll try."

"Thanks," Shawn said, her mind and heart already in L.A., as she impishly planned her surprise entrance into Matt's apartment.

When Matt entered the apartment early Friday evening, he did a double take. Patrice's lovely hair was piled high on her head, soft blond tendrils framing her delicate face. She, at last, looked the picture of health. As a matter of fact, she looked damned beautiful, with a rosy glow to her cheeks. The fuchsia dress she wore accentuated her well-being. Matt noticed thankfully that her shapely legs showed no impairment from the accident. They were as sexy and gorgeous as ever, and during the past week she had not displayed even the slightest limp. His guess that she would be well enough to be on her own, soon, appeared accurate.

"God, you look great!" he blurted. "How do you feel?"

"Wonderful," she replied. "Thanks to your pampering. Matt, I saw the doctor today, and he's declared me well. That's cause to celebrate, don't you think?" She reached up and kissed him, brushing her fingers across his forehead. "Now, you go shower and I'll fix you a cool drink. I've prepared the same special dinner that I did the night of the accident, only this time we're going to be able to enjoy it," she said with gaiety and a slightly suggestive gleam in her eyes.

A stab of uneasiness nagged him despite his delight with her professed health. "Honey," he said, "you shouldn't have gone to all that fuss. It's great enough, the news from the doctor."

"Nonsense, I wanted to. Anyway, I feel wonderful, so why not?"

"Okay. Why not, indeed?" he said. "I'll only be a minute."

Matt hummed a little tune as he showered, "Shawnie, how I love you, how I love you, my dear old Shawnie," then chuckled to himself about the melody that he was usurping to express his feelings. There was no correlation whatsoever except that now he would be free to pursue his love for Shawn. It was cause for celebration all right, and time that he spelled it all out to Patrice. She was strong enough now. He snatched a towel and wrapped it around his slim waist as he stepped out of the shower and vigorously dried himself from head to toe. He felt marvelous, as though he had been given a new lease on life, and in a way, Patrice's doctor had done just that.

"You needn't dress," she said from the doorway. "Why not just put on your favorite robe and slippers, and I'll rub your back before dinner."

She was gone before he could answer. She'd never offered that before, and it pleasantly surprised him. The idea sounded terrific, considering how tense he had been in the courtroom today. He pulled on a pair of pants, yanked a burgundy velour lounging robe out of his closet, and padded to the kitchen barefoot. The aroma wafting from the oven set his mouth watering, and as he entered, Patrice handed him a frosty, tall gin and tonic.

"I've built a fire," she said as she led the way to the living room where she curled up on the couch. "Let's have our drink first so you can unwind. Here, come sit by me," she urged, patting the soft velvet pile.

"To your health," he said, lightly clicking her glass as he

eased down beside her. "Does this mean that you'll be coming back to the office?"

"Yes, very soon," she said excitedly. She smiled and took a sip from the tall glass, then laid her head back against the soft couch. "Oh, Matt, it's been so wonderful staying with you!"

He didn't know how to answer that, so, instead, he said, "Um. This occasion calls for a bottle of the finest wine. I think I have just the one!" He made his way to the bar and selected a bottle of light French Chablis from the refrigerator, pretending to concentrate upon opening it while trying to formulate the words he had to say. Could he make it clear to Patrice that he would always love her as a close friend? Someone special. It was just that what he felt for Shawn was so much greater, so much deeper and soul-satisfying, an indescribable love.

Absorbed in the gravity of his thoughts, Matt abstractedly poured the wine, unaware that Patrice had momentarily left the room until her soft voice interrupted his reverie. "Matt, I'm ready for that wine."

As he turned to face her, she floated across the room in a blue gossamer gown that left absolutely nothing to the imagination. He was mesmerized by her loveliness, her blond beauty enhanced by the flowing blue of her shimmering gown. It was as if he'd never before been aware of her body; every curve was a sensual delight. Was he a fool to let her go? His frustration was suddenly overwhelming. Was it possible to love two women, each very dearly and each very differently?

"Dinner won't be ready for at least half an hour. Just enough time for that back rub I promised," she invited.

Overwhelmed by the sight of her, all thoughts of Shawn were strangely forgotten. Suddenly, what Matt wanted most of all was to possess the loveliness before him, though he couldn't understand the all-powerful force that had overcome him. His hand trembled as he caressed her cheek. "God, you're beautiful," he breathed. "But, Patrice, I really need to talk to you."

"Matt, darling, you're shaking! Now, you just relax. You can talk to me while I rub your back," she said enticingly as she untied his robe and slowly pushed him down to the carpet.

The long, harrowing day in court had taken its toll, and Matt didn't need much encouragement to let his body give in to her urging. Prone on the soft rug, he felt her fingers deliciously exploring his neck, his shoulders, and his back, sending a multitude of very lovely sensations up and down his spine, relaxing him thoroughly and seductively.

"The poor darling is probably sound asleep," Shawn mused, glancing at her watch. Then, reaching Matt's door, she hesitated but a moment. "Shawn McCullough will make a new man out of you, love," she said with a soft chuckle and surprisingly found the door unlocked, swinging wide open from her slight push.

Disbelief hit Shawn like a hard fist to her stomach at seeing the two near nude figures on the floor, lost in a private world of their own. Numbed with shock, Shawn could only hear the echo of her own shrill voice crying out, "My God, Matt, this explains why you couldn't leave Los Angeles." To Shawn, the words she sputtered seemed to come from another woman within. She blindly spun toward the door, seeking refuge in the impersonal hallway, anyplace to get away.

Matt jumped to his feet, his elbow accidentally jabbing Patrice's cheek as he scrambled toward the open door. "Shawn, please wait, honey, come back! I can explain this!" he shouted.

Propelled by a devastating hurt, totally unlike anything she'd ever experienced before, Shawn was oblivious to his frantic pleas. She flew down the stairs and disappeared.

Matt reluctantly shut the door. Shawn was gone, probably for good, and he had only himself to blame. The stricken look on her face would forever be etched in his mind, and he whispered, "Oh, Shawn, honey, come back!"

Patrice rose from the carpet, slowly recovering from the slap in the face that his words had given her, and the jolt his elbow had administered. She felt a horrible need to retch, and she ran from the room.

Upon her return, long minutes afterward, Matt was still standing motionless, his hand clinging to the doorknob. He looked at her blankly. "I'm sorry, Patrice, I've wanted to tell you for such a long time. But—"

A film of tears blurred her vision, and Patrice's voice was barely audible. "Matt, you've already said it all. I think now you need time alone. God knows I do. Do me one last favor and call a cab for me. I'll be out of your way as soon as I can pack." With that, she turned on her heel, leaving Matt in a state of stunned disbelief. Both women he cared for were, with one stroke of Fate's sword, excised from his life, and all he sensed beneath the numbness was finality. If only he'd heard the door bell, that plaintive warning from the outside that one's private moments are very transitory.

Chapter Fourteen

Without a thought of the hour, Shawn pounded on Elsa's door. When the door finally opened, a bleary-eyed Elsa said, "Well, Shawn! What are you doing here so late, honey?" Then noticing Shawn's desolate expression, she quickly came to life. "Shawn, what is it? What's wrong?"

All at once Shawn's numbness gave way to the pain she had held in check since her first horrifying glimpse of Matt and the unknown blond. "Oh, Elsa, everything's wrong!" Shawn cried as she fell sobbing into the older woman's outstretched arms.

Hugging her close, her friend murmured soothingly, "I'll put on a pot of coffee and we'll talk about it."

"Oh, Elsa, it's so late! Do you mind? I really do need you."

"Of course, I don't mind, honey, that's what friends are for. Now you go wash your face and slip into one of my nightgowns. You know where they are."

Shawn nodded tearfully and headed for the bathroom.

When she reappeared in a long flannel granny gown that reflected her mood, Elsa smiled. "Now you look more comfortable and cozy."

Shawn sighed. "I also look pretty awful, but what the hell, that's how I feel!"

Elsa picked up the coffee service. "You'd have to work harder than that to look awful," she said. "Let's go sit in the living room."

Shawn followed her lead and slumped disconsolately on the couch.

After pouring the rich brew, Elsa, with an expectant look, handed Shawn a steaming cup.

"I was feeling low and thought a trip and seeing Matt would cheer me up," Shawn blurted, "and all the time he was seeing another woman."

"How do you know?"

"I wanted to surprise him, so I went to L.A. It was a surprise all right, but only to me! The two of them were on the floor."

Elsa gave her a sympathetic look but kept silent.

"I guess for Matt I interrupted at a most inopportune moment. Oh, Elsa, she's so lovely!" she wailed.

"And all of a sudden you've turned ugly?" Elsa asked with a smile.

Shawn forced a faint grin. "You're quite prejudiced, you know."

"And why shouldn't I be? I love you."

"Oh, Elsa." She took her friend's hands and kissed them lightly. "I don't know what I would do without your friendship. You're a godsend. No wonder McCullough loved you as he did."

Elsa's brown eyes grew wistful at the mention of Jack's name, and for an instant, both women's eyes filled. Finally Shawn broke the nostalgic silence, and for the next hour, she poured out her heart while her friend listened attentively without once interrupting.

In Shawn's eyes, Matt had cruelly betrayed her trust and humiliated her. Even as a child, she had worshiped Matt, and the realization that he hadn't been honest with her, all the while professing his deep feelings for her, was devastating. It was her first experience of feeling degraded, and it was crushing.

When all her anger and hurt was spent, Shawn wiped

helplessly at the tears that continued to trickle, and stared woodenly at her friend.

"You'll see, honey, things have a way of working out for the best, whichever way they turn out. Did you talk to Matt at all?"

"No, and I don't intend to!" Shawn said vehemently. "If only he'd been honest."

"Perhaps you should give him a chance to explain."

"There's no explanation needed, Elsa. He's made a hundred excuses not to come up here. I think his message is pretty clear. That rotten, no-good—skirt chaser!"

"I don't know, honey. That young man had love in his eyes when he looked at you."

For a moment, Shawn was silent. Then in a small voice she asked, "Do you believe that a man can possibly love two women?"

Elsa smiled ever so faintly. "Yes," she said, and Shawn knew she was thinking of McCullough's love for her mother. He had never gotten over it even though he loved Elsa, too.

"I'm sorry," Shawn said. "I've really upset you, barging in here, waking you up and expecting you to have all the answers."

"Nonsense," Elsa insisted. "Nobody has all the answers. It's just good to have a confidant. Now, let's have a small brandy and get some rest."

"Elsa, is there something wrong with me?" Shawn asked ruefully. "Why do men treat me the way they do? Am I, somehow, unconsciously inviting abuse?"

"What do you mean?"

Shawn told her about Andrew Bellows's strange reaction on their last date. "I haven't heard from him since. Am I too honest and too open for my own good? I lost a good friend because of it, and now I've lost Matt, too! Elsa, you're my very best friend, *tell* me."

The older woman smiled. "Honey, that's what's so beautiful about you, and I love you just the way you are. I wouldn't change a hair on your head," she said. "Come on, let's have that brandy. I have absolutely no doubt that you'll find the answers."

Saturday morning, the Renegades stood snickering at Shawn's challenge. "Listen to this, will ya?" Spike, their leader, sneered as he read the sign aloud to his companions. "To the Renegades who are not brave enough to face a woman with their complaints but who prefer to be underhanded. Meet me at seven P.M. Monday night at the park, and let's get our feelings out in the open. I'm willing to settle this myself without the authorities, if you have the backbone to show up and talk. I intend to be alone. Shawn McCullough, McCullough Landscaping."

They all laughed uproariously. "Who does she think she's kidding?" Sammie derided as he picked up a clod of dirt and accurately targeted the sign, the other boys quickly following suit.

"Oh, hell," Spike said. "This is wasting time. Come on you guys, help me. We'll show her that she can't con us!" He seized the sign and started to wrest it from the ground. Laughing and cursing, they all joined in.

"Hey, you guys, what are you doing?" Jason asked as he rode up on his bicycle.

"Jason!" Sammie yelled. "What the hell are you doin' here? I told you before to butt out of our affairs!"

"But, Sam, what's this about a meeting?" Jason pleaded in a small voice. He walked over to the sign and peered down at the crumpled cardboard. "There's nothin' wrong with meeting her. She was really nice to me. At least you could give her a chance to explain. Are you guys afraid of her?"

"Afraid of her! No more than I'm afraid of you!" Spike interrupted contemptuously as he grabbed Jason's arm and flung him on top of the sign, pinning the small boy's neck with his boot.

Jason's eyes bulged with fright as he gasped for air.

"Now, I'll tell you exactly what we're gonna do to your friend. I have the perfect plan," Spike bragged, glaring down at the helpless Jason. "We'll meet her all right, but not the way she wants. While some of us keep her busy, the rest of us will soak her car with gas and have a nice little bonfire. We'll see how brave she is!"

"Hey, Spike," Sammie said, shoving Spike away from Jason. "That's enough. I'll take care of my brother!"

As the two bigger boys tumbled to the ground, exchanging blows, Jason scrambled to his feet and sobbingly stumbled across the ditches, looking back at intervals to gauge the progress of two of the gang in pursuit. His heart pounding and blinded by tears of fright, he was totally oblivious of the delivery truck rounding the corner.

The two boys chasing him stopped abruptly and stared in horror as the small boy, unable to stop, crashed headlong into the truck. There was a sickening thud, and Jason ricocheted grotesquely against the curb.

Monday morning, Shawn marched into the office after a miserable Sunday spent ignoring the incessant ring of the telephone. It had to have been Matt, and every ring had stabbed at her heart, but her pride had refused to let her bend. He had made his choice, and she was determined to leave it at that.

"Audrey," she said, "I'm not accepting any calls from Matt Monroe under any circumstances!"

"Oh? Okay," the secretary answered. "Guess I don't need to ask about your weekend," she added under her breath as she watched Shawn's hurried retreat to her office.

It was mid-morning when Audrey buzzed her. "I have a call from your real estate agent, Mr. Larken."

"Oh, shoot, I forgot all about getting back to him," Shawn winced as she punched the button. "Good morning, Mr. Larken," she said with a cheeriness that belied her mood, while rubbing her wrinkled forehead. "Have they accepted my counter offer?"

"Yes, with a few stipulations, but all in all, it's a very good deal. Can you meet me for lunch to go over the details?"

"Sure can, that sounds better than the sandwich I brought."

"All right, let's make it the Velvet Turtle in Sunnyvale, say about noon. I'll meet you in the lounge."

"I'll be there," Shawn said. "Thank you for calling."

After she hung up the phone, Shawn rested her head in her shaking hands. Her world was crumbling. Everything that was close to her, save Elsa, was gone. Her father, then Matt, and now the house, everything she loved—and even her budding friendship with Andrew. She felt a terrible loneliness closing around her. "Oh, to hell with this," she muttered and threw herself into her work. "At least these damn papers won't disappear!"

For the next hour, she concentrated on a set of specs, and it wasn't until she realized that it was time to meet the realtor that she remembered another problem. Where would she move if and when they finalized the deal on the house? None of the places she had checked had notified her of a vacancy. "I better get my act together," she reprimanded herself. "I'll call them after lunch." She sighed, picked up her purse, and left for the Velvet Turtle and her fateful appointment, knowing the sale would break all material ties to the past.

Tony and his foreman, Steve Nelson, had just devoured a huge combination pizza with a pitcher of beer and were driving back to Arcadia Lane. The storm sewers and underground electrical work was half-completed, and both men were pleased with their progress. It would mean a sizable check for McCullough Landscaping, and they had celebrated accordingly.

As they approached the entrance to the soon-to-be shopping center, Tony was impressed by the majestic backdrop of the Saratoga hills. Bellows, as usual, had really picked a winner, not only in choosing the site, which had been extremely difficult to arrange, but in the name he chose as well. Arcadia, ideally rural, rustic, having to do with quiet contentment. It was a paradox.

Soon throngs of people would disturb the tranquil setting, yet the design that Bellows had formulated would actually combine two ideas, incorporating the modern, fast-paced America with the leisurely past.

Just beyond the entrance, Saks, I. Magnin's, Macy's, Emporium, and all of the major stores would surround an attractive open area to be highlighted with sixty-foot palm trees, elaborate lighting and all the trappings of modern landscaping. The second and equally enticing concept was one of old-time America, separated from its modern counterpart by a stream featuring a huge waterwheel and a picturesque bridge to bridge the gap of a century. This Arcadia of quiet contentment was designed to rejuvenate the exhausted shopper by providing small shops, quiet restaurants, a park featuring an old-time bandstand, and benches to relieve weary feet.

Bellows even had plans for supervision of youngsters and a merry-go-round to occupy the children while their mother shopped. For teenagers, an attractive arcade to be centrally located would feature every kind of video game imaginable to entice young people. Nor had Bellows forgotten the older set. The Arcadia Lane of yesterday would have continual transportation on its streets in the form of old-fashioned surreys, powered unobtrusively by electricity.

The magnitude of this landscaping was extremely challenging to Tony. No matter what he had originally thought of Bellows, the man was a genius. If McCullough Landscaping could pull it off, what a fine tribute it would be to Jack. The whole enterprise was designed for convenience, relaxation, and enjoyment, not to mention the monetary potential. It would, indeed, be one of a kind.

Tony pulled up alongside the tractor. "Well, I guess it's back to work, Nelson. I gotta run by Sun Haven and check on the plumbing. I'll set up for the palm trees to be delivered next week."

"Right. I'll see ya tomorrow, boss," Nelson replied as he hopped out of the truck.

Tony made a U-turn and zigzagged around the stacks of plastic pipe that would eventually become miles of irrigation.

"Hey, Rizzo," Andrew Bellows yelled as he pulled up in his Lamborghini, "did you ever get that mudhole dried out at Sun Haven?"

Tony stopped opposite him and leaned out the window as Andrew, looking deeply tanned and relaxed, ambled over. "Did you have to ruin my day by mentioning that?"

Bellows laughed. "You mean to tell me you haven't got those kids whipped into shape yet?"

"No, and it doesn't look too promising, not after what they did to my truck." Tony related what had happened, and Shawn's planned meeting with the gang that evening at the park.

Bellows's brow furrowed. "Oh, Christ! That stubborn woman could get hurt! How in hell does she think she can deal with a gang alone?"

"Don't ask me, I only work for her, and she's serious about it whether I like it or not!"

"I think she's making a big mistake, but hell's bells, I know what you're up against."

Suddenly Tony noticed the darkening sky. "Well, I better hit the road. Sure like to get those trenches filled in within the next day or two. I might have to light a fire under my plumber!"

"Not a bad idea. Did you hear the long-range weather forecast?"

Tony winced. "If they're right, it's gonna be a wet one. See ya." He rolled up the window and drove off.

At Sammie's order the Renegades had gathered across the street from the park. "All right, guys, tell ya what we're gonna do," Sam stated. "We're goin' to that meeting tonight!"

"What?" Carlos screeched. "You gotta be kiddin' us, unless you want to use Spike's plan to burn her car?"

"Hey, man, Spike is past tense. I'm in charge now. The only plans we make I okay, and we ain't doin' any dumb stunts to get the cops on us. If any of you don't like it, let's settle it now!"

"Say, man, are you going soft?" the young Chicano asked.

"No, Carlos, but my brother's in the hospital and he might die. I think the least we can do is hear her out for Jason's sake. He was set on it."

There was a lot of grumbling among the boys, which Sammie ignored. "You be there, seven o'clock tonight," he ordered, "or else you deal with me. It sure as hell won't hurt to listen to her; if we don't like it, we can still get even."

It was six forty-five in the evening when Shawn arrived at Sun Haven Park after changing into sneakers, jeans, and a polo shirt at the office. As she looked at the hamburger and french fries that she had picked up en route, her mind wrestled with a thousand thoughts, the least of which was the food in front of her. Yet now that the house she had lived in all her life was sold, she would probably be eating a lot of hamburgers until she found a condominium that suited her. As forlorn as she felt at the moment, at least she could repay the bank loan, though right now she wasn't sure that the money was worth losing the one pillar of security that remained in her life.

She looked over to the small building at one end of the park where Tony was storing supplies. It was the only place where she would have light to show the Renegades the plans for the park. Suddenly Tony's warning came back to her. "You shouldn't go out there alone. Those little hoodlums can be vicious." But she was committed, and even though she wished now that Tony was beside her, she would not back down.

She rummaged through her purse for the building's keys, grabbed the plans and flashlight, and maneuvered the open trenches toward the solitary shed. "Damn," she muttered to herself. "Why didn't I set this up during the daytime?"

As she fumbled with the lock, she was startled by a

voice from behind her. "I'll show you we're not chicken." It was Sammie who loomed tall above her.

Shawn dropped the keys and whirled to face her antagonist. No matter how hard she tried, she could not control the sudden cold fear that riveted her to the spot as she stared at the youth. Her eyes darted past him to the shadowy figures beyond. In the flashlight's dim glow, they looked ominous, and she could barely keep her knees from shaking as she bent to retrieve the keys.

"I didn't think you were chicken, but it was the only way I knew to get you to come," Shawn said, assuming a confidence that she scarcely felt. "It seems to have worked."

"All right. We're here. Now, what have you got to say?"

The Renegades slowly surrounded her while Shawn, determined not to let her hand shake, unlocked the door. Flipping on the light, she laid the plans across some boxes of plumbing supplies. One of the gang reached back to close the door. Panic welled up in her throat. "No, leave it open," Shawn commanded with an authority that she didn't feel.

"Whatsa matter, Miss High and Mighty? You afraid of us?" one jeered.

"Well, who in the hell wouldn't be?" she quickly retorted. "I think I'm doing pretty damn good against the odds!"

A trace of a smile played in Sammie's eyes, but his words belied it. "Well, let's hear what you got to say, and it better be damn good!"

Despite her inner fear, Shawn unrolled the prints. "I want to show you what we're doing here."

While Shawn stretched out the plans before the sullen faces of the Renegades surrounding her, Tony lay cramped up in the mainline irrigation trench, in his hand the billy club he usually carried under the seat of his truck. His ears strained for the slightest sound of distress from the building. Off at the far end of the trench, unknown to one another, Andrew Bellows, clutching a heavy piece of pipe that he'd scavenged from the site, inched his way in the dark toward the small building. "I'd better get closer in case they try to pull anything funny," he muttered under his breath.

Tony's thoughts were focused on Shawn as he pictured the woman surrounded and outnumbered by the gang. Suddenly he heard what sounded like a shuffling noise in the ditch behind him, and his grip automatically tightened around his club. Tony's fine-tuned ears caught a rustling noise as it came closer, and in one quick movement, he leaped out of the trench, grabbing for the shadowy, advancing figure. "All right, I've got you! Get out of that trench, or I'll make mincemeat out of your head!"

Bellows scrambled from the trench toward the menacing voice with his pipe raised. "Try it," he yelled, "and there'll be one less delinquent for the cops to worry about!"

"Delinquent? Who the hell *are* you?" Tony roared as the two men closed in on each other.

"Oh, damn! Rizzo?" Bellows shouted.

"Bellows?" Tony replied. "What the hell are you doing here? I almost clobbered you!"

Back in the building, the muffled yells from the outside alarmed the gang and sent them running. Outside, Tony and Andrew saw the hoodlums scatter in all directions. They looked at each other. "Fine protectors we are!" Bellows said. "What the hell do we do now?"

Tony shrugged. "I think we already did it," he said glumly.

Shawn was stunned by the turn of events, and furious with whoever had ruined her plan. Suddenly all her fear evaporated in the heat of her anger.

"Damn you, take your hands off me!" she ordered Sammie, who had pushed her aside when he ordered his gang to run.

"You double-crossed us, lady! You already put Jason in the hospital, and now you're tryin' to throw me in the can!"

"Jason? In the hospital? Why?" she was shocked.

"Because he was defendin' you," Sammie sneered. "Now I'm gettin' out of here, and you just better get the cops off our backs or you're gonna regret it!"

"Hey, now, you wait a minute!" Shawn yelled as she grabbed his belt. "I'm going to prove to you that I haven't called the cops. If I'd wanted them after you, I'd have called them a long time ago! I don't know any more about this than you do."

Sammie snorted his disbelief. "Boy, lady, you must think I was born yesterday."

Ignoring his taunt, she purposefully headed for the door and ran smack into Bellows's muscular chest. Shawn's eyes flashed. "What are you doing here?" she demanded.

"Just trying to protect a damn-fool woman," Bellows sputtered.

Shawn's eyes narrowed as she realized Tony was behind him.

"We were just trying to see that you didn't get hurt," Tony said defensively.

"Well, you damn near accomplished just the opposite," she said irately. "Now stay the hell out of my personal life, both of you!"

Then, turning to Sammie, who was finding it difficult to conceal a budding grin, Shawn clarified, "They aren't cops, they're just meddlers. Now, you're going to take me to the hospital to see Jason. Where is he?"

Sam's brown eyes showed a mixture of uncertainty and a dawning respect as he stuttered, "Rosewood Memorial, but he's in ICU. I don't think they'll let you in."

Shawn's eyes flashed her irritation. "You'd better believe they will."

Bellows and Rizzo looked at each other sheepishly as she and Sammie abruptly departed. "God damn!" Bellows swore. "I feel like a dog. Every time I get close to her, I somehow get kicked."

Tony shrugged. "Well, I got a doghouse big enough for both of us. Join me?"

An hour later, after making certain that Jason would recover, Shawn stood before the hospital's glass exit door,

noting the glistening rain spattering the concrete. A chill
that had nothing to do with the cold rain on her face ran
up her spine, and she couldn't help shuddering when she
thought of the long-range forecast for an extremely wet
winter. It could compound her money problems, and like
her father, she hated it when the men were forced to draw
short paychecks because of weather conditions curtailing
work. Yet it was an inescapable reality in landscaping.
Her father had been overly generous, and she wondered if
she could really keep the emotional side of herself in
check. Lately, it seemed that every day brought a trauma
of some sort, business or personal.

She was so wrapped up in her thoughts that it was a
moment before she realized that Andrew Bellows, umbrella in hand, had stepped out of the shadow of the building
to walk beside her.

"Andy," she said, "what are you doing here?"

"That's the second time tonight, Ms. McCullough, that
you have asked me that, and I guess"—he shrugged—"it's
because I want to be here. Oh, hell, I'm not good at
apologies—seldom give them—but I *am* sorry that Rizzo
and I put a crimp in your meeting tonight. We damn well
didn't intend to. Friends?"

He was holding the umbrella over her head, looking
apologetic and pleading as the rain dripped from his nose
and saturated his clothing.

Shawn was genuinely happy to see him, and now that
her temper had cooled, a little ashamed about chewing
him out earlier. She grinned in answer and the two of
them huddled together under the protection of his umbrella as they splashed to her car. "Oh, Lord," Shawn said as
the rain picked up. "I thought they said light rain! Poor
Tony. I hope it doesn't cave in his trenches again."

"God forbid! He's probably still out there slapping that
pipe together by flashlight," he said, chuckling. "It's bad
driving weather. I'll follow you home," he said, opening
the door for her.

"Oh, Andy, you needn't. You're soaked."

"I'll dry," he said. "Anyway, I want to hear all about

Jason, and I don't see why we can't discuss him over a cup of something hot. Do you mind?"

"No," she said. "Jason's quite a little guy. I think he'll be fine."

"That's what the doc seemed to think."

"You talked to his doctor? How did you learn his name? Mrs. Brown wouldn't even tell me!"

"I have ways, my dear, rather devious ones," Andrew said with a devilish grin that Shawn was suddenly warmed to see.

All the way home, as Shawn maneuvered the Los Altos hills in the steadily falling rain, the sight of Andrew's headlights in her rearview mirror was comforting. She was glad that she wouldn't be entering the big, empty house alone tonight, and as she pulled up the winding driveway, a pang of sadness gripped her; the house would soon belong to someone else.

As she watched him get out of his Lamborghini, which he'd parked beside her car in the garage, Shawn couldn't help wondering how he had known about the meeting tonight, but that really wasn't important. Her earlier irritation regarding the whole fiasco suddenly seemed overblown. Andrew and Tony had risked her wrath solely to protect her. Now that's friendship, she thought, and smiled kindly at Andrew as he took the key from her hand, opened the lock with it, and ushered her in.

"Hey, it sure feels good in here," Andrew remarked. "Damned if that rain isn't cold!"

"Oh, Andy, you're soaked. Why don't you go upstairs and take a warm shower? I'll put the coffee on."

"You know, that sounds great! I think I'll do just that," he said, running his fingers through his unruly blond waves. "Now don't run off, we have a lot to catch up on. I've missed you, Shawn McCullough."

He said it in such a way that she instantly knew that he meant he had missed her friendship. "Well, to say the least, Mr. Bellows, life is never dull when you're around," she teased, and then added, "I'm glad you're back."

He flashed her a smile and bounced up the stairs two at a time. Shawn busied herself with coffee, and by the time he reappeared wearing her father's blue velour robe and slippers, the coffee was in the server on the silver tray along with two piping hot bowls of soup that she had heated from a Campbell's can, and crackers in a fancy crystal bowl. "It ain't Mama Luigi's minestrone, but it's hot and I'm hungry," she remarked.

"I'll never tell," he said. "Smells good. Where are you going with it?"

"In the living room. I thought we could build a fire and get thoroughly dry," she said over her shoulder as she thought how attractive he looked, his hair towel-dried, his strong thighs outlined by the robe.

"Um. Sounds wonderful. Where's the wood?"

Within minutes, Andrew had a cozy fire going, and they sipped their soup quietly while enjoying the sound of the rain on the windowpanes and the warmth of the blaze. Shawn felt some of her sadness about Matt begin to slip away as she acknowledged that she was enjoying Andrew's unusually quiet presence, and she somehow knew that he was a friend, the kind she had hoped he would be.

He rose to put another log on the fire. "Shawn—" he said.

"Yes, Andy?" she said, wondering how he would react if she were to lean over and kiss him.

"I just wanted to say that I may never like him, but I hope that son of a bitch knows what he's got."

She knew he was referring to Matt, and his ill-timed words snapped her upright and brought tears to her eyes. She rose from the sofa and walked to the window to stare out at the rain.

"Shawn?" He was beside her now. "I am sorry," he said softly. "Did I say something wrong again?"

She shook her head silently, desperately trying to fend off the unexpected avalanche of tears that were threatening to fall. What is the matter with me? she wondered as he raised her chin in the dim light and searched her face for an explanation. "I'm sure he's a nice fellow since you love him," he said. "Who knows? I might even like him, too."

A little sob escaped her, prompting Andy to ask, "What is it, Shawn? It can't be what I just said, can it?"

"No, Andy," she whispered. "Matt has another woman."

"I'm so sorry," he murmured genuinely. He studied her glistening eyes for long, silent moments, then squeezed her shoulder. "Thanks for the loan of the clothes. I'll change now and let you get some rest."

Chapter Fifteen

Jamison Park was beautiful this time of year. Its leafy finery fluttered a last defiance to November's oncoming chill. Winter was close at hand. Squirrels scurried about as if doing their last-minute shopping. An elderly couple, with their dog, strolled leisurely down the winding, leaf-strewn path. Children darted about, their shrill voices puncturing the natural quiet of the park. Amid the youngsters' exuberance, Patrice Guzman sat quietly on a bench, abstractedly feeding the pigeons. She was weary of dwelling on a situation over which she had no control.

Last week had been lonely and depressing with only an occasional call from T. J. inquiring about her health and urging her return to work. Patrice could give him no answer. Though her physical health had greatly improved, her mental state was simply not up to the hectic office environment, and since her dream of becoming Matt's wife had been shattered, she could not face the prospect of working with him day after day. Yet she owed T. J. so much, and for that matter, Matt, too.

If only Dr. Benton, with his calm, reassuring manner, was sitting beside her now and could offer a tailor-made solution to a broken heart. With the flutter of wings, bringing her out of her reverie, she noted that all the pigeons had disappeared, save one, who seemed to be staring at her expectantly as if he somehow knew that she still had more to give. Patrice glanced down at her clenched hand and opened her fist, allowing the crushed bread to spill to the ground.

The sudden movement immediately caused the pigeon to take flight. Dropping back to the ground at a slight distance, he warily eyed the bread. Patrice picked it up. "You're lucky, you can fly away from potential hurt," she said to the pigeon, who slowly inched his way back, his small beady eyes darting about cautiously.

"Come here, little fellow, you needn't be afraid of me," she said as she broke up the wadded bread and offered a piece from her hand.

The pigeon pranced around in a circle, gradually advancing toward her. "It must be wonderful to be a bird," she said aloud. "You seem to know instinctively what's best for you."

The fearless bird suddenly stopped as if pondering an answer and cocked his head curiously for her attention.

Patrice smiled at his coy mannerisms. "You look so intelligent. I'll bet you have all the wisdom of the ages."

The creature bobbed his head in seeming agreement. Patrice grinned as the pigeon stretched his neck to pick the proffered crumb. "If you were me, what would you do? No, don't tell me, I know," she said quietly. "You'd fly quickly away. Perhaps I should have sense enough to do the same. What possible good can come of staying miserable in a hopeless situation?"

Taking the last tidbit from her hand, the friendly little pigeon cooed his gratitude, or so it seemed to Patrice, before flapping his wings to rejoin the flock.

A quiet contentment came over her, and she leaned back against the bench, closing her eyes to enjoy the sun's fleeting warmth. Suddenly she felt someone's presence, and her eyes opened to the friendly face of a man perhaps in his sixties.

"I hope you don't mind, I've been watching you," he stated pleasantly. "Please don't take offense. I am a happily married man, but I have to tell you, you've got the loveliest legs I've ever seen!"

"Well, thank you," she said. "I could hardly take offense to that particular compliment. You have no idea how great that makes me feel! You see, a couple of months ago, I thought I might never walk again."

The man smiled in response and continued on down the path.

She watched him walk away, a good feeling sweeping over her as she rose from the bench. No more hiding in the solitude of her apartment. She was ready to face tomorrow and whatever it would bring.

At the same time that Patrice had made her decision and left the park, Matt Monroe was stretched out on a deck lounge on his apartment terrace, trying to enjoy an unexpected Friday off. Instead, questions very similar to those that Patrice had been asking herself plagued him. It had been a week since the shock of that eventful night, yet he had resolved nothing, nor was he sure that there was anything salvageable. Persistent though he had been, Shawn had been adamant about not speaking to him on the phone, and he strongly suspected that it would be no better if he tried in person. Knowing and admitting that this dilemma was all his own fault did not alleviate the pain he felt, nor could he erase the vivid memory of Shawn's shocked expression and Patrice's tears. God, he'd had it all, and now he had nothing.

Even his court battle had suddenly lost steam. Then, too, he missed the stimulating interchange of ideas with Patrice and longed for her moral support. She had been his valuable sounding board and only now was he beginning to realize how much he had relied upon her wisdom and, yes, support. There had been no doubt in her mind that he would win the case. Grudgingly, he admitted that her faith in him had been marvelous but nothing to compare with the more personal side of her that he had only briefly gotten to know, the warm, so completely generous, person that she had become. Seeing her in that blue gown, so

trusting and so beautiful, had excited him more than he
would ever have thought possible considering how he
thought he felt about Shawn. Damned if life wasn't
complicated. All that was left to him was the ache in his
chest, the lonely nights, and the pain of losing love and
something he had never thought possible to lose: self-
esteem.

Matt drummed his fingers on the arm of the lounge and
sipped his frosty drink. No matter how many times he
went over all the preceding events, the only sure thing
ahead of him was the trial, and he knew that winning the
case was one important step toward regaining his self-
respect. He no longer had the edge on the renowned
attorney, Pollard. They were even, he and Pollard, each
with their own personal can of worms. Matt's case was
excellent, but it would take all his concentration and
determination to win it. He could not allow the confusion
in his personal life to infringe upon his professional
prowess. Though it had turned out to be one hell of a mess,
time had a way of untangling human error, and time
seemed to be the only answer.

An hour after she left the park, Patrice nodded approvingly to her image in the mirror. The teal blazer and
matching skirt set off a bow-necked, white blouse, enhanc-
ing her beautiful slim curves. She quickly applied a touch
of lipstick before slipping into attractive pumps. She had
learned something from Matt. He had unlocked something
within her that had never before been stirred by her
former husband Richard or anyone else. He had warmed
her frozen heart and set it free to love again, to be hurt
again, and dammit, hurt it did. Even so, this time she
would not crawl into a safe little niche, drowned in her
work while life passed her by.

She had had to learn a sad, painful lesson, but she really
couldn't place the blame on Matt alone, nor could she
bring herself to hate him after once having known his love
and tenderness. Wallowing in self-pity as she had done the

past week was not the answer to her dilemma. Life would go on, and she didn't want to miss any of it. Someday, she would know love again, she knew that now. Next time there would be no hesitation or doubt. She would not fearfully fly away as had the pigeon. Patrice slowly picked up her purse and walked out of her apartment.

Downtown, at T. J. Lewis Enterprises, T. J. brightened at the sight of her. "Patty, my girl! You look stunning! Here, come sit," he sputtered excitedly. "Cup of coffee?"

Patrice smiled and nodded. It was so good to see him, this man who was like a father to her. "Just thought I'd fill out an application in case this outfit is looking for a girl Friday," she teased.

"How about Monday, Tuesday, Wednesday, and Thursday?" he joked.

"I guess we could stretch it a little," she said, chewing her lip in feigned thoughtfulness.

He grabbed the phone and reached for the intercom button. "Now, what the hell is her name? Mary? Marsha? No—Marty. Yes, Marty, please bring in a pot of coffee."

A short time later, the girl brought a steaming carafe to his desk and departed. Patrice rose to pour the brew. "No, you sit still and just let me look after you," he said as he quickly snatched the pot and poured two cups. "You don't know how much we've missed you, Patty. Does this mean you're back?"

He was the only one who ever called her Patty, the only one who ever really saw past the efficient, almost cool exterior that she presented, to the gentle girl within. Tears came to her eyes. It wasn't only Matt who had shown her what love is but also this kindly, brusque man whom she admired and loved. "Yes, T. J., I'm back."

"Oh, thank God!" he breathed. "I'll find another spot for what's-her-name, Marty, where she can do less damage."

Patrice laughed at his exaggeratedly serious expression. "I'll bet she's not half bad!"

"You're probably right. It's just that I'm accustomed to the best!"

She walked around the desk to kiss him on the cheek, then paced about the office, glancing at the technical magazines that decorated a lavishly carved mahogany coffee table in front of two elegantly upholstered matching chairs.

He watched her curiously. "Well, since this is Friday afternoon, is it safe to assume you'll be here Monday?"

"Yes," she said with a smile, turning to face him. "Just one favor, T. J.?"

"You name it!"

She lowered her eyes and tried to think of a delicate way to put it. Finally she blurted out, "I can no longer work with Matt!"

His heavy brows raised in shocked concern, and he was completely at a loss for words. Rising from the chair, he came around his desk. "Patty, look at me," he said, raising her chin with his fingers. "Has Matt hurt you? If he has, I'll thrash him!"

"Oh, no, T. J., no! Matt is an excellent lawyer and a fine man! This is partly my fault, too."

He looked at her incredulously.

She shook her head. "Yes. I've been afraid of too many things for too long, but not anymore. I know I'll eventually have to see Matt, but right now I can't work closely with him. Can you understand?"

T. J. blinked, then nodded. "Shouldn't be a problem. He's in court most of the time, winding up the suit. We'll get together for lunch next week and talk it out."

"Good, then I'll see you Monday morning," she said as she took a last sip of coffee and put the cup down on his desk. She was just closing the door when she heard Marty's intercom. From the conversation, she knew T. J. was already transferring the girl to another department. Patrice smiled. It was warming to feel needed again.

"Oh, I know where that is. I'll tell you what, Mr. Rollings, I'll meet you there," Shawn said, thinking how close it was to Arcadia Lane. "I really need to make another stop and that way it'll save time." Her voice was cheery though the idea of moving was still abhorrent to her.

"Fine, Ms. McCullough. The number is 1470 Wilburn Drive. About an hour then?" the realtor concluded.

"Right," she said, jotting down the address. "I'll be there." Shawn glanced at her watch. It was ten A.M. on Monday morning, and with Tony's glowing report on the progress at Arcadia, not a bad start for the week. She was curious about the palms and she hadn't been to the shopping center since working on the bid. This would be a good opportunity to see the site. She handed Audrey a letter on her way out of the office. "Please type this and I'll sign it later."

"You leaving?" Audrey said, noting Shawn's purse in hand.

"Yes. I might be awhile. There's a condo I want to see, and it's in the direction of Arcadia. As long as I'm there, I'll see how the job is going."

When she walked through the condo door with Bob Rollings, Shawn was ambivalent. The atmosphere was absolutely nothing like that of her beloved house. It was as though everything here was in miniature, and the second-floor location added to the claustrophobic feeling. Mr. Rolling's professional enthusiasm was wasted upon her. The walls were dirty and the carpeting badly worn, and as Shawn's obvious distaste became more and more apparent, the real estate agent was quick to emphasize the meager possibilities. "You could easily have it painted and recarpeted for a lot less than what the rest of these condos have gone for."

"Mr. Rollings, I don't know." Shawn said, shaking her head. "This place is pretty bad. I haven't enough money to recarpet and pay a painter. If I were rich, I'd have kept my house!"

He smiled. "I suppose so, but let me tell you the good news!"

"Boy, please do! I haven't heard any so far!"

He laughed. "You can assume this loan at a low interest rate, and about fifty thousand will cover their equity."

She rolled her eyes. "What do you consider low interest?"

"Nine and a half percent."

"Hmm. Well, let's take a closer look." Mentally, Shawn added up the cost of new carpet and paint. She could try her hand at wielding a paintbrush to save some money, and it would be one way of keeping busy now that Matt was no longer a part of her life. She could also see where decorating could raise the property value considerably. It did have all of the modern conveniences in compact form, and the view from the living room that overlooked the small town of Saratoga was a saving grace. The native trees of all descriptions and the quaintness of the square light fixtures on black iron poles lining the streets made Shawn visualize what an attractive scene it would be at night. "What's the bottom line, Mr. Rollings?"

"They're asking two hundred thirty-five thousand," he said, as though it were a steal.

"That's totally out of line, considering the condition this place is in."

"I'm sure they'll take less. The owner has been transferred to the East Coast."

Shawn sighed. Condominiums were certainly expensive. She hadn't looked at anything under two hundred thousand. The location was a plus, close to the office, and as she reevaluated the price and also the rapidly closing date of her house sale, she shot him a figure. "I won't pay a cent more than two hundred thousand, and that's only if I can take possession almost immediately so that I'll have time to put this place in order. I only have thirty days before I have to vacate."

"Well," he said, "I don't know if they'll drop the price that much. Depends on their commitments." He shrugged. "But this is a funny business. It won't hurt to try."

"It's their choice. I can store my furniture and move in with a friend until something better comes along," she stated matter-of-factly. She knew he was also thinking of his own diminishing commission.

"I see. Well, there's always the unexpected. They might just go for it."

En route to Arcadia, Shawn could not work up any enthusiasm over her offer, yet at the same time, it would be a great sense of relief to get her housing problems settled. She knew that paint could make a world of difference, and her mind explored all of the condo's possibilities. Before she realized it, Arcadia Lane was upon her, the sight of which came as a total surprise, so deeply was she engrossed in her redecorating plan. They had barely started raising the huge buildings when last she had seen it, and now the ultramodern shopping center was growing by leaps and bounds. Driving through the entrance, she could see that work was steadily progressing. The satisfying scene generated a euphoric feeling of excitement and accomplishment. The progress was impressive. Andrew Bellows did nothing small-scale, and what a tremendous vision he had had in Arcadia Lane.

Shawn drove around the site's perimeter, dodging equipment, stacks of pipe, and open trenches. Workmen were scattered about in clusters, sitting on piles of lumber or in their trucks, their attention devoted to lunch pails, cigarettes, radios, and card games. Shawn hadn't thought about lunch, but she would eat something later. Right now, she was anxious to see the palm trees. As she rounded the first row of buildings she spotted five forty-foot flatbed trailers loaded with red-flagged palms that extended a considerable length beyond the trailer beds. Tony's truck was nearby. Shawn parked her Spitfire alongside his truck and got out.

"Well, hello, boss lady," Tony said as he walked over to her car. "I haven't seen you on a site since the mud bath at Sun Haven."

She laughed. "My curiosity got the better of me. I've never seen sixty-footers planted. Anyway, I was in the area looking at a condo."

"Well, stick around," he said as he took a bite out of his submarine sandwich. "You had lunch?"

"No, not yet."

"Catering truck's right over there. Can I treat ya?"

Shawn glanced at her workmen, who were all sitting around with Nelson, the foreman, eating their lunches between Tony's and Nelson's trucks. "No, you go ahead and enjoy your lunch with the men. I'll get it myself. What's good?"

"Not a hell of a lot. It all tastes about the same—it just eases the hunger pangs."

She laughed. "You're terrible, Tony," she said over her shoulder as she carefully picked her way across the rough terrain toward the caterer.

"What the hell is she doing here, Tony?" Nelson asked with a frown.

"Oh, she's just curious. Wants to see how you're going to drop those palms in."

"Just what we need is a woman who doesn't know a damn thing about it to supervise us," he muttered in disgust.

"Hey, you got her all wrong. She's pretty damn savvy. Anyway, she won't interfere."

"Her being here is interference enough," he snorted. "She'll get the men all uptight."

"Naw, you're making a big deal over nothing."

"Oh, yeah? Listen to those wolf whistles from the guys over there."

"Hell, why not? She's a good-looking lady." Tony laughed.

"Rizzo, you know damn well the guys won't concentrate on their work with a skirt watching them."

Tony gave him a typical Italian shrug. "What can I say? She's signing our checks. Relax, Nelson, don't be so tense!"

Shawn ignored the whistles and the innuendoes of the other workmen as she walked back to Tony's group. Though she felt very conspicuous in her tight-fitting blue angora sweater and navy side-slit skirt, she tried to maintain a certain amount of dignity despite the precariousness of her high heels. She wished that she had worn jeans and sneakers.

"Here, Shawn," Tony said, opening his truck door. "Sit here."

She was all too aware of the men watching her and the obvious lag in their conversation. She wondered if she would feel so out of place if she worked with them every day. Now, there were women doing just that. Turning to Tony, who was leaning on the truck sipping coffee, Shawn remarked, "It's sure quiet around here all of a sudden. What's the matter with these guys?"

"They're just not used to seeing a good-looking gal around here, makes 'em a little nervous."

"I'm not going to bite them or seduce 'em."

"They'd go for that," he said, laughing. "Don't worry. They'll settle down."

Within minutes, the site came to life. The men followed their foreman and Rizzo to the flatbeds, and the cherry-picker operator yelled suggestively at Nelson. "Hey, buddy, she a friend of yours? I'd sure like a date!"

"Hell, no, she's the big boss!" Nelson returned with disgust.

"That's interesting. I'd much rather plant her than these damn trees." He laughed.

"We're not paying you for lip service, my friend. Let's get this thing rollin'!"

Tony grinned. "Don't get so excited, Nelson. We got to get these trees in the ground this afternoon so we don't have to pay for another day on the rigs."

"Well, I think you better get her the hell out of here then."

"Shit, Steve, she's the boss. *You* tell her to leave."

"Dammit, Rizzo, we're gonna have trouble because of her." Nelson snorted as he walked off and started lining up the men for the backfilling that would be required. He was a man who considered *all* women bad luck on a job.

Shawn gobbled the last of her sandwich and was getting out of Tony's truck when her supervisor returned. "We can sit in the truck and watch," he said as he climbed behind the wheel. "I'll drive up on the hill so you'll have a better view."

"Are you trying to tell me something, Tony? I want to see this firsthand."

"Well, Shawn, it's like this. These guys aren't used to working with a woman around, especially one dressed like you. In case you don't know it, you're quite a sexy lady."

It was not taken as a compliment by Shawn. Didn't they understand her interest? Her presence certainly wasn't to impress the men.

"Damn, Tony. What is the field of landscaping? A man's private domain?"

He shrugged. "Okay, boss lady. You're calling the shots. Follow me."

Shawn was intrigued watching the operator wrapping a web sling around the trunk of the first huge palm and deftly maneuvering it off the flatbed with the cherry picker. He had placed the sling in such a manner that upon lifting it with the boom, the weight of the palm tree's ball automatically righted its position for transportation to the awaiting eight-foot hole that had been prepared earlier. The whole operation was much simpler than she had imagined with the machine doing almost all of the work. Of course, it was obvious that the operator was a crackerjack and well worth his wages even if, at this moment, he was spending too much time staring at her. Tony had made her well aware of the distraction she had caused, yet she was just stubborn enough to ignore this warning and Nelson's obvious irritation as he scowled at the offending operator.

While wrapping the second and larger tree, the workman's eyes strayed once again to Shawn's inviting curves. Shawn chatted with Tony as the two of them watched the operator lift the mammoth tree from its resting place. The cherry picker barely had the palm raised free of the flatbed when the sling slipped and the tree crashed to the ground with a thud.

"God dammit; stop staring at her and pay attention to what you're doing!" Nelson yelled as he ran over to inspect for damage.

Shawn turned to Tony. "Maybe I'm costing us money. It really annoys me, but I guess I can see them when they're all planted," she said, disgruntled.

"By God," a familiar voice from behind her said, "you're the prettiest damn thing I've seen in these parts!"

"Damned if that doesn't seem to be a universal problem," Shawn returned sourly. "I was just leaving!"

"Well, I didn't mean to insult you," Bellows replied with a wide grin.

"Normally, I wouldn't be insulted, but 'pretty' seems to be a detriment around here. How are you, Andy?"

"Better now that I've seen you. Actually, you can't blame 'em for enjoying a pleasant change of scenery. Don't rush off; as long as you're here, I'll show you around the site."

"I'll take it," Shawn said decidedly.

Andrew ushered her to his car while the workmen stared after them. "You are a definite distraction, aren't you?" he agreed with a rather proud grin. "Eat your hearts out, fellas," he teased under his breath.

Shawn laughed. "This time it's probably the great Andrew Bellows they're staring at."

"I rather doubt that," he said, pointedly eyeing her revealing sweater.

They drove around the entire area. "I remember from the plan that it was big, but, Andy, this place is gigantic! How have you been able to keep control of all these projects? There's everything in the world going on here!"

A smug grin lit his face. "It's easy. I just pay for the best and let 'em do what they're best at. Pretty simple really."

"I should have known you would say that. Does that include McCullough Landscaping?" she teased.

"Of course." Andrew stopped the car. "Shall we take a little walk? I want to show you the Arcadia Lane of yesterday. It's not as yet so congested with workmen in this back area. It's eventually going to be the main attraction as well as my favorite part. Right over there"— he pointed—"is where the merry-go-round will be, and if you remember from your landscaping plans, the man-made stream will run right along there."

"Oh, yes, I recall. That's where the bridge goes and the stream recirculates into a huge pond down at that end. It should be lovely with the waterwheel and the lilies. Those flowers were a problem in bidding. We had a heck of a time finding the correct strainers and bafflers to slow down the water flow so as not to disturb them. Will it have goldfish, too?" she asked exuberantly.

"Sure, what's a pond without fish?"

Shawn smiled. "The landscape plans hardly do it justice. Oh, Andy, it's going to be magnificent."

"I hope so. This is my pet project. I've built lots of shopping centers, but I've always wanted to build one that's unique, one that everybody would find enjoyable," he said.

"Looks to me like this one's a certainty. Andy, you've thought of absolutely everything. I love your idea of baby-sitting for the preschoolers."

More and more she was discovering Andrew's affinity for children. She looked at him, remembering that he had donated an old truck to the Renegades at the meeting last week. Now the boys could haul trash and do cleanup work in order to earn money for a video game and pool table to use at Sun Haven. He'd even gotten the city to go along with the idea and volunteered his supervision one night a week upon the completion of the recreation center.

"You really do like kids, don't you, Andy?"

"Well, I wouldn't go so far as to say that," he said noncommittally. "This is just good business."

"If you say so, but I think there's more to it than that." She could still see Jason's beaming smile the day he had come home from the hospital and stared in disbelief at the new bicycle provided by Andrew as a coming-home surprise. He could barely wait to be well enough to ride it.

"Oh, did I tell you about the electrically driven surreys?"

"No, but Tony did, and I think they're a fantastic idea. Think of it, getting a ride to your car when you have a bundle of packages. Gosh, Andy, where did you get all these brainstorms?"

"What can I tell you? Just brilliant, I guess."

She swatted his arm playfully. "Some woman is going to be really lucky to get you one of these days."

He laughed. "I tried to tell you that."

"Andrew Bellows, you are something. What an ego!"

"Bellows," a cantankerous voice interrupted from their right.

Andrew and Shawn whirled around to see a little old man making his way toward them. "Who's that?" Shawn asked.

"Oh, hell, it's that little old geezer who lives up on the mountain above us. He's trouble."

"What do you mean?"

"You'll see. He's been dead set against this development from the beginning. Tried to stop us by riling up all of the local residents and gave me a real hard way to go."

"What do you suppose he wants?"

"Who knows? He bugs the workmen continuously. The old guy lives only in the past."

"What do we do, grin and bear it?" Shawn asked.

Bellows nodded as the interloper stopped directly in front of them, a scowl on his face.

"What kind of a fool idea have you got now, bringing South Sea Island trees into my valley? If you have to build this monstrosity, the least you could do is stick to what's native to the area," he snorted.

"Mr. Krugger, this is Shawn McCullough," Andrew said in hopes of distracting the man.

Ignoring the introduction and Shawn, the crochety old man spoke directly to Bellows. "What I want to know is how many other oddball schemes are you people gonna come up with to ruin this place?"

"Look, Mr. Krugger, if I'm not mistaken, I own this

property, and I have a very legal permit for everything that I'm doing here," Andy said patiently. "But I'm tired of placating you, and I'm getting extremely annoyed with your continual harassment of the workmen."

"You can't threaten me. This is still my valley! You'll see, the people in this area won't shop here. I'll see the day when they tear all of this down!" he snarled vindictively. Then with an abrupt turn, he stomped back up the hill.

"Gets excited, doesn't he?" Shawn said. "Where is his house?"

Bellows pointed. "See that old place up on the hill over there just above where the pond will be? His wife is dead, and he's all by himself except for his dog. The house is in bad shape, so I tried to buy him out." He shrugged. "Older people sometimes find it hard to accept progress. Who knows, maybe I'll get that way myself someday. But there's not much I can do, he simply wouldn't hear of moving."

"Hm, I would think he'd get awfully lonely up there. You'd think he'd enjoy a little activity. It's not as if this is going to be an all-night disturbance."

Andrew's brows raised. "Don't be too sure of that. The Bullhorn might kick up quite a ruckus with all the loud country-western bands, not to mention the movie theaters. So far, I don't think he's aware of that."

She grinned. "I would strongly suggest that you don't mention it. Well, Andy, thanks for the 'Cook's tour.' I should get going. I've been away from the office longer than I'd planned, looking at a condo before I came here."

"Did you like it?"

"Not particularly. But then there's no way I'm going to find anything I like as much as my house," she said wistfully.

"You do love that house."

"Yes," she said. "I grew up there, and it holds all my memories."

"Well, I wish you'd let me help you."

"Did I hear you volunteer? If I get this place, it needs painting throughout. How are you at mastering a paint-brush?"

"I hire experts."

She laughed. "You're no fun at all!"

Chapter Sixteen

Holding the heavy silver coffee service, Patrice paused a moment outside the boardroom before opening the door. Matt would undoubtedly be inside. "Oh, well"—she shrugged—"sooner or later I have to face him." Nudging the door open with her hip, she maneuvered the huge silver tray into the walnut-paneled room and deposited it on the mahogany serving table in the corner as quietly as she could.

Matt was sitting next to T. J. Lewis at the far end of the conference table. Her stomach tightened at the very sight of him. She clutched the edge of the table for support, beads of perspiration slowly forming under her soft blond bangs.

She was thankful that the board members' attention was devoted to Craig Murray's presentation, and she took advantage, listening to the speech in an effort to calm herself.

After what seemed an eternity but was in actuality but a few minutes, she slowly became aware of Craig Murray's droning voice. "If you find the report favorable, I would then propose sending Monroe to the site direct, in order to investigate the legal ramifications regarding a possible purchase of the chromium mine. Matt? Any objections to South Africa?"

Patrice was surprised. When she'd asked T. J. for a different work assignment for Matt and herself, she hardly expected Matt to be sent so far away. She watched Matt's eyebrows arch at the news. "I have no objection, provided that I'm not still tied up here in the courtroom," he said.

T. J. Lewis cleared his throat, and acknowledging Patrice's presence, he said, "I don't know about the rest of you, but I could use a coffee break."

"None for me, thanks," Matt replied. Then, becoming painfully aware of Patrice's presence, he hastily jammed his papers into his briefcase. "I've got to get to the courthouse."

As Matt approached the door, for one brief moment he was face-to-face with Patrice. In a quiet voice, concern showing in his eyes, he asked, "How have you been, Patrice?"

Her voice was a mere whisper. "I'm fine, thanks for asking."

"I'm glad. Sometime we must talk."

"If you'd like—sometime."

Shawn opened the trunk lid of her car and reached for the eighteen-pound turkey she had been forced to buy due to her last-minute decision to cook Thanksgiving dinner for Andy. Unfortunately, one of the smaller turkeys, which she would have preferred, hadn't lain around the market waiting for her tardy brainstorm. Why had she, as usual, let her inherent impulsiveness dictate her actions? It was insane to think that she could, at the last minute, come up with a traditional dinner while in the midst of painting the hastily acquired condominium.

She tugged awkwardly at the resistant bird. "You are coming with me," she stated emphatically while eyeing the darkening skies above, "before we both get drowned." She clasped the fowl to her breast and lurched backward. On reaching the stairs, Shawn took a deep breath, glared at the huge turkey in her arms, and muttered, "Well, let's give it a go." And up the stairs the incongruous pair staggered, swaying from one side to the other, the thought of a more manageable five-pound Thanksgiving ham becoming ever more desirable in Shawn's mind. She was well aware of how she must appear to any passerby, a ninety-nine-pound weakling wrestling with an eighteen-pound bird.

With a sense of extreme relief, she finally reached the top of the stairs, congratulating herself as she rummaged through her shoulder bag for her keys. "Dammit. I left the keys in the trunk lid." Halfway down the stairs, she suddenly realized that in her indignation she had neglected to leave the turkey at the doorstop and was still carrying it as she reeled back down the stairs toward the car.

The first sight that greeted Andrew Bellows as he swung into the parking lot was the turkey resting on the hood of Shawn's car while she stood, arms akimbo, glaring at the object of her frustration. The minute she saw him walk toward her, she accused, "Bellows, where were you when this damn bird was fighting me every inch of the way up the stairs?"

Andrew looked at the innocent bird quizzically. "Looks to me like he couldn't fight his way out of a paper bag—and didn't."

She shot him a fiery glance. "Just what I need is a smart aleck."

Shawn grabbed the turkey and literally slammed it into his stomach. "Here," she said, "let's see if you have better rapport with Tom."

"You just haven't shown the proper respect to the old fellow," he said laughingly. "Look at him. He's all beaten up."

Shawn grinned despite herself. "Just keep talking, and there'll be two birds worse for wear around here."

He laughed uproariously.

After several trips from the car, the kitchen had taken

on the appearance of dinner in a hardware store. The well-worn turkey lay sprawled on the counter surrounded by stuffing mix, canned cranberries, a bag of potatoes, salad greens and dressing, fresh vegetables, and two bottles of good white wine. Paper plates and cups added to the informality. The imitation slate linoleum was littered with cans of paint, brushes, mixing paddles, paint rollers, and rags.

Two hours later, Andrew pulled a small paint-speckled cigar from his polo shirt. Leaning back against the only unpainted wall of the living room as he lit the cigar with white-blotched hands, his gaze rested on Shawn, who was on tiptoe three-fourths of the way up a ladder, stretching to catch a missed spot on the ceiling. He grinned. By God, he thought, whenever she makes up her mind, she stops at nothing. She was a surprisingly good painter—fast, thorough, and neat. There seemed to be no end to her talents, and eyeing the firmness of her breasts and buttocks as she brought the paint roller evenly across the overlooked spot, he could not help but still yearn for more than friendship. He felt so totally alive when he was with her. She was the essence of everything that he had ever envisioned in a woman—beauty, strength of character, intelligence, and a lot of admirable spunk—and every time he was near her, he fought the same inner battle. Was there a chance for him? Was this Matt character definitely out of her life, and how could he find out without opening up old wounds for her? As frustrating as it was, all he could do was enjoy the times that he shared with her, times that he knew could end at any moment. He took a long drag on his cigar and slowly blew out the smoke as though trying to expel his dismal thoughts.

"Well, shoot, Andy, you don't have to hold up that wall. Can't you do two things at once?" Shawn said, grinning devilishly. "What do you think I pay you for?"

"To supervise your work," he returned. "Hey, there's another little spot you missed over there. See, in the corner?"

Shawn scanned the ceiling. "I'm going snow-blind. All I

can see is white paint. Oh, Lord, my neck's killing me!"
She rolled her head around and rubbed the back of her
neck. "Tell ya what, Andy. You get up there and *I'll*
supervise."

A teasing gleam lit up his eyes as he strode across the
room. His huge hands encircled her tiny waist, and he
swooped her off the ladder, depositing her upright on the
floor.

Shawn's eyes flashed indignantly. "Now that you've
displayed your muscle power, let's see your creativity on
the business end of that roller."

"So you want me to show you how to paint?" he teased.

She rolled her eyes. "Whatever's right. I had better get
old Tom into the oven or we'll have to go out after all, and I
don't think we're exactly dressed for the occasion."

When Shawn returned, Andrew was putting the finishing touches on the dining alcove that adjoined the living
room. "Andy," she remarked in amazement by all that he
had accomplished, "you're not a half-bad painter."

"Sure, when I don't have a distraction," he replied as he
made the last pass with his roller. "Get the bird all taken
care of?"

"You bet. We'll eat around six."

"Six? What about lunch?"

Shawn's eyes grew wide. "Oh, my gosh, I intended to
cook earlier; time just got away from me."

"Well, come on, woman, a working man's gotta have
sustenance."

Shawn racked her brain. Last week when she had
cleaned some of the filth off the walls, she had left some
cheese in the refrigerator and a few crackers in the
cupboard. "How about a wine-and-cheese party?"

"Wasn't exactly what I had in mind, but beggars can't be
choosers. Let me get some of this paint off and I'll crack
the wine."

They sat on newspaper-covered paint buckets in the
middle of the empty room, munching cheese and crackers,
sipping wine from paper cups, and thoroughly enjoying
their makeshift picnic.

Suddenly Andrew's gaze grew serious. "You know something?"

"No, tell me something."

"I wouldn't have missed this for the world, even if it is a lot of work."

She touched his arm gently. "I hope you know how great it is to have a friend like you."

He didn't answer but squeezed her hand in reply. "Come on, let's hit the bedroom," he said in a lighter vein.

"Andrew Bellows, I thought we had an understanding about that subject," she teased, determined to keep the tone light.

"What? You don't want to paint it?"

"You know very well what I mean."

He smiled evilly. "You're no fun at all."

"Stop stealing my line, and let's transform the bedroom."

"I wouldn't touch that with a ten-foot pole," he said, snickering.

It was five-thirty P.M. when Andrew pulled the golden brown turkey out of the oven and transferred it to a platter. Potatoes were steaming on the stove, and the smell of fresh vegetables comingling with the aroma of the turkey blotted out the odor of the fresh paint. Shawn opened a can of whole cranberries and scooped them into a small glass bowl. Next, she pulled the salad greens from the refrigerator, and while Andrew watched with pure admiration, she deftly tossed a crisp, colorful salad. Then grabbing a hot pad, she drained the potatoes and watched the steam curl to the ceiling and cloud the window above the sink. "Andy, it's raining."

He stood behind her and peered out at the dark gray sky. "So it is." He frowned. "It's been threatening to all day."

For a moment, they stood gazing out silently while beads of water splattered and danced against the window. The very act reminded her of her father, who had so often been mystified by nature's fleeting patterns. It was the first holiday that she had spent without McCullough, and memories of much happier times gripped her. If she were to let herself, she could easily have a good cry over the two men who were missing in her life, but she silently resolved not to spoil Andrew's day.

Andrew seemed to sense her wave of melancholia as she turned abruptly from the window, picked up the pot of potatoes, and busied herself with mashing them. "What can I do to help?" he asked. "I carve a mean turkey."

She smiled, her eyes glittering with unshed tears. "Oh, Andy, I was hoping you'd volunteer! My dad always made an art of it, and I'm afraid I haven't had much practice. I'll make a deal with you. If you cut up the turkey, I'll stir up some gravy, and we'll be all set."

"Sure, why not," he said. Then with tremendous insight and compassion, he said, "You miss your father a lot, don't you?"

"Yes," she mused. "It's very strange, a holiday without McCullough." For a moment, she was engulfed by private thoughts, wishing that she could shake the empty feeling that had infiltrated her being. "I'm sorry it shows, Andy, but I loved him very, very much."

There was a catch in her voice, and he couldn't resist wanting to enfold her in his arms and kiss away her sadness. Instead, he picked up the electric knife and said, "Don't be sorry. He must have been quite a man. I wish I had known him."

"You would have liked him, Andy. He was a lot like you. He lived life to the fullest, physically and emotionally." She sighed wistfully. "Still, he wouldn't want me to be sad," she said, and with a noticeable effort, she set about making gravy. While Andrew heaped thin slices of turkey on the platter and scooped out stuffing into a heated bowl, Shawn spread a bright-red checked tablecloth on the dining room floor, then poured two glasses of the already open wine while intermittently stirring the gravy.

"I saw that," she accused, catching Andrew sampling a tasty morsel. "Is it good?"

He grinned. "Mighty fine," he said. "You've done an admirable job of this, too."

She smiled. "You're just hungry. It's all that paint," she said teasingly. "Come to think of it, I'm starved. The cheese and crackers wore out about an hour ago."

"Well, what's holding up dinner?" he asked as he laid down the knife and smiled expectantly.

"Just a second, you stay here," she said, and started carrying off all the food into the other room. After several trips, she smiled at Andy's perplexity. "Okay let's eat. Grab the rest of the wine, huh?"

He followed her curiously to the dining room and smiled his approval at the sight of the tablecloth neatly spread over the carpeting. She had turned down the overhead chandelier, giving a soft glow to the still-wet paint that surrounded them. It was a picnic and a banquet all at the same time. Like Shawn herself, it had a touch of class under the most adverse circumstances. For an instant, Andrew's expression grew serious. "I'll always remember this day. Do you know it's my first real Thanksgiving dinner?"

"Oh, Andy, you're kidding! With all the elegance that you're accustomed to?"

"It isn't just the meal, you know. Thanksgiving means much more than that." Without giving her a chance to reply, he raised his wineglass in a toast. "To your first holiday dinner in your new home."

Shawn smiled faintly as she reached for her glass. "I'll drink to that, though I really wish it were still the old house."

While Shawn and Andrew sat Indian style on the carpet and gorged themselves on the delicious dinner, the wind-driven rain pelted the windows, lending an unexpected coziness to the empty room. Yet a feeling of ambivalence overtook Shawn. She suddenly rose and walked to the window, peering into the darkness.

Andrew frowned. Had he said something to disturb her? "I hope you're not deserting me yet," he said lightly. "As good as he is, old Tom's company isn't anywhere near as pleasing as yours."

"I'm sorry, Andy, it's just the storm. I'm concerned about the jobs. I guess I've grown up in a world where rain can be a real problem. It's just utterly depressing thinking about the men losing pay by not being able to work. But I shouldn't be bothering you with my problems after all the help you've given me." She turned to face him as he rose from the floor. "And I suppose Matt's still on my mind, too," she said, too softly she thought, for him to hear.

He stopped abruptly, then turned and went to the kitchen and reappeared with the Chablis in hand. Filling the two glasses, he said calmly, "I have a big set of shoulders if you want to talk about it."

"It's not fair to unload my problems on you when there's nothing you can do."

"What's fair in this life? You either win or you lose, but never give up too easily if what you're fighting for is important to you. Have you made any attempt to talk things over with him?" She knew he was talking about Matt.

"No. He's tried to call me but, Andy, I don't want to talk to him yet. I've lost faith in anything he says. He's not as honest as you are."

Andrew gave a slight chuckle. "I'm not sure that's a compliment. I've often been accused of being just down-right blunt."

Shawn grinned. "That you are at times, but at least I know where I stand with you. I can't explain the way I feel about Matt. God, I've idolized him since I was ten years old!"

Andrew frowned. "Idolization isn't love."

She looked at him helplessly. "I know, but it's *not* like an irrigation system. You can't just turn your heart off with the twist of a valve."

"True, but you can sure replace the valve."

She pondered the idea while she stretched out on the carpet on her stomach, sipping her wine, chin cupped in

her hands and resting on her elbows. "You're right, Andy,
I haven't given him a chance to explain. We Irish are
too damn proud and emotional, but how would you feel
if you had seen someone you loved in a compromising
position?"

His look was incredulous. "You're asking me? Hell, I'm
as damn emotional as you are." He joined her on the floor.
"The point is, things are not always the way they might
seem.. I've had to eat crow more than once."

The wine had brightened her mood, and she laughed as
she reached for the half-full bottle, refilling both their
glasses before easing herself back to her comfortable
position. "I'll bet you have," she remarked. "Still, I like
you just the way you are, and come to think of it, I really
don't know much about you. You're quite a mystery, you
know. Everybody knows of your success in business, but I
wonder how many people know the real you?" She smiled
at him. "You're quite a guy, Andrew Bellows. Tell me
about your growing-up years."

His response was interrupted by a flickering of the
light, and suddenly the room was plunged into darkness.
The power failure's timing struck her as incongruous, and
she quipped, "Your young years couldn't have been that
bad!"

"Worse," he said. "But that was a long time ago. I
learned to live with it."

He said it so matter-of-factly, yet there was palpable
hurt in his voice. She wished that she could see his
expression, but the room was pitch-black. "What do you
mean, worse?"

Andrew had had just enough wine to unburden the
long-kept secret traumas of his youth. "You want to know
about my childhood?" He snorted. "I'll tell you. It was hell!
I was raised in the slums of Chicago. All I can remember
was seeing things falling apart, disintegrating around
me. The kids made a game out of teasing me about my
drunken father."

She could hear the long-ago frustration of the little boy
in the man's angry voice, and she knew that, were it not

for the darkness, he never would have revealed these confessions to her.

"Oh, Andy. I'm so sorry. I shouldn't have pried, but I'm really honored that you feel you can share the past with me."

The sincerity of her words affected him deeply. He had always been regarded as invincible by his peers, and he didn't know how to respond to Shawn without showing the vulnerability that he had long since denied and so he was silent.

Without warning, the lights came back on. "How about another touch of the grape?" he asked lightly. "We can't let the past rule our lives."

She nodded, the serious tone gone. Still she said, "You know something, Andrew Bellows? I admire you very much."

He smiled wistfully. "You're not so bad yourself, Shawn McCullough."

She grinned as she rose from her comfortable spot. "Well, I guess nobody else is going to clean up this mess. I'd better get cracking if I'm going to paint again tomorrow. Shall I reserve a paintbrush for you?"

Andrew mentally ran through the next day's schedule. There was a meeting in Denver that he, himself, had scheduled. He had never missed an important board meeting except the one recently when he'd gone to San Juan, and they had all managed to survive without him. Still, this particular meeting was significantly more important. Millions of dollars were on the table. Could he send Jim Kraff in his stead? Andrew had taught him everything he knew, and this was as good a time as any to let his protégé try his wings. Besides, time with Shawn was infinitely more valuable to him than anything his money could buy. "Can I count on a turkey sandwich?" he bargained.

Shawn laughed. "You sure can, and if you're nice, I might even whip up some turkey à la king for dinner."

"I'll take it," he said laughingly. "And now, Ms. McCullough, we had better stash away this food. I have a few calls to make when I get home, and this is one hell of a storm, so I'll follow your car and make sure you're safe for a future bout with the paintbrush."

"Considering the sad state of my neck and shoulders, you've got a deal."

As Andrew followed the red glow of the Spitfire's taillights in the gusting rain, he relived the day in his mind. Though he hadn't done any painting in years, today had been enjoyable. He'd almost forgotten during the last few years the feeling of accomplishment that comes from doing something as mundane as pushing a roller. But then he'd always liked working with his hands. As a teenager, when he had taken long walks across town to get away from the slums of Chicago, he'd whittled on scrap blocks of wood filched from building sites and had stood awestruck watching a skeletal framework become a beautiful modern apartment house or sleek office building.

Construction had gotten into his blood, and he had a hatred for the squalor of the slum that sickened him. Someday he would build streamlined stores and apartments, and one day he would come up with a unique concept in design. There was something stimulating and vital about construction, not just the physical, finished product, but, to Andrew, who had had so many negatives in his life, it set his spirits soaring.

He had spent every spare moment shadowing the workmen on any number of construction sites, assimilating firsthand knowledge at each opportunity. When he was fourteen, the foreman of a huge project took a liking to him and gave him a summer job. At first, he "fetched and carried" for the journeyman carpenters, the masons, and whatever trade was involved at the time. At lunch hour, while the other men sat together joking and eating, Andrew studied the blueprints, and by the end of the summer, he was pounding nails with the same "one, two, drive it home" rhythm as his experienced peers. The desire to become a success in the building trade by the time he was thirty-five became an ever-present goal, and he seized every chance to learn, despite being shuffled from one

foster home to another. At least it beat the orphanage
where he had been warehoused upon losing his parents.
And so he lived for his jobs, the only constructive and
dependable thing in his life.

The years had gone by swiftly, and now, here he was,
about to realize the culmination of his dreams in Arcadia
Lane. But now he had a completely different yearning
that no amount of knowledge, drive, or desire could
satisfy. Now Shawn McCullough had gotten into his blood.

Andrew frowned, trying to remember his rationale
about Shawn, which he had formed upon leaving San
Juan. He pulled up into the driveway behind Shawn and
watched her get out of her car. For all of his frustration, a
strange kind of peace overcame him before he joined her at
the door.

"Quick, Andy, you'll get drenched!" she urged laughingly. "Want to come in for a brandy?" She swung the door
wide, flipped on the light, and tossed her purse on the
foyer table.

"No, thanks, I'll pass on the brandy. Don't forget, I must
make my calls. Anything I can bring tomorrow?"

"Just the great Andrew Bellows," she said brightly.
Then, taking his hand, she added, "Thank you, Andy, it's
been a very lovely Thanksgiving after all."

"The best." He leaned to kiss her forehead gently. "See
you in the morning, honey," he said, leaving.

Shawn watched him all the way to the car. Then she
shut the door and leaned against it hard, a wayward tear
trickling down her cheek. If only she loved Andrew.

Chapter Seventeen

It was ten A.M. Monday morning when Patrice Guzman opened the door to courtroom number seven and quietly entered, taking a seat in the rear of the huge, half-empty room. The trial was in its eighth week and according to T. J. Lewis, Matt was hoping for a verdict soon, if not today. But it wasn't solely for T. J. that she was here; she had been involved from the very beginning in working on this case with Matt, and no matter what had transpired personally between them, she wanted to see the lawsuit to an end.

At that moment, the renowned Mr. Pollard was delivering his summation to the jury in his most impressive manner. In a three-piece, charcoal-and-white pinstripe suit, he exuded the confidence of a man who was accustomed to winning. Patrice could well understand why women were attracted to the attorney. Despite his years, Norman Pollard was a very handsome and dapper gentleman. His command of his voice as he carefully and systematically delineated his case was enough to sway even the most doubtful juror, and Patrice felt a budding apprehension. He had a powerful mastery of language and a most effective delivery, forcefully verbalizing his thoughts, then pausing for effect as he deliberately turned his back on the jury to pace the floor. Having given them

enough time to ponder his point, he would abruptly turn
to eye them fiercely in a well-calculated move, much like a
tiger stalking its prey. Patrice could not mistake the
spellbound look on the faces of the mesmerized jurors. A
quick glance at the judge showed his apparent accord, and
a sinking feeling began to overwhelm her. No wonder
Matt had been so nervous. Pollard really knew how to put
on a first-class show, and his prodigious reputation was
obviously well deserved.

This case of supposed collusion between T. J. Lewis
Enterprises' representatives and specified members of the
board of directors of Tec-Amtel Corporation regarding a
recent conglomerate acquisition contained so many gray
areas that, in fact, in no way could the entire truth
possibly ever be known. She was aware that the jury's
decision would depend solely upon the attorneys and their
respective credibility.

Patrice's reverie was suddenly interrupted by the judge.
"Mr. Monroe, are you ready to deliver your summation?"

Matt slowly rose from the chair. "Yes, I am, your honor,"
he said to the heavy-jowled thin-lipped judge as he approached the jury.

"You may proceed," the judge said.

The strain of the past weeks showed clearly on Matt's
handsome face, and compassionately, Patrice ached to
reassure him. She desperately hoped that the verdict
would go to T. J. Lewis Enterprises, yet there was no
denying Matt's opponent's strength and charisma.

Matt faced the jurors, then turned, and his eyes quickly
scanned the room, coming to rest upon a young blond
woman seated near the rear exit. Patrice! The sight of her
was like the first ray of sun after weeks of gloom, her
presence greatly reinforcing his courage. He began to
speak.

When he finished, his eyes sought Patrice, and hers
replied in private communion. It seemed there was still a
tacit bond between them.

Matt smiled before seating himself. Several jurors were
nodding their approval of his words. Judge Thomas Ed-

ward Vaughn then gave the jury their instructions. "This court is now in recess until such time as the jury renders its decision." It was finally out of Matt's hands, and relief overcame him. Yet there was still one more gray area to resolve. He strode toward the rear of the courtroom, but she was nowhere in sight.

At three-thirty P.M., the buzzer sounded, announcing that court was reconvening. It wasn't until Judge Vaughn prepared to ask for a verdict that Matt lost his newfound calm. If the jury ruled in Pollard's favor, it would certainly be a personal blow to Matt's sense of justice. Just then he noticed T. J., who had just entered with Patrice. He was so lost in his own thoughts that he barely heard the judge, but he returned his attention when he heard, "Mr. Foreman, you will please tell the court your verdict."

"Your honor, we, the jury, find the defendants not guilty."

For an instant, Matt was stunned. "Not guilty" echoed in his head, bringing a most pleasurable release from the pent-up hell that had tortured him all these weeks. It was a dream come true! He had actually beaten the sharpest attorney on the West Coast, and more importantly, a new precedent had been set. He couldn't even remember the exact words of his closing summation, only that his true beliefs had been voiced and the feeling was marvelous.

There was a buzz of voices in the courtroom. Judge Vaughn sharply struck his gavel. "Order in the court! At this time, I would like to thank the jurors for their time and effort. Court dismissed."

Appearing considerably annoyed, Norman Pollard approached Matt. "Well, Monroe, it looks as though you've won this time. But I'm on to you now, and you'll play hell beating me again," he said with a condescendingly wry smile.

"Anytime, Pollard. I'll look forward to another contest," Matt returned as he brushed hurriedly past him in a search for Patrice and their employer. A beaming Lewis met him halfway down the aisle, hand outstretched.

"Well, goddamn! You did it!" he said jubilantly. "I'm

mighty proud of you. Patrice told me your closing speech was a dandy." He grabbed Matt's hand and pumped it vigorously.

Matt smiled, but his eyes wandered about the room. "Speaking of Patrice, where is she?"

Lewis arched his heavy brows. "She said something about a little air. She must be outside."

"I need to talk to her," Matt said. "There's another speech that's long overdue."

Lewis became serious. "You'd better choose your words carefully. I know it's none of my business, but that little girl means a lot to me. Winning attorney or not, I just want you to know that you'll have to answer to me if you ever hurt her again."

Matt's expression was rueful. "For whatever it's worth, T. J., I never meant to hurt her. She's probably the best friend I've ever had."

For a moment, Lewis's dark eyes bored into Matt's unflinchingly. Then, slapping the younger man's back, he said, "Go to it if you think you can dodge the reporters. They're lying in wait outside the door. You're quite a celebrity, you know. I think Pollard, in all his long, illustrious career, has only lost one other case. You're the new 'David' of the press, and far better copy than 'Goliath.'"

Matt grinned. "I'm really not so sure, but I certainly did learn something in this courtroom," he said as though he had discovered a great secret. "Well, I'll see you in the morning, T. J. Right now I need to thank a lady for her moral support." With that, he left the older man. Shrugging off the reporters who besieged him with cameras and note pads, he pushed his way through the crowd.

"Got a statement, Mr. Monroe? What are your plans for the future? Do you intend to stay with T. J. Lewis Enterprises?"

Matt gave them a pleasant smile. "Ladies, gentlemen, please! I need a breath of air. It's been a rather difficult day."

"What do you think of Pollard?"

"As an attorney, he's one of the best."

"Do I detect an undertone?" the news hound jibed.

Matt frowned impatiently. Then, spying Patrice who was sitting on a bench at the foot of the courthouse steps, he quickly closed the attempted interview. "That's all I have to say at present. Mr. Pollard is a most worthy opponent, and I look forward to future confrontations with him. Now, if you don't mind, there's someone I must talk to."

As Matt neared, Patrice rose and extended her hand. "Congratulations, Matt. You were superb," she said sincerely, and with a laudatory smile.

He took her proffered hand and happily grinned, and while the cameras flashed, he half-whispered, "Let's get out of here. I've had my fill of this place."

For a moment she hesitated, then she shook her head. "I came here with T. J."

"I think he knows that you're in good hands." And with his arm protectively about her, he ushered her quickly away from the reporters before she could protest further. She allowed herself to be pulled along, stopped suddenly, and turned to face him.

"You," she said slowly, her eyes glistening, "will always be dear to my heart. Don't ever forget that. I think, in time, I can be your friend, but I can't be second-best, much as I might be tempted, if you know what I mean."

Her words told him that she wouldn't be going with him this time. He studied Patrice's face silently, nodded to her, and his lips brushed her forehead before he turned and left.

Patrice turned away with a sigh. No use pining for what might have been. All her tears had been shed. It was time to get back into the mainstream of life. She turned back to the courthouse to look for T. J., and walked briskly toward him where he was surrounded by reporters. She was finally putting all the past to rest.

Chapter Eighteen

Shawn's mind ran in circles as she walked into the office earlier than usual on Tuesday morning. She had taken a three-day weekend to supervise the movers and to straighten out cupboards, closets, and generally put her new home in order. There were still a lot of loose ends, things that she couldn't part with but really had no space for. She could not shake the depression that assailed her from going through her father's things and having to dispose of belongings that brought back a flood of memories recalling their time together. It had been extremely difficult, and if not for Andrew's helping hand and cheerful attitude, she would have spent the weekend in tears.

As spent as she was, it was almost a relief to return to work. The impersonal trappings of the office seemed to stiffen her backbone, and she immediately attacked her work, catching up on a mountain of details that had piled up from the previous day.

"Well, good morning, boss lady. I see you've favored us with your presence today," Tony Rizzo teased as he walked in.

Shawn smiled. "I would much rather have been here than in the throes of moving. How's it going?"

"Not bad. The sub is putting the finishing touches on the

recreation building at Sun Haven, and we're near ready to plant, providing we don't get any more rain."

She agreed. "Rain has been a problem, hasn't it? I don't know how you've managed to get the irrigation and back-filling finished with all the mud."

He shrugged. "Oh, hell, I probably wouldn't know what to do with dry ground anymore. I think I'm growing webbed feet!"

"How's the building look?"

"Pretty good."

"Great. Any trouble with the kids?"

"Hell, no, they're too busy since you and Bellows got them in line. The most I see of them is when they tool by, hauling loads of trash in that clunker of a truck Bellows gave 'em. Except for once, they did meander over to check out the recreation building. At the rate they're going, they'll have converted enough junk into cash for that pool table and whatever else they want. They're sure anxious for the building to open. It's been a lot easier running that place since you met with them. Maybe you missed your calling. You should have been a counselor for delinquents."

She smiled. "They're not really bad kids, Tony. In fact, I rather like them, especially Jason. Now, there's a nice little boy."

"I suppose you're right. All they needed was someone to care about them, but I would have sworn they needed a few swift kicks."

"I darn near agreed with you at one point. Now, tell me about Arcadia."

"Well, Nelson's having the same problem with the rain, but he's got the trenches all dug in the parking lot for the irrigation to the planting areas. He's hitting it hard. The rains are the worst in January and February, so if we can get the pipes and the touch-up grading done before the weather decides to really get serious, hopefully we can get in the curbs and the asphalt between rains. There's just no getting around it, winter puts a damper on the best-laid plans."

"Yes," she said, "it does. Still, it sounds like you're making a great deal of progress."

"Yeah, if we can keep this momentum, then when Sun Haven's finished and we throw all of the men on Arcadia, we'll meet that April sixteenth opening day."

"I like that kind of talk. Keep up the good work, Tony. We're committed."

Shawn's intercom buzzed. "Don't forget, I'll be leaving for my dental appointment at ten o'clock," Audrey reminded as Tony waved his way out of Shawn's office.

"Glad you jogged my memory," Shawn said. "No problem, I'll catch the phone. I have to go to the bank this afternoon, but I'll be in the office all morning."

Shawn's spirits soared at the thought of fully paying off the loan. It was the only thing that had made selling her beloved home worthwhile. Now the business would really be hers, debt-free.

Her thoughts were again interrupted by the familiar buzz from Audrey. "I have Elsa Sommers on line one, and I'll be leaving now."

"Thanks, I've got it. Have fun!"

"Sure," Audrey said sarcastically.

Shawn laughed and punched the button. "Good morning, Elsa. How are you?" she asked warmly.

"That's exactly what I called to ask you," Elsa returned. "You must be on the verge of moving. What can I do to help?"

"Oh, nothing, dear heart. I'm already in—moved over the weekend, and took Monday, too."

"You mean, you didn't even let me know? How did you manage all by yourself?"

Shawn laughed. "It wasn't easy, but I had help. I really couldn't have done it without Andy."

"Andy? Who's Andy?"

"Andy's a long story. He's just a great friend."

"Oh, a friend." She laughed. "I see. That's good. I'm glad you're getting out more."

"I have to. I've shed enough tears over Matt." Then, changing the subject, she inquired, "When can I expect a visit from you? The condo isn't anything to brag about at this point, but it'll keep me dry," she remarked as she noticed the rain forming a soft mist on her office window. "Tell you what, if you're free, why don't you come and spend a couple of days with me? I'd love to see you, and I could certainly use your expertise in the decorating department."

"Sounds great! Would Wednesday night be all right? I can stay till Friday evening."

"Terrific. I'll leave the office a little early and expect you for dinner about six, okay? 'Bye, Elsa."

Shawn had no sooner replaced the phone when it jangled anew. "Well—busy, busy," she muttered as she reached for the instrument. "Good morning, McCullough Landscaping, Shawn McCullough speaking."

"Good morning, Shawn," Matt replied.

Hearing his deep voice was like a dousing with ice water, and her first inclination was to hang up. If she hadn't been so stunned, she would have. Shawn held the phone in midair and stared, unseeing, at it. What could he possibly have to say to her, and short of hanging up, what could she say to him?"

"Shawn?"

"Yes."

"Please don't hang up. Hear me out."

"I don't see what you can possibly say that will matter now," she stated coolly.

"It will matter a lot to me," he said, deadly calm. "Even the accused deserve a hearing, Shawn."

There was a resolve in his voice that brought her up short. "Okay, Matt, I'll hear you out."

"I have to see you in person, even if it's finished for us. I'm flying in Friday night. Can you meet me at the airport? I have to talk to you. I want you to know that I care for you very much, no matter what you now believe."

"I'll allow you the time between flights," she said evenly, ignoring his tender words, "but I can't give you any more time than I've already foolishly given."

"That's all I ask. I'll be on the commuter flight."

There was a soft click and he was gone. Shawn dazedly held the phone for a moment. What had she let herself in for? More heartache? Yet she couldn't slow the adrenaline that the mere sound of his voice had generated, just as it had when they were much younger. Somehow he had the uncanny ability to break through her resolve and . . . manipulate her? She brushed away the thought as soon as it occurred to her, and her thoughts flashed to Matt's gentleness and consideration in the days after her father's death. He had been a support *and* her idealized friend since adolescence, for God's sake, she admitted. Their love affair had been a crushing failure, perhaps, but he *had been* a friend nonetheless.

"But it's finished. I must be a fool to even give him the time of day." She dropped the receiver back on the cradle, thinking there was something distinctly different in his voice that she'd not heard before. What had happened to him? Had the beautiful blond deserted him? Yet his matter-of-fact tone seemed incongruous for a man on the rebound.

"Damn you, Shawn McCullough, one phone call doesn't mean anything! You have work to do. Quit trying to second-guess."

By two o'clock, she had nearly succeeded in dismissing Matt's call from her mind. There was no sense spending the entire week wondering what he would say on Friday. She picked up her purse and tucked a check into the zipper compartment. This particular check was too important to mail. She would hand deliver it.

As she entered this time, the austerity of the bank could not undermine her confidence. She was a woman about to make good her promise. Shawn smiled charmingly at the same stuffy loan officer who had originally attempted to thwart her meeting with the bank president. "I would like to speak with Mr. Kendall," she once again stated.

"Ms. McCullough, I believe," he said, still patronizing.

"You remembered my name, Mr. Trusdale."

"Ah, yes," he said with an air that implied, how could I forget. "I believe he's tied up at the moment. Is there any way I can assist you?"

"No, I'll wait a few minutes. I really prefer to deal with Mr. Kendall. No offense, you understand," she said sweetly.

Shawn took a seat outside Kendall's door and crossed her shapely legs, swinging her foot a bit impatiently.

Trusdale frowned as he walked past her into Kendall's plush office. "Ms. McCullough is here to see you," she overheard him say.

Kendall's eyes raised from the documents he'd been studying. "McCullough? McCullough? Oh, yes, Shawn McCullough. As I recall, that charming little lady waits for no one. Perhaps you'd better send her in."

"Ms. McCullough," Kendall said, standing when Shawn entered his office, "please have a chair. Now, then, how can I assist you?"

She smiled, her blue eyes sparkling. It was a much more comfortable atmosphere than she had encountered at their first meeting. "No, it's not a problem that brings me this time. I merely want to express my gratitude for your support and give you this." Beaming, she handed him the check that paid the debt in full.

Kendall glanced at the amount and smiled approvingly. "Wonderful," he said. "I want you to know, Ms. McCullough, you can feel free to call on me anytime."

By five P.M. Wednesday evening, Shawn was busy preparing dinner for Elsa, who was due to arrive within the hour. This time she would surprise her friend with a savory gourmet meal instead of chili dogs; that is, if she could find all the fixings that she had hurriedly unpacked during the move. "Let's see," she questioned herself, "where did I hide all the seasonings? Aha! They're still in the carton." She searched through the packing crate's contents, pulling out onion powder and garlic.

Within a few minutes Shawn had potatoes au gratin put

together and in the oven. She had just washed romaine
lettuce for the salad when the buzzer sounded. Shawn
glanced at her watch; five-twenty. How nice! Elsa was
early. They could enjoy a leisurely drink while she finished cooking. She hit the security door release to the
outside, and by the time her visitor had gotten upstairs,
Shawn had dried her hands and opened the door.

Hearing footsteps on the stairs, she called, "Come on in,
Elsa. I just have to stir something." Then, dashing to the
oven, she grabbed the hot pads and mixed the bubbling au
gratin casserole. "There, that should do it," she said,
hearing the front door shut. "I'm out here, Elsa."

"Now, do I look like an Elsa?" an annoyed masculine
voice asked.

Shawn whirled around in surprise to face Andrew.
"Well," she said, eyeing him exaggeratedly from his
golden-bronze wavy hair to his broad shoulders and down
to his expensive suede shoes. "I think not. As a matter of
fact, you look very handsome indeed," she teased. "Quite a
change from our weekend grubbies."

"And you, Shawn McCullough"—he looked her up and
down in the same deliberate fashion—"could drive a man
mad by wearing that slinky lounging outfit. I don't
know what color you'd call it, but it's passionate pink to
me!"

She laughed. "It's magenta, my color-blind friend. Oh,
Andy, it's good to see you. I thought after all that moving,
it'd be a while before you wanted to see this place again."

"On the contrary, I feel I have an investment." He
grinned. "Actually, I thought you might like to sneak
away from the unpacking and have a quick dinner with
me, but I can see that you have other plans."

"That was a very nice thought, but you're right, I have a
good friend coming over to stay a couple of days. Tell you
what. Why don't you join us for dinner? I'd love for two of
my favorite people to meet. You'll like her, Andy, she's a
dear! What do you say?"

"I really shouldn't. I have to be somewhere by seven-
thirty." He glanced at his watch. "It's already five-thirty."

"Oh, come on, dinner'll be ready by six, and I promise you won't have to do dishes tonight. Just fix us a drink."

"Sold," he said, heading for the liquor cabinet. "What's your pleasure?"

"Um, let's see—a martini sounds good for a change, very dry."

"Dry it is," he said just as the buzzer sounded.

"Must be Elsa this time," Shawn said as she once more clicked the door release and went to let her friend in. "Oh, Andy, make one for her, too, please?" she called over her shoulder.

"Right."

Elsa was comfortably clad in ivory slacks and a rust-colored cowl-necked sweater, and her smile, as usual, was warm. Shawn hugged her. "It's so good to see you."

"And you grow prettier every day," Elsa remarked fondly.

"I'll second that," Andy's male voice interjected.

Elsa's brows arched at seeing an immaculately dressed, suave, handsome man carrying a tray of drinks toward them. "You didn't tell me we were entertaining a gentleman, or I would have dressed for the occasion."

Bellows laughed. "Well, ma'am, most gentlemen would prefer a beautiful lady not too dressed, if you know what I mean."

"Andy," Shawn said indignantly as she nudged his arm.

"Careful now, or the martinis will be extra dry!" he teased. Setting the tray on the coffee table, he handed a drink to Shawn's guest. "Sorry about that remark. I just couldn't resist. I'm Andrew Bellows, and I presume that you're Elsa."

At the mention of his name, Elsa was startled. Her mind flashed. So this is the Andrew Bellows McCullough had raged about, the infamous building magnate, seducer of women, breaker of men. "So you're the legendary Andrew Bellows," she voiced aloud in surprise, studying him with a steady gaze.

He laughed. "That's just a tag the media loves to hang

on me. Actually, I put on my pants the same as any other man."

She grinned. "It rather looks that way." She liked him, she decided and wondered about Shawn's feelings for him.

Andrew handed Shawn a martini and picked up the last glass. "To good friends." He clinked their glasses.

Shawn's smile embraced them both. "May we long remain."

Elsa took a sip, then, looking around, she remarked, "Shawn, I like the place. It's much nicer than you described."

"Do you really approve? I guess I'm just prejudiced. Andy, why don't you show Elsa around while I put the finishing touches on dinner."

"Oh, no, dear. There's no hurry. I can see it all later. We'll join you in the kitchen."

Later, they were enjoying a leisurely cognac after a most pleasant meal. Shawn was pleased to find that Elsa and Andrew fell into easy conversation as though they had known each other for ages, talking about everything from the building trade to politics and Christmas gifts.

Good heavens, Shawn thought, Christmas is only two weeks off. What will I do for the work crews? She was vaguely aware of her dinner guests' conversation while making plans. A Christmas tree for the office. She would have Tony pick up one tomorrow, plus a small one for her new home as well. Perhaps gift certificates for the employees this year instead of turkeys. McCullough had always made a big thing of handing out turkeys, and she didn't want to remind the men or herself of his absence.

"Shawn?" Andrew said, "you're awfully quiet. I'm afraid I've monopolized the conversation."

"No, Andy," she replied. "I've enjoyed you and Elsa getting to know each other. I was just thinking about Christmas. It sure has crept up on me this year! I usually love spending a lot of time decorating the house and"—she looked around—"I haven't the vaguest idea where the decorations are." She put her hand to her mouth. "You don't suppose I gave them to the Goodwill by mistake? Oh, Andy, I must have, now that I think of it. I haven't seen them anywhere."

"You can have some of mine, dear. I have plenty," Elsa said.

"You're an angel, Elsa. You know how I love to decorate the tree."

"I should," she said with a laugh. "Remember, dear, how we used to string popcorn and tie big red bows, and you always insisted on Christmas music. Lord, that was fun! I think your father and I got more pleasure out of watching you than from Christmas itself."

"Yes, McCullough always said that I should have been one of Santa's elves," she said wistfully.

Andrew could see her eyes glisten momentarily, and he was again overwhelmed by her wholehearted passion for life and her strong attachment for her father; he knew that Christmas would be even more difficult for her than Thanksgiving had been.

Later at Shawn's door, as Andrew was leaving to make his evening business appointment, he gently kissed her on the forehead, and gave Elsa a light hug.

"I enjoyed meeting you, Andy," Elsa said with sincerity. "I can see that Shawn has a good friend in you."

By his suddenly serious expression, Elsa could tell that she had struck a raw nerve.

Shawn smiled, oblivious of Andy's wince. "Yes. Don't tell him, but he *is* pretty great." Then turning to Andrew she said, "I'm glad that I talked you into joining us for dinner. It was fun. Good night, Andy."

"I'll call you tomorrow," he promised as he left.

When he was gone, Elsa stood eyeing Shawn for a silent moment. "Jack may have disliked that man, but he reminds me so much of McCullough."

Shawn grinned. "Doesn't he?"

Chapter Nineteen

San Francisco Airport loomed in the distance: a maze of concrete, lights, construction barriers, buses, taxicabs, and people. A string of jets on final approach cast their luminous shadows on the moonlit bay. San Francisco Airport traffic was at its evening peak, and the controllers were spacing aircraft tighter than usual. As Shawn neared the parking garage, she said to herself, "Some things never change. This place is always in a turmoil." Around and around, from one level to another, Shawn and her Spitfire searched for a temporary slot. Why was she hurrying like this? It would serve him right if she was late. Yet her very blood was rushing in anticipation, and she could not still the excitement that vibrated through her with every breath. Why couldn't she feel this way about Andrew? she mused, surprised at the thought.

Shawn jammed on the brakes as she saw the backup lights of a Firebird relinquishing a space. The Spitfire slid easily into the vacancy, and she hurriedly locked the car door and headed for the terminal.

On the moving sidewalk that seemed to be going in slow motion, she shifted her weight from one foot to the other. Impatient with the conveyance's snail's pace, she quickly bypassed the other travelers and their baggage, leaving the slower moving patrons in her wake.

At the foot of the escalator, she hesitated but a moment, choosing the stairs as a more expedient route. A fleeting glance at the board revealed that flight 902 would be ten minutes late. "Damn," she swore, "after all this rush!" It was ironic, but right now she needed Andrew to bolster her courage.

She slipped into the bar and ordered a sherry, downing the amber liquid in hopes of steadying her pounding heart and calming the storm within.

Ten minutes later, Shawn stood in the waiting area, watching the passengers of flight 902 coming up the ramp. The procession seemed endless, finally dwindling down to a scattered few. Had something come up, like another blond, to have made him miss the flight? Disgustedly, Shawn paced back and forth and finally slouched into a chair, tapping her fingers on the arm. She was about to leave when the unmistakable voice of Matt Monroe turned her resolve to butter.

"Shawn," he said, "beautiful as always! Where can we talk?"

The long-awaited sight of him abruptly unleashed the torrent of feelings that she had sought so hard to suppress. A part of her wanted desperately to melt in his arms, and yet another wished he had not come. "Matt, I don't have anything to say to you, but I am willing to listen because of what we once had," she said tersely.

"That's all I ask," he said with a resolute calm. "Shall we have a drink in the bar?"

"All right," she agreed quietly.

He made no move to touch her other than taking her hand to help her to her feet. His touch sent immediate shivers up her arm, and her eyes deliberately avoided his. If she could only ignore the entreaty in his gaze, she might be able to sort out her emotions logically. The power he still held over her was frightening, and she wasn't sure she could hear him out without falling victim to his charm.

When they were seated in the dimly lit lounge, she could stand it no longer. "It's your sixty minutes. Say what you have to say and let's get on with our lives," she said in a firm voice that belied the tumult boiling within.

He grimaced ruefully. "I deserved that. You know, all the way up here, I've thought about what I could possibly say to you, and it comes down to whether or not you can understand the situation I was in."

Her sapphire eyes met his green, imploring gaze across the candlelight, but she said nothing.

"The truth is, I did love you and I do love you now. At one time I was ready to love Patrice, but when I found you again— Well, that was it for me. All I wanted was to have you forever. I forgot about everything and everyone else until the flight back to Los Angeles."

She looked at him expectantly. "And . . . ?"

"Well, then I realized that, although I was not committed to Patrice, I did owe her an explanation. You see, we were very close, and she was picking me up at the airport. My intention was to take her to dinner and honestly explain about you. I had hoped that she would understand. But the accident wiped out any chance of my explaining."

"Accident? What accident?"

"Patrice wanted me to drive, and I won't deny that I was extremely nervous about telling her because she was acting so much warmer than she had ever been. It was as if she had decided she was in love with me and had only realized it while I was gone. That made it even harder; I didn't want to hurt her."

"Since we're being so honest," Shawn said with a tinge of sarcasm, "what was your relationship with Patrice before I came along?"

Matt flinched imperceptibly. "Do you want me to tell you that I made love to her, that we spent a lot of time together at work and socially? Does it really matter? That was before you. After you, everything changed."

"Matt, you don't understand. If you loved me, how could you possibly not trust me to understand?" Her hurt showed, and she knew it, but there was no way she could conceal it.

Matt shrugged. "I don't know. I was so confused, so upset. I know I handled this whole thing badly, but don't you see, Shawn? There was the possibility she might never walk again, and it was my fault."

"So, you sought to do penance by destroying two other lives—or is it only mine being destroyed?"

Matt sighed helplessly. "You'll never know the hell I went through trying to understand my own feelings, and more importantly, deal with my obligations."

She studied his face, and the honesty rang clear in his straightforward answers. Her heart was tugged, yet she was reluctant to fall under his spell, and that would have been oh, so easy. She picked up her purse. "I'm not sure that you actually know what love is. If only you had told me, I would have understood. You gave me no credit." She shook her head. "Matt, I will not be hurt anymore. Please, just go back to L.A. and sort out your feelings. I get the impression that you're still not really sure."

He looked at her sadly, then nodded dejectedly. "If that's what you want. Then, that's what I'll do." He took her hand and said, "Believe me, I do love you, and thanks for listening."

Shawn watched him walk away, a small tear trickling down her cheek. Was it for Matt or herself? Perhaps it was for the sadness, the heartache of words unspoken. She rubbed at her eyes angrily as she walked from the lounge. She could not stop her tear-blurred gaze from chasing down the corridor after Matt's retreating figure. Suddenly all her resolution evaporated, and in a voice that she barely recognized as her own, she cried out, "Matt, come back!"

He spun on his heel and in quick, long strides was beside her, covering the distance in seconds.

Shawn said sheepishly, "I don't know why I called you back. I only know that I can't let you go like this."

"It doesn't matter. I can take the next flight or stay with the folks. I'm here as long as you want me. Where shall we go?"

Shawn shook her dark, curly head. "Let's get away from all this. I can't think with so much confusion."

"We can have privacy in your car, if you don't mind having to drive me back here or to the folks'."

She nodded. "That's easy enough."

They were silent as they headed away from the airport. Finally Shawn broke the long silence. "Oh, hell, Matt, this is ridiculous. It's too cold to sit in the car, and we need a quiet place to talk if we can ever make any sense out of this. Do you think we could go to my new place and just talk it out?" She glanced over and squarely met his eyes. "I can't just forget everything that quickly. What I'm saying is that settling this is too important to put a time limit on what we need to say. I'll warm up some chili, and you can stay in the guest room if you wish."

He nodded. "Sounds fair to me, but what's this about a new place? You mean that offer on the house was firm?"

"Yes. I'm in a condo now."

"How do you like it?"

"It's the pits."

He laughed and twisted in the passenger seat to face her. "Not like a house, is it?" he asked.

"No, but it's not really so bad. I'm just spoiled. Saratoga is quite a nice picturesque little town. I'll get used to the change eventually."

An hour later, the smell of chili wafted into the living room and soon they were both eating quietly, each absorbed in his own thoughts, Shawn wanting to know more about the accident that had not yet been explained, and Matt torn by indecision as to how to best handle the next few hours.

"That really hit the spot," he said as he finished up the last of the chili. "I'm glad we came here, it's a whole lot better place to talk."

She smiled tentatively, beginning to relax in the familiar warmth of Matt's company. "Would you like an after-dinner brandy?"

"With chili?" He laughed. "Oh, well, what the hell. Remember when we had pizza and wine?"

She giggled. "Not bad, was it?"

For a moment their eyes met and locked. It was as though yesterday and all the memories they had shared since childhood came rushing back to test them. If he touched her right now, there would be no stopping him, and they both knew it.

Shawn abruptly left the table and went to the liquor cabinet. Pouring two brandies, she said with her back to him, "Let's sit in the living room and relax."

Matt joined her silently, still groping for the right words while his arms physically ached to hold her close. She was so beautiful, even in her present unrelenting mood.

Where Shawn would normally have put the drink in his hand, now she set it on the coffee table and fled instantly with her own drink to a rattan chair on the opposite side of the room. Matt picked up his glass and took a recliner chair several feet from her.

Shawn twirled her brandy, took a tiny sip, then looked up. "Tell me about the accident, Matt."

"Well"—he hesitated, showing her it was still difficult to talk about—"it happened when we left the airport on the way to my place. I'd been thinking about how to tell Patrice about us. It was one of those things you least expect. An older lady lost her brakes and swerved in front of me. It was so quick I never had time to stop. When I came to, Patrice was pinned under the dashboard, crumpled in a pool of blood. Oh, God, how awful it was! I thought she was dead, this vivacious woman who had been so animated a few seconds before." He hesitated, again reliving the scene with a shudder.

Shawn's expression was sympathetic. "It must have been dreadful," she murmured.

Matt cleared his throat and sipped his brandy. "As it turned out, Patrice had been critically hurt, and I felt like an irresponsible jerk and doubly blamed myself for having tried to bolster my courage with gin on the flight. Even so, I still don't know if I could have prevented the collision if I had been completely sober. All I know is that it happened and it was hell! All that time in the hospital, waiting to see if she'd live or die— I can't explain the guilt, the agony. Shawn, do you know what it's like to think you may be responsible for someone's death, especially someone who's dear to you?"

"No, Matt, but I can imagine. It must have been terrible. What I can't for the life of me understand is why you didn't tell me all of this? Are you really sure that you didn't love her?" Shawn's words hung in the silence of the room, then she said softly, "Is it possible that you loved both of us?"

Matt stared into his brandy glass and reflected a moment before answering. "That thought crossed my mind, but what I feel for you is something far different, something I've never before felt with anyone." He shook his head. "It's possible that I did love her. I don't know. All I know is I had to take care of her, see her through. No matter what I felt for you, Shawn, I couldn't hurt her on top of the accident and all. And yes, I think I do love her in many ways but not the way I love you."

"Are you really certain of your feelings now, Matt?"

His emerald eyes locked with hers, and the seriousness of his gaze was unmistakable. "Yes, I am. After the first few attempts to reach you, I knew I had to be positive to be fair to both of you and myself as well. I had already hurt the two most important people in my life, and I needed time to think things through. After a couple of weeks of sorting out my guilt feelings, I told Patrice how I feel about you. But Shawn, no matter how much I love you, Patrice will always be a special person to me, she knows that. And I don't want you to think otherwise. It wouldn't be true."

Shawn sighed wistfully. "She must love you very much to understand and support you that way," she said, and suddenly thought of Andrew. Was it possible that Andrew loved her in the same way?

Matt nodded. "Yes, it would seem she does, but I can't be responsible for the way Patrice feels."

"That may well be, but put yourself in my place when I walked in to find the two of you on the floor. How would you have felt if you had walked in on me and another man in the same situation?"

He reached for her hand. "If it had been me, I'm sure I'd have found it hard to handle, too, but it wasn't the way it seemed. She was only rubbing my back. I'd had a tense day in court with the case winding down, and I was exhausted. Oh, I won't deny that I could have easily taken advantage of the moment, but it was you I loved, Shawn, only you. I won't lie to you: I was tempted but I couldn't. Believe it or not, I was trying desperately to tell her about you that very night, and I had meant to get her situated back in her own apartment and out of mine."

"Oh, come on Matt, a back rub in a low-cut gown? That's pretty hard to swallow." She pulled her hand away.

"I know how it must have appeared, and all I can say is that there's only one woman in my life, if she'll have me, and that's you. I hope you can understand how much Patrice needed a friend, and that's all it was."

"Yes," she acquiesced, thinking of Andrew, dear Andy, who always seemed to foresee her needs. "I do understand, Matt. I have a good friend, too."

He nodded. "Then forgive my inability to call you? That's all I ask for now."

She slowly shook her head from side to side. "I don't know—I'll try, Matt, but right now I'm so terribly tired. I think I'd like to turn in. We can talk in the morning."

"Yeah, I'm pretty bushed myself. Get a good night's sleep, and please think about what I've said. God knows it's the truth. I could have invented a more convincing story if I were going to lie to you."

She nodded as she rose. "Take the first bedroom to your right," she said. "Oh, by the way, what's happening with the case?"

"It was tough but we won. I'll be off to South Africa the first of the week. That's one of the reasons I wanted to see you tonight."

"Congratulations, Matt. That's great; the case I mean. What about South Africa?"

"T. J. Lewis Enterprises is thinking of buying a chromium mine there. I'm going to check out the legal technicalities. But how about your business? How's it going?"

Shawn was pleasantly surprised. It was the first time that Matt had mentioned her work of his own accord. Perhaps her interests were important to him after all. "Not bad. Things are going better, especially at Arcadia Lane. It's going to be quite a unique shopping center one of these days. I'll have to show it to you sometime."

"I'd like that," he said sincerely. "I want to know everything that's happened to you, but it can keep till morning." He stretched his lean frame to his full six feet. "Good night, honey," he said as he left the room with no attempt to touch her.

Shawn watched him leave, her mind a jumble, wanting to believe that Matt was sincere about his feelings but unable to sort out her own.

Saturday morning at the airport, Matt and Shawn stood hand in hand next to the window in the boarding area.

"Shawn, I love you. Let me love you, please?" he pleaded in her ear.

His whispered words almost blotted out what was left of her resistance. Their fate was in her hands, and though she believed he loved her, the wound was still too fresh, too painful. Shawn pulled away. "Matt, I do believe you love me. It isn't that," she tried to explain.

His smoldering eyes intensely searched her face, but he was silent.

"I'm still hurt," she said, pleading for his understanding and yes, testing his love. "It's like starting all over again. We need to build trust in each other. I don't want to be ruled by desire, only love, real and honest love."

Though he ached inside, he knew that he alone was to blame for the shattering of her trust, and his face mirrored his acceptance. He lightly kissed her forehead and murmured, "I love you, Shawn, in time you'll know." Then with all the strength he could muster, he added, "But when I get back from South Africa, we'll be together for the rest of our lives, if I have my way. Then we can really make plans."

She looked up at his handsome face. "We'll see. I hope so, Matt." Then, recalling the unhappy silences of before, she couldn't stop herself from saying, "You will call me and write this time, won't you?"

"You know I will. This time nothing's going to stop me."

"Last call to board flight 710," an impersonal voice announced over the loudspeaker.

He reached for her hand. "God, if only I could take you with me. Hey, wait a minute, why can't I?"

She laughed. "I can't just run off and leave the business. Who would run the place?"

"It'd only be for a month or so, honey. Christmas together in South Africa, wouldn't that be something?"

"Matt, you're plain crazy! I can't be gone that long right now. Too many things on the agenda need my attention."

"Well, if I can't talk you into it, my love, I shall have to depart, or that plane will be minus one passenger." He leaned down and kissed her soundly, then raced down the ramp, leaving Shawn gazing sparkle-eyed after him. Perhaps their separation had been a blessing in disguise. It had forced them to go a little slower, to really test their love. The physical desire, when it was finally satisfied, she knew would be pure heaven. How different she felt from last night. "Matt," she whispered, "please don't let it all be a dream."

Chapter Twenty

Monday sailed by quickly for Matt. He felt certain that Shawn and he could begin their marriage plans when he got back from the firm's negotiations in South Africa. It would be so wonderful once the landscaping business was sold, and she could concentrate on being his wife. Coming home to a beautiful wife each night, sharing the trials of the day together, somewhat the way he and Patrice had, would be wonderful. And later, making love to their heart's content—oh, God, just the thought was exciting. Shawn, beautiful Shawn, would finally be his completely, and he meant to take good care of her. As Patrice had said, he could write his own ticket now that he had beaten Pollard.

At the time that she had said it, he'd given the possibility little thought, but after the call this morning from Allan Woodhall, the aerospace tycoon and well-known political manipulator, Matt suddenly realized the bounty of opportunities that could be available to him should he decide to enter the political arena. Woodhall had indicated his support and backing for a seat in the state legislature. This could open the door to his becoming state attorney general and eventually, perhaps even governor, Matt mused.

It was quite an offer, and Patrice had been more on

target than she could have realized. He had wanted to see her before he left but somehow had not been able to catch her for even a few moments during their busy schedules throughout the day. Not being able to share his happiness or discuss the wonderful new opportunity with her was disappointing.

Matt glanced at his watch. Six P.M. His bedroom was a shambles due to his haphazard and hasty packing. Perhaps she was home now, and he might reach her by phone. He stuffed an assortment of socks into his bag, snapped it shut, and dialed her number.

An hour later en route to the airport, he was glad to have, at last, caught her and happier still that she was seeing him off. It was almost like old times but without the tension of their last meeting. They had shared so much in the past that confiding in Patrice was a habit, and he could hardly wait to tell her about his visit with Shawn and Woodhall's call.

He spoke briefly about Shawn. Patrice made no reply, but her knuckles whitened on the steering wheel.

However, her reaction went unnoticed by Matt in his present euphoric state, and he continued. "That's only part of my good news. There's a possibility that I may run for state legislature next year. Woodhall called me this morning and gave me his backing, carte blanche. He said Roy Whatling is going to give up his seat after this term, and Woodhall thinks that I'm hot press right now."

"Oh, Matt, that's wonderful! Woodhall has quite a political machine behind him. If that's what you want, I don't see how you can lose. And the good you could do in that position is unlimited."

"Do you really think so?"

"Of course. You're perfect for the job, and that office could certainly use you."

"Hm. The idea is intriguing, though financially I'd be better off to stick with T. J."

"Yes, but, Matt, there's no end to the things you'd be

able to accomplish. Corporate law might pay well, but it's really more or less a dead end. In politics, you could make a lasting contribution to the entire state."

Matt grinned wryly. "You know, at one time I had dreams of becoming state attorney general."

"Why not, you might even go for governor."

"Governor," he said thoughtfully, visualizing Shawn, thinking of the responsibility that asked of a wife, all those political and social obligations. Matt nodded thoughtfully. He would have to think long and hard about this decision because it would mean giving up time and privacy for both he and Shawn. "I don't know. It's a big step. Maybe this trip is just what I need to be able to give it some serious thought," he said.

"I'm sure you'll make the right decision, Matt. Well, we're almost there. This is off the subject, but I hope it doesn't take forever to find a parking spot, or you'll miss your plane."

"Oh, don't bother. Just drop me off and I'll take it from there. It's easier."

She agreed, though she knew this might be the last time they would ever be alone. She reluctantly pulled to a stop before the TWA terminal. Matt hastily kissed her on the cheek before reaching for his luggage in the backseat. "Thanks for the lift. Stay well, honey."

Patrice touched his face for a brief moment, then quickly let her hand fall away. "It's always sad to say good-bye," she murmured.

Matt gazed at her long and tenderly. "It's never good-bye for us. I'll see you at the office in about a month," he said as he handed the bags to a skycap and shut the car door. With a smile and a wave of his hand, he was gone.

Now she decided she would really have to lay her dreams to rest. She quickly pulled away from the curb and entered the flow of traffic.

Matt paused at the sliding door of the terminal and looked back at her rapidly disappearing car. "There goes

one hell of a woman. The man she marries will certainly
be a lucky son of a bitch."

Shawn sat in her office leisurely sipping coffee, as if the
mountain of work would somehow vanish before her eyes.
It was a good Tuesday morning, and in spite of the
unusually heavy rains of the past few weeks, Sun Haven
was virtually wrapped up and Arcadia Lane was showing
amazing progress. This morning, Tony had made another
glowing report. The business outlook was exhilarating
and very much in keeping with her present mood. Still
basking in the afterglow of her visit with Matt, she was
almost sorry she'd put such a tight rein on their relationship, but it would take time to rebuild the trust she'd so
freely given in the beginning. Until then . . . Yet his call
from the airport had reinforced her belief in his sincerity,
and she was luxuriating in his evident adoration. Life was
wonderful; finally, everything had come together, and
those depressed and frightening days after McCullough's
funeral were now a part of the past.

As soon as Andrew returned from his New Orleans
conference, she would thank him for urging her to clear
the air with Matt. How great it would be if the two men in
her life could be friends. They might even share the
holidays together. She would introduce them at the first
opportunity.

Shawn was still relishing her newfound happiness when
the intercom jolted her.

"Yes, Audrey," she said, her happiness spilling into her
voice. "What can I do for you this fine morning?"

"Beats me, but you had better think of something," the
excited voice came back. "It's like Christmas Eve out here.
The whole reception area is full of packages, all from
Ornaments Galore. What'd you do, buy out the place?"

There was a sharp click and almost simultaneously
Shawn appeared, looking perplexed. "What on earth?" she
exclaimed. "I didn't buy anything!" Suddenly, she remembered her lost ornaments. "Don't tell me he took it upon
himself to replenish my supply of tree trimmings!"

"Replenish? I don't know about you, but this looks to me like a clear case of overstocking!"

There were ten bright red boxes bearing the exclusive logo of Ornaments Galore on their corners. The secretary handed Shawn a card. "I don't know who he is, but he's some kind of Santa's helper."

Shawn laughed. It had to be Andy. Only he and Elsa knew that she'd lost her Christmas trimmings in the move from the house to the condo, and only he would send ten boxes of expensive replacements. "I should have known," she said happily. How could she be cross with someone for helping to decorate her tree, especially when she was feeling on top of the world? Shawn opened the card with Audrey curiously peeking over her shoulder as she read Andrew's greeting. "Just a little thank-you for dinner. Love, Santa himself."

Shawn smiled and shook her head as she quickly opened a box, displaying all the anticipation of a child as she delicately fingered the lavish assortment of shiny red, gold, and green globes, each unique with its fancy, glittering, jeweled trim. "How like him. Let's open just one more," she said excitedly, "and see if it's the same."

It was eleven-fifteen A.M., and the reception area looked like a department store after a post-Christmas sale. Shawn had just finished examining all the contents of every box with an astounded Audrey beside her, and ornaments were strewn everywhere. "I love it, I love it! Isn't this fun, Audrey? I wish I had the tree here to decorate right this minute!"

The secretary gave her a grimacing smile as she surveyed the scattered boxes and the mountainous wrappings.

Giving the girl no time to answer, Shawn rattled impulsively. "Audrey, see if you can get a reservation for two at Altier's for one o'clock. I know a certain gentleman who deserves lunch."

She dashed to her office, leaving Audrey befuddled and stuttering, "B-but who?" as she surveyed the demolition of the reception area.

"Santa Claus, who else?" Shawn giggled before shutting her door. Then grabbing the phone, she quickly dialed Andrew's office.

"Bellow Enterprises," Jill answered.

"I'd like to speak to Andrew Bellows, please," Shawn requested.

"I'm sorry ma'am, he's not in at the moment. May I take a message?"

"No, I'll call back. When do you expect him?"

"Oh, hold on, he just walked in. May I tell him who's calling?"

"Just tell him it's one of Santa's elves."

There was silence on the other end as Jill pulled the receiver away from her ear and looked at it. She shrugged. "What is it about Christmas that makes everybody crazy?" she mumbled.

"Any important calls, Jill?" Andrew asked as he approached her desk looking extremely weary, loosening his tie as he spoke.

"Well, this one's a winner."

"Who is it?"

Jill raised her brows. "I don't know—some little elf?"

Andrew smiled. "I'll take it in here," he said, and the sudden bounce in his step as he entered his office was definitely noticeable.

"Hi, little elf," he said. "How are you?"

"I'm just great! I'll see you at your office in half an hour. This elf is buying you lunch, so don't take off your jacket as I won't take no for an answer. I have some great news that you have had a whole lot to do with."

Andrew grinned as he hung up the phone. Shawn sounded as though she couldn't wait to see him, and she had said that her good news had to do with him. Could it be what he'd been hoping for the past weeks?

"Hot damn!" he chortled as he burst from his office and grabbed Jill in a whirling bear hug. Then, plopping the flustered girl into her chair, he gave her a resounding kiss on the cheek. "No calls, Jill, I'm still on my trip." With that, he turned and dashed back to his office.

"I'll say you're still on a trip," she remarked.

Twenty minutes later, Andrew emerged from the clever hideaway beyond his office, clean-shaven, freshly dressed in a charcoal gray suit. Glancing at his watch, he walked briskly to the lobby, ignoring Jill's arched brows as he paced from the coffee machine to the doors that separated his exclusive office from the hallway and the rest of the many Bellows Enterprise offices.

When Shawn arrived, he grabbed his coat and was out the door, propelling her in his wake.

"Andy, hold on," she protested. "Did the jet fly you or did you fly the jet?"

He turned to look at her and impulsively hugged her to him. "I don't know, does it matter?" He laughed. Then, in a more serious tone, he half-whispered in her ear, "God, I missed you. Now, what's all this excitement about?"

"Well, first of all, thank you. I'll accept your generous gift on one condition."

"And that is?"

"That you come over tonight and help me do the tree. Oh, Andy, it'll be such fun! We can have Christmas music on the stereo and eggnog by the fireplace. I can hardly wait!" she blurted out in one breath as they hurried off the elevator.

"Hey, hold on—I'd love to, but you're forgetting something. Sam and the kids are counting on us at Sun Haven. Still . . . hell, I wish it were any other night we'd promised them."

Shawn stopped walking and turned to face him, disappointment clearly showing in her frown. "Oh, that's right." She pulled out her car key, at the same time searching her mind for some alternative.

Andrew took the key from her hand, unlocked her door, and went around to the other side. "Tell you what," he said when they were both in the car, "if you have no plans for Christmas Eve, why don't we do it then? It's only three days off, and I've always wanted an old-fashioned Christmas."

"That's not a bad idea. Oh, Andy, they're the most beautiful ornaments I've ever seen! I'm going to go crazy waiting!"

He laughed. "You know, I bet you will."

She grinned in response. "You know me very well, don't you, Andy?"

"Not well enough to read your mind. Now, what's this great news you have to tell me?"

"Oh, it's like good wine, it gets better with age. I'll tell you over lunch when I don't have to worry about this mass congestion of Christmas shoppers," she said as she carefully picked her way out of the parking lot.

Andrew smiled contentedly to himself and smoothed his hair with his hands as he adjusted his large frame to the confines of her Spitfire. "By the way, where are we going?"

"We're almost there," she returned in mock mystery.

Later, after being seated in the restaurant, the waiter asked, "Can I get you a drink?"

"Yes, the gentleman would like Chivas Regal on the rocks, and you may bring me an old-fashioned," Shawn was quick to reply. "Today it's my treat."

"My God, what's happening? You're certainly on a wonderful high," he chuckled in amazement.

"Yes," she said. "I'm on top of the world, and you helped put me there."

Andrew waited impatiently for her to explain, but Shawn just kept smiling silently and gazing out of the window, savoring a secret that she was not quite ready to share.

Andrew lit the small Havana cigar he'd been toying with, emitting tiny puffs as he studied the flushed excitement on her delicate face. She wore a beatific smile of inner contentment.

When the waiter placed their drinks before them, Shawn's attention focused on Andy. She raised her glass. "To you, Andy. You've changed my whole life."

He clicked her glass. "For the better, I hope."

"Oh, yes, Andy dear! I've never been so happy!" She paused. "You remember Matt?"

He nodded, not daring to speak, lest his happy anticipation vanish. Finally, Andrew could stand it no longer. "Yes?" he inquired as he attempted to sip his drink nonchalantly, his penetrating eyes never leaving her face.

"Oh, Andy, he loves me, he really loves me. And I have you to thank for making me listen to him. You are a very wise man, indeed!"

Andrew choked explosively on his drink. The hell I am, he thought. I'm a damn fool who should have left well enough alone. Somehow the words he knew she was waiting to hear stuck in his throat, and he toyed with his drink, unable to respond, for what he really wanted to say was to hell with Matt. *I* love you above and beyond everything else. Can he match that? But his pride and his ego kept him silent except for the involuntary grinding of his teeth.

Shawn noticed the muscles in his jaw tighten and saw the pain in his eyes. How could she have been so blind? Suddenly the picture became clear. She was stunned. All the time she had thought he was simply lusting for her body as he had said so many times, but his true feelings were all too evident as she looked at him. Andrew loved her, too, so deeply that he had put her happiness above his own. She instinctively reached for his hand. "Andy," she said quietly, "I didn't realize. Oh, please forgive my stupidity."

He squeezed her hand tightly. "It's all right. I'm happy for you. It's just that I'm beat. This trip has been twenty-five hours a day, constantly on the go." And all at once, he was extremely tired. Her declaration had hit him in the stomach like a red-hot iron, cauterizing his hopes, forever putting an end to a beautiful dream. He was a damn idiot to have dared think that by some miracle Shawn would love him, instead of Matt. He wanted to curse and he wanted to hold her so tight to his heart that she could never escape him, but he hadn't settled for crumbs since clawing his way out of the slums, and he wouldn't settle for pity now.

Though her news was utterly devastating, Andrew
drew on his years of corporate role-playing, assuming a
mask of composure that carefully concealed his aching
frustration throughout the uncomfortable meal, and
neither Shawn nor he were able to recapture their cam-
araderie.

Chapter Twenty-one

Tonight was Christmas Eve, and as Shawn drove home from the office, she was filled with ambivalence. The day had gone well, and the men had seemed to appreciate the gift certificates she had given them as well as the buffet lunch and the afternoon off. And now her thoughts turned inward. Would Andy still help her decorate the tree tonight, or was she expecting too much from him after their last tense parting? Still, she had never known Andrew to break a promise.

As she absently pulled into her parking spot, she reflected upon all the changes in her life during the last six months. Christmas certainly would not be the same in her new home, and to make her feel even lonelier, Elsa was back East visiting her sister. Though she could not repress her emotional dependence on her good friend, she knew that her thoughts were selfish. Elsa deserved the trip, and she should be happy for her. Oh, if only Matt were here. What a wonderful holiday they could have together. She mentally kicked herself for not going with him as he had wanted, but then she, too, had a commitment. Arcadia Lane would be the fulfillment of everything that McCullough had hoped to accomplish, and his presence was still very much with her.

"Stop feeling sorry for yourself," she ordered sternly.

"You've got the best of everything—jobs going well, a man who loves you, and you couldn't ask for two better friends than Andrew and Elsa." She swung the car door open, picked up the bag of groceries, and marched up the stairs. If Andrew did come, it could still be a lovely evening. Entering the condo's kitchen, she deposited the groceries on the counter and stashed the eggnog in the refrigerator.

A shower did wonders to refresh Shawn, and the anticipation of decorating the tree filled her with excitement. Here she was, twenty-six years old, and she felt as though she were ten. Wearing her jet-black jump suit accessorized with gleaming silver jewlery, she walked quickly into the living room and smiled at the awaiting tree. "You'll be the most beautiful tree ever," she promised with delight.

By six-thirty, the kitchen counter was littered with scraps of celery, cheese wrappers, an empty water-chestnut can, toothpicks, and bacon. Shawn took the bowl in which she had been soaking the water chestnuts in soy sauce and sugar, and artfully began wrapping each chestnut in bacon, piercing it with a toothpick, then arranging them on a baking sheet. Glancing at the clock, she decided there was enough time to whip up some additional zucchini appetizers while the bacon-wrapped chestnuts simmered in the oven.

By seven-thirty, the aroma of zucchini and parmesan cheese mingled with the tantalizing smell of the bacon to fill the kitchen with its mouth-watering fragrance. When the hot hors d'oeuvres were done, she pulled them from the oven, cutting the zucchini into tiny squares and transferring them along with the bacon canapés to a Christmas platter, all ready to pop into the microwave for a last-minute warming. Then she stepped back to admire her culinary effort. Everything was ready for a festive evening. The only thing missing now was Andrew. She glanced at the clock, which read seven forty-five. They had not set a time. Shawn reached for the telephone and started to dial. Perhaps he didn't intend to come after all. She dropped the receiver back into its cradle and sighed. Suddenly the possibility that she might well be alone this

evening seemed utterly crushing. Shawn wandered into
the living room, her eyes drawn to the barren tree and the
boxes of beautiful ornaments on the floor.

Tears welled, and she felt completely deserted. Matt
hadn't called either, and though she told herself that the
lines were probably all tied up, it was no comfort. There
would never be another Christmas with her father, and
neither Matt nor Andrew could fill the void tonight,
though they might have softened the loneliness.

Andrew Bellows, drink in hand, paced back and forth in
his luxurious penthouse. It really was decision time.
Could he handle an evening alone with the all too tempting woman he idolized but could not possess? It was a hard
pill to swallow. Though he had gotten over his anger, he
could not get over the frustration that was eating him
constantly, and especially when he yearned for Shawn's
tantalizing curves, her expressive blue eyes, and that
smile, like none other, that could light a room with its
radiance. Could he put himself through it all again
tonight? Yet if he didn't show up, would she understand?
Could Shawn ever possibly realize the depth of his love, a
love that was absolute, that made everything else in his
life second-rate?

Andrew snatched the phone, hesitated a moment, and
then slammed it down again. "Hell, it's no good. I simply
have to see her." He pulled his sport coat off the chair and
stormed out the door.

Shawn absently fingered the delicate ornaments as she
carefully removed them from the box. It was eight-thirty
and pretty clear that Andrew wasn't coming. For the first
time in her life, she would spend Christmas Eve alone,
and even the carols on the stereo did little to improve her
desolate mood. If only Matt would call.

The sound of a bell brought a surge of hope. "Matt, oh,
Matt!" she cried to herself as she rushed to the phone, but
the instrument emitted only a dial tone. It had to be the
outside buzzer. Shawn quickly pushed the security re-

lease. "Andy!" She raced to the door, hurrying to open it. "Oh, damn, I forgot, it's bolted!" Her fingers excitedly fumbled with the latch. "Andy, oh, Andy," she exclaimed as she rushed to hug a very surprised Bellows.

His arms instinctively enfolded her, the feel of her sending a gnawing surge of longing through him, before he reluctantly pulled away. "Is there something wrong?"

"Yes, you idiot, you're late and you know I'm dying to do that tree." She smiled and held his arm, pulling him into the living room. "Oh, Andy, I'm so glad you're here!"

Andrew smiled faintly. "If I had any sense, Shawn McCullough, I wouldn't be."

She took his hand. "Andy, please don't say anything now. Christmas only comes once a year. Let's enjoy it," she entreated quietly.

"You're right, it is Christmas and I'm famished," he said. "Mind if I sample some of those munchies?"

"Of course not, silly. I made them for us. How about an eggnog chaser?"

"Sounds good. I'll do the honors."

While the stereo poured out seasonal joy, Shawn and Andrew ate ravenously and sipped their eggnog as they trimmed the tall spruce. Shawn was so caught up in the holiday spirit that she was unaware of Andrew's growing restlessness and the way that he watched her every movement as though trying to frame a picture of her in his mind, a picture he could hold forever.

After Shawn placed the last ornament to her satisfaction, she turned, beaming happily, to face him. "It's gorgeous, the most beautiful tree I've ever had. Merry Christmas, Andy, and thanks so much for your present and all of your help. I only wish I had something to give you in return, but there isn't anything that you don't already have."

Her words were the fuse to ignite the fire of his passion that had been held so tightly in check, and he realized he could no longer honor his promise to remain her friend. All the control that he had consciously sought to maintain in order to preserve their friendship was suddenly overruled by his all-consuming love, and he couldn't subdue his overwhelming need of her. He took her hand, and his eyes were filled with a tenderness that Shawn had never before seen. "There's one very important thing I don't have, Shawn—your love."

There was such infinite sadness in his statement that Shawn was cut to the quick. He was so handsome in the dim light from the tree, his bronze hair slightly rumpled from tangling with branches, his sharply defined features strangely softened, and his eyes glistening with the fervor of his emotion. And somehow he was especially dear at this moment.

Shawn gently touched his cheek. "Andy," she whispered, "oh, Andy, my dear, what are we doing to each other?"

He took her hand, which was still against his cheek, and pressed it to his lips. "I don't know. I only know I can no longer ignore my love for you. I can't pretend we're merely friends when you are everything I desire," he groaned as his lips sought hers with great urgency and soul-baring need.

"Please, Andy, this will destroy our friendship," Shawn begged as she took a backward step, clumsily bumping into the side of the chair.

"Then tell me to go," he demanded as his strong arms encircled her, pinning her against the chair, his eyes smoldering with volcanic yearning as his lips again sought hers.

The effect of the drinks had released her inhibitions more than she thought possible, and the heady masculine scent of him overpowered her senses. For once, she was at a loss for words. As their lips met, his tongue sought hers, and her first impulse of resistance was subjugated by an all-engulfing passion, a passion which, until this moment, she thought could only have been kindled by Matt. The gentle strength of his kiss demanded response, and Shawn lost herself in answer. There was only the tingling sensation of his fingers, caressing and warm, on her skin as he slowly pulled at the zipper that ran from her collar to her navel. She felt as though she were a spectator watching herself being disrobed from afar, drugged by his kisses, helpless with sheer pleasure. The ardor of their kisses, like a mingling of their life's blood, would not be denied as he ever so gently eased her down on the couch and at the same time removed her lacy bra and panties so sensitively that her skin felt as if it were brushed by the wings of a butterfly, elusive and gossamer.

In the colorful light of the Christmas tree, Andrew's handsome face, transfigured by love, even his expression somehow a caress, was all she could see, spellbinding in its adoration of her body, of her. "Oh, my darling, you are so very precious, you are everything to me," he murmured. And his seeking hands stroked her breasts, her thighs, all of her. She tried to think of Matt, but it was impossible. Andy filled her senses with such delirious desire that she gave herself to him shamelessly, matching his ardor with her own in helpless surrender. Every tantalizing movement stimulating her until they moved as one.

She was his goddess, and he worshiped at her shrine, his rhythm masterfully gentle, in perfect time with her every pulsing need. "Oh, my beautiful darling, you feel so wonderful," he murmured, and her soft, responding moans filled him with delight. She was everything he had known she would be, and he wanted to preserve this moment forever. His control was unbelievable, prolonging her pleasure as he did, until Shawn could bear it no longer.

"Oh, Andy, oh, God!" she cried, and a wave of ecstasy engulfed the two lovers, transporting them out of themselves to an unbelievable pinnacle, a summit that until now had only existed in fantasies for either of them.

When they at last descended back to human level, they lay entwined, Andrew brushing tiny specks of kisses on her nose, her eyes, her silken shoulders, and the pink-tinged aureoles crowning her delicate milk-white breasts. Neither spoke lest they break the rapturous spell. For a long while they were content within each other's arms, exploring each other in an almost childlike fashion, loving the feel of the other's flesh, almost awestruck with one another and by what they had just shared. It was Andrew who finally spoke. "My God, how beautiful you are!" he uttered in wonderment. "With you, it's a whole new dimension. I feel as if I've never really made love before."

She couldn't put into words the way she felt; almost dazed, waiting for the shock of what she would have once thought illicit pleasure to set in, yet constantly amazed as she lay in Andrew's arms, to feel so wonderful, so fulfilled. Strangely, even the thought of Matt brought no guilt. She had been irrevocably drawn to Andrew, and she could no more have stopped what had just happened than she could have stopped the sun from rising, nor had she wanted to.

Three hours had passed, in which she had been loved in almost every way conceivable. At last, Andrew reluctantly sat up, gently pulling her with him, kissing her fingertips as his eyes adored the near perfection before him.

Trying to regain some normalcy she murmured, "It's so pretty, Andy. The tree, I mean."

"Um," he said lazily. "I can see nothing but you."

She smiled, and her blue eyes were dreamy in the soft glow from the tree before she rose to gather up her clothes and retreat to her bedroom. When she returned in her lavender robe, Andrew was dressed.

"Thought you might enjoy a brandy," he said, handing her a snifter.

"Thanks," she said, studying his face as if she had never seen him before.

"Shawn."

"Yes?"

"I know you still love him, but I can't say I'm sorry. How can anyone apologize for being recreated, for loving someone? Too many people search a lifetime, in vain, for what I've just discovered with you."

"I don't know," she whispered. "But I'm truly not sorry, either. All I can say is that it's not fair for both you and me to gang up on me. You're a most desirable man, Andy."

He smiled wryly. "And you are the damndest woman I've ever met."

She took his hands and brushed his cheek with her fingertips. "Andy, dear Andy, you've known my feelings all along. I've never meant to hurt you or to lead you on. I don't know what came over me tonight, but it was beautiful. I wouldn't change it, but please, help me to see that it doesn't happen again."

"You still love him?"

Her mind was befogged, still reeling in amazement, still waiting for the guilt she surely would feel when she was released from Andy's spell. She didn't answer.

Andrew set his brandy down, picked up his sport coat, and looked at her long and penetratingly. "If you ever need me . . ." His voice became ragged and he turned away. "I won't cross the barrier again. Merry Christmas, my love," and he was gone.

On Christmas morning Shawn was roused by a distant ringing, which she tried to ignore in favor of snuggling into her pillow and savoring the warmth of the satiny down comforter. Who would be calling at this ungodly hour? She pulled the coverlet over her dark curls and breathed a drowsy sigh of contentment, but the caller was persistent.

On the sixth ring Shawn lazily withdrew her hand from under the pillow. Wanting to silence the irritating noise, yet reluctant to give up her cozy nest, she remained curled in the fetal position, only her hand protruding as she reached for the phone, drawing the receiver under the bedclothes as she mumbled a sleepy greeting.

"Merry Christmas, darling," Matt's voice surprised her. "Did I wake you? I've been trying to get through since last night, but the damn lines were all tied up."

"Matt, oh, Matt!" she cried, instantly wide-awake. "Merry Christmas! How are you?" she asked as she sat halfway up in bed and glanced at the clock. It was six-thirty A.M. and dark outside, the wind-driven rain pelting the windows incessantly. It was one of those mornings when she felt relieved not having to relinquish her bed at such an early hour and trudge off to work.

"Bet you're still in bed."

"Uh huh," she admitted.

"God, how I miss you, sweetheart! You wouldn't be sleeping if I were there," his deep voice promised.

Shawn said nothing. It was marvelous hearing from him, though she was completely bewildered and absolutely amazed that the sound of his voice hadn't triggered the slightest guilt in her. Who was this woman who had more than willingly surrendered to Andrew, yet who now felt so relaxed and at peace? If ever she should feel guilt or at least some kind of remorse regarding her indiscretion, it should be now, in talking with Matt. Yet his familiar voice did nothing to shatter the marvelous well-being that her night with Andrew had produced. Andrew had a special place in her heart that she had not been aware of until last night, a place that even Matt couldn't touch.

"Oh, Matt," she said before the silence went on too long, "when are you coming home?"

"It won't be long, honey. Seven or eight weeks, I reckon. Save all that love I hear in your sweet voice for me, my darling."

"I will," she said absently, wondering at her surprisingly flat response to his words.

"Good," he replied. "I just wanted to wish you Merry Christmas. Shawn, I love you."

"Yes," she murmured quietly. "Take care of yourself."

"Yes," he said, "and I'll write. 'Bye now, sweetheart."

Shawn replaced the receiver and inched back under the covers. Last night was a pleasant memory of two people who had a desperate need for loving closeness, and she would leave it at that, with her heart still intact. She would never hurt Matt by telling him something that could only shatter him, something she couldn't explain even to herself. Within minutes, she was, once more, fast asleep, while the rain drummed on the window and a smile played on her contented lips.

Chapter Twenty-two

Several weeks had passed, and work at Arcadia Lane had slowed considerably due to the incessant rains. Had it not been for the farsighted planning on the part of Tony Rizzo and Steve Nelson, who had reserved particular tasks for such an event, McCullough Landscaping would have found it necessary to lay off a number of men. All in all, they had lost only a few days of work to date, despite the throes of winter.

Shawn was pleased with Tony's daily reports, and now that she lived closer to the job, she often stopped by on her way home from the office for a firsthand glimpse. It was moving right along, and by all indications, they would make the April sixteenth opening day deadline.

Life in general had been going well. Notes from Matt filled her in on his excursions with the geologists, his dealings with the South African lawyers, and his professed love for her. The nights were lonely, especially since Andrew had become such an important, but now missing, part of her life. She had seen him at Sun Haven on their weekly evening of supervising the recreation center, and he remained a friend, greeting her warmly enough, but it was not the same as before. He had honored her request, making sure they were never alone, even for

a moment. He no longer popped in at her condo or offered
to see her home, yet he was the same Andrew, kidding and
fun-loving with the group of boys, shooting pool with
Shawn.

Time passed, and if a certain spark was missing, she
attributed it to the gloom of winter and Matt's absence.
She spent late hours at the office and more and more
nights with the kids at the center. But tonight she would
have a nice diversion. Elsa was coming for the weekend,
and she looked forward to the visit. As she sat in her office
mentally planning the menu, a surge of anticipation
cheered her. It would be good seeing Elsa. She answered
Audrey's buzz with a lilt in her voice.

"Someone wants to get in touch with Tony," Audrey
informed her. "She says it's urgent. I thought you'd better
handle it."

"Thanks, Audrey," Shawn replied, and punched the
button. "Shawn McCullough," she stated. "Perhaps I can
help you."

"Where is my son Antonio," the woman demanded in
broken English between sobs. "Poppa is gone," she wailed
between great gulping sobs. "Oh, God, oh, God! Where is
my boy?"

It was five minutes before Shawn could get Tony's
mother, the grief-stricken Mrs. Rizzo, to make any sense.
When at last she had gotten the hysterical woman somewhat coherent, it was to learn that Tony's father had died
very suddenly, and for a moment after she hung up the
receiver, Shawn was stunned by the news, reliving her
own father's sudden death. Poor Tony, how could she tell
him? She still didn't know when she got him on the radio
and asked him to meet her at Arcadia Lane for a cup of
coffee in twenty minutes. Her heart sank to hear his
familiar kidding, which made her task even harder.

When she pulled up alongside Tony's truck, he was
studying the grade plan with Nelson. He flashed her a big
grin as she walked toward him, her insides churning.

It had finally stopped raining, and the sun had peeked
out just before noon, giving everyone on the job a much-

needed lift. Lord, how she hated being the one to tell him about his father. She'd be supplanting the sun with gloom, and she felt heartsick.

"What do ya think, boss?" Tony questioned in response to her serious look. "Making good time, aren't we?"

Of all days, he was in such a happy mood, and her heart sank even lower. Shawn nodded but could no way match his enthusiasm with what was on her mind. "Yes," she said absently. "Tony, let's go get a cup of coffee."

"Sure," he said. "Hop in the truck and let's go."

Shawn wanted to drive under the circumstances, and her reluctance was evident.

Tony picked it up before she could answer. "On second thought, maybe you better chauffeur, the truck is pretty damn dirty. Lead on, boss lady," he gestered with a flourish.

Nelson, who had been sullenly listening to their conversation and behaving as if Shawn was interrupting a crucial development, gave her a disdainful glance, rolled up the plan, and walked briskly toward his crew of men, who were staking trees.

"Put it on hold, Steve. I'll be back shortly," Tony called after him.

There was no reply.

Tony shook his head. "Damn, talk about a chauvinist," he said.

"Yeah," Shawn commented. "I'm glad you have to deal with him and not me."

"Aw, he's all right. Just has this thing about women. Thinks they're all superfluous," he conceded. "Someday he'll figure out that you're not a bad head."

Shawn gave him a doubtful glance.

After they were seated in a private rear booth that Shawn had chosen, Tony ordered coffee. The superintendent smiled as he reached for the sugar. "Since the work is going so smoothly, it can't be that. Have we got some kind of money problem? You look so serious," he noted.

"No, I wish it were something that materialistic." She laid her hand on his. "Tony, there's no easy way to tell you;

your father has passed away." She hesitated, watching
Tony's face pale, the muscles in his cheeks twitch, and the
sparkle in his eyes extinguish. For a moment, he couldn't
speak and could only stare unseeingly at the spoon in his
hand. She softly continued. "Your mother called. She
needs you, Tony. I'm so terribly sorry," Shawn murmured
as tears clouded her own eyes and she tightly squeezed his
hand. "I didn't want to tell you on the job."

Tony nodded. "But I just talked to him on the phone at
Christmas and he was fine," he protested futilely. "How
can this be? Was it a heart attack?"

"I don't know. Your mother said it was sudden but she
was too upset for details."

"I see," he murmured. "Poor mama. She was so dependent on him. Dad always took care of everything. If only
she wasn't clear back in Nebraska." He shook his head
sorrowfully. "I loved that old son of a bitch."

"I know," Shawn almost whispered. "I have Audrey
checking airline reservations for you and your family. If
you don't want to take the kids, I'd love for you to leave
them with me. I can find someone to care for them during
the day."

"I appreciate it, Shawn," he said sincerely, "but I have
lots of aunts back there, so we'll take 'em along. Thanks
for checking out the flights. I'll give Audrey a call on the
radio and see what she came up with." He pushed his
untouched coffee aside and flipped some money on the
table. "Mind if we go?"

She rose and followed him. In the car, Tony stared
straight ahead, and Shawn's heart went out to him.

"You know, it's crazy," he muttered just before getting
out of the car. "I know what you just told me is true, but I
can't believe it. Death is so"—he groped for the word—
"final. It's impossible to believe he's really gone."

"Yes," she said softly. "I still can't believe McCullough is
gone. But, Tony, loved ones are never really gone; a part of
them is with us always."

He brushed her cheek with a light kiss as he moved to
leave.

"You have a company credit card," she said. "Charge the tickets, and we'll call it a business expense. You go home to your family. I'll tell Nelson."

He opened the door and turned toward her. "You know something," he choked, his dark eyes brimming with tears, "you're one hell of a friend. I'll be back as soon as I can."

She watched him walk woodenly to his truck. When he got in, his back was to her, and as he rested his head in his hands, his shoulders shook uncontrollably. What a far cry from the happy buoyant man of an hour earlier. It was a full minute before the truck came to life and Tony sped away. Shawn got out of her car with a heavy heart and walked toward Nelson.

"Steve," she said. "Tony's father died, and he's taking a trip back to the Midwest for a few days. I'll be checking with you daily till he returns, so call the office if you have any problems."

Making no effort to reply, Nelson frowned as he nodded his agreement.

On Monday morning, Shawn was rejuvenated from having spent a lovely weekend with Elsa. Her good friend was one of those extraordinary people, who, if Shawn hadn't seen her in months, could make her feel as though no time at all had passed, almost as if she had but briefly left the room and then returned to continue the conversation. There was a certain glow about Elsa, a zest for life and a way of discerning her friend's secret feelings, always lending a positive note to things. Shawn had mentioned the death of Tony's father, and just talking about it seemed to relieve the sorrow she felt for her superintendent. Elsa had asked about Matt and Andrew, and somehow drew out Shawn's feelings regarding both men. And as usual, Shawn felt so comfortable with her that she talked unashamedly about her night with Andrew.

"You know, honey," Elsa commented, "I'm delighted that you can confide in me. It's quite a compliment. You know, life has a way of continually testing us, of making us feel so obligated to others that we pass up marvelous experiences, an act that we later regret because we were afraid to give in to our emotions. I'm glad you don't feel guilty, that tells me it was right. Things happen for a reason, dear, and someday you'll know it." Then, in a lighter vein she said, "Now, tell me how the jobs are going."

Shawn hugged her impulsively. "Oh, Elsa, you're one in a million. Lucky me to have you for a friend." And they had gone on till the wee hours, talking about Arcadia Lane and all the events of Elsa's trip. As usual, Shawn hated to see her leave on Sunday, and she felt a twinge of loneliness as she watched Elsa's car fade from sight.

Monday morning seemed to be an extension of the weekend, playing out the five-day forecast of sunshine, dawning bright and clear, one of those days when the mockingbird in the fir tree near the street below Shawn's condo was experimenting with his own delightful rendition of an Irish jig as he flitted from one branch to another, strewing melodies in the air like daisy petals on the wind. Shawn smiled as she watched the bird's performance, jumping and twirling and finally soaring from her view with a loud, trilling burst of song.

Later, in the office, Shawn quickly ran through the stack of papers on her desk, cancelled an unimportant appointment, and drove to Arcadia Lane. It was ten A.M., and if overseeing the jobs was, for the moment, her responsibility, she'd better get familiarized.

As Shawn's Spitfire approached the entrance to the shopping center, a smile and more than a little pride shone on her face. She was truly a part of a tremendous joint effort that was gradually shaping into a very impressive sight. Friday, with Tony's dilemma on her mind, she had been unaware of all the progress. The outer shell of the front buildings had been transformed into an artistic ultramodern facade like none she had ever seen, classic in its design. The shopping center was a daring man's vision come to life, Andrew's vision. How proud he must be watching it grow, and for the first time, she thought of opening day, not as a worrisome deadline, but as a momentous occasion, one of which she, too, would be proud.

Shawn drove the perimeter, taking in all the activity, then carefully made her way to the central area where men on scaffolds were painting buildings and installing windows, and the continual muffled buzz of saws from the inner confines, along with the rhythmic tap of hammers, told her the finishing touches were being applied. The landscaped areas that her crews had planted now flourished in the morning sun, and she beamed with pleasure at the man-made stream separating the modern section from the one of the past. Shawn was impatient for the waterwheel to be installed and the bridge built. How pretty it would be when the stream bed was full of water, fish, and flowers. Her men were doing an excellent job, and she was mighty pleased.

She got out of her car and walked the length of the stream, ignoring the whistles and suggestive remarks of the workmen, whose attention was drawn to the beautiful woman wearing designer jeans that, while protecting her legs, scarcely concealed the round firmness of her hips. Her pale blue denim shirt was topped by a navy cardigan draped carelessly over her shoulders, the arms tied about her neck just in case she needed to slip it on.

"Come on over here, I'll give you a job," one workman remarked.

Shawn laughed. "Thanks, but I don't need a job," she replied. "Anyway, my best effort with a hammer is hanging pictures."

He grinned. "Doesn't have to be with a hammer, honey."

"You're right, it doesn't have to be," she said sweetly as she raised her fingers and wiggled them "good-bye," then proceeded on down to where her foreman, Nelson, was supervising the picnic and playground area. The bright yellow Massey Ferguson had already been gouging the earth the better part of the morning, and a considerable amount of soil had been trucked out of the area to the far end of the site for fill.

For a moment, Shawn watched Nelson operating the tractor. He was a pro whose fair skin was deeply tanned and leathery from years of weathering in the outdoors. As much as she didn't care for the man's blatant rudeness, she had to admit that he handled equipment well. He was so engrossed in his work that he failed to notice her. Shawn walked over to his truck to refresh her mind with the grading plan he had draped over the hood of his pickup and anchored with several small rocks. Nelson was loading a dump truck when he caught a glimpse of her backside.

"Oh, hell, here comes trouble," he grumbled. He went right on grading.

Shawn walked the grid stakes twice before she put her finger on it. Her uncanny instinct told her intuitively that something was wrong with the elevations. If they graded it the way that Nelson had it set up, which was, she presumed, according to the plan, the drainage would be too severe. She closely scanned the layout again. There was no way that the detail on this area plan could mesh with the surroundings. Nelson would love to hear that. He wasn't fond of her to begin with. "Oh, well," she sighed in resignation, then waving her arms at the foreman, she yelled, "Shut it down for a minute. I need to talk to you."

"Oh, damn, here we go," Nelson griped as he shut down the Fergie and motioned the truck driver on his way. "Damn females always gotta have their say."

"Good morning," Shawn said.

"Yes, isn't it?" he remarked sarcastically, not at all pleased with her presence.

She reached for the print, and when she turned back, he was studying her boots, jeans, and shirt, a scowl creasing his hatchet face.

"I thought I'd dress the part today," she said brightly, vowing not to let him unnerve her.

"Yeah? Well what can I do for you? When that Fergie's not working, it puts the dump on standby and the cleanup crew over there just lean on their shovels." He glanced at several laborers who were standing around under a huge

oak tree close to the foothill of the mountain beyond.
"That all costs money, you know."

"I'm quite aware of that fact, Mr. Nelson, but if I'm right
in what I stopped you for, we might waste one hell of a lot
more time and money straightening out a bad problem.
Now, if you can forget that I'm female for a minute, let's go
over the grade elevations."

"There's nothing wrong with those stakes. I shot the
grades myself," he defended with a reproving glare.

"You may be right, but I damn well want to know it."
Where did he come off telling her what cost the company
money?

Nelson stood glowering while she checked and rechecked all the elevations. They were correct according to
the grade plan. She shrugged her shoulders in dismay, but
she still wasn't satisfied. There was something wrong.
What was it? If only Tony were here. But he had been
around when Nelson had staked it out. Could she be
imagining things? She glanced at Nelson, whose sneer
infuriated her. By now the rest of the crew had walked
over to see what was going on, and the truck driver had
returned, climbing out of his truck and ambling toward
them.

"Got a problem?" he asked.

"Only one," Nelson retorted, imperceptibly tossing his
head in Shawn's direction. "Now, if you don't mind, Ms.
McCullough, I'll get back to work. I'd like to get this
grading finished before another storm moves in. If it didn't
have good drainage, we'd play hell working it even today."
He walked off with the men following. Making no attempt
to lower his voice, he grumbled, "Maybe now she'll go
back to the damn office where she belongs. Ain't no fool
woman gonna tell me how to run a job."

Shawn was furious with his attitude. Damn! What a
smart S.O.B. he was, trying to make a fool of her like that
in front of the men! Fuming, she went back to comparing
the detail plan with the overall grade plan. She was still
puzzling when she looked up to see Mr. Krugger, the little
old man who lived up the hill. She was in no mood for his

tirades, which had become legend to the workmen, but she was cornered with the plans in hand and could not gracefully leave. Anyway, she still wasn't satisfied that Nelson was right, and she meant to study the situation further. She returned her attention to the blueprint.

"Do you have something to do with this—this abomination?" Krugger demanded. Then, going on as if it didn't really matter whether she did or not because he was going to tell the whole world, anyway, he said, "Of all things, now they're tearing away at the foot of my mountain here, gonna cause a landslide, that's what they're gonna do. I know this valley like the back of my hand, and it don't pay to disturb the lay of the land. You'll see." He shook his finger in her face.

Shawn took a backward step. "Mr. Krugger, a team of engineers and geologists have gone over the entire layout and it has met with their approval. Everything that's being done here has been documented as safe."

"What do they know." He sniffed contemptuously. "Those college boys with their fancy gadgets? They weren't here years back when we had that little earthquake, and the whole side of the mountain came down. It was wet, just like it is now."

"Where, Mr. Krugger? Where did the mountain slide?"

"Down yonder about six hundred yards. You can't tell now. It's all grown over in trees and brush. You mark my words, you people shouldn't be changing things! Meddling, I call it!"

She glanced up at his rickety home, which perilously clung to the side of the mountain, and a shudder ran through her. It didn't appear safe under any circumstance, and suddenly she was concerned about the stubborn old man. "Mr. Krugger, why don't you move if you're so worried? Andrew Bellows offered you a good price."

"Never! I won't move," he ranted vehemently. "I was born and raised in that house, and I intend to die there!"

Shawn thought of her own sentimentality regarding her lost home, and she said sympathetically, "Mr. Krugger, sometimes we can't hang on to the past, as much as we might like to. Please reconsider Andrew Bellows's offer to buy you out."

He shook his head adamantly. "The house will have to slide down the mountain first, and if you don't stop disturbing things with all that high-powered equipment, that's just what will happen. I warn you, stop before it's too late! A pretty young woman like you ought not to be out here working with the men, anyway."

With that, he stormed off leaving Shawn to sputter, "Men. God, who do they think they are? What makes them think I don't enjoy what I'm doing?"

Did they think she was completely lacking upstairs? There was determination in her stride as she crossed the dirt field to where Nelson was loading the dump truck, and she yelled at the top of her lungs, "Nelson!" But the growl of the tractor drowned out her voice, and Steve scooped up another load with the bucket, dropping it into the truck with a resounding thud. "Nelson," she repeated, not sure whether he hadn't heard her or had deliberately chosen to ignore her. Still, she was hesitant to get any closer to the moving equipment.

Finally the truck driver noticed her and honked his horn. Nelson immediately shut the tractor down, looking to the teamster who pointed to Shawn about thirty feet away. The tight-lipped foreman jumped to the ground. Hands on hips, he stood looking daggers at her. "What is it *now*?" he demanded, letting her know she was wasting his time.

"I'm shutting you down till I talk to the architect," Shawn announced. "Take the crew over to the other side and finish staking all those trees. I should have an answer later today."

"What the hell's the matter now? You just proved the grades are right!" he sputtered indignantly. "Don't you believe in plans and specs, lady? Christ, there ain't no room for female intuition on this job!"

She could hear the other men snicker softly, and Shawn's blood began to boil. She might waste some time and money, but she had to see it through. Nelson had already belittled her in front of the men, and if she was wrong, so what? They all thought she was a dumb broad, anyway. "You heard what I said, Steve. I may be female, but I'm still signing your check, so park that Fergie and don't give me any more of your lip. I'll let you know when the architect can meet with us."

The men's brows arched in amazement. She was calling his bluff. Nelson, face red with anger, stared long and hard at Shawn.

Oh, Lord, what would she do if he quit? She had let her Irish get the best of her, and yet she was the boss, so it was best he learn it right now.

Nelson hopped on the Fergie, jerked the key out, jammed it in his pocket, and yelled to the men, "Hold up for now. Gather up your tools and get in the truck. We'll go plant posies till somebody makes up their goddamn mind!"

Shawn turned on her heel and left. For two cents she'd fire him, that bullheaded, insolent bastard, but good foremen were hard to find, and Tony would be upset. She had to admit her job would also suffer. By the time she reached her car, she was steaming hot, despite the cool winter air. Shawn radioed the office. "Audrey, please get in touch with Richard Ramsey. Tell him that I need to meet with him as soon as possible. I think we have a problem with the detail grade print on the picnic area at Arcadia. I'm on my way to the office. Over and out."

"Right. I'll call him immediately. Out."

Shawn heaved a disgusted sigh. Her first day overseeing jobs, and what a lousy substitute for Tony she was, letting Nelson get to her like that. Suddenly she spied Bellows's car on the perimeter road, and the urge to talk with a friend was strong. "No, Shawn McCullough," she lectured. "This is your problem. Andy can't save you from big, bad, burly Nelson." She flipped the key in the ignition and drove away.

Three hours later, the landscape architect was on the job, scribbling in his notebook while Shawn waited, shifting her weight from one foot to the other, fretting. Nelson stood to the side, hard hat cocked back on his head, a smug look on his thin face. His eyes on her were piercing and defiant, and worse yet, he'd brought several of the men with him, whose faces showed obvious annoyance with the delay and the interference of an incompetent broad.

She was so intent upon the outcome, and so afraid that her intuition could be wrong and she would surely have to eat her words, that she barely noticed Andrew Bellows walk up.

"Got a problem?" he asked.

She glanced to where Andy stood, frowning, arms folded, and her confidence level dropped to zero. She couldn't help remembering his earlier remark about a woman running a landscaping business being asinine. Was he right after all? She nodded. "I seem to be a minority of one."

"Never hurts to check. Can save a lot of headaches," he remarked.

Shawn was silent. What made her feel there was an error?

Ramsey looked up from the transit. "Grade elevations all check out, Ms. McCullough. I don't see any problems."

Her color deepened, and she refused to look at Nelson. He would surely be gloating.

"All right, let's hit it," the foreman said to his men. "Shit! We've lost enough time already."

"Just a minute," Shawn said quietly, a light going on in her mind. "I remember we once had a problem with conversion on a detail plan. Is it possible that when you enlarged the thirty-scale drawing to sixteen, you could have made an error?"

Nelson stopped momentarily, frowning as if to say, "God, she doesn't give up, does she?"

Ramsey pulled a pencil from his shirt pocket and started scribbling in his notebook. He looked up and whistled. "Damned if you aren't right, Ms. McCullough. I sure slipped up on this one. By the time you got to the pond, nothing would have matched up. We can't be right all the time, but that doesn't excuse this. I'm sorry. I'll get right on it and work up an elevation change."

Shawn let out a deep breath in relief.

"You have a good eye," the architect praised her. "I'll see that you get the change order first thing in the morning."

She smiled. "Thank you, Mr. Ramsey." Then, looking at Nelson, whose brow wrinkled in amazement, she said very calmly, "I know Mr. Nelson is anxious to get on with it. Now, I'd best be getting back to the office." She shook his hand. "I'll be expecting the change early." Shawn turned and walked toward her car without a word to Nelson, and she smiled devilishly to herself over the remarks the men were now aiming at her foreman.

"I guess you showed that broad," one of them said, and they laughed raucously.

"Son of a bitch!" Nelson exclaimed. "Stop your silly-ass laughing and get in the damn truck!"

When Shawn opened the car door, a hand touched her shoulder. "Nice going! You proved a damn good point," Andrew commented from behind her.

"Thank God! If I'd been wrong, it would have been tragic," she said in all seriousness. "Oh, Andy, this has been one hell of a day! I have such a headache that I can feel every root of hair poking in my brain!"

He laughed. "Come on, you know-it-all broad, I'll buy you a cup of coffee and a couple of aspirin."

Shawn giggled. "Thanks, *friend*," she said.

Chapter Twenty-three

About ten A.M. the next day, the architect showed up at McCullough Landscaping's office with the promised change order on the detail grading plan, again apologizing for the error. Shawn accepted his apology graciously, saying that she might just as well have been wrong, and thanked him for his promptness.

An hour later, she handed the revision to Nelson, who wore a begrudging smile. "Okay, Ms. McCullough," he said. "We'll get right on it. They're forecasting more rain for the end of the week."

Though it appeared that she had won a new respect from him, she still wished Tony was back to deal with him. Work was already falling behind at the office, and she was extremely uncomfortable knowing the men were watching her every move. Her own crews were cooperative and subdued since yesterday, and she knew that word had gotten around that she wasn't such a dumb broad after all, but the other workmen on the site still made passes. Damn them, anyway; why shouldn't a woman be just as interested in construction as any man?

"There's still one heck of a lot of work in the other section across the stream," she pondered aloud. "It's going to be tight meeting the completion date, especially if it doesn't stop raining."

"We'll make it," Nelson said confidently.

Shawn smiled. Maybe his bullheadedness was good for something after all. "Tony should be back on Thursday," she said. "Call me if you run into problems."

He nodded.

That same evening, Tony phoned her at home from Nebraska. "Boy, do I miss you. How's it going?" Shawn asked, "and when are you coming back?"

"Not for a bit. My mother had a bad breakdown after the funeral today," he said sadly. "I'm having one hell of a time if you want the truth."

"Oh, Tony, I'm sorry. What a shame. Your poor mother. I wish I could help."

"You *are* helping, with the job."

"Some help. I got into an argument with Nelson the first day."

"That damn stubborn Swede! What the hell's the matter with him?"

"Nothing now. We got it all straightened out."

"What was the problem?"

"The picnic area. Detail drawing was wrong."

"I thought there was something cockeyed there. Was just about to check it out when you came on the job Friday, but I forgot all about it after that."

"Hey, don't worry, everything's under control. Get your mother squared away. That's what's important now."

"Thanks, boss lady. I hope Steve doesn't give you any more trouble."

"I believe we've come to an understanding," she stated. "I can't overcome being female, but I think I have overcome being stupid." She laughed.

Tony chuckled. "Hang in there. They'll find out just how smart you are. I'll call you the end of the week."

When Shawn hung up, a sinking feeling washed over her that she couldn't explain, a kind of foreboding she couldn't shake. She absently turned on the TV, her mind still on the job, going over the plans and specs, trying to stay one step ahead of Nelson. Finally, she got out the set of prints she had been carrying since Tony's departure and studied them in detail once again. There was really one hell of a lot left to go just as she had told Nelson. Mulling over the absent Tony, who might be gone a couple more weeks, she only half-heard the weather, calling for heavy downpours in the next few days.

"Oh, great!" Shawn said disgustedly. She punched the off button and went to bed. She lay there about an hour, still thinking about the job. Finally, she drifted off to sleep with the hopeful thought that the weather might clear before the weekend.

Wednesday the job went well. Nelson had finished the grading by noon, as he'd promised, and started laying out the walkways in the picnic/playground area. Some of the crew were pounding stakes and setting forms while a couple of laborers followed up by hand-grading the soil inside the forms and laying a base of rock. Rain wouldn't bother the walkways, the foreman assured her, and they could pour concrete even in a light rain if necessary.

Shawn noticed a slight thaw in Nelson's iciness and a tinge of respect from the men that gave her a lift. She felt the sun on her face and heard the chatter of a squirrel in the huge oak tree. Everything was working out, and her feeling of apprehension was gone. Her step was light as she walked to the trailer, and she even smiled to herself at hearing the workmen's whistles and catcalls.

It was 4:30 P.M. when Shawn locked up the trailer. By now, it was getting dark, and the shadow of the mountain was like a drawn shade, covering the day's work with a lavender-gray hue. Her focus was drawn to the sudden ascent of a hawk, its graceful flight culminating on the cliff beyond Kruger's old house. In the dusk, it looked as though a stream of water were cascading down the face of the rock above the decrepit home, and a sudden chill enveloped her. Was Kruger's warning prompted by a vision of things to come? Nonsense, she thought. The old coot's getting to you with his gloom and doom. Nothing more than winter's seepage or shadows playing tricks. Shawn got into her car and headed for the exit.

*   *   *

Sometime during the night, Shawn was startled awake
by a rumbling noise that in her sleepy condition she
mistook for thunder, until a sharp jolt shook her bed, and
the sliding closet doors began violently rolling back and
forth. "Earthquake!" She bolted from the bed to brace
herself in the doorway before gingerly reaching for the
light switch on the wall. She could hear the rattle of dishes
from the kitchen, and she stood, petrified, watching the
moving doors until they gradually slowed to a halt. "Good
Lord!" she exhaled slowly, noticing the crystal teardrops
on the lamps still tinkling together in a chimelike sere-
nade.

For several minutes after the rumble, Shawn was
terror-stricken. Although she had experienced earthquakes before, she had never been alone, and her heart
pounded with fright. Was this lull the end of it—or the
beginning? She had no idea how long she'd stood in the
doorway, but when she looked at the clock, it read five-
thirty A.M., almost time for her alarm to go off. Her hand
shook as she hit the button to switch on her bedside radio.

Within seconds, an excited newscaster interrupted the
soft music. "As most of you are no doubt well aware, the
Bay Area has been hit by a good-sized quake. At this time,
Berkeley is estimating a magnitude of somewhat over 5.5
on the Richter scale. The epicenter is believed to be in the
western vicinity of San Jose. We have received a report
from the California Highway Patrol that Highway 17
between San Jose and Santa Cruz is now closed due to
slides. So far, no other damage reports have been received.
Stay tuned for further details as they come in. Now back
to our regularly scheduled program."

With the return of the music, Shawn finally got up
enough nerve to check out her apartment. Several pictures had crashed to the floor, and one cupboard door hung
open in the kitchen. Half a dozen or more glasses had
toppled onto the countertop and shattered, sending frag-
ments of glass in all directions. She set about cleaning up
the debris, her heart still pounding in her throat, her ears
fine-tuned, straining to hear another awesome rumble,

even though she knew aftershocks rarely occurred until
several hours later. But this one might be different.
Earthquakes were still unpredictable despite all of the
sophisticated equipment.

The office! Was it closer to the fault line? And what
about Arcadia Lane? Oh, no! All those huge panes of glass
they had just installed yesterday? And water mains? She
had visions of the irrigation systems all uprooted, gushing
out tons of water, flooding the entire site. The damage
could be stupendous. She thought of Elsa and Andrew, but
she knew the telephone lines would be all tied up. That
was the first thing everyone did after a quake, call family
and friends.

Shawn jerked a pair of Levi jeans from a hanger, pulled
on a sweat shirt, ran a comb through her hair, then
quickly brushed her teeth while hopping from foot to foot,
trying to get her boots on in a hurry. She was out the door
in record time, only to run smack into Andrew Bellows as
she rounded the corner of the building en route to the
parking garage.

"Oh, Andy!" she cried. "Lord, am I glad to see you."

"Where's the fire, Shawn McCullough?" he teased.

"That's all we need," she said. "Did you see much
damage on the way over?"

"That was not my primary concern. Are you all right?"
She gave him a shaky nod.

"Helluva feeling, isn't it? Where were you going just
now?"

"To Arcadia Lane. I hate to think what might have
happened there."

"That was my next stop. Why don't I drive you?"

"Please do! I hate to face destruction all by myself," she
said in all seriousness.

"Better ride with me. You're still pretty shaky," he
suggested.

In the car, she squeezed his arm. "Thanks for being
concerned about me," she said.

Concerned, hell! That was sure putting it mildly, but
his voice was teasing as he said, "Well, I can't afford to

lose the best subcontractor I got. We'd miss that opening day!"

"So there's a method to your madness!"

He grinned, and his quicksilver blue eyes sparkled with mirth, but there was a certain softness reflected there that belied all humor.

Shawn returned his smile and then turned her attention to the shops along the street. Driving through downtown Saratoga, they could see a few shattered display windows, and already the police were patroling the streets, watchful of looters, stopping everyone for identification. A number of store owners were assessing their damage.

When Shawn and Andrew pulled into the huge center, it was obscured by darkness. "Damn hard to see much," Andrew remarked. "You game for a walk-through?"

"Why not?"

Andrew parked next to McCullough Landscaping's trailer and flipped the door and trunk release. He pulled a huge flashlight out of the Lamborghini's trunk.

"That's not a flashlight, that's a torch," Shawn remarked.

The trailer appeared the same as it had the night before, except for a few boxes of plumbing supplies that had toppled over, creating a pile of assorted hardware in the middle of the floor; probably only a half-hour job to sort the jumbled sizes once again. Further investigation showed one cracked window.

"Looks pretty minimal," Shawn said. "Let's check on all those huge windowpanes they installed yesterday. I'll straighten this out later."

Andrew lighted the way as they walked to the front-side buildings where several mammoth windows showed cracks. Shawn walked closer.

"Stay away from them!" Andy warned. "Glass is tricky. They could fall out at any time."

"Oh," she said. "I feel sorry for the guys who have to replace these. They looked so great last night."

"Yeah," he said, "but it could be a damn sight worse.

They could all be broken. Anyway, they'll get paid to do it again."

Shawn nodded. "You're right, of course. Let's take a look at the other side." To her dismay, it was far worse. A number of large panes were shattered, gigantic shards of glass still hanging from the edges. "There's no rhyme or reason to it," she said. "Why didn't they all break?"

Andy shrugged. "It's a strange thing. Possibly the way they were set in, some more tightly than others, no give, or else, inferior glass. Who knows? I'd say we're damn fortunate that all the glass in the center wasn't in. This will cost a few bucks."

Since they were already installed, she knew it would cost Andrew rather than the glass contractor. "I'm sorry," she said sympathetically. "I guess they aren't insured?"

"Against earthquake? No. That would have cost a bundle if it were available, and more than the damn windows, that's for sure. Don't worry, I can afford it. I'm just glad the buildings are standing. Come on, let's take a look at that stream your crew constructed."

Shawn followed his lead toward the man-made stream, shivering in the brisk, early morning wind that seemed to be increasing in velocity. "Here," he said, peeling off his jacket and handing it to her.

"Oh, no, Andy," she said hesitantly, "you'll freeze in that pullover."

He shrugged and said, "No, I'm fine. I've been a lot colder than this." He draped his jacket around her shoulders.

The lining was already warm from his body heat, and she slipped her arms gratefully into the garment.

He smiled. Her hands were completely hidden by the overlong sleeves. "God, you're so little," he remarked.

"But mighty," she reminded with a grin. "Lead on, oh, great bearer of light," she teased, feeling somewhat relieved that no irrigation leaks had been spotted.

He laughed, also feeling greatly relieved. The damage seemed to be slight, and broken windows were not a grave concern. At least the buildings had suffered no apparent structural damage. Bellows had adhered to the strictest building codes demanded anywhere, and for good reason. This was earthquake country and no place to scrimp on safeguards. The center was his longtime dream, and he insisted on superior construction and every known safeguard.

"I think it's finally morning," Shawn said. By now, the sky was lighter, but no trace of the sun was yet visible, only the overcast, hanging like a gloomy pall over the top of the mountain that rose skyward from the picnic/playground side of the shopping center. The short reprieve in the weather was about to end, and the wind whipped Shawn's thick, ebony hair around her face, sending a shudder through her as she lagged behind Andrew, gazing at the mountaintop that was barely visible in the half-light.

"What's the matter, Shawn McCullough, still cold?" he called to her.

She buttoned the supple brown leather jacket to stave off the chill and hurried to join him. "It is mighty frigid out here," she said. "I'll bet you're freezing!"

If he only dared tell her how he'd like to get warm. God, how warm they had been the night they'd made love. Just the thought of it aroused him, and he dared not dwell on the idea. He had meant what he'd said. He would not cross that barrier again, and he refrained from the most innocent reference, knowing words could make them both uncomfortable and put a strain on their friendship. "Wind's picking up," he said, not acknowledging her comment. "Looks as though the weatherman is right for a change."

"Yes," she said, stopping at the far end of the stream. There was a considerable amount of water in the bed, dark, murky water, unlike the two or three inches of rainwater of the day before, and Shawn stiffened. "Andy, look at this! Last night it had only a couple of inches of clear water in it!"

He hurriedly joined her, his brow narrowing.

"It can't be rainwater," she said. "It hasn't rained!"

They could see the water level rising ever so slowly, tiny swirls eddying in their direction, indicating a source at the other end. "Strange," he muttered. "It's being fed from somewhere."

The same ominous feeling she'd had last evening returned, and Shawn frowned. "I don't like it! It looks like mud," she said.

"Yes," he replied, and they both began running along the stream toward the opposite end. The soil that had been freshly graded the day before was eroding from beneath the sidewalk forms, and the rock base that the men had prepared for concrete had disappeared under what looked like chocolate cake batter, lazily covering the whole area. Their eyes traveled further to where liquid mud was slowly cascading down the mountain slope in thick rivulets, inundating the entire picnic/playground section in a sea of muck and feeding into the gradually filling stream like creeping quicksand.

"Oh, my God!" Shawn exclaimed, staring dumbfounded at the awesome sight before her.

"Christ Almighty! What the hell is happening here?" Bellows said.

Even as they stood rigid with disbelief at the edge of the man-made stream, the jellylike mud covered their boots and continued to follow the path of least resistance, oozing down the concrete side of the unnatural pond. It seemed to originate somewhere above Krugger's old house on the hill, which looked forlorn and even more fragile with the water now flowing around it, eroding the soil in its path as it proceeded on down the slope, gathering patches of grass and brush in its wake to deposit in clumps at the foot of the hillside. Andrew's keen mind considered every possibility. The problem had to be a natural source, perhaps a deep-seated artesian well or spring of some sort, which the earthquake had unleashed. "It must be underground water brought to the surface by the quake," he mused aloud.

Shawn stood immobile. How could this be happening?

She had never seen anything like it before. It was as if nature had suddenly created a waterfall to stave off the builders, and it was as if the old man had willed it. "Mr. Krugger," she said excitedly. "Good Lord, Andrew! That rickety old house. We have to warn him." She started across the field. She had barely taken a step when, in one swift movement, Andrew blocked her way.

"We can't," he said. "That whole mountainside could come down at any minute. You sure as hell can't stop an avalanche, and neither can I! He's probably already out, anyway."

"No, Andy. I don't think so. He's such a very stubborn, old man. He told me he was born in that house and he intends to die there." She attempted to wriggle free of his grasp.

"No you listen to me, Shawn McCullough. That old man might die in that house, but you're not going to join him. I'll call the police and have them send a helicopter with a loudspeaker to warn him."

"But there isn't time," she pleaded. "There's a road leading up there. Can't we drive up quick?"

"It's too risky," he warned. "The whole damn mountain is undoubtedly unstable. Let the police handle it. They're equipped. We'd better divert this water and concentrate on how in the hell to save the center. The storm sewers won't handle all the debris that's washing down for very long. You know what will happen if the drains plug."

She was still staring at Krugger's house. Andrew took her hand, pulling her with him, Shawn resisting his urgent tugging. "For God's sake, woman, be reasonable."

She knew he was right. The police were better equipped to warn the old man than she and Andrew, and it was true, the whole place could turn into a full-blown disaster unless they quickly counteracted nature's wrath. Shawn gave in to his urging though she couldn't put Krugger from her mind as they quickly made their way back alongside the slippery banks of the muddied stream. Two days ago she had fought with Nelson over the grades on this very same section, and now grade elevations seemed so inconsequential. Nelson. She had better call Nelson; she had better get the whole damn crew out here. Somehow they would have to keep the drains running free, or Arcadia would surely drown. If only the rain would hold off. Shawn gazed skyward at the dismal overcast. Time was of the essence, and she quickened her pace to match Andrew's long strides.

Back at McCullough Landscaping's trailer, Andrew quickly alerted the police. "Can you get a helicopter up there to warn him?" he asked after tersely summing up the situation for the dispatcher. There was a pause, then Andrew commented, "I know you have other rescue missions, just do the best you can and fast." Rapidly redialing his superintendent, he said, "Samuelson, get the hell out to Arcadia. We got problems," Bellows emphasized, "big problems!"

"I'm on my way."

Andrew handed the phone to Shawn, who immediately called Nelson. Then glancing at her watch, which said 7:10, she listened for one more ring and dropped the receiver back in place. He was probably en route by now.

Only five minutes had passed as Shawn stood impatiently in the trailer's open doorway, hoping to catch Nelson, while at the same time listening intently to Andrew's conversation on the phone, first with the geologist and then with his pilot. From the sound of it, he was arranging for a firsthand look at the problem from the air. The moment she caught sight of Nelson's pickup, she rushed out the door.

The foreman's eyes darted about the site, and his face fell as he looked at his fresh grading that nowhere resembled the clean cuts he had made the day before. "What the hell!" he stammered to the two laborers who always rode with him.

Shawn pointed to the mountain slope. "It's coming from above the house on the hill. We think the earthquake set off an artesian well. Andrew Bellows is getting a helicop-

ter to go up and take a look. There's grass clumps and
brush washing down from above," she said excitedly.
"Better get the dump truck and catch as much debris as
possible. We *have* to keep the storm sewers running until
we can solve the problem, or everything will be flooded!"

"You're telling me," he said emphatically. "Hey, you
guys, grab the flat shovels from the pickup and let's go."
The laborers wasted no time, and the three of them headed
for the dump truck on the other side of the trailer.

A sudden gust of wind tousled Shawn's tangled tresses,
and she impatiently brushed the hair out of her face,
straining her eyes toward the mountain. How in the hell
do you stop an underground spring, a big one from the
looks of things? And with the soil already saturated from
the continual rains, it wouldn't take long for the whole
place to be under water.

As she stood staring at the continual flow, wishing more
than ever that Tony was here, Shawn felt large drops of
cold moisture on her face. The storm was starting. Mr.
Krugger! Where was the helicopter that had been promised? "I was born there and I'll die there," rang through
her head. She was sure the old man was still in the house,
and as she gazed at the ancient wooden structure, she
could visualize it slipping, hear the cracking of rotted
wood. Oh, Lord, somebody had to get him out. Shawn
walked over to Nelson's pickup. He had gotten so worked
up that he had left the keys in the ignition. Andrew was
about fifty feet away, gesticulating with Samuelson, and
the two men were deeply intent on developing a plan of
action.

By now, the rain was coming down in full force, pelting
her from all sides, rising wind tearing at the jacket
Andrew had loaned her, the moisture turning the leather
a glistening dark hue. She couldn't stop thinking about
the aged man. Impulsively, Shawn yanked the door of
Nelson's truck open, climbed in, and turned the key. It
was, after all, McCullough Landscaping's pick-up, and
somebody had to get that stubborn old man out of there.
She put the truck in gear and sped toward the exit.

The mountain road was rocky and full of ruts. Shawn could barely see with the rain beating furiously against the windshield and the wipers unable to keep pace as she manuevered the difficult curves. Mud was everywhere, and only the rocks, pounded into the earth from years of wear and weather, provided a base that was passable. She dared not look at the edges of the narrow roadway or she would surely give up her mission of madness. What if he wasn't even there? But she knew he would be. Shawn stared straight ahead, straining through the blurry windshield at the road, only the road. She would make it if the wind and rain let up, but the gusts, even in the three-quarter-ton pickup, made steering difficult, and the truck bounced through the ruts, growling its protest at the abuse. Shawn downshifted. The house was still one hundred yards away, and despite the wind, she could hear the creak of the old structure.

So intent was she on watching the house that she failed to realize the ruts were deeper in this stretch and brimming with muddy water, leaving no way to gauge their depth. A sudden drop of the right front of the pickup jolted her grip on the steering wheel, and the truck was mired in the spot. "Oh, come on," she pleaded. "We're almost there." But the spin of tires as she pressed the accelerator told her it was hopeless.

"Oh, hell," she cursed, striking the steering wheel with her small fist. There was no time to waste trying to rock it out. Shawn leaned on the horn a long minute, shut the engine down, and bolted from the truck. "Mr. Krugger," she yelled as she stumbled over the bumpy terrain, barely able to stand up with the wind assailing her full-force and her feet sinking in the quagmire. "Mr. Krugger, dammit, I know you're in there! Get out!"

But there was no answer, only the loud barking of a dog. Shawn pulled the jacket tight about her rain-soaked body, and with determination born of fear, she struggled toward the front door, trying the knob, but it was locked.

"Mr. Krugger," she shouted, banging on the door with

both fists. "You stubborn, idiotic old man, get the hell out of there! Don't you see it's time to give up?"

Finally, when her fists were becoming raw, the door opened, and she all but fell into Mr. Krugger's arms. "Don't you have even a lick of sense?" Shawn sputtered. "This house is on the verge of collapse. *Listen* to it!"

The old homestead creaked and groaned a sad, defiant protest to the wind, and a small spotted terrier stood yapping at intervals at the intruder. "Oh, shut up," Shawn said forcefully to the animal. "You're just as stupid as he is."

The surprised dog cowered behind his master, whose angry expression erupted into angrier exclamations. "Now you listen to me! This is my house! I was born here," he repeated with outrage.

"Yes, you told me, and you're going to die here, too, if you don't listen to reason. For God's sake, man, can't you see all that water coming off the face of the mountain? It's going to wash this house right down the slope like a match box!"

"Go away," he shouted, "and leave me be! It's none of your business! What do you care about an old man, anyway?"

"I'm not going to leave unless you come with me, and believe me, I can be just as stubborn as you," Shawn said resolutely, her sapphire eyes flashing in anger and fear.

He walked to the window and looked out at the raging storm, then turning to her, he said, "Why did you come up here in such a storm? That road's full of ruts. No place for a woman."

"I guess I'm a damn idiot, too," she said, "or maybe I understand what it's like to have to give up your beloved home. But you must!"

Even as she spoke, the old structure, whose frame was stressed beyond endurance, shifted, and the sickening cracking of wood as Shawn and Mr. Krugger struggled to maintain their balance served as a final warning. Fear clutched at Shawn's heart. "You're wasting precious sec-

onds," she said angrily. "Do you want the three of us
buried at the bottom of the hill?"

He shook his head solemnly, and she knew in that
instant that he had sadly resigned himself to leaving.

"Come on," she said, a little more patiently, suddenly
wondering how in the hell they were going to get off the
mountain with the truck out of commission. Did he have a
car? Even so, the pickup was in the way.

"Just a minute," he said almost pleadingly. "I'll just get
Emma's picture."

"Your wife?"

He nodded.

Shawn stood in the doorway, watching him disappear
into the other room, his shoulders slumped. A lump filled
her throat. She knew every second counted, but she
couldn't deny him his last link to the past even though
fear had become a raw ache as she listened to the house
creak and shudder as if drawing its last rasping breath.

While Shawn had fought her way up the treacherous
hillside road, Arcadia Lane had come to life. It was
seven-thirty A.M., and a continual flow of workmen were
arriving. The site was mass confusion with carpenters,
plumbers, electricians, and all of the various tradesmen
exclaiming about the storm, some hurrying out of the
weather to an inside job, and others, unable to work in the
downpour, simply putting in an appearance, checking
their particular phase of work for damage. However, they
all had one frightening question in common. Anxiety was
palpable and filled the air like thick, muffling smog. What
was happening on the mountainside? Was all of their work
destined for ruin?

Andrew Bellows had put the word out that he wanted to
see all workmen on the inside of the mall, beneath the
enclosure between Saks and Macy's. When the men were
gathered in out of the storm's fury, Bellows took charge.
"All right, men," he said, "you all have a choice. I won't
pull any punches. This is no picnic going on here! I have a
helicopter en route and a geologist on his way. We're going
to see if we can figure out a way to safely divert the water

coming down the slope. I've given Samuelson orders to blockade the major part of the parking lot. There's every possibility of a slide, and I don't want anyone even close to the foot of that mountain. Do you understand?"

There was a lot of mumbled exclamations and heads nodding.

"In that case, you can stay if you like, we sure as hell need your help, but I don't want anyone around who isn't going to take this turn of events seriously. Samuelson and I won't have time to play policemen. Never mind which contractor you work for. There are only two bosses here today. My superintendent and myself. If you have a quarrel with that, I suggest that you leave immediately." Noting with satisfaction that not one man moved, Bellows continued. "Now, there're only two places I want to see vehicles of any kind, either heading toward the exit or on the opposite side of the center. No foolish moves. Do I make myself clear?"

The usually boisterous men solemnly nodded their agreement.

"Good," he said. "All right, Samuelson, I'll leave the ground operation to you for the present. I'll be all tied up with the geologist and the chopper as soon as they arrive. Right now I'm going to see what I can do about getting hold of the fire department for some high-powered hose to keep the mud from plugging the storm sewers. If you need me, I'll be at McCullough's field office. It's closer than ours." With that, Andrew turned on his heel, and in long quick strides, disappeared into the pelting rain.

"Let's hit it," the superintendent said. "Johnson, you grab a couple of guys and go pick up the dump trucks we have in the yard. Run by the County Flood Control and fill those suckers with all the sandbags they'll give ya. They know you're coming." Then turning to Ace Concrete's foreman, he said, "Severin, I want you to buy up all the burlap bags you can find and charge 'em to Bellows Enterprises. The big boss has a couple of ten-wheelers

full of sand en route. Now, Nelson, collect all that crap
that's coming off the hill. Drop it in the 'bone yard' for
now."

"Way ahead of you. The broad already gave us orders to
that effect. Got a half a load of debris right now."

"No shit! Sounds like she's got more going for her than
the wiggle of her cute little ass!"

Nelson laughed. "Could be," he said.

"The rest of you guys," Bellows's super said, "are all on
standby. You'll be needed for a chain-gang operation of
filling bags and toting sand. Meanwhile, grab your rain
gear and pick a sewer drain. I don't care if it is raining like
hell and blowing like a son of a bitch, we have to keep
those mothers running as long as we can stand up in this
gale!"

The men all took off toward their respective vehicles, and Samuelson headed in the direction of the landscape trailer. When his super entered, Bellows slammed
down the phone. "How'd you make out?" Samuelson
asked.

"They weren't too anxious to tie up their equipment, but
it looks like we'll get at least one truck," Bellows said.

Samuelson shrugged.

Suddenly Nelson burst through the door, sputtering
angrily, "You guys know who took my truck? I had it
parked right over there."

"Hell, no," Samuelson said. "It probably floated away."

Somehow, Andrew knew instantly. He had been wondering what had happened to Shawn since his return to
the trailer. "Where's Shawn McCullough?" he demanded.

"She was in the doorway of the trailer the last time I
saw her," Nelson offered.

"Oh, damn!" Bellows exclaimed. "Well, she's not here
now. She's on that mountain, sure as hell!"

He charged out the door with Samuelson and Nelson
following in his wake. "She took your truck up the
mountain to warn Krüger, I'll bet anything! Christ on a
crutch, you can't tell that woman a goddamn thing."

"She's got guts, I'll say that," Nelson remarked.

"I'm taking the four-wheel-drive," Bellows snapped at Samuelson. "Where are the keys?"

As the superintendent pulled the keys from his rain-drenched coat pocket, another rumble filled the air.

"Jesus, that's all we need, thunder and lightning," Nelson griped.

"That's not thunder!" Andrew yelled as the ground began to tremble. "That's an aftershock!" His eyes flashed toward the mountain. Could he make it up there in time? He grabbed the keys from Samuelson's hand, but before he could move, a massive roar from the distant mountain froze the three men in horror. Their heads jerked up in unison, and they stared unbelievingly at the avalanche of mud sweeping the rickety, timeworn house in its path.

"Oh, my God, Shawn!" Bellows uttered.

The trio of strong men watched helplessly, awestruck by the horrendous sight before them, powerless to stop nature's onslaught.

Chapter Twenty-four

At the same instant on that mid-February morning that Krugger's house was being swept down the mountainside, Matt Monroe was entering the massive doors of T. J. Lewis Enterprises. It was eight A.M., and even though it had been a long sleepless flight home from South Africa, the thought of seeing Shawn soon was revitalizing.

He was certain the board members would be pleased with his painstaking research and the purchase agreement that he had negotiated. He would hopefully wrap up his presentation by noon and be on tomorrow morning's flight to San Francisco and Shawn.

Matt smiled to himself when he thought about her. No more painful partings. He had given Woodhall's offer a lot of thought while in Africa, and the prospect appealed to him. Picturing Shawn, he mused what a great legislator's, or even governor's, wife she would make. Now she could get rid of the landscaping business. She would be far too busy helping him campaign, and if he had his way, Shawn would be returning to L.A. as his wife. Happy plans whirled through Matt's mind kaleidoscopically as he walked down the hall toward his office.

"Well, hello there, stranger," a cheery, familiar voice arrested him.

Matt spun around. "Patrice. God, it's good to see you, honey. You look fantastic. Got a hug for an old friend?"

Matt hugged her tightly, and Patrice, feeling his warm arms around her, became overwhelmed by his sheer masculinity and the sudden return of her passionate yearning.

Releasing her, his hand slipped about her waist. "Come on into my office and let me look at you. It's been too damn long."

Oh, this is pure hell, she thought. All the time she'd missed him being here, and now that he was, she almost wished he was back in Africa.

"Now tell me, what have you been up to?" Matt urged.

Patrice shrugged. "Nothing that exciting. You know, the same old routine. T. J. always manages to keep me busy. You're the one who must have all kinds of stories to tell. And what a tan you've acquired."

His grin set off his even, white teeth, and the gold flecks in his hair gleamed. "Get's pretty hot on that continent, especially for attorneys."

She laughed softly. "I can imagine, but I take it that your negotiations came out well."

"Yes," he said. "They bought the whole deal—lock, stock, and barrel. You know, Patrice, it just seems that lately everything's falling into place for me, thanks to your and T. J.'s encouragement," he added more seriously. "I couldn't ask for more supportive friends."

Patrice absently toyed with the stapler on his desk. Matt's good looks, his charm, his very presence were destroying all the backbone she had managed to muster since their parting. She had to get away from him. "Matt, I don't mean to rush off like this, but I do have several urgent errands to attend to," she said in panic as she bolted toward the door.

"Patrice, wait." Matt took her hand, preventing her flight. "What's the matter? You're trembling. Do you feel all right, honey?"

"Oh, it's nothing, just nervous energy. T. J. has had me

running a lot this week. Guess I'm all geared up," she rushed on, attempting to make light of her distress.

"Hey," he said seriously. "Do you need a warden? Must I always stay around to make sure that you take care of yourself?"

"No, really, I'm fine, Matt," she said as convincingly as she could manage.

"Okay, if you're sure," he said. "But you can't leave till I tell you my fantastic news."

She knew before he said the words that the time for their final parting had come. She smiled, though the ache within her was eating away at her, and her voice belied her facial expression. "You're going to marry Shawn," she stated flatly.

Matt was too ecstatic to note her dejection. "Yes, I'm leaving shortly for San Francisco to ask her to marry me. I really want you to meet her. After all, the two of you are the most important women in my life. You'll like her, Patrice."

Somehow Patrice got out her congratulations, then turned once more to leave.

"Just a minute, I haven't finished my good news."

Oh, for God's sake, what more does he want from me? she thought.

He went on exuberantly. "You remember what I confided in you before I left? Well, I've decided to accept Woodhall's offer and go into politics."

"That *is* good news," she said sincerely. "You'll be a great legislator."

"And you'd be my perfect campaign manager," he said enthusiastically.

"I'm sorry, Matt, but nothing's changed," she said firmly. "I really am glad for you, but we just can't be one big, happy family." With that, she squeezed his hand and abruptly left his office, quietly closing the door behind her.

Matt stared at the closed door, and despite his feeling of exultation, there was suddenly a painful emptiness growing within him. He would miss her. God, how he would miss that beautiful lady.

The moment she had shut the door, Patrice bolted down the carpeted hallway. She charged by the receptionist, on through her own office, and burst into T. J. Lewis's domain without her usual light knock.

Lewis was sipping coffee, his attention devoted to the file that was spread out across his desk. He looked up slightly startled. "Oh, good morning, Patty."

"Remember that talk we had about a Dallas transfer?" she blurted out without so much as a greeting. "Well, I've thought about it, and that's what I want. You know my situation with Matt. Oh, T. J., I've tried, but I just can't work it out here. I have to get away, do something new, a change of scenery," she babbled, out of control.

For a moment, the entrepreneur simply gazed at her in his analytical way, the heavy dark brows arched, the eyes deeply compassionate. There was no getting around it, Patrice was dead-serious this time. He was going to lose her one way or the other, and it wasn't the corporation that would suffer as much as he would. Somehow he could manage to find an efficient assistant, but he could never replace this loved one. Damn that Monroe, anyway. How in hell could he not realize what he had so cavalierly thrown away?

"Relax, Patty, relax," he said in the soothing voice that he often, of late, found himself using with her. "I'm sure we can work out something. Let me get through this board meeting, and then we'll have a leisurely lunch. I know we can arrive at some solution."

"No more stalling, T. J. I only agreed to stay on long enough for you to find a replacement, remember?" Her golden brown eyes flashed in indignation. "I need a complete change, and I'm not going to find it here in L.A."

Lewis stroked his beard while gazing pensively at Patrice in that familiar way he had of buying himself time to formulate a fitting reply. "Don't be so presumptuous, my dear. I may be able to offer you something better than a transfer. Let's discuss it at lunch."

"Can't you tell me now?" she demanded impatiently.

He rose from his chair and came around the desk to take

her hands. "Trust me, Patty," he said most beseechingly, his dark eyes imploring. "I need to think about this myself for a little longer. Just wait until lunch, please? We can take the whole afternoon if necessary."

Suddenly all the wonderful things he had done for her, the special way that he alone had of making her feel good about herself, flooded her mind and shamed her. Trust him? How could she not, when he had been the most stabilizing influence in her life, this wonderful teddy bear of a man. He was so dear to her, and here she was, inflicting her pain on him. It wasn't fair. "All right," she said softly, touching his hand. "I'll wait for lunch."

"Good," he nodded, smiling as he walked her to the door.

When she had gone, Lewis seated himself once again. Picking up the contract, he stared at it unseeingly for a long moment before putting it aside. A whole new contract of a completely different nature was forming in his mind. Did he dare?

As Patrice walked out of T. J. Lewis's office, stomach churning, a more conventional type of storm continued to batter the San Francisco Bay Area. Bellows, Samuelson, and Nelson stood motionless in the parking lot at Arcadia Lane, transfixed by nature's terrifying display. Despite all Bellows's power, he felt helpless, gaping at the monstrous juggernaut that, in the space of seconds, was ravaging the side of the mountain with a thunderous roar. Krugger's house seemed to sail like an ancient galleon atop the mass of mud and rocks, twisting and quivering as trees toppled and fell with the insignificance of toothpicks in the wake of the avalanche.

Krugger's old house, engulfed in mud and entangled with uprooted trees, shuddered violently. Then it folded like a ruptured accordian with a resounding crunch as it all but disintegrated under the huge old oak tree that seemed to stand in sole defense of the picnic/playground area below.

In Bellows's mind, there was but one crushing thought as he powerlessly watched the tons of mud now an

ominous invader, threatening his concrete world, its
spreading tentacles enveloping all that stood in its path.
Shawn! Oh, my God, Shawn! Could she have survived this
colossal destruction? He gazed at the ugly brown scars on
the mountain where the treacherous slide had changed
the shape of the green hills, carving a mammoth swath,
and his cry of anguish was a barely audible prayer. "Oh,
God, protect her, please—please!"

"Holy shit!" Samuelson exclaimed. "Would you look at
that?"

"Hell's afire!" Nelson gasped. "I've never seen anything
like it!"

Even as he stared at the encroaching mud, debris, and
splintered remains of trees and Krugger's homestead,
Bellows reacted. "Samuelson, see if that damn fire truck
arrived. Tell them to send for more help. Then get the
bulldozer and the dump truck over here in one hell of a
hurry. Nelson, get a crew together. We'll need your
backhoe, skiploader, and the Fergie. Shawn and Krugger
must be in there somewhere," he said urgently. "We have
to get them out!"

Lunging forward, driven by dread and a love he'd never
known before, Bellows struggled against the creeping
brown ooze.

Clothes drenched and clinging, Andrew attacked the
rising mass of rubble, barely aware that Nelson was
beside him, fighting the obstacles in their path. Was
she still alive, buried by tons of mud and wreckage? Please
let her be safe, he silently prayed. Bellows hurled
huge boards and barely recognizable household goods
aside with a strength born of sheer determination as
he slipped and slid in the mud, at times sinking to his
knees in his desperate attempt to reach the collapsed
structure.

Within minutes, the fire truck barreled through the
mud, a platoon of workers racing along behind. Carpenters, plumbers, electricians, laborers—all pitched in to
comprise a team of anxious rescue workers to be led by
Bellows himself.

While the wind assailed them full-force and the pelting rain added to the unstable footing, Andrew directed the equipment operators with the expertise and caution of a superior construction boss.

When they had painstakingly cleared a path through the mound of mud in front of the old house, they carefully worked their way through broken furniture, which had been pushed out by the explosive force of the mud. Bellows strained to hear the slightest indication of life. Were his ears playing tricks? He hesitated. "Hold it," he shouted above the howling wind. "You guys hear anything?"

Almost miraculously, within the same breath he heard, "H-e-l-l-l-p." It seemed to come from the center of the almost completely collapsed structure. Spurred on by the faint cry, the men redoubled their efforts. Bellows and the firemen tried the front door, but the attempt was useless. Wreckage had jammed it shut, and the windows as well.

"Son of a bitch!" Andrew swore. "We can't break it in! The whole damn thing is probably just hanging together by what little support is left of the framework. If we dislodge that, we'll never get them out."

"The roof," one of the firemen said, pointing. "We can chop a hole through it." They both hurried to the truck, returning with a ladder and several axes. With ax in hand, Andrew wasted no time scrambling to the rooftop, chopping and hacking at the shingles. "Hold on, Shawn! We'll have you out in a minute," he cried as he tore at the shingles like a wild man.

When he had cut a hole large enough to accommodate his body, one of the two firemen on the roof gently pushed him aside. "Whoever is in there may need CPR. If you don't know the procedure, better let us go in."

Bellows nodded. "All right," he said impatiently, "but get moving!"

Suddenly the debris beneath them shifted and buckled, knocking all three men to the ground. Andrew was instantly on his feet, completely mud-covered, resetting the ladder. The firemen picked themselves up, futilely wiping mud from their hands onto their muddied rain gear.

"H-e-l-l-l-p," came a second soft, muffled cry. And before either of the firemen could respond, Bellows was up the ladder and onto the roof, lowering himself through the hole. "Shawn," he yelled frantically as he dropped into the muddy quagmire below. "Where are you, Shawn?"

Twisted, mud-covered flooring was everywhere; beams hung from the ceiling like streamers; plaster lay in jagged pieces scattered about like huge hunks of confetti amidst the mud. Battered and broken furniture, strewn in piles, jammed the front door. Strangely, the only thing left intact was the roof, and no telling when that would go.

Suddenly the whining of a dog startled Andrew, and he carefully turned to glimpse a small terrier pitifully wriggling free from the muck. By now, the two firemen and Nelson were at Andrew's side. Bellows cautiously picked up the shivering, slippery mongrel and handed him to Nelson, who in turn relayed him to the nearest fireman.

"I didn't come here to save a mutt," Nelson grumbled.

But the dog struggled free, climbed on an overturned couch, whining pathetically as he pawed at the pile of mud-encrusted furnishings beneath him.

"H-e-l-l-l-p." It was almost a whisper now, and Bellows jerked at the debris frantically. "There's someone under here!" he shouted. "Give me a hand!"

The three men yanked and pulled, throwing broken pieces of furniture aside until at last the victim was free. "Krugger," Bellows said despairingly, unable to hide his disappointment. "Where's Shawn?"

But for the moment, the old man was too stunned to speak. "Damn you! I said, where's Shawn?" Bellows roughly shook the old man's shoulders. "Was she here?"

"The girl?" Krugger said dazedly as the firemen helped him to his feet.

"Yes, the girl," Bellows snapped.

The old man shook his head. "She was right about here in the doorway when it hit. I just wanted to get Emma's picture," he rambled as he gazed numbly at the surrounding shambles, his hand still clutching the photo. "I was in the bedroom. The force threw me out here to the front. That's all I know."

"Christ almighty! She must have been thrown from the house," Bellows said, desolation showing through his words. "She could be anywhere, even underneath this whole damn mess. Oh, my God!"

As he spoke those words, there was a formidable cracking sound, and more chunks of plaster fell from the ceiling.

"There's no sign of her in here," one of the firemen reported.

"We have to get out," the other firemen warned. "This whole place is a death trap."

"You go on," Bellows said to the firemen. "I have to have one last look around."

"Better make it quick," the first fireman said as he tore off a good-sized piece of a bedraggled curtain, wrapped it securely about the suddenly complacent dog, and tucked the animal under one arm. "This is no place to loiter!"

"I'll stay with you," Nelson volunteered.

"What? Are you crazy? Get the hell out of here! I'll be behind you in a minute."

When he had convinced them and they were gone, Andrew searched the rubble like a man possessed, ripping and tearing, hands bleeding. There seemed little hope that he would ever see her alive again, and his keen mind was dulled by grief. So overwrought was he that he but vaguely heard the helicopter overhead. Grieving for Shawn, he nevertheless realized that he was needed to direct the men. Arcadia Lane would be a total washout if a lot of quick thinking wasn't immediately applied, but right now it all seemed so meaningless. The dream he had envisioned was fading, and now all he could see was the face of Shawn; beautiful, spirited Shawn, who couldn't bear to let a stubborn old man die.

Andrew slumped on the overturned couch, his head in

his hands, trying to think. He couldn't ask the men to keep digging through the rubble. With the continual rain and the rising underground water, there was no way of telling how many more slides to expect. He couldn't endanger other lives, even if it meant the life of the only woman he'd ever loved. Could she have possibly been thrown clear? But he knew that was wishful thinking. Even if it were possible, Shawn could have been thrown clear of the house only to be buried in the massive slide. Oh, God, it didn't matter that she wasn't his; all that mattered was to know she lived. "Shawn, I loved you so," he whispered, "more than life."

Lost in grief, the next thing he knew, a hand was touching his shoulder, startling him.

It was Steve Grodecki, his pilot, who stated flatly, "You were wondering where the hell I was with the chopper."

Andrew didn't reply, but Grodecki already knew that was not the crushing concern at the moment.

"Come on, old buddy, there's nothing more you can do here. She may be out on the slope somewhere. Let's take a look with the bird, huh?" He pulled his friend to his feet, and the two men crawled out through the hole in the roof.

Back on the ground, they fought their way to the firmer footing of the asphalt parking lot. Andrew turned for one last look at the old house, then miserably turned away.

Grodecki gave him no time to dwell on it. "Come on," he ordered. "The geologist is waiting for us at the chopper."

"I don't give a damn about the geologist. Everything and everyone can wait! You got a rope or a sling on that chopper?"

"Yeah," Grodecki said.

"Good, we'll take a look from the air, and if we can't see her, I want you to set me down up there where the house was."

"You didn't find Shawn McCullough?" Samuelson asked as he and Nelson walked up. "I'll go with you, Bellows."

"Me, too," Nelson offered solemnly, but his sober look as he faced Bellows gradually blossomed to a full-blown grin as his sharp eyes caught a small figure advancing toward them.

"Thanks, fellas. Anybody who wants to join the search on the hillside for Shawn McCullough," he said to the other men standing by, "I'll make it worth your while."

One by one, he noticed they were all grinning, and he felt a light tap on his back. Andrew spun on his heel.

"Are you looking for someone?" piped a meek little voice.

She was alive! Standing there. Mud from head to toe. For a moment he was overcome. Then he burst out, "Shawn! Thank God! You have *never* looked so beautiful!" He picked her up and spun her around until she gasped. Quickly, he returned her to earth.

She looked down at her filthy apparel, and her black hand went to her mud-caked hair. The only clean spots visible were her white teeth when she grinned and the velvet blue of her eyes. "Some taste you have," she quipped to cover her embarrassment by his openly affectionate display. Then she swayed from sheer exhaustion.

He noticed her teeter and quickly reached to steady her. "Oh, Andrew," she breathed before collapsing into his arms.

"Samuelson, don't just stand there. Call the damn paramedics!" Andrew bellowed.

When Shawn's eyes fluttered open, her senses were immediately assailed by the icy chill of the wind-driven rain, and she burrowed her head more deeply into Andrew's protective shoulder while he carried her toward the field office. She was exhausted from fighting the mud on the mountain, and her body ached all over. For the moment, she wanted only to stay in the warm comfort of his arms and clear her light-headedness. Over Andrew's shoulder she became aware of the group of men staring after them, and she was embarrassed. Now they would surely consider her trouble. What a dumb thing to do, faint in front of all the workmen; especially Nelson, who thought her an utter nuisance simply by virtue of being female. This would really clinch it.

"Andy, put me down. I can walk," she sputtered weakly.

"Sure you can, Ms. McCullough," he said facetiously. "I think you've done your quota of walking for this morning. Just relax, the paramedics are on their way."

"Paramedics? Oh, Andy, I'm all right!"

"We're going to make damn sure of that," he stated firmly, not loosening his grip the least bit as he nudged the door of the trailer with his foot, then kicked it open. He gently lowered her to the battered, old office chair. "Now, you sit right here like a good girl till they check you over, understand?"

"Andrew, don't patronize me," she said indignantly. "I'm perfectly all right. Just a little tired." But the solid set of his jaw told her he offered no choice in the matter, and she was inwardly relieved to be able to rest. Every muscle throbbed as if she'd been cycled through a washing machine. It was miraculous that no bones had been broken when she had been forcefully ejected from the doorway of Krugger's house by the impact of the slide. "Krugger! What happened to Mr. Krugger? Is he alive?" she asked anxiously.

Andrew grinned. "Yes, we pulled him out of the house. He's fine and in one piece. The old bird's too mean to die."

"Well, damn. To think I risked my life to get that stubborn old goat out, and he still slid down that godforsaken mountain in that rotten house!" she exclaimed indignantly.

Andrew laughed. "Shawn McCullough, you are something."

"And so are you, my friend," she said seriously. "Thanks for worrying about me. I didn't mean to cause so much trouble, but I simply had to warn him. I could never have lived with myself otherwise." Just remembering how frightened she had been sent shivers through her, and her skin felt like ice. "Lord, Andy, I'm so cold. That rain must be coming from the North Pole."

He wanted to hug her tightly enough to stop her shivering, but instead, he searched about the trailer, sidestepping the jumble of hardware that was still strewn all over the floor from the earthquake. "Here," he said, pulling a crumpled fleece-lined Windbreaker from a top shelf. "Not too clean, but it'll stop your teeth from chattering. Must be Rizzo's."

"I'll take it," she said, struggling to pull her arms out of Andrew's tattered leather jacket.

He saw her wince, and he knew she was in pain. "Here, let me help," he offered, and she gratefully accepted.

Once snugly wrapped in the dry garment, she sighed. "Oh, does that feel better." Only then did she become aware of Andrew holding his torn and ruined jacket distastefully at arm's length as if at a loss as to what to do with it. "Andy, I'm so sorry, your beautiful jacket . . ." she offered ruefully.

"That's the very last thing I care about," he said, dropping the filthy coat into the wastebasket.

By now the paramedics had arrived, accompanied by Samuelson. Seeing that Shawn was conscious and alert, the superintendent remarked, "Glad you're okay, Ms. McCullough. Like Nelson said, you're some gutsy lady."

His remark warmed her more than the fleece lining around her. "Thank you," she smiled.

Samuelson grinned, then turned to Bellows. "The geologist and Grodecki are waiting for you. They're ready to crank up the chopper and brave the wind for a look-see."

"Yeah, I know," Andrew said. "Hold up and I'll join you." Taking Shawn's hand, he spoke so that the paramedics could hear, "Promise me you'll let them check you thoroughly, and if they want you to go to the hospital, you'll go."

"You got the first one," she said. "But not the second. I'm not leaving."

"She's in your hands, fellas," he said with a helpless shrug, "but I warn you, she's one stubborn lady!"

Satisfied that Shawn was in competent hands, Andrew

Bellows diverted his attention to the immediate problems with renewed vigor. Thank God Shawn was safe. Not only was she alive, she was her normal feisty self, and he was damn happy. He strode purposefully toward his men, scarcely feeling the chilling wind or battering rain.

T. J. Lewis opened the door of his silver-gray Cadillac for Patrice, who gracefully slid onto the seat. "The board meeting went well, I presume," she said as she got in.

"Oh, yes, the deal is all set," he said, glancing over at her with a pleased expression. "But let's forget about business for the moment. I'm more concerned about you, not the business," he explained. "We can get back to that later. I thought we could drive out to the ocean and just talk awhile, then perhaps have lunch at one of the restaurants along the beach. What do you say?"

Was he stalling again? Even though the knowledge that she was valuable to him was flattering, she couldn't help feeling a bit annoyed that he seemed to be hedging, completely out of keeping with his behavior regarding all other business matters. Still, she did need to talk to someone, and who better than a beloved friend whose interest in her was genuine? She gave him a faint smile and settled back in her seat.

While T. J. concentrated on driving, Patrice tried to imagine a new life in Dallas. It was going to take time to forget Matt and to get everything in her life back into proper perspective. She had really tried for friendship, but after this morning, she knew it wouldn't work. Had he ever really loved her as he had at one time professed? she wondered. Not that it made any difference anymore. Matt had found a new love. She had to really make an effort to put all her memories aside; the good and the bad. She was barely aware that T. J. had pulled to a stop along a quiet stretch of the beach. "See those rocks?" he pointed downward. "How would you like to take a walk?"

Patrice looked down at her high heels. "In these?" she sputtered.

"Oh, hell, take 'em off. That's what I'm going to do." He opened the door, got out, kicked off his shoes, pitched them on the floor of the car, and rolled up his pant legs.

"But my nylons?" she said helplessly.

He laughed. "Sometimes you worry about the damndest things! Take 'em off, too. My back is turned and no one can see you in the car."

A few minutes later, he gave her a steadying hand to help her down a grassy knoll, and they walked silently along the shore, each enjoying the lapping waves that repeatedly teased their toes with cool, frothy bubbles.

How many bosses would go to such lengths for an employee? She knew she was special to him, yet she had seen him react just as kindly on numerous occasions with other employees. What a kind, perceptive man he was, she mused. She would really miss him.

"Well," he said, bending over his slight paunch to pick up and examine a bleached shell as he rolled it in his palm. "Do you feel like talking about what has upset you so?"

"You already know," she said, picking out a sturdy piece of driftwood and lowering herself on it with a sigh. "Oh, T. J., if only I could love someone who would love me in return, in all the gentle, kind ways that are so important; someone who would never want another woman," she said, feeling selfish. She attempted a wistful smile. "Right now I'm so scared, so tired of trying to be brave and expected to be magnanimous, when all I want is love and security and a couple of kids before I get too old to safely have them."

He put his hands on her shoulders and tilted her chin up to face him. Then, dark, honest eyes boring into hers, he said, "Patty, honey, you could have that with me. Don't you know I love you, my sweet? Marry me, and you'll never have to be scared or worried again. You can stop working and have those kids."

At first she thought she had heard him incorrectly. She blinked back tears as her brimming eyes focused on his

face, the serious face of someone very dear and caring. She
realized from the love and compassion mirrored there that
she had actually heard him right, and she drew in a sharp
breath, too stunned to speak. She could only stare wide-
eyed at the man she had loved like a father for so long.
Never once had she suspected his secret love for her, but
now it lay naked in his adoring gaze.

She opened her mouth to speak, but his fingers touched
her lips, beseeching her silence. "Please," he said, "I know
the way you feel about Matt, and I know that you don't
love me in that same way." For a fleeting moment she saw
a sadness flicker over his face, and he turned away. "But I
can live with that," he said.

She waited for his gaze to return, and she searched his
face, the face of a man who had never willingly hurt
anyone, let alone someone he loved. Her thoughts tumbled
like dice in a cup, and it was a long moment before she
digested what he had offered her. "T. J.," was all she could
say, the tears flowing freely now, running down her
cheeks. "I don't know, T. J., I just don't know what to say.
God love you, my dear friend. I never knew you felt that
way." She hesitated. "Even if I said yes, it wouldn't be fair
to you."

"I'm willing to take that chance," he said, and then
speaking low, his voice under tight control, he went on, "I
know I'm twenty-five years your senior, but I can give you
the love and security you need, and I've never looked at
another woman since the day I met you. My dear, you're
the most beautiful part of my life, and I can't let you go
without telling you. You talk about being fair to me. I'm
not in the first flush of youth, and I'll be happy to accept
what you are willing to offer, and I will never ask for
what you're not prepared to give. Don't you think I know
that you don't feel the same passionate love for me
as I do for you? But there is love there, a deep caring
kind, and it's enough. Sometimes it's by far the better
kind."

"T. J., I can't." She burst into sobs. "It would look to
everyone as though I'm marrying you for your money."

"What does it matter if you enjoy some of the comforts I can furnish now or later? You know, everything I have is willed to you and a favorite charity, anyway. My lovely lady, you're all I have, the one person deserving to share in what you might say we built together."

She couldn't deny that it was she who had spent countless nights working up reports with him, putting together stacks of paperwork to close deals, and putting her whole heart into helping him. It wasn't until Matt had joined the firm that the pressure had eased. But she also knew that without this kindly, brusque man, she would never have had the business opportunity. She shook her head in mute bewilderment, blurred eyes staring out at the sea for a long minute before she spoke. "And if I say no?"

He lightly kissed her forehead. "It doesn't change anything. I'll always love you, I have ever since we met. You can still transfer to Dallas if you wish, but I couldn't let you go without trying to win you." He took her hand and raised it to his lips. "And if you decide in favor of marriage, you have my promise that if you ever want out, freedom is yours, and if there are children, they, and you, will be well provided for, no matter what. I'll put it in writing."

He was so incredibly unselfish in his love, and she knew he was as good as his word. "I don't know." She shook her head. "I couldn't give you an answer this minute, but I do know that if I decide to marry you, there's no need for a contract. There never would be between us," she added softly.

He smiled. "When can I expect your answer?"

"In a day or two," she said. "But, T. J., I think we'd better pass on lunch. I'm too unnerved at the moment to eat. It isn't every day a girl gets such a handsome proposal."

His face flushed above his well-trimmed beard, and he stammered, "Oh, I know I'm no Don Juan, and certainly no Matt Monroe. But no one could love you more. Think about it and let me know."

It was the first time she'd ever seen this wonderful man embarrassed, and her hand rose to lovingly touch his cheek. "I think you're beautiful in all the ways that count," she said, "and I'm truly honored."

At four o'clock that afternoon she reached for the phone and said yes to the one man she was sure would always really love her.

Chapter Twenty-five

Friday morning at eight, her body still aching, Shawn pulled into the far end of the parking lot at Arcadia Lane amid a beehive of activity. Some of the men she recognized as the same ones she had left working there five hours earlier. Andrew had split the workers into two shifts so that the battle against the encroaching mud could continue uninterrupted throughout the night. Shawn noticed that the construction trailers had been moved to the far end of the parking lot, and the huge floodlights that he had set up had been turned off now that the morning light was penetrating the thick overcast. The rain had measurably lightened, but the weatherman had proclaimed only a short respite. Another storm of considerable intensity was due to hit by late morning. Despite the rain's slowing to a heavy mist, the underground flow had not eased and mud continued to build in the parking lot, the threat of more slides remaining constant.

Yesterday, when Andy had gone up in the helicopter with the geologist, they'd discovered that the quake must have disturbed the bedrock and tapped the water table. Water was gushing out of the ground at two hundred gallons per minute. They'd decided to cap it just like an oil well. Now, if only they could get the well capped before the second deluge. Thank heaven Andrew's Texas office had been able to contact Johnny Pope, one of the best independent cappers in the business. Pope had agreed to help them out when Andrew had started talking five figures.

As she surveyed the damage that was continuing to mount, Shawn was heartsick. A big portion of the work that her crews had completed was literally down the drain. It would be a monumental task to undo the damage and complete the contract by April 16. Just the cleanup alone would take days. The situation was bad enough, but her heart sank even lower when she thought of the cost it entailed. She'd already received progress payments for the majority of the work completed, work that would have to be redone at her expense.

For the second time in her short career as head of the company, she was faced with the threat of possible bankruptcy. It wasn't fair. If only McCullough and Tony were here, she could go back to her cozy office and stick to estimating. What on earth had ever made her think she could run a landscaping business? When the chips were down, she evidently just wasn't tough enough. She remembered Nelson saying she had guts, and it brought an ironic smile. Right now there was nothing but knots in her stomach. What was it her father used to say? You can't keep a good Irishman down? Well, good Irishman or not, she'd sure like to know how to get up. She was so lost in the doldrums that she scarcely noticed Andrew approaching.

"Good morning," he said, smiling cheerfully. "I see you managed to scrape all the mud off. How're those bruises this morning?"

How could he smile when the whole project was a disaster? This was his lifetime vision in ruins. Andrew was the one who truly had guts, and she felt ashamed of her self-pity, yet she couldn't match his cheerful greeting. "You want the truth?"

"Seems like that's what I always get from you." He grinned in approval. "Give me the straight dope, huh?"

"I feel like I've been slammed against a brick wall," she

told him. Then, noting his concern, she added, "But all things considered, I guess I'm lucky to be alive. Oh, Andy, this is a hell of a mess. How can you be so damn cheerful? You probably didn't even get four hours of sleep."

"No, but I did manage to get cleaned up a little, and after all, I wasn't in the middle of the slide. Now stop worrying, we're going to lick this thing, Shawn McCullough. Come on, I'll buy you a cup of coffee. Catering truck's just around the corner, which reminds me: Tell your crew that the tab is all taken care of for as long as this mop-up takes."

Just then their conversation was drowned out by the noisy clatter of a helicopter, and they simultaneously peered skyward. The impressive Sikorsky S-58 was a sight to behold with the derrick needed for capping the water flow dangling from its skyhook as it circled the back parking lot and slowly eased its cargo to the asphalt before releasing it.

The arrival of the chopper lifted Shawn's spirits further, and she matched Andrew's long strides with double-quick short steps. By now the workmen had congregated in a circle around the helicopter that had just landed. Samuelson and Nelson were talking with a stranger, who by his drawl, Shawn supposed was Johnny Pope, the Texan rigger.

Bellows ambled over to them. "What do you think, Pope?" he asked. "Will that derrick suffice?"

"Oh, hell, yes. This is gonna be like taking candy from a baby," the tall lanky Texan remarked. The men, whose tired faces reflected the strain of the past hours, brightened visibly with his declaration, and Andrew slapped him on the back jubilantly.

"I believe we have everything you requested."

"Awright, let's get on with it before that second front moves in. I got to be back in Houston tonight. Got a date and it's not with a well!"

Two hours later, the scene was set. A tow truck had been driven up the fire trail on the far side of the mountain and stationed on the flat mesa to form the base

from which to hook lines to the men below. The diesel
engine had been lowered to the trouble spot and secured
by chains from above, and a stack of pipe had been placed
in a crevice just above the well via the chopper. Huge
lengths of fire hose had been taken up to hook to the valve
after capping to divert the water. Johnny Pope's enthusiasm and daring had rubbed off on the men, and he had
collected a number of volunteers, including Samuelson
and Nelson. Both men being pilots, Andrew Bellows and
Grodecki would work as a team, Andrew on the slope with
a walkie-talkie and Grodecki flying the chopper with a
co-pilot. Everything was all set up and none too soon. The
wind was picking up and the sky had darkened angrily,
foreshadowing the expected storm.

Shawn eyed the helicopter sitting on the far side of the
derrick and for a fleeting second wished she were going
with them. Andrew and the others were already on the
slope, and the chopper would be taking the derrick up
next. Grodecki and his co-pilot were climbing into the
whirlybird. "Wait," Shawn called as she hurried over to
them. "Is there any way that I can listen in on what's
going on up there?"

"Sure," Steve said, stepping back to the ground and
reaching behind the seat to pull out a hard hat with a
built-in radio receiver accompanied by a plug-in radio. He
flipped the dial. "Stay on this frequency. Bellows is on it
and we will be, too."

"Thanks," she said, "and good luck."

Grodecki gave her a bow and a mock salute before
climbing aboard.

Shawn pulled on the yellow hard hat and retreated a
safe distance to watch the craft depart. Could they pull it
off or would the whole mountain slide out from under
them, derrick and all?

Rig attached to the hook, the Sikorsky rose skyward, its
cargo dangling and swaying in the wind as Steve manipu-
lated the craft like the expert he was. "Come on, baby.
Easy does it," Grodecki coaxed as if talking to a favorite
girl friend. His feet worked the pedals, and his right hand

gently rotated the stick to correct a slide to the right as the wind gusted and the craft buffeted in the turbulent air. "Man, this'll keep you awake," he said to the co-pilot, who looked over and frowned.

Both men kept a constant vigil on the instruments. A stall could be fatal. There would be little chance for recovery in this wind with the attached load unless they could quickly jettison the derrick. Beads of sweat glistened on the pilots' faces as they neared the RPM redline, and Grodecki eased up on the throttle, silently praying that the natural updraft would give them an air cushion as they scaled the slope.

"Nice going, so far so good," Bellows's voice clearly encouraged from the radio. "You're almost here. Just ease it on up, Steve. Another two hundred feet and you've got it."

"Two hundred feet. Holy Christ! It might as well be a thousand."

On the ground, Shawn and the men watched the maneuver from the parking lot and listened intently as Andrew skillfully guided the pilot to a position directly above the well.

"You're getting close," Bellows said. "Ease it about ten feet to your right."

"Nothing easy up here today, buddy." Grodecki cracked. "Trying to make this bird hover is like patting your head with one hand, rubbing your stomach with the other, and trying to stay in two hop-scotch squares. You savvy?"

"I believe it." Bellows laughed. "You're almost right on now. Correct a foot or so left. That's it, on target. Push that magic button to release the charges."

Shawn could hear the explosives that were to drive spearlike anchors down through the derrick legs into the bedrock.

"Good shot." Pope's drawl came through. "It's anchored solid. This baby isn't going anywhere."

Shawn and the firemen, who had all been listening, smiled at each other as they watched the helicopter descend to the parking lot. "Great," Shawn said. She barely had the word out before she felt a sudden surge in the wind, and the darkened sky opened up as if in rebellious counterattack to their progress on the mountain.

Shawn pulled her slicker tighter and fought the rain and howling wind that threatened to blow her meager ninety-nine pounds away as she trudged away to check the storm sewers. She could hear Andrew and Johnny Pope on the radio and the noisy sputter of the diesel engine in the background as it turned the bit that was boring down to the water table in the heart of the mountain. Just then she saw sodden grass clumps and brush tumbling down the hillside just as they had before the first slippage, and Shawn shuddered with fright.

She was suddenly struck by a horrifying thought: Oh, my God, Andrew and the men on the mountain! "Andrew!" she yelled into the radio. "I think we have the makings of another slide. We're getting an increase in tumbling debris from the mountain down here."

Almost as she spoke, there was an ominous rumble that was clearly recognizable to Shawn, who would remember that sound forever. "Look out! Get the hell out of there!" she screamed to her men in panic. Then into the radio she cried. "Andrew, another slide!" As Shawn shouted warning into the radio, Andrew reacted instinctively.

"Watch out! The damn mountain's giving!" he yelled. "Grab onto whatever's solid!" At that same instant, on the lower side of the derrick where Johnny Pope stood, the earth gave a wrenching shudder and fell away flinging him violently against the cold, hard steel of the structure, while Andrew and the others desperately clung to the newly entrenched support.

"I hope this sonofabitch holds," Bellows muttered.

After what seemed like forever, but was only seconds, the mountain was innocently quiet once more and the derrick stood undaunted.

"Is everybody all right?" Andrew asked anxiously.

The men all nodded except for Pope who was grimacing with pain and holding his right arm at an awkward angle.

"Aw shit, this sure as hell will ruin my date tonight," the rigger complained with disgust.

"To hell with your date, you can get a rain check. Are you OK?"

"Yeah, but I don't know if I can operate with this arm."

"I told you to forget about your date," Bellows chuckled. "Is it safe to proceed with the capping?"

"Christ, yes, we're not stopping now. That derrick is anchored in China! If you've got the muscle, I've got the know-how. Those lines from the tow truck will hold. There's still firm footing on the topside of the derrick and the rigging is still intact." He smiled ruefully. "You're about to get some quick on-the-job training."

While Shawn and her crew began their desperate efforts to save the drains from the new seepage of mud, Johnny Pope could be heard over the radio, instructing Andrew and his team as they strove to cap the well. It seemed like days, but it was early afternoon before a cry of jubilation from the mountain boomed loud and clear over the radio. They had done the impossible.

Suddenly, Shawn was terribly anxious to see Andrew. She watched the chopper lift off, thankful for a slight lull in the wind, and she headed to the parking lot, unaware that she was smiling. It didn't matter that there was a second slide to clean up. Now the water would be flowing through rerouted channels, and soon the men would be safely off the mountain. Even though the rain was still coming down in sheets, Andrew's words came back to her. "We're going to lick this thing, Shawn McCullough."

"You bet we will. We're one hell of a team," she said determinedly as though he could hear her.

In his rented car, Matt Monroe glanced down at his map of Saratoga. The next right should be Arcadia Lane. He was impatient to see Shawn, and his hand on the steering wheel tapped in time with the lively beat on the stereo. At first he'd been disappointed when she hadn't answered her phone last night, but her surprise in seeing him unexpectedly might be even better. Shawn's secretary had indicated that there had been difficulties at the shopping center that required Shawn's attention and that she would probably be there all day. Well, to hell with those kind of problems. Shawn would have a much bigger challenge today, one that involved only the two of them. Perhaps this time she would be ready to really consummate their love. He could vividly picture the events to come—picking out the ring and making plans in which she'd share his political life. He would be the envy of all, to have her beside him as he strove to fulfill his goals, and he never once doubted that Shawn would have the same goals.

Matt guided the car through the entrance of the shopping center, his attention immediately drawn to a helicopter that was just setting down. What was going on? He'd heard about the earthquake aboard the flight from L.A., and obviously the rain had created flooding from the looks of the mountain of sandbag barriers along the storefronts, but why the chopper? Still, what did it matter? Shawn was his only concern. He would ask someone in the group of men standing around the aircraft that had just shut down. Matt got out of the car and made his way to the circle of workers, who seemed to be caught up in excitement.

He hesitated for a moment, his curiosity piqued by the shouts of, "Nice going" and "Congratulations." Happy himself, Matt smiled at their exuberance and watched as the mud-drenched passengers stepped out of the aircraft one by one and the men noisily greeted them with slaps on the back, handshakes, and effusive words of praise. There was a tall, dark, lanky fellow who spoke with a southern drawl, and a ruggedly handsome blond man who seemed to command the most attention.

"All right, gang, this calls for a celebration," the muscular blond fellow said. "Beer's on me. Samuelson, go round up a couple of kegs. This is one working day when booze on the job is permitted."

As the men dispersed, a small figure wearing a yellow hard hat, muddy rain gear, and a happy smile splashed across the parking lot toward the chopper.

It had to be Shawn, Andrew decided. Nobody else was that small, and damned if she wasn't completely covered with mud again. She certainly had a knack for getting herself in the middle of things, yet if not for her earlier warning, there could have been a dire tragedy on the mountain. She was absolutely incredible, a woman of such vitality and determination, which only added to her feminine charm. Even covered with grime, she was the most attractive female he'd ever known. He was eager to talk with her and thank her for the timely warning. Perhaps they might have lunch together in some nice warm restaurant while they thawed out and planned the renovation of the site. With opening day looming all too near and Shawn's penchant for standing on her own, he had no idea of what kind of help she might accept, if any. Still, his smile broadened to a full-blown grin as he again marveled at her spirit and independence. With or without his help, she would manage. Bellows's feet instinctively carried him in her direction.

He heard a masculine voice ahead of him call, "Shawn," and Andrew's face sobered when she at first hesitated, then ran into the tall, dark stranger's arms.

"Matt, oh, Matt, I had no idea you were here," she cried as the man lifted her in his arms in an embrace that chilled Andrew's heart.

Matt Monroe. So here he was, larger than life. The finality hammered home by actually seeing his rival erased every speck of hope that Andrew unconsciously still harbored.

"Darling," he heard Matt say. "God, I can't wait to get you alone. Come on, let's get out of here."

Andrew felt shattered, and Shawn's exuberance paled somewhat upon glimpsing the pain etched on Andrew's face as he stood staring at them. She couldn't define the sudden stab in her heart that strangely dulled her joy in her reunion with Matt. "Wait, Matt. There's someone I want you to meet. You remember the friend I told you about?"

"Oh, yes," he said, "but can't it keep?" He was nearly

bursting to tell her his plans and impatient with the delay.

She took his hand and pulled him along with her. "Congratulations, Andy," she said enthusiastically. "I'm so proud of you and the men. You were fantastic up on the slope today." Then, not giving him a chance to respond, she said, "This is Matt Monroe, Andrew Bellows."

The two men stared coolly at one another for a long, strained moment. "Well, for heaven's sake, can't either of you speak?" she demanded.

"Bellows," Matt finally got the name out. "I understand you're a good friend of Shawn's." There was a slight emphasis on the word *friend,* as though it were necessary for him to define the relationship between Shawn and Andrew aloud.

Andrew accepted the proffered hand, picking up on the innuendo immediately as he nodded. "That's where it's at, Monroe. But it's not by choice. You must be the better man."

"I see," Matt said. "Well, thanks for your honesty."

"Quite all right. Now, if you'll excuse me, I have some pressing business. Take good care of her, you lucky so-and-so," he said while thinking *son of a bitch.* With that, Andrew turned abruptly on his heel and strode toward Samuelson. "What the hell are you gawking at? Can't you see that there's a hell of a lot of work to do?"

Samuelson, mouth open and speechless, watched the big boss angrily step into his car and splatter mud in all directions as the Lamborghini spun around in the sludge and then, gaining traction, sped toward the exit.

Chapter Twenty-six

"Just a minute, Matt," Shawn said. "I need to talk to Nelson before we leave." With time running out, every day would count, and no matter what, she was determined not to let Andrew down on a business level. From the look that had crossed his face, it would seem that she had really lost what she treasured most, his friendship. Rain or shine, the cleanup would continue throughout the weekend. She would be there bright and early to talk to Andrew and work up a plan of attack with Nelson.

"Steve," Shawn said, "I know it's asking a lot to give up your weekend, especially in this weather, but can you and the men work tomorrow?"

"Already planned on it," he returned.

"Good," Shawn said. "Tell them I really appreciate it. And Steve, I'll be here first thing in the morning."

"Fine, Ms. McCullough. Now why don't you take a break?"

His attitude was vastly different than it had been earlier, and it cheered her. "Thanks, Nelson." Her sincerity rang through. "You've been super through all of this. I want you to know I am very grateful." He nodded self-consciously, and for the first time, she saw a smile on his hatchet face.

Shawn returned to Matt. As pleased as she was with

293

Nelson, her feet felt weighted, and even Matt's presence did little to raise her spirits. What was the matter with her? She should be overjoyed now that Matt was here, yet the feeling of elation she had anticipated from his arrival was strangely missing. But what could she expect? She was physically and mentally spent from the overwhelming strain and lack of sleep. A nice warm soak in the tub would certainly help, and that would be her first priority. As she drove to her condo, though, she wasn't able to shake her strange mood.

Only a bit more collected, she got out of the car and smiled tentatively at Matt, who had followed in his rental car. "I can barely wait to get into your arms, Matt, darling, but I'm afraid I'd contaminate you. Lord, do I need a tub of hot water right now."

"No problem, I'll help you," he volunteered.

"Oh, no, you don't," she said with a laugh. "This is one bath I need just to soak my weary bones. Lord, I ache all over. Do you mind?"

"No, sweetheart," he said, a bit disappointed. "Take all the time you need. From what I heard listening to one of the workmen, you had a damn rough day yesterday—and today, too—with that slide. My God, Shawn, you had no business up on that mountain under those conditions. What on earth were you thinking?"

"Of an old man," she said, unlocking the condo door.

"What do you mean, an old man?"

"Just an old codger who lived on the mountain; it was a perilous situation. I had to warn him."

"Darling, you could have been killed," he said protectively, then less adamantly he went on, "well, all that is past. I'm here to see that you don't pull any more stunts like that. You're far too precious to me."

His statement rankled, but she let it pass, knowing that she was tense and overly sensitive. "Matt, why don't you fix us something warm while I soak? I could sure use a nice hot drink."

"Sure, how about a hot toddy?"

"Sounds good. Teakettle's on the stove, liquor's in the cabinet. We'll have a nice dinner later."

"Great," he said. "Nothing like you and a good meal, too. Now don't worry, just go get cleaned up. Damn, honey, at the moment, you're one solid mud ball." He laughed.

She didn't reply as she headed down the hall toward the bathroom. Incongruously, his statement had brought back Andrew's words regarding her muddied exterior. "Shawn, you have never looked more beautiful."

"We're just going to have to shape you up," Matt teased as he followed her to the doorway. "A legislator's wife shouldn't be out playing around in the muck."

Playing around in the muck, indeed. Did he really think that summed up her work? Surely not. She just didn't feel like joking right now, and though she had every right to be on edge, she was baffled that Matt hadn't snapped her out of it. Biting back a sharp retort, she turned to ask. "Then you've decided to enter the political scene?"

"Yes," he said, "and you're going to make one hell of a governor's wife one day."

"If I get rid of the mud?" she asked pointedly, immediately hating herself for the catty remark.

The slight sarcasm was lost on Matt, who laughed. "I'm afraid, to some extent, our life will become public domain."

She smiled ruefully, ashamed of her unnoticed minor outburst. "I won't be long," she said, shutting the door.

While Shawn let the frothy bubbles and the warm water perform therapeutic miracles, she tried to imagine herself as a governor's wife. She loved wearing nice clothes and enjoyed people, but she was very outspoken and honest. Matt would be splendid in that political position, but she was another matter and would definitely have to work at keeping her emotions under control and her foot out of her mouth. Would it be like walking a bed of nails for someone of her disposition?

When she finally stepped out of the tub, Shawn felt like a new woman, and she pushed her negative thoughts to the back of her mind as she sprayed herself with Chanel and donned a soft blue angora sweater and white pants. She ran a brush through her hair and gave it a few gentle pushes with her fingers, then padded barefoot to the living room.

Matt rose to his feet at the sight of her. "Now, that's more like it. You look beautiful, my darling," he complimented, letting his eyes travel over her curves appreciatively before taking her in his arms.

A strange, sudden chill crept over her at his touch. Was physical beauty all he saw? Why hadn't he thought her beautiful when she had been mud-encrusted? Was her outward facade more important than the qualities within that really made her tick? She knew she was being petty, and she didn't know why. Still, she couldn't help comparing the way that Andrew had looked at her when she'd been paint-spattered or covered with mud. "Shawn, you have never looked more beautiful." It hadn't been merely his words; his expression had said it all. Each time he had said, "You really are something, Shawn McCullough." It told her that Andrew loved the whole complexity of her, not the clothes, not the looks, but everything that made up Shawn McCullough.

She began to realize that she didn't really know this man. He was different somehow, or, in honesty, was it she who had changed? The thrill of Matt's kiss, the arousal from his touch that she had so vividly remembered had somehow vanished, and in bewilderment, Shawn pulled away. "Oh, Matt, my dear, don't be cross with me please, but let's just relax for a bit. I don't know what's wrong with me. I guess I'm more tired than I realized."

"Sure, honey," he said, disappointed. Then, trying to recover his aplomb, he handed her one of the steaming toddies. "I'm sorry, I didn't mean to rush you. I know you've had a nasty time of it these past two days." He picked up his own drink and clicked it against hers. "Darling, here's to a quick sale of your business and an end to your problems."

The hand holding her drink froze in midair. She

was absolutely stunned. Sell the business? "Matt," she gasped. "You can't be serious. No one would buy it in its present state of near bankruptcy even if I wanted to sell it."

He frowned. "Surely you don't intend to keep working? If it won't sell, then perhaps you should declare bankruptcy. I'm perfectly able to take care of you. You don't need the business anymore. Believe me, you'll be far too busy helping me campaign, my love. Anyway, landscaping is scarcely the type of thing in which such a beautiful woman should be involved."

She looked at him incredulously. He had no earthly idea what the business meant to her: the loyal crews out there the past two days, struggling to save McCullough Landscaping, working nonstop in the icy wind and rain, chilled to the bone and uncomplaining. She should tell them she was filing bankruptcy? Just like that, shut the door on the office and go play lady of the manor for the rest of her life? It all seemed so simple to Matt. Was he really that self-centered, or was he just unaccustomed to sharing interests? The revelation came to her in a flash. There actually was no way that he could put himself in her shoes, and there was even less chance that she could ever be a prim and proper governor's wife. It was simply out of character for them both; a different world, and dammit, yes, Matt, too, was different. Had she been blinded by loneliness and need in the beginning of their relationship to the extent of seeing only what she had wanted to see? Had she been so caught up in a childhood fantasy of a handsome prince who could solve all problems that she had failed to acknowledge Matt's all-too-human shortcomings? It had been a lovely reverie, but suddenly she had outgrown the confinements of the castle. Had the last few months made a big change in her? It was hard to say. The only thing she did know was that she could not live within the restrictions of political life.

"Matt," she said regretfully, and her hand lightly touched his. "I'm afraid you don't understand me at all. I could never turn my back on my employees. Those men put their heart and soul into their work the past two days. I can't just walk away from them, leave them jobless."

His smile was condescending. "Honey, you make it sound so tragic. It's really not, you know. No one could expect you to do the impossible. Why, under the circumstances, any other landscaper would do the same. It's not as if you owe the men anything more than a paycheck. They can find other jobs."

She knew that logically he was right, but the men weren't paid to take chances like they had today. They could have refused to work under such hazardous conditions, yet they had not turned their backs on her any more than she could shut the door in their faces. It wouldn't be easy to pay the bills—she would be back in debt—but she had to go with her feelings. She was, after all, her father's daughter, and like him, stubborn to a fault, willing to fight for what she believed and loved. She sank to the couch. "I can't, Matt," she stated wistfully. "What you're asking me to do just isn't me."

He knelt beside her and took both her hands in his, dark eyes imploring. "Shawn, does it mean that much to you, honey, that you would put the business ahead of us?"

"Matt, it really has nothing to do with us. Can't you see? If I walked away now, it would never make either one of us happy. I have a contract with Andrew that I must fulfill if it's humanly possible. I owe him and the men a great deal."

His steady gaze bored into her, and he gently said, "It's certainly obvious that Andrew Bellows is in love with you. Shawn, is it possible that you love him, too?"

She shook her head, momentarily at a loss for words. Then, eyes brimming with tears, she said, "I really don't know what I feel this minute, except that I can't be what you want me to be. We would both be miserable. Our priorities would never mesh. Physical love would not be enough to sustain a marriage. Eventually we would be torn in opposite directions. Oh, Matt, do you understand what I'm saying?"

He paused for a moment. Was she right? Had he been so

captivated by her charms that he had missed seeing the
determined woman beneath? Now she was telling him her
innermost feelings for the first time, feelings that they
had never before discussed.

"Yes, my love," he said sorrowfully. "I guess I was trying
to make you into something you're not, and it wouldn't
work. I'm much too selfish to share you with anything or
anyone. Perhaps Andrew Bellows was wrong," he said
sadly. "You need a much bigger man than I am."

"Oh, Matt," she cried, then pulled away to look into his
glistening eyes. "Oh, Matt, dear, Matt. We'll always be
friends, won't we?"

He saw love in her eyes that somehow diminished the
hurt of a dream gone astray, and she smiled ruefully.
"Forever," he promised as he lightly kissed her forehead
and resignedly rose to leave. Then, smiling genuinely, as
if really trying to put their changing relationship into
proper perspective, he said, "And there's still no one I'd
rather share Oreos with."

She gave him a small smile and watched him leave. The
feelings they had shared had been part of a beautiful
dream that somehow had faded, but understanding and
loving friendship was something that would always remain, and she felt comforted.

Shawn did not return to Arcadia Lane that Friday night
but sat for a long while thinking and trying to understand
her new feelings. Then she called Elsa.

As usual, after talking to Elsa, she felt more at peace
with herself. To give her a further lift, Tony had called to
tell her that he was back.

Now, Saturday morning, as she pulled into Arcadia
Lane, she was anxious to see her superintendent, and she
knew Nelson would be happy, too. She hadn't gone into
detail about the problems. They would cover all the bases
this morning, and then she would turn the cleanup project
over to Tony's very capable hands so that she could
concentrate on another matter that had become priority
number one.

She spotted the Lamborghini. Great! Andrew was here.
She parked alongside and glanced around hopefully. It
was still raining softly, but the workmen who were busily
attacking the residue of the past two days had traded their
cumbersome rain gear for water-repellent jackets. Though
today was not a normal workday, it appeared that most of
the crews were here. Shawn smiled to herself. The construction trades, as much as they had petty gripes with
one another, stuck together in times of crisis, and it was a
wonderful feeling. Some of Bellows's men were helping
her own crew haul out debris, and she glimpsed Andrew
talking with Samuelson at the catering truck. Shawn
grinned at the sight of him, and she could hardly wait to
get him alone. Dear Andy, did she love him as Matt had
wondered? She had almost decided to walk over when
Tony pulled up.

"Morning, boss lady," he said cheerfully.

"Tony! Lord, am I glad to see you."

He flashed his sunny grin and jumped out of his truck,
quickly surveying the site. "I can sure see why. Hell's
bells, I knew I was valuable, but I didn't think everything
would fall apart the minute I left," he quipped.

"You don't know how valuable," she said good-
naturedly. "Do you think we can put it back together in
time?"

"I don't know, but we'll sure give it hell." He glanced
around to spot Nelson and the men at work. "Early, aren't
they?"

Shawn shrugged. "They've been here around the clock."

Tony shook his head. "Damn good men."

"Yes," she agreed. "Even Nelson."

He laughed. "Well, you can relax now, Shawn. From
what I heard about you from Bellows as I drove in, you've
done a damn good job, too. Why don't you take a well-
deserved break from this mess and catch up on the
paperwork. There must be stacks of it. I'll get back to you
bright and early Monday, and we'll figure out how we can
catch up and regroup. I need to get a handle on this first."

"Some break," she scoffed. "As soon as I talk to Andrew Bellows, I might just do that."

"Good," he said. "Now I better get my butt in gear, or these guys are going to claim all the glory."

She laughed as he hopped in his truck and drove over to Nelson. Then she walked to the catering truck to join Samuelson, who was lingering over a cup of coffee. Andrew had suddenly disappeared. She smiled cheerily and said, "Good morning. Where's Bellows?"

"He just left. Said he had a lot to catch up before he leaves for a board meeting in the East."

"When is he leaving?"

"Don't know, but he'll be back Monday afternoon. Don't worry, Ms. McCullough. I think Rizzo, Nelson, and I can get it all together now."

She smiled ruefully. "I'm sure *you* can," she said, and she added softly to herself, "I hope we can, too."

Chapter Twenty-seven

Shawn spent all day Saturday at the office, catching up on mounds of paperwork and still trying to sort out her thoughts and feelings. If only she could talk to Andrew. Surprisingly, the expression on his face when she had introduced the two men bothered her more than the breakup with Matt. In the manner of dreams, when she had awakened to reality, she'd felt a tinge of sadness in finding their relationship was not all she had hoped for, yet the empty feeling she had expected simply hadn't materialized. Why? Why hadn't she been completely devastated? Had Matt hit upon the reason? Was she in love with Andrew?

Shawn got up and went to the first-aid kit, took out two aspirin, and swallowed them with some water. Talk about a headache! Business was a disaster and her personal life as well, but right now she would have to tend to the demands of the corporation. To add to that, she couldn't bear to hurt Andrew again, so she would have to give herself time away from him and be damn sure this time of what she felt. Right now it would be enough to know he was still her treasured friend.

Sunday morning saw Shawn struggling: going over bills, signing checks for the bookkeeper, writing letters, and keeping her calculator clicking in an effort to gauge the cost of putting Arcadia Lane back on track. If she could delay paying for materials, the money problem would be eased somewhat, and the amount needed to insure the men's paychecks brought down to a level that she could manage with a small loan. There was always Statewide Bank.

It was dusk before Shawn left the office, but she felt optimistic despite the multitude of problems that remained unsolved. She knew that the men were behind her, and Tony's return was like a governor's reprieve. Thinking of her capable crews and her crackerjack superintendent, Shawn's confidence was bolstered.

She nearly slept the clock around, waking easily on Monday morning at the sound of the alarm. By seven A.M., Shawn was back in the office, anxiously awaiting Tony's appraisal of the damage.

The front had played out, and the sun had burned its way through the remaining wisps of clouds. Shawn sat at her desk, appreciating the morning sun's warmth on her shoulders as she sipped coffee and collected her thoughts.

"Good morning, boss lady." Tony sauntered in, set his coffee on the edge of her desk, and dropped into one of the gold chairs opposite her.

"Hi, Tony! How goes it?"

"Pretty damn good, I'd say, if you add up all we accomplished over the weekend—but then again, if you consider what all's left, we're in a hell of a shape. It all depends on whether you see the glass as half-full or half-empty."

"I think I'll go with the first one," she said.

He grinned. "Might as well, doesn't cost any more to be optimistic."

She smiled. "You're so right. Now give me your expert opinion. Can we do it?"

His brow furrowed, and now that he was no longer smiling, she could see new, tired lines cobwebbed around his eyes and a weary slump to his shoulders. For a moment she feared he would tell her they couldn't possibly meet opening day, but instead, his face brightened, and he remarked, "You damn betcha! Hell, I think we've already moved half the mountain. Drains are all free and the best I can tell, the only water coming off the slope is just the normal seepage after a lot of rain."

Shawn sighed, relieved. Tony pulled a list of replacement items from his shirt pocket, and they spent the next hour going over costs and studying solutions.

"Now don't you worry, Shawn," Tony admonished as he was leaving, "we *will* be ready to open April sixteenth, come hell or high water."

"Bite your tongue," she said, as he flashed his familiar grin.

Tony had just left when Audrey buzzed Shawn. "Mr. Kendall of Statewide on line one."

Shawn smiled to herself and picked up the phone. "Mr. Kendall," she said, "how are you?"

"Oh, fine," Frank Kendall said, "but I'm not so sure about you. I heard about the slide out at Arcadia Lane. Tell me, how does all of this affect your job?"

"Badly," she said, "it's certainly put a crimp in the works. But I really have faith in our ability to put it all back together and still come out ahead. Still, I do have a monetary problem as you can well imagine. My men are putting in a lot of overtime that's going to eat up my small reserve."

"I see," he said, again impressed with her honest determination. "What kind of money are you talking about?"

"One hundred thousand would be a godsend," she said.

"I'll see that it's transferred to your corporate account today and get the paper for you to sign in the mail. Would ninety days be all right?"

"Yes, fine. Thank you, Mr. Kendall. I sure appreciate the call, and you can count on the loan's prompt return," Shawn said, smiling as she unconsciously heaved a sigh.

"I have no doubt," the bank president said. "Good luck on your project."

Time passed slowly that afternoon and evening. Shawn wanted so badly to call Andrew but reminded herself that she'd already hurt him too much. She would let it ride for now and try to get her own feelings straight. Or had she lost the friendship of a man who had been important to her? In any case, it was out of her hands, and by ten P.M., she crawled into bed, vowing not to dwell on decisions that were not hers to make.

Tuesday morning driving to the office, Shawn couldn't help remembering Andrew and all they had shared, so many good times, laughing together, and the bad times as well, when he had been so supportive. Never once had he expected her to be anything other than she was. Earlier occasions passed through her mind like a silent movie; nights with the kids at the park, painting her condo, his patience with her regarding Krugger, and the way the men admired him and how they had followed his lead because they, too, believed in him. He was one of a kind, and she felt the loss of his friendship more deeply each day. Was she in love with this dynamic man? If she ever decided, this time it would be for keeps. She would never hurt Andrew again.

That evening when she pulled up at Sun Haven for their weekly gathering with the teenagers, Shawn wasn't surprised to see Andrew's Lamborghini. He was a man to be relied on, no matter what. Shawn's step was suddenly light as she entered the recreation building.

Two hours later, when the door had shut behind the boys, Shawn caught Andrew's stare. The veil had lifted, and the hurt in his eyes was unmistakable. "Andy," she said, "I need to talk to you."

He remained silent.

"I hope we can always keep our friendship," Shawn said softly.

The muscle in one cheek twitched, and he smiled pensively. "That's given."

"Thank you, Andy. I'll always treasure it."

"That is," he qualified, "if Monroe can tolerate our being friends. By the way, when is the big date?"

"There isn't going to be one."

He looked at her incredulously but didn't question further.

"It's my fault, really. I guess I was looking for something that never was there," she explained sadly.

"Shawn," he said, momentarily at a loss. "What can I say?"

It was all she could do not to run to the comfort of his arms, to again know the tenderness of his kiss, yet she dare not give in. Andy must never feel used or second-best. If ever again she went into his arms, he must know that it was for always. "Please don't say anything right now," she said, lightly pressing her fingers to his lips. "It's enough that we're friends."

He looked at her a long moment, a part of him wanting desperately to envelop her in his arms, and part of him still meaning what he had said. He would not cross the barrier again. The next move would have to be Shawn's, and if and when it was right, she would have to decide. "Come on, I'll walk you to your car," he said.

Pausing beside her car, she took his hand. "Thank you, Andy, for not asking. I can tell you it just wouldn't have worked for Matt and me. I thought I knew him and learned that I did not."

He nodded understandingly, then gently kissed her forehead and opened the door for her, resisting the ritual of following her home. Right now, she needed time, and he would give her that, though it would take every bit of restraint he could muster.

The following weeks passed quickly; everything going full-speed at Arcadia Lane. The men had been working ten hours a day for weeks now, and the past eight days, had put in as many as sixteen hours so that Arcadia Lane could open on Saturday. Andrew and Shawn had seen each other every Tuesday night at Sun Haven and various times at the shopping center where they had discussed business, sometimes talking for an hour or two, checking problems when Tony was too busy with the men. Their relationship was comfortable on the surface, yet both

fought inner turmoil when in the other's presence, Shawn
a bit unsure of her feelings, and Andrew once again
nurturing a faint ray of hope.

Friday morning, Shawn sat in her desk chair contem-
plating tomorrow's grand opening of Arcadia Lane. Her
job there was almost done. Now she struggled with what
she had avoided these last hectic weeks. Once her professional contact with Andrew ended, what would happen to
their friendship? She sat silently for long minutes, the
thought of losing daily contact with Andy filling her with
such sadness that she finally faced the truth. She grinned,
leaned back in her chair, and broke the silence. "I'll be
damned," she said, and laughed.

Shawn drove directly to Exclusively Hers, an ultraex-
pensive boutique.

She went directly to the size five loungewear and
fingered swiftly through the expensive garments, finally
selecting a few to try on. If Andrew still loved her as he
once said, it wouldn't make any difference what she was
wearing, but the woman in her wanted to be the very best
she could be.

Shortly after, she was out the door with her selection
and on her way home, doubts running rampant. What if
his feelings had changed? Would it be fair to put him on
the spot, and would it make him uncomfortable now if she
told him that she loved him, that she at last woke up to
realize she had loved him for a long time and was too blind
to know it? A smile of sweet remembrance swept over her
lovely face with the memory of the night they had made
love. Lord, how could she have wasted so much precious
time? He was everything she wanted: gentle, understanding, handsome, and so very dear. Shawn parked her car
and raced up the stairs. She was barely inside the door
when she reached for the phone. Rapidly dialing the
number, she kicked off her shoes and shrugged out of her
jacket.

"Bellows Enterprises," Jill's voice came cheerily over
the wire.

"I know Andrew Bellows isn't there, but if he calls in, would you please tell him that Shawn McCullough needs to talk to him right away? It's *very* important," she stressed.

"Yes, of course, Ms. McCullough. Where might he reach you?"

"At home. He has the number."

"I'll see that he gets the message."

"Thanks."

For the next hour, Shawn busied herself, soaking in a scented, foamy bath, imagining his gentle touch instead of the bubbles caressing her skin, shivering with delight in remembering his embrace. Lord, how blind she had been not to have realized that she loved Andy until the possibility arose of losing him. She stared at the phone she had brought into the bathroom and silently implored it to ring, but the instrument remained mute, agonizingly so.

She had just wrapped herself in an oversize towel and was checking the clock for the fourteenth time when the long-awaited ring startled her. "Hello," she said eagerly.

"Hello," a pleasant voice responded. "I'm Margaret Spelling, calling for Welfare Mothers. Our truck will be in your area next Tuesday. Do you have any discards to donate?"

"No, I'm sorry; I'll have to pass," Shawn said, and disappointedly dropped the phone with a resounding clunk. She hadn't taken her hand off the receiver before it rang again. "Oh, it's probably that same darn woman. They lose their place on their lists. Hello," she said with some irritation. "I told you my answer was no."

"I've heard that before," Andrew Bellows's deep voice announced.

"Oh, Andy! I thought you were the woman from some unheard-of charity who just called a minute ago. I'm really sorry. I shouldn't have been so abrupt."

He chuckled into the phone. "No problem. My secretary told me that you called and that it was extremely pressing."

His voice was openly concerned and so dear. "Yes, Andy,

I have a problem, a big problem, and I need your expert advice. Could you possibly come over when you're free?"

"Shawn, what is it?"

"I'd rather not discuss it on the phone, Andy, if you don't mind."

"I'll be there within the hour," he promised. Hanging up the mobile phone, he mused aloud, "I wonder what's troubling Shawn."

When Shawn opened the door for him, Andrew involuntarily drew in a ragged breath. She had always been beautiful, but the vision before him was absolute perfection in gorgeous low-cut ivory. She had the classic look of a Greek goddess, her gown's graceful, silky folds cascading from a wide, shirred neckline and a silk cord gathering them in, accentuating her lovely breasts and small waist. Cleverly cut side slits on both sleeves and the skirt gave provocative glimpses of her firm arms and softly rounded calves to complete her breathtaking allure. She sure as hell didn't portray a woman with a problem. A dismal thought struck him. Was she all dressed up for Matt and ready to return to him? Well, she hadn't better expect him to second the motion this time.

"Hello, Andy. I'm so glad to see you," she said sincerely. "Come on in."

"Hello, Shawn," he said, not daring to look straight into her eyes lest she surely learn that his willpower was struggling vainly to control one hundred eighty pounds of excitable virility. He walked slowly past her into the living room, buying time to compose himself before he could ask what was bothering her.

Shawn followed. "Sit down, Andy," she urged.

When he was seated on the couch, she stood behind him and bent over his shoulder, her hair lightly brushing the back of his neck. "Would you like a drink?" she inquired.

That's not all I want, he thought. Hell, this is pure torture! She looked seductive wearing mud, but damn, this is too much! "Yes," he said aloud, "I certainly would. Make it a double; it's been a very taxing day."

"Why don't you take off your jacket and relax? I'll only

be a minute," she said, and her throaty voice made him want to seize her and say, Forget the damn drink, I know something that would please me one hell of a lot more, but he made no comment. Instead, he removed his jacket and carelessly draped it over a chair.

Shawn poured the drink, came back to the living room, and handed it to him, managing to innocently touch his fingers in the process.

"Thanks," he said, feeling almost stung by the slight contact. Then, not wanting to prolong the agony, he opened the conversation as he stirred the ice with his finger. "Now, Shawn McCullough, what is the problem, and how can I help?"

"Oh, Andy, I knew I could count on you." She sinuously eased down on the couch beside him, a waft of her perfume tempting his senses. "I don't know how to tell you this," she continued. "It's really quite a dilemma."

"Has it something to do with Arcadia Lane?" he asked hopefully.

"Oh, no, it's much more personal than that, but still, it is a big problem."

Shit, it was that damn Monroe again! "Yes? How big?"

"A little under two hundred pounds."

Andrew took a sip of his drink, dreading what was to follow but making every effort to conceal his feelings. Why was she being so coy? It was very much out of character, and he was puzzled.

"Is the drink all right?" she asked, innocently snuggling closer to him. "You're beginning to look a little more relaxed, and you'll need to be to help me."

About as relaxed as a whore in church! What the hell was going on here? Was he imagining this? He refused to look at her. He meant to keep his promise about not crossing the invisible barrier, but damn, she wasn't making it at all easy when she was close to him like this. He took a big gulp and set the drink down hard. A little under two hundred pounds? It had to be Matt. "Shawn, about this problem. What in hell do you mean, a little under two hundred pounds?"

"Oh, Andy, he's absolutely wonderful," she said with a wanton gleam in her eye.

Andrew frowned in response but couldn't bring himself to ask further.

"Andy, you seem so tense. Come on, relax. *I'm* the one with the problem. Here, let's make you a little more comfortable." Before he knew what she was up to, she had gently unknotted his tie, letting her fingers lightly brush against his neck with what he swore were fleeting caresses as she smiled innocently, dropping the tie on the coffee table.

Christ on a crutch, what was she trying to do? Or was his imagination running wild? Andrew hastily reached for his glass and drained it.

"Andy," she went on, "have you ever felt your heart beat words of love throughout your entire body? It's the loveliest sensation that I've ever known, and that's the way I feel about this special man in my life." She sighed dreamily as she unbuttoned his shirt slowly, sensually stroking the dark gold hair on his chest with her delicate fingers.

"Shawn, please," he rasped helplessly, his trembling hands and anguished expression telling her that his desire for her was as strong as ever. She could no longer mask her feelings.

Her sultry eyes and seductive smile filled him with indescribable joy. There was no mistaking that radiant look. He was suddenly seeing a woman who, he realized, loved *him!* My God, it's *me* she's talking about!

"Please, what, Andy?"

"Please go on," he said, deciding to play and wanting to see just how far she would carry her little game. "I want to hear all about this man. How tall is he—six feet?"

"Give or take a little," she said, deliberately eyeing the length of him.

"Hm, is he blond?"

"Yes. He has very attractive, thick waves," she said, running her fingers through his hair and down his neck to create a tingling sensation that shook him all the way to his toes.

"I see. Perhaps he has blue eyes?"

"Uh huh," she murmured as she touched his eyelids with the tenderest of kisses and then lightly brushed the tip of his nose with her lips.

"And I would imagine, hair on his chest?"

"Oh, yes, lots." Her fingers caressed Andy's wiry, golden mat and traced the well-delineated pectoral muscles beneath.

It was all he could do to control himself, but this was her game and he was a willing player, enjoying her seductive advances and very much surprised by the sheer delight of her. If this was a new parlor game, he could highly recommend it. "This man," he said, continuing the playful charade, "is he nearby?"

"Indeed," she said, taking his hand and gently coaxing him to his feet, then easing the shirt from his arms and carelessly letting it fall to the floor. And she actually felt reckless as she slowly caressed his arms, his shoulders, and the back of his neck.

His gaze burned into her smoldering eyes, and his lips touched her satin-smooth exposed shoulder, sending a flush of desire coursing through every vein in her body. Then, drawing back with a lecherous grin, he asked, "You wouldn't care to tell me his name?"

She smiled teasingly. "I think they call him the Big Boss."

"Sounds like a man with a lot of clout. Would you be inclined to accede to his wishes?"

"Depends on whether or not I like them."

"Well, suppose he wanted to make love to you right here and now—and every chance he gets in the future?" he asked with a deep yearning in his low voice, which had all at once gone serious.

She was brimming with desire, and her arms closed about his neck, her body answering for the words that were not spoken.

"Shawn, oh, Shawn," he groaned in her ear, and his lips became fire, igniting her flesh as they brushed her ear, her cheek, her neck, and traveled to the fullness of her moist lips, drinking in the heat of her as their tongues met in searing union.

"Andy," she gasped between kisses. "God, I have been so blind. I must have loved you from the beginning."

His words were a whisper. "Darling, you are my love, my life." One hand caressed her bare back while the other moved possessively over her hips, drawing her closer, closer still, until he thought he would explode with wanting her.

Then, drawing back, he probed deeply into her eyes, which had turned violet in the candle glow, the loving expression in his own hypnotizing her. Hands gentle, he slowly, sensuously undressed her, his eyes openly adoring every curve of her, his fingers moving tenderly over her flawless skin. When the gown had slithered to the floor, his passionate eyes drank in her nude beauty in the dim candlelight for a long, deliberate moment. "Venus herself could be no more beautiful," he breathed in wonder. "Shawn, my lovely love." His seeking hands caressed her throbbing breasts and traced circles about the suddenly erect nipples, then he softly kissed each one in turn and gently teased the pink tips with his tongue, even further stimulating the aching desire of every vibrating cell within her. His fingers moved to the insides of her thighs, driving sensations of intense pleasure into every nerve. Fire leapt from her flesh to his as his lips again demanded hers, and her boiling blood and taut nerves radiated an all-consuming heat that whetted his passion to fever pitch. He quickly discarded his clothes to lie beside her, all the while savoring her beauty.

"Sweet Shawn," he groaned, "you are perfection."

"Andy, oh, Andy, I love you so. Please, please—make love to me before I die from wanting you."

Love had transfigured his face; his expression wild, yet gentle as he granted her plea, his blood rushing furiously through his virile body as she offered herself with supreme shamelessness and he entered her soft folds. Her wonderful love, her beautiful body were his, exclusively his, and the feeling was deliriously wondrous as their bodies, their very souls, merged into one. "Shawn, oh, God, Shawn, I have never truly loved before this moment," he cried.

"Nor I, my darling."

And their love was an insatiable hunger. He thought he would never get enough of her as they rose to heights unknown to mere mortals, simultaneously crying out in fulfillment.

Later, they lay entwined on the lush carpet, Andrew tracing her face with small kisses, softly stroking her body, and Shawn, content within his arms, loving the feel of him. For a long time neither spoke, lest they break the rapturous spell.

Finally, Andrew reluctantly sat up, gently pulling her with him, kissing her silken shoulders as his eyes nakedly exposed his deep love for her.

"Oh, Andy, I've never been so gloriously happy," she breathed as she pulled his head down to softly kiss him.

He smiled. "Mm, I think we've completely solved your problem, Shawn McCullough," he jested.

"Completely?" There was a wicked glint in her blue eyes before she stretched her lithe form to rise with feline grace, and her very movements again aroused him.

Andrew was on his feet immediately, sweeping her up in his arms to carry her effortlessly to the bedroom. "Come to think of it, that's a problem I sure as hell don't want to ever completely resolve. I could easily stand a lifetime of working on it."

When next Shawn opened her eyes, the morning sun had brightened the room, and Andy was lovingly studying her face.

"I love you," she said honestly, and it was the nicest good morning he had ever heard.

"Well, I can't say I love you," he said, touching her cheek.

"You can't?"

"No, the word doesn't begin to say enough, you mean everything to me, Shawn. I idolize you, I—"

She smiled, kissed her fingers, and then placed them on

his lips. "Um, I'll take it," she said, "but don't touch me again or we'll never make it to the opening."

"Oh, Christ, I actually forgot." His thoughts raced to the award ceremony to come and how surprised she was going to be, and he could hardly wait to see her reaction. "Better move that beautiful body, sweetheart, or we'll be late."

Arcadia Lane, resplendent in design with its fresh paint and gorgeous trappings, sparkled in the April sun as if it could anticipate the admiration of the festive Easter shoppers who would be enjoying its attractions. This was opening day, and a sleeping, lifeless giant was about to be awakened. This shopping center was one of a kind—magnificently so.

Already there was a continuous stream of cars filling up the parking lot, and avid shoppers impatiently awaited the glorious moment when the doors would open to display the tempting array of wares. Andrew Bellows's vision was about to be shared with the multitudes.

Shawn and Andrew hurried to cross the bridge. "Wait a minute, Andy," she said, stopping to take in the beauty around her. "This is the first time I've seen the water-wheel working."

He smiled and put his arm about her. "It is rather quaint, isn't it?"

"I love it! You know, there was a time when I was afraid I'd never see this completed. It's amazing, Andy, no one would ever guess what a disaster we had here."

"That's for sure. No one but the old oak over there, and it's not about to tell."

Her eyes focused upon the ancient tree majestically towering above the picnic/playground, then, remembering the slide and the demolition of Krugger's house when the old oak, alone, had stood undaunted, she said, "It's a splendid tree, don't you think? I'm so glad you didn't remove it, Andy."

He laughed. "That would have been positively blasphemous. Come on, we'd better get to the bandstand. Mayor Finley is planning the opening-day ceremony for nine-thirty sharp." He took her hand to hurry her toward the bridge.

Shawn kept pace, all the while keeping an eye on the huge goldfish lazily swimming around and under the lily pads, the attractive shrubs on the bank of the stream, and the refreshing water splashing as the waterwheel turned incessantly on its million-mile journey to nowhere.

Close to the bandstand, a good-size crowd was milling about, and a gray-haired, distinguished looking gentleman was adjusting the microphone on the outdoor platform. The wooden base of the stage was gaily decorated in shiny red plastic bearing huge white block letters on all four sides that proclaimed, ARCADIA LANE WARMLY WELCOMES YOU. Streamers of the same red and white were wound around each of the myriad lantern-type light poles that dotted the entire area, and hundreds of helium filled balloons were fastened in bunches halfway up each ornamental fixture. The soft cooing of doves could be heard though no bird was in sight.

"Good morning," Shawn and Andrew said in unison, recognizing the mayor of Saratoga as he finished regulating the microphone.

"Yes, it is lovely. You couldn't have planned it any better," Mayor John Finley agreed.

Shawn smiled and let her gaze continue to wander, taking in the vast array of buildings with their elegantly dressed windows, the ever increasing crowd of curious shoppers, and the charm of the old section with its electrically driven surreys trimmed in bright red-and-white stripes.

"Isn't that Krugger over there by the surrey?" Shawn asked Andrew as she observed the oldster, in a red-and-white uniform, climb behind the wheel.

Bellows grinned. "Yeah, I decided he'd make a better friend than enemy. I couldn't bear the thought of him standing on the hillside shaking his fist and scowling all day, so I talked him into a job."

She knew Andrew was concerned about Krugger's losing his house, and she strongly suspected that he would find a solution to that problem as well. "Do you know, Andrew Bellows, you are really a very nice man," she said with sincere delight.

By now, all the strategically scattered benches were filling, and a chorus of appreciative remarks could be heard from the crowd. It was heartwarming, and she could scarcely believe that after all the long months of struggling, opening day was finally here. Yet Arcadia Lane was more beautiful than she had ever thought possible, looking as exquisitely picture-perfect as if there had never been any doubt that opening day would be anything but a smashing success, and right on schedule. The band had arrived and was setting up on the platform, and she glimpsed Tony, laughing and kidding with their crew of workmen, who, it seemed, had all turned out. It was the first time she'd seen the majority of the men in anything other than work clothes. They looked mighty spruced up, and their presence touched her deeply. "I'll be right back," she said to Andrew, and made her way over to them.

"Good morning," she said brightly. "I can't tell you how pleased I am to see all of you. I thought by now you'd be fed up with this place."

"Oh, hell," Tony said. "They've been sleeping and eating Arcadia for too long. You don't expect them to break a bad habit overnight, do you? Anyway, today they can enjoy it."

"And well they should," she admonished. "See ya later," she said with a wave of her hand. Tony grinned in response.

When she returned to Andrew, the band was finishing up "Seventy-six Trombones," and the crowd's attention was diverted by the mayor taking the stand.

"Ladies and gentlemen, I'm mighty proud to be here at Arcadia Lane today to welcome you to the finest shopping center on the West Coast. First I would like to introduce the man who is responsible for this work of art. Andrew Bellows. Mr. Bellows, would you kindly step up here?" he gestured with a flourish.

As Andrew made his way through the crowd, the reporters stationed themselves where they would have easy access for pictures. The building magnate stepped onto the platform and accepted the older man's outstretched hand as the crowd applauded vigorously, the news cameras flashed, and Shawn beamed with pride for Andrew. On cue, Boy Scouts, each near a lamp pole, released bright helium-filled balloons, all bearing the name of Arcadia Lane and the date. Caught up by the light morning breeze, the gay spheres wafted skyward in a colorful flurry, drifting above the building tops and glistening in the glorious sunshine.

"Here he is, folks," John Finley said into the mike. "Andrew, I have here a token of our esteem on behalf of the city of Saratoga. We're very honored and proud that you chose our fair city in which to build such a magnificent shopping center. Congratulations on your most worthy project," the mayor said exuberantly as he presented Andy an enormous key inscribed with CITY OF SARATOGA and the date.

The band led off a loud hip, hip, hurrah, finishing with a drumroll as the Boy Scouts then released doves by the flock from the bridge and every corner of the park. The soft flutter of wings brought a delighted *ah* from the crowd as they watched the birds circle the area in breathtaking flight, some catching the gentle breezes to soar to the heights of the buildings, others to perch amid the freshly planted trees or to light on the railing of the bridge in hopes of cadging a tidbit from a passerby.

A red-faced, smiling Andrew stared at the mammoth key in his hand for a moment, watching the doves, the symbols of peace, before he cleared his throat to speak. "Thank you, Mayor Finley. I am deeply honored. I'm not going to thank all the people who really put this together because they know the great job they have done. However, I would like to point out my superintendent, Ken Samuelson, a man who has worked hard at developing a big aspirin habit. Please stand up, Ken."

The laughter of the crowd filled the air, and Samuelson, looking rather alien in a pinstripe suit, waved enthusiastically to the crowd.

"Thank you, Ken, and thank you one and all for the tremendous effort you put forth to make this all possible. I'm accepting this award on behalf of each and every one of you. You're a great team!" Bellows declared before relinquishing the mike to step back.

The mayor smiled as he again took command. "And now, ladies and gentlemen, we have a special guest here today, a Mr. Dan Cunningham, president of Golden West Landscapers Association. Would you please step up here, Dan?"

The question crossed Shawn's mind as to why Cunningham was here today, but she shrugged it off.

"Thank you, mayor. I consider it a great honor to be here today, and I would like to ask Shawn McCullough of McCullough Landscaping and Richard Ramsey of Ramsey, Potter and Martin to please join me on the platform."

Shawn was dumbstruck, and she stood gaping, first at Cunningham, who motioned her to the microphone and then at Andrew, whose grin told her that whatever was happening was no surprise to him. Somehow her feet turned to lead.

"After you, Ms. McCullough," Ramsey urged, firmly propelling her toward the platform. The crowd had begun a chanting clap and shouts of "We want Shawn," from Tony and her crew, filled the air. Reluctantly, Shawn preceeded Ramsey to the stand, surprise overwhelming her pretty face as she began to put two and two together.

Dan Cunningham offered his hand. "Ladies and gentlemen, Shawn McCullough," then grasping the architect's hand, "and Richard Ramsey."

Shawn wondered if her wobbly knees would buckle as she listened to Golden West's president, and her eyes flashed in consternation into Andrew's. "You *knew*," she whispered, "and you didn't tell me!"

He said nothing, but his smug grin showed his enjoyment.

Cunningham looked directly at Shawn and Richard. "It certainly is my pleasure to give this special recognition award for the most unique design in landscape architecture to Richard Ramsey and for the execution of that design to Shawn McCullough. Both parties have done a splendid job and can be proud of their tremendous accomplishment."

Tears of happiness rolled down her cheeks as her crew cheered enthusiastically. Andrew Bellows stood, arms folded, grinning broadly and shaking his head in pleased admiration. She was something, all right.

John Finley chuckled. "She's quite a woman!" he said before closing the ceremony.

The eyes of the crowd were directed skyward to watch the graceful airplane overhead as it wrote a fluffy smoke message across the bright April sky. "Arcadia Lane Shopping Center Grand Opening."

Shawn turned to Andrew. "Grodecki?"

"Yeah," he said, "he just had to get into the act."

"Well, I guess he deserves to be," she said, and they both laughed.

Elsa, who had been watching their happy antics, smiled knowingly and said with obvious double meaning, "Congratulations, you two."

Shawn whooped with delight at the sight of her. "Oh, Elsa, I'm so glad you came. If only McCullough could have been here, it would have been perfect."

"Yes," she agreed. "But somehow I think he knows."

A wonderful feeling of elation stole over Shawn; she was so lucky and so deliriously happy. All her fears and doubts of the past had vanished with the certainty of Andrew's love, and this glorious opening day was icing on the cake. Arcadia Lane: quiet contentment. It was paradoxical, for even in the buzz of activity there was something about this marvelous electric wonderland that Andrew had created, which sang of harmony. Did anyone else feel it, or was it merely that she had reached a point in her own life where she had finally found her own Arcadia Lane?

Andrew studied her with pure delight as she walked

back to him. "Come on," he said. "I want to show you something."

"What is it?" she said.

"I can't tell you. You'll have to see it." He took her hand and headed toward the bridge.

Midway she stopped to gaze again at the waterwheel. Putting his arm about her waist, he let her enjoy the flowers and the fish, the two of them completely oblivious of the passing traffic as they stood by the railing.

"Oh, Andy, I've never been so marvelously happy." She sighed in contentment, her eyes on the scenery, but more aware of his strong arm about her and feeling especially close to him at this moment.

"Nor I, my darling," he whispered in her ear. Then, taking both her hands in his, he said, "There's only one thing that could make me happier, and I think you know what that is."

She turned to face him, and her hand caressed his cheek. Her eyes were a blue sparkle of love in the midday sun as she smiled joyously. "Is that a proposal, Andy?"

"Well, I think that's a close definition," he teased.

"Yes, oh, yes, Andy, my love," she said excitedly, her face the focus of all the radiance from within.

"You're so beautiful," he said huskily, and kissed her soundly as he whirled her around in a bear hug.

"Put me down." She laughed merrily. "Everyone is staring."

"You don't expect the happiest man on earth to care, do you?" With that, he scooped her up and carried her the entire way to the car while heads turned and chuckles followed after them, but the two lovers were oblivious to all but each other.

"Where are we going?" she asked when in the car.

"You'll see," he said mysteriously.

He recklessly held her hand as he drove, allaying Shawn's natural curiosity for the moment with adoring glances at safe intervals. Noticing a smug smile on his face as the car took the winding Los Altos curves with ease, she remarked, "This is familiar territory."

"I would imagine."

"Andy, tell me where we're going."

He only grinned.

"Why, this is my old street," Shawn said in surprise. "The street where I used to live."

"Yes, isn't that a coincidence?"

She eyed him suspiciously as he pulled up the long, winding drive to her childhood home. "Do you know the people who bought it?"

"Yes, as a matter of fact, very well."

"Oh, Andy, do they like it?"

"Absolutely."

"But should we bother them?"

"No bother, I think the guy who bought it would enjoy showing you the place."

"This is insane, but I really do love that house, and I'd like to see how they've furnished it," she said as he helped her out of the car. "Are you sure they won't mind us dropping by?"

"I can guarantee that they won't," he promised, opening the gate.

"Oh, Andy, wait! I don't want to miss the garden; the flowers are so beautiful in the spring." She walked across the grass to admire the daffodils and tulips, stooping to finger a pretty flower. "The place looks well-cared-for; at least that makes me happy. Oh, how I wish we could live here," she said wistfully.

Andrew bent down beside her, smiling in secret delight. He started to say, "We . . . " but was abruptly silenced by the automatic sprinklers, which quickly soaked them both before they could escape to the patio.

"Seems like I remember a similar circumstance once before," he said with a soggy grimace.

"Me, too, only the sprinklers weren't automatic then."

"Yes, I know," he said, wiping his wet face ineffectually with his hand.

"Oh, Lord," Shawn said laughingly. "They'll never let us in now."

"You want to bet?"

"You must know them pretty well," she said.

"Yes." He pulled a key from his pocket and inserted it in the lock while Shawn watched in disbelief.

Swinging the door open, he said with a wide sweep of his hand, "It's ours: an early wedding present, my love."

She was stunned. "Oh, Andy," she breathed, and tears of joy filled her eyes. It wasn't the house so much as his unselfish love; his concern for her and the things she loved. He could have easily bought her a mansion, but he understood her sentiment for her childhood home with its fond attachments. The tears streamed down her pretty face unashamedly.

"Why are you crying, darling Shawn McCullough?" he questioned.

"Because we've wasted so much precious time."

"I'll see that that never happens again," he promised firmly, his own eyes slightly damp with moisture, which had nothing to do with the sprinklers. There was a long, meaningful pause, then he ceremoniously picked her up and carried her in. Kicking the door shut behind them, he kissed her more deeply than she had ever been kissed before, differently than she had ever known, and he continued the kiss as he determinedly carried her up the familiar staircase. She was quivering uncontrollably from the passion of a kiss such as she never dreamed existed. Pressing her back upon the soft bed, eyes never leaving her beloved face, he swiftly and masterfully unclothed her.

Then lowering his superb body to hers, he entered paradise—and took her with him.

This is the special design logo that will call your attention to Avon authors who show exceptional promise in the romance

THE AVON ROMANCE

area. Each month a new novel—either historical or contemporary—will be featured.

HEART SONGS Laurel Winslow
Coming in April 85365-5/$2.50

Set against the breathtaking beauty of the canyons and deserts of Arizona, this is the passionate story of a young gallery owner who agrees to pose for a world-famous artist to find that he captures not only her portrait but her heart.

WILDSTAR Linda Ladd
Coming in May 87171-8/$2.75

The majestic Rockies and the old West of the 1800's are the setting for this sizzling story of a beautiful white girl raised by Indians and the virile frontiersman who kidnaps her back from the Cheyenne.

NOW & AGAIN Joan Cassity
Coming in June 87353-2/$2.95

When her father dies, a beautiful young woman inherits his failing landscape company and finds herself torn between the fast-paced world of business and the devouring attentions of a dynamic real estate tycoon.

FLEUR DE LIS Dorothy E. Taylor
Coming in July 87619-1/$2.95

The spellbinding story of a young beauty who, fleeing France in the turmoil of revolution, loses her memory and finds herself married to a dashing sea captain who is determined to win her heart and unlock the secret of her mysterious past.

A GALLANT PASSION Helene M. Lehr	86074-0/$2.95
CHINA ROSE Marsha Canham	85985-8/$2.95
BOLD CONQUEST Virginia Henley	84830-9/$2.95
FOREVER, MY LOVE Jean Nash	84780-9/$2.95

Look for THE AVON ROMANCE wherever paperbacks are sold, or order directly from the publisher. Include $1.00 per copy for postage and handling; allow 6-8 weeks for delivery. Avon Books, Dept BP Box 767, Rte 2, Dresden, TN 38225.

Avon Rom 5-84

VELVET GLOVE

An exciting series of contemporary novels of love with a dangerous stranger.

Starting in July

THE VENUS SHOE Carla Neggers 87999-9/$2.25
Working on an exclusive estate, Artemis Pendleton becomes embroiled in a thirteen-year-old murder, a million dollar jewel heist, and with a mysterious Boston publisher who ultimately claims her heart.

CAPTURED IMAGES Laurel Winslow 87700-7/$2.25
Successful photographer Carolyn Daniels moves to a quiet New England town to complete a new book of her work, but her peace is interrupted by mysterious threats and a handsome stranger who moves in next door.

LOVE'S SUSPECT Betty Henrichs 88013-X/$2.25
A secret long buried rises to threaten Whitney Wakefield who longs to put the past behind her. Only the man she loves has the power to save—or destroy her.

DANGEROUS ENCHANTMENT Jean Hager 88252-3/$2.25
When Rachel Drake moves to a small town in Florida, she falls in love with the town's most handsome bachelor. Then she discovers he'd been suspected of murder, and suddenly she's running scared when another body turns up on the beach.

THE WILDFIRE TRACE Cathy Gillen Thacker 88620-4/$2.25
Dr. Maggie Connelly and attorney Jeff Rawlins fall in love while involved in a struggle to help a ten-year-old boy regain his memory and discover the truth about his mother's death.

IN THE DEAD OF THE NIGHT Rachel Scott 88278-7/$2.25
When attorney Julia Leighton is assigned to investigate the alleged illegal importing of cattle from Mexico by a local rancher, the last thing she expects is to fall in love with him.

AVON PAPERBACKS

Buy these books at your local bookstore or use this coupon for ordering:

Avon Books, Dept BP, Box 767, Rte 2, Dresden, TN 38225
Please send me the book(s) I have checked above. I am enclosing $______
(please add $1.00 to cover postage and handling for each book ordered to a maximum of three dollars). *Send check or money order*—no cash or C.O.D.'s please. Prices and numbers are subject to change without notice. Please allow six to eight weeks for delivery.

Name ____________________

Address ____________________

City __________ State/Zip __________

Velvet Glove 5-84